A Broken Hallelujah

Melanée Addison

BALBOA.
PRESS

A DIVISION OF HAY HOUSE

Balboa Press books may be ordered through booksellers or by contacting:

Balboa Press
A Division of Hay House
1663 Liberty Drive
Bloomington, IN 47403
www.balboapress.com
1 (877) 407-4847

Because of the dynamic nature of the Internet, any web addresses or links contained in this book may have changed since publication and may no longer be valid. The views expressed in this work are solely those of the author and do not necessarily reflect the views of the publisher, and the publisher hereby disclaims any responsibility for them.

The author of this book does not dispense medical advice or prescribe the use of any technique as a form of treatment for physical, emotional, or medical problems without the advice of a physician, either directly or indirectly. The intent of the author is only to offer information of a general nature to help you in your quest for emotional and spiritual well-being. In the event you use any of the information in this book for yourself, which is your constitutional right, the author and the publisher assume no responsibility for your actions.

Any people depicted in stock imagery provided by Thinkstock are models, and such images are being used for illustrative purposes only.
Certain stock imagery © Thinkstock.

Print information available on the last page.

ISBN: 978-1-5043-4411-1 (sc)
ISBN: 978-1-5043-4412-8 (e)

Balboa Press rev. date: 02/06/2017

PROLOGUE

The jubilant couple wades through a sea of parting hugs and kisses. Just before hopping into their car, they tease the cheering crowd with one last smoldering kiss.

"Wow, that was fun! The man exclaims as they head off. I feel like I could do it all over again but next time...we'll start with that kiss. That'll get the party started much faster! Seriously hon, the place was great. We should go back again soon."

"Yeah..." The woman dreamily stares out the window. "Between the food, chill reggae music, and bright, beautiful decorations, it really felt more like we were in a Caribbean resort than celebrating at a restaurant in the 'burbs."

The man breaks into a slow smirk. "Well, babe... that may have had more to do with all those tropical drinks everyone was sucking down than the island soundtrack or colors in the room."

She nods, giggling. "For sure! That rum punch was responsible for a lot of interesting speeches tonight. Who knew your straight-laced family could be so raunchy?"

He joins her in laughter. "I, for one, didn't. What a rip-off! To think I could've shed this shy geek image years ago. However, now that we've confirmed where my hidden wild side comes from, watch out baby: your lion is publicly on the prowl!"

He lets out a loud roar and pretends to paw at her, sending her into screeching peals of laughter. "Stop playing and drive!"

A few moments later, his eyes begin to appreciatively glide over her body.

"Speaking of which… this dress looks amazing on you. What do you say we pull over to see if it is just as beautiful on the inside?"

Playfully, she slaps away his groping hand. "Oh no…you've already marked this territory, 'Mr. Leo'. Anyway, you need to save all your energy for tomorrow, so I suggest you drop me off at the hotel as planned, then take some catnip and calm down. I would ask what's gotten into you tonight, but that much is *Cristal* clear. What I will ask, though, is how many drinks did you have and should I be driving instead?"

He holds her eyes with a sinister grin.

"Sweetheart, what you are seeing is a man drunk solely on the elixir of your love. Anyway, what did you expect after that kiss? It's taking all my power just to try to stay in the lane."

"Well, clearly you can do that if you focus more on the road than my cleavage. It's only temporary anyway, so don't get too excited."

Squeezing her hand, he gives her a slow, sensuous peck.

"Darling, please know that I will gladly take you in any form and love you all the more. You have given me so much to live for, especially now, and I—

There is an abrupt explosion of shattering glass and twisting metal, then complete silence.

Trying to open swollen, seared eyes, she can barely make out the paramedics hovering over her stretcher calling out instructions to each other. She strains to comprehend their words but they seem distorted and far away. The tube down her throat causes her to gag with each attempt to speak. While frantically struggling against the restraints, her mind races with a flurry of unanswered questions just before everything goes black.

CHAPTER ONE

Residents of Oakwood stream into the library with an air of excitement. Laughter spills forth as children bounce with enthusiasm, couples chuckle over private exchanges, and singles work the room, striking up animated conversations, hoping to identify worthy partners. Even the elders are enlivened as they proudly share time-honored strategies with those wise enough to listen. The crowd leisurely makes their way into the community room and begins setting up their tables.

Sometime later, a man closely followed by five teenagers rushes in and looks around searchingly. As scrutinizing looks are cast their direction, he briefly doubts having come. Spotting a woman with a bright, friendly face, he approaches her, hoping this will turn out to be a good experience for the kids like he envisioned when bringing them all the way across town for this event.

"Good Evening, my name is Rob Stephenson from the U.N.I. Youth Development Center. I'm looking for Stephanie Martin."

She flashes a welcoming smile. "That's me! I assume you are here for Scrabble Night?"

"Um…yes. I'm sorry we're late, but there was some traffic along the way. Are we still able to play?"

"Sure! We are set up for people to either join a group or come as you have with your own games. Feel free to choose any open table. Dictionaries are located on the back shelf. We are just about to start, so do you need help with anything else?"

No thanks!" Confidently exclaims a caramel skinned, curly headed girl with a duct taped 'Deluxe Edition' of Scrabble under her right arm, and a sizeable scar running through her left eyebrow. "We've all played at the center before, but just so you know, *I* am the Scrabble aficionado and have only come here to publicly serve these amateurs!" she says with a bright eager smile.

The others promptly respond with a swarm of retorts, challenges, and wagers, as Rob looks on with feigned skepticism.

"Well, Mariana, I sure hope you can spell all those words correctly, because if not, it will be *your* head on a platter tonight."

Bursting into laughter, everyone enthusiastically moves toward the tables.

After making sure the group is settled, Stephanie walks to the front of the room and taps on the microphone.

"Good Evening Ladies, Gentlemen, and Scrabble Aficionados alike."

She gives a nod and wink in Mariana's direction, who broadly smiles at her acknowledgement.

"I am Stephanie Martin, Director of Outreach here at the Oakwood Public Library. Thank you for attending our very first 'Scrabble Night'! From the looks of things, I don't think it will be our last.

Applause and hoots of confirmation follow.

"Scrabble Night will be held every third Tuesday of each month here in the community room from 6:30-8:00 p.m. "I hope you enjoy your experience tonight. If so, please tell us, and others. So, without further ado…let the games begin!"

* * *

When their game is finished, Mariana waves Stephanie over.

"Ms. Martin, guess who won?" She asks with a smirk of disappointment. "Rob! But I was only 10 points behind, so he'd better look out next time." She declares, eyeing Rob with playful competitiveness.

"Oh yeah, Mariana?" Counters a tall, lanky, smooth brown boy with tight braids, loose pants and a mischievous gleam in his eye, "I was only 5 points behind you, so you and Rob both better watch out!"

"Yeah Tim…you really surprised me", says a short, stocky guy with straight black hair in a buzz cut and a tribal tattoo covering his entire right arm. "I didn't even know you could read, nigga, let alone spell correctly!"

"Oooh!" the kids taunt, slapping the table in mirth.

"Aiight, Fabian…that's why the most points you got in your game was for the word 'weed'." More cackles and hoots follow.

"Okay guys…that's enough." Rob lightly cautions, casting an apologetic glance toward Stephanie. "Fabian, what did I tell you about using that word, man?"

Fabian knits raised eyebrows, clears his throat and in a mock British accent says, "Using your given names with each other is a sign of acknowledgement and respect."

Laughter erupts again.

"Okay then. I don't care how you say it," Rob maintains with a placid smile. "If you know it, then show it."

"Uh oh!" Chimes a fair-skinned girl with half her jet-black hair dyed bright blue. She is wearing dark, heavy eye makeup and several facial piercings. "Mr. Rob is a poet and he don't even know it!"

"*Doesn't* even know it, Clarissa", Mariana quickly corrects.

"Fuck you, you 'know it all' bitch!" Clarissa hisses. "Clearly, I know that, because *I* won *my* Scrabble game. I was saying it for effect. You need to learn your own fucking language before you start trying to correct others on theirs."

"Hey!" Rob booms loudly, and they quickly become quiet. He gives Clarissa a stern stare that instinctively informs her next action.

"I'm sorry, Mariana," She mumbles, glancing quickly at the girl before looking down at the table. "I was just saying I already knew that, so please don't correct me."

Rob's face softens. "Thank you, Clarissa, for acknowledging your infraction and expressing yourself correctly. That is very mature of you."

Clarissa looks at Rob with relief, gratitude, and more than a little pride in his compliment. She smiles apologetically at Mariana, who grins back with forgiveness.

A thin framed boy with a round, gentle face and straight black hair falling just above his slender, almond shaped eyes approaches Stephanie with extended hand and thick accent. "Hello, Ms. Martin, may I introduce? My name is Chen and though I got least points, I am glad to be here now. Thank you."

As Stephanie shakes his hand in return, Rob proudly squeezes Chen's shoulder.

"Chen has recently arrived from China but is quickly picking up on the English language. So, this is who we all need to look out for!"

Stephanie fondly smiles at them. "Well, Mariana, Tim, Fabian, Clarissa, and Chen, it is great meeting you and I look forward to seeing you all at the next Scrabble Night. You've each made this a special experience for me." She extends her hand to Rob and gives it a slow, firm squeeze. "Rob, I really appreciate you coming out this evening. It truly means a lot."

Rob looks at her and instantly a surge of energy swells through him. Everything stops as their eyes latch. Sharply inhaling and clearing his throat, he offers a restrained smile. "It's my pleasure, Ms. Martin. Take care." Under the pretext of time he quickly excuses himself and the kids with apologies for missing the public announcement of each winner.

* * *

On the way back, while the kids continue their playful jostling in the van, Rob's thoughts begin to run. What the hell just happened back there? Each time he recalls Stephanie's deep, smoky brown eyes boring right through him, his heart begins to skip with excitement. Maybe he is finally feeling the effects of his singleness-- i.e. loneliness. It has been two years since his divorce from Karen, and even longer since she walked out on him. He didn't think he could feel anything like this again, and up to this point, he hadn't.

Still, whatever it is, he is determined to let that boat pass. After 26 years of marriage he doesn't have much left to offer anyone, and what he does have, he needs for himself. He'd given his best and all to Karen, who ultimately stepped on it like a dirty old rag worth nothing. Just recalling this makes his heart grip with pain and resentment.

He takes a deep breath to collect himself so the kids do not sense his emotions. They tend to hone in to every little thing, which is no surprise. In the areas they live in, they have to. He just hopes they also didn't pick up on that brief interchange with Stephanie, because for sure, he will hear about it nonstop. They always are trying to fix him up with someone.

He glances at them through the rearview mirror, noticing they are beginning to droop from the day's excitement and gentle sway of the van. Chen is already asleep, with head bent forward and hair swinging over his face. Smiling wistfully, Rob wishes he would've had his own children to experience moments like this with.

Thoughts of Stephanie begin to surface again. Rob is moved by her genuine fondness and respect for the kids, which considering their display tonight, is no small thing. He smiles to himself. She must be a great mother. He also noticed that she wasn't wearing a ring, and wonders of her relationship status. Having been drawn in by her warm charm and authenticity, he relishes the idea of having a woman like this in his life. However, the sobering reality is that anyone as caring and vibrant as Stephanie most likely desires and deserves more than what a love wary, brokenhearted man, like himself has to offer.

CHAPTER TWO

Stephanie is snuggling in bed with Fred, when he abruptly gets up, claiming to be late for an appointment. Confused, because it is the middle of the night, she asks where he has to go at this late hour, but he does not answer. When she asks again, he continues moving as though he doesn't hear her.

Suddenly there is a knock at the bedroom door and when it swings open, Rob is standing there, staring at her with an expression as if pleading for something. For some reason, she can't look away and they remain there with eyes locked. When she finally does turn to Fred, he is gone. A bright light catches her eye and she turns back to see warm rays of sun shining through trees from a large picture window where the door had been.

Startled by a loud wail she looks down to see a tiny baby in a pale yellow blanket wildly flailing on her lap. She gently sways side to side to comfort it, to no avail. Desperate, she feels around the bed and is surprised to find a bottle filled with fresh milk. As she watches the hungry baby feed, a feeling of love and joy washes over her.

The shrill ring of her cell phone jolts Stephanie and she pops up from the couch in a daze. Grabbing it from her purse, she sees the number and groans.

"Hi Lehti", she hoarsely mumbles. "I am so sorry I overslept. If I had known how draining last night was really going to be, I'd have scheduled a different morning."

"It's ok, Stephanie," Lehti says in her soothing lilt. "I understand. However, we do need to reschedule another time for you to come in and debrief with me about last night. It was a big night for you. Are you free this evening?"

Stephanie sighs and absently grabs a pen from the table. "I hate to be difficult, Lehti, but I am usually drained after work. It's so hard for me to process anything. Can we stick to mornings—any day would be fine."

In the silence, Stephanie restlessly clicks the pen and waits. Finally, Lehti responds. "I don't want to wait too long to process this, so I'll make space for you tomorrow at nine. In the meantime, please take the time to reflect on yesterday and write down your thoughts so we can discuss."

Stephanie sighs with relief. "Yes, of course! I'll do it now. Thanks again, Lehti. See you tomorrow."

Falling onto the sofa with a long stretch, she rises and sets a pot of coffee to brew during her shower. Later, snuggled in a bathrobe with steaming mug in hand, Stephanie begins to review the day's events.

While pondering, her earlier dream flashes back to memory. Although she slightly wonders what it means, there are more pressing, real life matters to work out with Lehti. Further, the more she considers it, she is convinced that it is related to yesterday's events and all the emotions that came with it—missing Fred, her instant connection with the kids, and even Rob's crazy stare last night during their handshake.

Nevertheless, as her mother would have encouraged, she records all the details anyway. Her mom could find meaning in anything. To her, nothing was coincidental or happenstance. How ironic then that her life ended the way it did. She misses her, especially at times like this.

* * *

The moment Rob walks into the center and sees Clint's laughing face he already knows what's up.

"Heyyy there, Loverboy! I heard you caught a BIG fish yesterday!"

Rob maintains the usual impassive posture necessary when dealing with Clint's antics. "Wow, it's good to see that you have a life, Clint."

Clint smiles undeterred. "Come on, man! You gonna let another one get away? How many panties have you passed up by now? If you ain't gonna use them, at least toss a few my way.

Rob sits down and turns on his computer. "Spoken like a true gentleman. Now, is there anything work related that I need to know about?"

Clint lounges in the chair by Rob's desk and distractedly studies a sheet of paper. "As a matter of fact, there is. I need to leave early today, so... um... can you take over the group for me this afternoon?"

Rob resists the urge to roll his eyes. "What's up this time?"

Clint stands up and begins tossing Rob's stress ball in the air. "Nah, I got an appointment to take care of...something...serious."

Rob studies Clint for a moment and then breaks out in laughter. "Oh yeah...? An 'appointment', you say? Did one of your 'panties' pass something onto you--again?"

He looks at Clint's transparent face and laughs even harder. "You, my man are the number one reason for passing up 'panties', especially ones you don't know anything about. Even so, have you never heard of a condom? How in the hell do you advise kids and live like this? Keep this up and one day you're gonna get something a shot or a pill can't cure."

Clint looks penitent. "Yeah, I know, but sometimes I can't help it. When it's that good, it's the last thing on my mind. And I do carry a condom, but just got caught up this time. Man, the stuff that chick did! Plus, she *was* HOT. Every dude in the place wanted her, and--"

"You got her." Rob finishes, shaking his head incredulously. "Congratulations! Now you're probably fire throwing pee from all that 'heat'." He resists the urge to laugh again. "Alright, I've got you this time man, but no more...especially for this dumb stuff. Either keep it in your pants or wrap it up. Furthermore, don't be coming in here and sitting your crab ass on my chair spreading some new strain of crotch fever in my office." This time they both crack up laughing.

Clint smiles and gratefully slaps Rob on the back. "Yo, thanks, Rob. You're good peeps. Check you tomorrow."

Once Clint leaves, Rob begins to reflect on their conversation. Having been married for so long, thankfully these were things he didn't have to deal with. Although Karen began secretly seeing someone else toward the end of their marriage, thank God she never brought anything home. Still, it is pretty heartless to be screwing another guy while your husband is out working his ass off trying to provide for your extravagant lifestyle.

Looking back, he realizes he may have been spared any potential predicaments because the beginning of Karen's new 'arrangement' also seemed to coincide with her sudden disinterest in and the abrupt end of their sex life. Either way, he supposes it was a blessing in disguise, as Karen could be quite ruthless in getting what she wanted. For a long time, he even doubted if she really thought she was pregnant when they had to hastily get married in order to protect her reputation and the honorable position of her Father. Oh, and what an 'honorable' wedding it was! It cost her father loads of money that he made clear was not going to go to waste, having paid twice as much for making arrangements on such short notice. It didn't help that she had gotten 'pregnant' in between prom, graduation, and wedding season.

Nevertheless, in the end, she got everything she desired, right down to the 18K gold trimmed china that had to be specially shipped in for the occasion. Even the exclusive 5-carat diamond and platinum Tiffany wedding ring she insisted upon had set him back a pretty penny, but at the time he didn't care. This was the dream he had been working so hard for in the first place: a loving, beautiful wife who would give him a family to care, protect, and provide for. Hah! The joke was clearly on him.

In retrospect, he wishes he would have been wiser. Although already a savvy businessman at twenty-four, in affairs of the heart he was still inexperienced and so blindly in love that it never even crossed his mind that a 'sweet' pastor's daughter could be so devious. Well, having learned his lesson, he definitely will not be picking up anybody's 'panties'. Even if he had been inclined to consider it before, Clint's situation certainly stopped that thought process dead in its tracks.

* * *

As soon as Stephanie walks into Lehti's office, she feels a nervous excitement run through her.

"Hi Stephanie, it's good to see you," Lehti greets with a smile.

"Thanks," Stephanie responds, as she kicks off her shoes and luxuriantly sinks into the high backed, plush eggplant colored velvet couch she wishes were hers.

"So, where do you want to begin?" Lehti inquired.

Tucking her legs underneath, she leans forward to take a sip of coffee. "Well, let me start on a positive note. Scrabble Night was a complete success! We had nearly fifty people show up and everyone liked it so much that it may grow even larger. Who would've figured that part of my therapy would create such a stir?"

Lehti seems pleased but not surprised. "I am glad you have been able to create a meaningful emotional outlet that you can share with others. I am also proud of you for having the courage to step out and create a positive experience from something that could have kept you stuck in painful memories from the past. How do you feel about this?"

Stephanie ponders Lehti's words for a few moments as tears begin to fill her eyes. "It still hurts, maybe even more because here's a special moment and I can't share it with Fred the way I want to. I wish we both could have been involved in putting this together. It would have been so much fun!

I also feel alone in not having anyone as excited about the success of this event. I mean, I know that my boss and co-workers are pleased, but that's mainly because of the increased numbers and positive feedback. But on a personal level, Fred would have been overjoyed to see so many 'Scrabbled Eggs', as he used to call them, turn out with such excitement and passion. On the other hand, I felt like his spirit was there giving me strength throughout the day. So to sum it up, it was bittersweet. However, I think it will get easier with time. I really hope it will.

Lehti nods knowingly. "That was a very good assessment, Stephanie. You clearly expressed the difficulty of this process while still celebrating your success and envisioning the hope that lies ahead. This is a good place for you—a great place. Is there anything else?"

"Well, actually there is," Stephanie confesses. "There was a youth group that came to the event, and these kids were really...hmm...how do I put it? Well, let's just say they were very uninhibited in their presentation on every level, complete with tattoos, piercings, baggy pants and Goth makeup. Yet they were so real with themselves and each other, you know? And their group leader was this huge tough looking guy who actually turned out to be a softie. Well, to get to the point, as soon as we met, I instantly took to them so much that it has me feeling mournful of another loss connected to Fred: Teaching."

Listening intently, Lehti begins to jot in her pad. "Go on."

Taking a deep breath, Stephanie continues. "Well, after Fred's death, I swore I would never return to teaching. It was another thing I wanted to keep sacred to him—to us. But upon watching Rob—that's his name—interact with the kids, it created this strong desire to connect with young people again in that capacity."

Lehti looks up from her pad. "I see. So, what do you want to do with these feelings that have resurfaced for you?"

Stephanie pauses a moment, then sighs. "I really don't know. I still don't think I am ready to return to teaching and I like my job at the library, but being with them was so special that it unexpectedly touched a part of me I thought had died with Fred."

Lehti discreetly glances at the clock behind Stephanie and puts her pen down. "Well, Stephanie, you've uncovered a lot here. Let's continue to explore this more on your next visit. In the meantime, remember to journal your thoughts and feelings as often as possible."

Sliding back into her shoes, Stephanie begins to rummage through her purse. "Thanks, Lehti. I know it is a lot, but I already feel lighter by getting at least some of it off my chest."

Lehti smiles with encouragement. "Stephanie, you have covered a great deal of ground during our sessions, and I have no doubt that you will continue to make great progress over time. Inner work is challenging and takes a lot of patience, but the rewards are invaluable."

Stephanie hands Lehti a check. "I agree. For the first time in a long while, I'm content with where I am. It's not always easy and the pain never completely goes away, but overall I feel stronger than ever. See you soon, Lehti."

CHAPTER THREE

Inside Lifebreath Community Café, the quiet hum of conversation muted lighting, and low rhythmic music creates a hypnotic atmosphere that makes Rob feel as if he is somewhere hidden and exotic. This is why it has quickly become his favorite local escape. Lounging in a plush brown leather armchair, he takes a sip of lemongrass tea. Surveying the surroundings, he quietly chuckles to himself. If a year ago anyone bet him that he would wind up a regular in a place like this, complete with tribal music and sandal sporting neo-hippies, he would have confidently wagered his entire savings account.

However, one day when walking by, he saw a flyer in their window advertising a discussion on relationships that featured the author of a book he recently read. He attended and wound up striking up a conversation with a guy named Dalton who he later discovered was of all things--a Catholic priest. This blew his mind because the image he had always carried was that of an older man in a long black robe and a large crucifix, whose hand is to be kissed in greeting.

On the contrary, Dalton is 14 years younger and usually dressed in jeans with a plaid shirt. He looks like a model from Abercrombie & Fitch; yet when he speaks you feel like this 'kid has been here before', as his mom used to say of old souls in young bodies. As a person, Rob finds Dalton to be very down to earth, open and non-judgmental, which was why he not only enjoys his companionship but often seeks him out for advice.

Feeling languid and mellow, Rob briefly glances at the front door and instantly breaks out in a sweat. Walking in is none other than Stephanie

Martin. He wonders if he should pretend not to see her, but in that moment, she looks at him with a hesitant smile, so he cheerfully waves to her.

"Hi, Rob--fancy finding you here." Stephanie approaches with a cryptic smile.

Nevertheless, she is so unsuccessful at trying to hide her amusement that Rob has to laugh despite himself.

"Yeah...well, in case you didn't hear, the 'Annual Soul Train Dance-a-Thon' was cancelled, so I had nowhere else to go."

Stephanie gratefully joins him in laughter. "I would've thought you to be in a sports bar instead, but between Scrabble Night and a neo-hippie hangout, I'm no longer quite sure where I'll find you next."

Slowly, Rob raises his right eyebrow with an impish smile. "Really...? Well, I guess we'll just have to wait and see, huh?"

Now it is Stephanie's turn to be flustered, and she involuntarily lets out a nervous chuckle. "Yeah, I guess so, right?" Well anyway, it was good seeing you, Rob. If I don't meet you coming from the local synagogue first, hopefully, I will catch you and the kids at next month's Scrabble Night."

Watching Stephanie squirm gives Rob a satisfactory redemption from their last interaction. With a mysterious wink he says, "Sure...but as you say, anything's a possibility with me, so...take care, Stephanie."

As Stephanie walks away, Rob notices Dalton making his way over and heaves a sigh of relief that he doesn't have to deal with any introductions or awkward questions.

"Heyyy, what's up?" Dalton greets, as they exchange a cupped handclasp.

"Same ol'..." Rob replies nonchalantly. Dalton's eyes briefly dart toward Stephanie as she places her order. 'Damn', Rob thinks to himself, 'He doesn't miss a thing. He and the kids must be on the same eye hustling network.'

"I see." Dalton sits and smiles.

Rob shakes his head, laughing. "Man! What is this--confession? Why don't you get your usual coffee and scone first, so you can at least have something to eat while I entertain you?"

Dalton points at Rob suavely. "Good call! I'll be right back."

As he begins to get up, Rob clears his throat and draws in close with an attempt at menace. "I trust you'll invoke your priestly duties of discretion and confidentiality, right?"

Dalton briefly pauses before offering a wide, conniving grin. "Hmm… this must be good. Should I get a large coffee instead of medium?"

Rob waves him away dismissively. "Whatever, man. Just remember, I'm watching you; but more importantly…so is God."

"Ooooh!" Dalton mimes in wide-eyed fear as he walks away. Thankfully, Rob's apprehension quickly melts when he sees Stephanie walk off with her order just as Dalton approaches the counter.

* * *

"So Rob, what's all the mystery here? Dalton asks, sipping his large sized coffee.

Rob nonchalantly shrugs, shaking his head. "Seriously, it's nothing. She's just a woman who works at the library and runs an event that I bring the kids to. That's all."

Unfazed, Dalton replies, "Oh is that it? Well, okay then. Yeah…maybe it was just my imagination that I saw sparks flying out your eyes while you were speaking. Moreover, I could be misapplying my 'priestly' training as you put it, but did you really start your statement with 'seriously' and end it with 'that's all'? He starts laughing. "C'mon man, you work with kids--that's the basic law of deduction. I sure hope you've never advised them to accept a ride from a stranger whose line is, 'Trust me, I'm not a serial killer--really'."

Rob has to laugh in spite of himself, even though Dalton has pulled his card yet again. "Okay...okay", he concedes. "I am attracted to, and do like her, but the truth is I am in no place right now to even attempt entering into something I won't be able to carry to completion, so it's best just to leave it at shameless flirting."

Dalton grunts in response. "Well, I'd hate to tell you this, but with most women, that *is* the first step to entering into something. After what I just witnessed, she might be out choosing wedding rings by now."

"Yeah, well I may not know her that well, but one thing is for sure—Stephanie is not like most women. There's something about her that makes me know she's a well-grounded woman and definitely not the type to fantasize about marrying every man who flirts with her. I like her—she's very intelligent—intellectual even, but you can tell she's not high on her horse. When I brought the kids to her Scrabble Night event, Clarissa and Mariana almost got into a fight. She didn't even blink twice and in fact invited us back again. Most people in her position would've thrown us straight out or at least put on a fake front of tolerance. You can tell she really respects them."

Dalton nods understandingly. "She does sound special; perhaps someone even worth taking an emotional risk for?"

Rob leans back in his chair. "Nah, Stephanie is not the type of person you want to take a 'test run' on. With her I can tell, you either need to bring it out fully loaded or keep it in the showroom."

Dalton persists. "Okay, but if what you say about her is true, then just make sure that when she does leave the showroom in another model you will be fine with it and not kicking yourself for at least not trying."

Rob stares pensively into his empty cup. "I think I'd be fine with that more than having to be the cause of a total wreck."

Dalton looks at Rob and sighs heavily. "Listen, I know you've been through a lot and it has not been easy, but I also think that you do not give yourself enough credit for what a great guy you are. You keep comparing yourself to things that are deficient as though it is a total write-off, and while no one comes out of a betrayal after 26 years unscathed in the confidence department, please know that we are all flawed—even Stephanie; but that's the beauty of life and love—finding acceptance and grace in the midst of our imperfections."

Dalton's words stir something deep inside of Rob and he begins to feel a wave of emotion rising. Quickly, he excuses himself to the rest room and tries to compose himself, but the tears keep flowing. Suddenly he is angry with himself for crying like a baby over someone who cares nothing for him, and for ignoring it when he knew he should have left a long time ago.

He's tried so hard not to be 'that man', and where has it gotten him in the end--cowering in a public bathroom like a five-year-old who just wet his pants. Well, he doesn't care if Stephanie is made of diamonds and pisses pure gold; he is never going to let anyone put him in that situation again. At times like this, he can understand why Clint leads the life he does. Although he doesn't always go about it the smartest way, at least he's not weeping in a bathroom stall over some woman who took his heart and kicked it aside like an old rusty can.

Suddenly he is gripped with a thought that makes him break out in wild, silent laughter. He doesn't know which is worse: crying in a bathroom stall because of a broken heart or because you're pissing fire. With that unexpected but welcome comical reprieve, he wipes his eyes from what are now tears of amusement, splashes cold water on his face, and returns to the table feeling much lighter.

Noting the expression on Rob's face, Dalton says, "Wow, I thought only coffee ran through people like that."

Rob smiles. "Yeah man, you should try it some time. Lemongrass tea is really cleansing."

CHAPTER FOUR

As Stephanie sits at her desk studying the pile of papers before her, her mind begins to drift. Ever since Scrabble Night with Rob and the kids, she is finding herself less enthusiastic about her work at the library. She really misses teaching. There was always a level of wonder and newness to it; being able to listen to the stories that fascinated, challenged and perplexed her students always gave her a fresh perspective and approach to life. At night, she would exchange stories with Fred who was just as enthralled by his students, and it just seemed as if life was finally coming together for her and making sense. She had found her passion, her love, and her future all in one place.

Sometimes she wishes she had died in that car accident too. In a lot of ways, she feels like she did. How could she ever duplicate the life she experienced with Fred? She wouldn't want anything less than what she had--it was perfect. Although she sorely misses being with children, before this, she could never have imagined herself ever returning to work in a school. With whom would she share her stories? Who would give her the insight and encouragement to face the challenges of teaching? Each time she'd excitedly want to share an accomplishment would be another realization of how alone she really was without Fred in her life.

'This is too much', she thinks to herself. 'After all the work I've done and pain I've been through, it seems like there's always a fresh new batch waiting for me. It never ends—just like these papers. I need to get out and grab a coffee at Lifebreath.'

Recalling her last interaction with Rob there, she shakes her head in dismay. Underneath all that warmth and sensitivity he shows with the kids, clearly, he's still just another man on the prowl. He probably does this with all the women who cross his path, watching with amusement as they swoon over him, which would not be surprising, as he is really handsome. At the café, without the distraction of competing kids and a program to run, she was able to study him more closely. In addition to his magnetic presence are the prominent features of a strong broad nose and deep-set chocolate eyes that match his smooth skin; not to mention that electric mega white smile he kept seductively flashing at her. Feeling a wave of heat run through her, she quickly reaches over to take large, thirsty gulps from the bottled water on her desk.

"That's it!" she emphatically asserts. "Now I KNOW I've got to get out this office. I'm going stir-crazy AND having hot flashes".

She grabs her purse and stops at the front desk. "Aline, I'm running out to get some coffee. Do you want anything?"

Aline smiles wistfully. "No thanks, Steph. I'm trying to cut back on caffeine and sugar, and right now those are the only two things I do want."

Stephanie nods sympathetically. "Okay. I'll be back shortly." Once outside, she deeply breathes in the fragrant air from the flowers in the courtyard and stops to admire them. While gazing, she notices the sparrows playfully flitting about without a seeming care in the world and remembers the song her mom used to sing to her when she was little, about God watching over them and us. Stephanie closes her eyes and recalls how her mom's melodious voice softly caressed her fears away as she lay enfolded in her arms. She was so beautiful and special; she seemed like a rare bird herself. Too bad her wings were broken before she could really fly. Stephanie wonders what she would say about her life now. Her mom always had a perspective that made things better.

"I'd pay a million pennies for those thoughts."

Startled, Stephanie looks up with a mixture of excitement and apprehension.

"Hey…Rob!" She hails with a forced smile.

Rob takes one look in Stephanie's eyes and immediately drops the façade. "Are you okay?"

Stephanie chuckles with what she hopes is lightness. "Yes, but it's been kind of a rough day. I was stepping out for coffee, but clearly haven't gotten too far."

Rob nods knowingly. "Well, I'm no stranger to rough days myself, so I understand. I can go and get some coffee for you if you'd like."

Stephanie now smiles with genuine appreciation. "Thanks so much Rob, but I kind of need the walk. I'll tell you what, why don't you come with me instead?"

"That sounds great".

They walk along in silence until finally, Stephanie speaks. "I know this may sound like an obvious question, but what brought you to the library today?"

Rob starts to say 'Fate', but quickly catches himself, realizing it is not the time for his playful wit. This is their first real conversation, and he doesn't want to mess it up with another ill-chosen line. "Well, today is my day off so I went to the local bookstore to buy a book that a friend recommended to me, but of course they only carry the most current releases and those frequently requested, so I decided to come and try good ol' Oakwood."

Perhaps it is just her mood today, but Stephanie can't help but feel a rise with that statement. "Just so you know, Rob, Oakwood Public Library has some of the most extensive catalogs of books and media in the region. Not only do we carry current releases, but also classic manuscripts--many in their original and revised editions. We go far beyond Scrabble."

Damn! He wasn't even fully out the gate yet and already stepped on a land mine. "I'm so sorry Stephanie; I didn't mean it like that. I guess I'm not as educated about the library's resources as you are, but thanks for informing me. Maybe I'll check out Oakwood more often now".

Stephanie feels the heat of embarrassment run to her face and is compelled to apologize. "No Rob, please forgive me for jumping on you like that. As I said before, it's been a rough day, but that's still no excuse". Then quickly changing the topic, she asks, "So…what book are you looking for, anyway?"

Relieved for the shift in direction, he promptly answers. "The Epoch, by L.F. Vachon."

Stephanie abruptly stops and spins to face Rob. "Really?"

Not sure of how to respond, he answers with a slight trepidation. "Um, yes…do you know of it?"

Squealing, Stephanie begins gushing like a teen-aged schoolgirl. "Omigod! That's my all-time favorite book! I even have a signed copy of the original edition that I found online, but yes, we do have it at the library. It's an amazing book that surprisingly doesn't get borrowed too often."

Rob is pleased with Stephanie's swift transformation and even more so that he had something to do with it. "Well, with a recommendation like that, I'm even more eager to read it. Maybe once I've finished, we could compare notes, if you don't mind. I'd love to hear your thoughts on it."

Stephanie smiles. "I would really enjoy that".

When Stephanie returns to her office, everything seems bright and welcoming again. She and Rob decided to stay at the café and continued to have a wonderful conversation, exchanging experiences on her work at the library, and his involvement with the kids. His input has not only given her new perspective but also sparked some great ideas for her to implement at the library.

Perhaps Rob's appearance was purposeful after all, she muses. Recalling her thoughts the moment before he showed up, she smiles with tears in her eyes.

"Thanks, Mom."

CHAPTER FIVE

Rob sits on his deck overlooking the abundantly landscaped terrain, contemplating his conversation with Stephanie. The more time he spends with her, the more he truly admires her. Aside from the initial bumps, he really enjoyed their interchange today. She has the kind of personality that makes you feel safe telling her everything, because not only does she care about what you are saying, but who you are as an individual. That is rare in people, especially nowadays. He loves the way she intently listens and either asks thoughtful questions or shares her powerful perspective through a memorable story.

In many ways, Stephanie reminds him of Dalton. Even though she hasn't let on, she can also probably see through him just as easily. If so, it would be no surprise, as transparency has been his trademark for as long as he could remember. He was never able to hide anything like his brothers and as a result, his mother always knew to go to him if she wanted the real story. This is why he decided it easier, to be honest upfront, rather than face the embarrassing inevitability of being uncovered afterwards. Furthermore, dishonesty reminds him too much of his father's betrayal. Lying to his mom for years, destroyed her soul and forever fractured their family.

Rob's earliest memories of his mother were of a happy woman who loved to sing while cooking. He delighted being with her during these times because she would often share stories of her younger years as a dancer. Sneaking out, she would go to the night spot and show off her moves, which is how she caught the eye of his father. He quietly watched from the sidelines until on one memorable occasion, he decided to join her, and they instinctively moved like magic. In that moment, everyone stopped to watch, mesmerized.

Encouraged, they entered and won many contests, making a name for themselves. When they were offered the exciting opportunity of becoming part of a travelling revue, she found she was pregnant, so he got them an apartment and went on the road, with the promise of when he had enough saved, he would marry her and buy a house for their new family to live in.

She remained patient, even as he started coming home after longer breaks with less money, eventually having to apply for welfare when Ricky was born. By the time Roger came along, his father was nowhere to be found. She was disturbed when she heard rumors around town that he was shacking up with other women but continued to hold out hope. However, when she learned he married another woman and left town without so much as a wave goodbye, she began a rapid descent into despair.

Her only consolation was cooking. She loved to prepare feasts of fried chicken, steak; smothered pork chops with buttery mashed potatoes, macaroni & cheese, and buttermilk biscuits to sop up the gravy. The only vegetables she served were carrots, corn and collard greens with ham hocks. Desserts were sumptuous peach cobblers, banana pudding, and sweet potato pies.

She delighted watching her boys 'eat up', and as they did, each year they expanded a little more. Eventually, they were openly called "The Fatty Family" by the kids, and probably secretly by some adults.

When his mom wasn't in the kitchen, she was in her room crying or zoned out on TV. Trying his best to keep things together, Rob made a point of having her as busy as possible, even offering to help, because he'd rather see his mother happily bustling about the kitchen than tearfully buried in her bed. Soon food became not just Rob's way of comforting his mom but also distracted him from the pain of his father's absence.

In an effort to relieve his mother, he excelled in school and took on the responsibility of being a caretaker for his brothers, but it was too little, too late. She would often remain in bed, watching TV and eating, eventually becoming so large that she could barely move without assistance.

When Rob joined the football team in high school, it helped to channel his growing anger and lose weight. In the course of his freshman year, he went from blubbery to buff. Having a six-inch growth spurt didn't hurt either. No one dared say anything to him anymore—at least to his face. His transformation inspired his brothers who began incessantly playing basketball with the kids outside and eventually shed their weight too. He tried to get his mother to be more active too, but her motivation was gone. He took care of her as best he could, especially when she developed diabetes and often had complications.

Each year they got older, money became tighter, and Rob suggested that his mother file for child support to help with their expenses. However, she was adamant about having to go begging 'that man' for anything. As far as she was concerned, they were her kids and she would take care of them. Rob worried as he looked over their second hand clothes, and heard his brothers' complaints. Not having the 'right' gear in their neighborhood was often followed by an invitation to attain them by any means necessary. Therefore, he quit school at 17 and took a job in construction so he could buy his brothers whatever they needed.

Despite this, it couldn't save Ricky, an honor student with various basketball scholarship offers, from being tragically killed by a bullet meant for someone else while playing on the courts outside their building. This blow caused his already despondent mother to become completely unresponsive.

He continued to care for his little brother and mother until one left for the Navy and the other died of a stroke. It was an easy transition, therefore to take care of Karen for years until he realized he had been just as duped as his mother was with his father.

The difference is that he will not fall apart. For the first time ever, he has been able to focus on himself. He has spent most of his life taking care of others, and this was his time. As much as he appreciates Stephanie and looks forward to continuing to know her as a friend, he just doesn't have space for another relationship at this stage in his life.

CHAPTER SIX

At the end of the second Scrabble Night, the kids wave Stephanie over.

"Okay", she excitedly blurts, holding up her hand before anyone could utter a word. "Let me guess who won this time." She looks at Mariana whose eyes are popping out of her head, and asks, "Hmm…Mariana, by any chance, was it you?"

"Yes!" Mariana explodes, no longer able to contain herself. "I won by 35 points, Ms. Martin!" Stephanie glances over at Rob, who is beaming like a proud Papa.

"Yes, you did a great job, Mariana! It looks like I'll have to brush up on my vocabulary skills a little more for next time."

Meanwhile, Tim hunches in the corner scowling. "Awww, she just got lucky with her letter pick this time. She got the 'Z' and a triple letter spot."

Rob shakes his head at Tim with a look of admonition. "Tim, you know the expectations for the games here are the same as at the center. It's called 'playing' because it should be enjoyable. The true objective of this game is for you to achieve YOUR best, not just beat someone else. In reality, life is not always a series of 'wins' but of lessons that allow each of us to grow into our full potential, and when that happens, we all win. We are all on one team, so you know what to do."

Tim nods, conceding. "Yeah…congratulations, Mariana."

Mariana smiles brightly in response.

"As for you, Mariana…Rob adds, "You need to learn how to handle success graciously, and to also stop focusing on beating others. It's no fun to play with a gloating goblin."

There is an awkward pause before the kids explode in side-splitting laughter.

"Gloating goblin??" Clarissa gasps wiping her eyes. "Where the hell did you get that one from, Rob? You definitely should sharpen your vocabulary skills a little more. Oh, man—'gloating goblin'!

Rob joins in the laughter although slightly embarrassed in front of Stephanie. "Yeah…I guess I've got to stop falling asleep with the cartoon channel on".

"Please, man," implores Fabian. "You're supposed to be our role model, and we've got reputations to protect here." He says this nodding in Stephanie's direction, who good naturedly steps in to defend Rob.

"Well, I'm sure I've said worse in an unguarded moment, myself. You just wait until you get to be our age; you too may be surprised at some of the things that come out of your mouths."

Rob looks at Stephanie gratefully, and then over to Chen. "Hey Chen, for the record, please strike my last phrase from your list of popular sayings."

Chen smiles and nods his head knowingly. "Oh, I already did, Mr. Rob…I already did". Everyone begins chuckling again.

Mariana looks over at Stephanie. "Hey, Ms. Martin-- why don't you come to the center and play Scrabble with us some time?"

"Yeah!" The kids chorus in agreement.

Deeply moved, Stephanie smiles. "Thanks so much. I believe I will."

After saying their good-byes they begin to file out, when Rob abruptly turns back toward Stephanie and utters in a smooth, low voice, "I'm personally holding you to that, Ms. Martin."

* * *

There is a knock on the door and Stephanie looks up to see Stacie in the doorway. "Hey Steph, its quitting time on Wednesday, and you know what that means! Are you ready?"

Stephanie reviews the stack of papers she had been engrossed in and shakes her head. "Sorry, not tonight. I've really got to finish this report."

Then Aline, who is standing behind Stacie, comes forward. "Are you serious, Stephanie? That report's not even due until the end of the month. Stacie, I told you she was going to say this! Steph, stop being a workaholic and get out tonight. Plus, we want to ask you about that guy who's been coming to Scrabble Night with the kids. We've seen you talking to him, and Stacie wants to make sure the runway is clear before she comes in for her landing."

Stephanie laughs, shaking her head in bewilderment. "Stacie, what happened with you and Steve?"

Stacie rolls her eyes. "See, that's why you need to come out tonight. You've got to hear this story, girl." Aline nods with conspiratorial confirmation as Stacie continues. "So, what is the deal with that handsome hunk? I noticed he didn't have a ring on, so is he up for grabs or what?"

Stephanie's eyes widen with surprise. "Up for grabs? Are you trying to find a man or a game of pick-up basketball?"

Stacie raises her right eyebrow. "Girl, I'd play hockey on thin ice in the middle of Alaska as long as he was on my team! Well, anyway, I know how you like to be, umm…shall we say, discreet in *your* affairs, Stephanie, so I'm basically just trying to make sure I'm not encroaching upon private territory here."

Stephanie maintains her composure despite the pulsating heat rushing to her face. "Encroaching? Well, with a vocabulary like that, why don't you just come to Scrabble Night and find out for yourself? I'm sure he'll let you 'join his team' if that's what you want. And for the record, since being here I have had no affairs to be 'discreet' about, but you're probably right—if I did, *mine* wouldn't be on the six o'clock news broadcast, so thanks for checking."

Aline quickly intervenes. "Well, there you go, Stace! It sounds like he's free and clear—all ripe for the picking—ha ha! So listen Steph, we're gonna head out now. If you change your mind, you know where to find us."

Stephanie responds with a forced smile. "Sure thing, ladies! Have a great time tonight."

Once they leave, Stephanie immediately breaks into deep her breathing exercises and a couple of yoga poses. That Stacie is something else! On the surface, she tries to appear fun and lighthearted but clearly, cannot hide the deviousness that manifests itself in thinly veiled digs toward her. Knowing this, Stephanie usually manages to adeptly sidestep them, but for some reason, she was caught off-guard this time. Why should she care if Stacie wants to fawn over Rob? He probably would love it, as she is most likely his type. Heck, she is every man's type, with her clothes perfectly tailored to fit her Barbie doll figure; not to mention the long bouncy hair she loves strategically flipping while batting her long eyelashes and pouting with the studied confidence of a panther stalking its prey.

Actually, she hopes Stacie does go for it. Then Rob surely would have a more receptive recipient for his flimsy flirtations. Stephanie looks down at her papers and tries to focus, but it is too late. Furthermore, what about that 'discreet affairs' insinuation--as if she furtively goes around with every Tom, Dick, and Harry. Not everybody is like Stacie, creeping about, howling like a cat in heat. After heaving a few more deep breaths, Stephanie turns off her computer and heads home for a nice soothing bubble bath, soft music, and candlelight to clear her mind.

CHAPTER SEVEN

After reading 'The Epoch', Rob comes up with the idea to have a book discussion at his house with Stephanie and Dalton, which not only gives him the opportunity of reviewing this phenomenal book from various perspectives but also allows him to do one of the things he really enjoys— hosting others. This way he can spend time with Stephanie and not have her get the wrong idea that he is having her over for a date—or more.

Knowing he is attracted to her, he wants to be careful with their interaction. Out of respect for his marriage, he never cultivated any opposite sex friendships, so really, Stephanie would be his first experience in doing so. Thank goodness this time he is too wise to fall under the spell of the first woman to capture his interest.

The doorbell rings just as he places the Chardonnay in an ice bucket. It is Dalton.

"Hey man, thanks for coming. So, let me ask you a question—since we'll soon be in mixed company, do I have to now refer to you as 'Father Dalton'? To Rob's surprise, Dalton doesn't laugh as expected.

"Well, to be honest, I have recently been called into discussions at the Diocese over my 'super casual approach'. Still, without knowing Stephanie's background or how she'd feel learning I am a priest, I'd prefer not to hinder her expression in our discussion tonight, particularly around these topics. I am not ashamed of my faith or position, but this is one of the main reasons I have chosen to be more casual in my attire and discreet in revealing my vocation. Unfortunately, the traditionalists don't see it that way.

Rob looks perplexed. "So, what's the big deal?"

They perceive my actions as disrespectful but I feel in certain social situations the black attire and collar creates a wall that doesn't allow me to know who people truly are or what they really feel and think. As has been proven with doctors, most patients don't fully reveal their lifestyles or ailments because they feel either ashamed or intimidated. For some, this can be the difference between life and death. We share more with those we consider friends than who we perceive as 'officials'.

Rob nods with enlightenment. "Now I see why you didn't tell me you were a priest right away—and that was wise—because if you had, or even been wearing your collar, I don't think we would've developed the rapport we did, nor the friendship we now have. Your approach seems more realistic for someone who is in the service of people to be able to truly connect with them."

"Exactly," Dalton agrees. "So let's not mention anything until we can get to know a little more about her."

Rob shakes his head in admiration. "Wow, you would've been one hell—pardon—one *heck* of a ladies' man, Dalton."

Dalton smiles facetiously. "Who says I'm not?" They both break out in laughter.

"Come out back," Rob says. "I've got a veritable vegetarian feast out here. I don't know if Stephanie is vegan, so I whipped up both vegetarian and vegan fare."

Dalton surveys the table that could've been plucked off a page of a magazine in amazement. "You sure are talented, Rob. Not only do you design, construct and renovate beautiful structures, but you can also cook like a top chef with an impeccable flair for presentation. This is definitely not like sports night with the guys."

Rob smiles appreciatively though appearing somewhat uncomfortable with Dalton's effusive compliments. "Yeah well, I've got to up my game now

31

that there's a woman coming. You know how persnickety they can be about these things. With Saturday Sports Night all I have to worry about is the food being plenty, having a clear TV image with booming sound, and keeping the drinks flowing. Can you imagine if I pulled something like this with the guys? My reputation would be ruined!"

Dalton laughs. "I imagine so, but to be perfectly honest, I personally prefer this setup to the other, and am no less of a man. Neither are you."

"Yeah, but like you just said, I've got to know the audience I'm catering to in order to provide the best service possible."

"Well said, my friend...well said. So when is Stephanie arriving?"

"Oh," Rob says casually, "I had you come a little earlier so we could just chill first."

"That nervous, huh?" Dalton says with his usual perceptive but understanding smile that Rob doesn't even fight this time.

"Yeah", he sighs. "I guess I am. I'm sure it'll lessen once we get to know each other better. It's just the jitters that come in the beginning of anything new and exciting, which I've decided will only be a friendship. I've spent most of my life taking care of others. It's time to live for myself and do what I want, when, and how. Having a relationship means that you have to put all that away to completely be there for someone else. I am just not willing to do that at this point in my life."

Dalton looks like he wants to say something, but decides to leave it alone. "I understand, Rob. You have to do what feels right for you. That's what's most important."

Rob nods with relief. "Thanks for understanding, man." At that moment the doorbell rings and Rob's heart flutters with anticipation.

Sensing his apprehension, Dalton says, "Hey, relax man. Just be yourself, and everything will go fine— especially if you stay away from the corny one-liners."

Rob laughs, thankful for Dalton's presence. "No, I'll save those just for you, sweetheart."

Stephanie looks absolutely radiant in a belted yellow and white sundress that flounces just above the knee with strappy sandals. However, it is her dazzling bright smile, sun kissed skin and sandy brown hair with copper and gold highlights that causes Rob's breath to catch in his chest. He has to resist the urge to reach out, take one of those beautiful ringlets, and twist it around his finger.

"Hi, Rob. Thanks for having me over."

Rob instantly reverts to an infatuated pubescent boy. "Hi St-stephanie, glad you could make it. Um...I'd like to meet you—uh...I mean...for you to meet my good friend Dalton."

Dalton extends his hand with a welcoming smile. "Stephanie, I'm so glad to meet you."

Stephanie takes his hand, squinting. "Don't I know you from somewhere?"

Dalton shrugs obliviously. "I don't know, but as I understand we're both vegetarians, it could be from Lifebreath Café. I go there often."

Stephanie brightens with recognition. "Yes, it definitely could be. Isn't their food awesome? I go usually for the coffee and pastries in the morning but have recently been coming through for their lunch as well. I love it."

Dalton agrees. "My favorite pastry is the butterscotch scone. It is delicious, but I suspect we haven't had the best vegetarian fare Oakwood has to offer yet—right Rob?"

Rob smiles sheepishly. "That's up for you to decide. Come on out back and let's see."

As soon as she steps out onto the deck, Stephanie's jaw drops. "Wow... Wow, Rob...this is beautiful!" You must tell me who your caterers are so I can use them for our special events at the library.

Dalton shoots Rob an 'I told you so' look and broadly smiles at Stephanie. "The 'caterer' is the none other than the householder himself."

Stephanie stares flabbergasted. "What? Rob, did you do all this yourself?"

Rob is really embarrassed now. "Well, it wasn't that much effort. I just threw together some veggies and dessert, you know. Anyway, please sit down. For starters, I have some maple glazed grilled root vegetables. The entrée is grilled falafel burgers topped with portabella mushroom gravy—I can also top with Swiss cheese if you'd like, but wasn't sure if you were a vegan. To go with that I made curried potato salad on a bed of romaine, but it has eggs in it, so I also created a creamy cucumber dill salad made with tofu. I have a non-alcoholic lemon-basil sparkler as well as a chilled bottle of chardonnay. Dessert is a berry rum soaked pear flambé topped with a scoop of coconut cream sorbet and gingersnap wafer."

Stephanie looks at Rob with incredulity. "Are you kidding? How can you choose between that? I'll take it all!" They laugh and begin.

Later, with the meal devoured and chardonnay sipped amidst a lively conversation on 'The Epoch', Rob finally brings out his 'piece de resistance'. Dalton was right, his initial jitters and awkwardness had almost immediately disappeared in Stephanie's presence. She has such a way of putting people at ease. Feeling as if he'd always known her, he is now comfortable to the point of silliness. So, with great dramatic flair, he presents the pear flambé as Stephanie and Dalton coo, giggling like children when the flames shoot up.

Rob serves with the solemnity of a great magician. "I had to wait for at least sunset for this one to be pulled off properly."

Stephanie is drunk with pleasure as she dives into the dessert. "Mmm... Oh my god, Rob--this coconut sorbet is the perfect complement to the pear flambé."

Dalton agrees. "It's the ideal finale to a sumptuous meal." Suddenly his cell phone goes off. "Excuse me," he whispers, as he picks up the call and goes inside.

Rob watches as Stephanie lingeringly finishes the last of her plate, looking relaxed and glowing underneath the warm sunset. "Wow, that was by far the best culinary indulgence I've experienced! Rob, as I've said before, you surprise me a little more each time we meet but also must admit, I do find it quite exhilarating."

Their eyes lock and Rob feels like he is yet again floating under her spell, but this time doesn't try to stop it.

Dalton rushes in apologetically. "Hey, I hate to cut this short, but I have to handle an important matter. Rob, everything was perfect this evening, particularly the company. Stephanie, we have to do this again soon."

Stephanie quickly sits up from the chair she had been reclining in. "Oh well, I should get going too."

Rob looks at her in such a way that she instantly recalls her dream of him. "Hey, what is this, 'eat and run'? Although he says it laughingly, Stephanie detects more than a little hurt in his eyes.

"Oh no, Rob-- it's been so delightful, I feel like I could stay here forever, but don't want to wear out my welcome so soon."

Now Dalton intervenes. "Stephanie, please don't leave on my account. Believe me, if I were you, I'd get all I could of this royal treatment. If I didn't have to rush off, I would've easily been here for another couple of hours."

Stephanie looks over Rob's face and relents, "Well, you don't have to beat me over the head to stay, but you may have to do so to drag me out."

Relieved, Rob laughs a little more heartily than her comment warrants. "Well, we've got a plan then. Okay, Dalton, I'll talk to you later, and thanks again for everything."

Stephanie stands and shakes Dalton's hand with a comfortable smile. "It was such a pleasure meeting you Dalton, and I look forward to the next time."

Dalton smiles back warmly. "The same here Stephanie. See you soon."

Stephanie takes a sip of her wine and stares at the moonlit sky. "Rob, you have such a magical place…it's absolutely beautiful." She says dreamily.

'That's exactly how I feel about you', he wants to say as he gazes at Stephanie, mesmerized by the way the moon illuminates her face, giving her an otherworldly appearance. He wouldn't be surprised at all if she began floating into the sky, like the angel she looks to be, so serene and luminous.

Suddenly she turns toward him with those piercing eyes, and he quickly has to do something to regain his composure. "Hey, let me show you the rest of the place. Some of it is not ready yet and probably won't be for a while, but I don't mind taking my time to get it just right."

Stephanie stretches then gets up to lazily pad after him. "Well, that's why you had such a successful construction business. You put the time and effort in where it matters most, and people value that."

Rob bashfully glances down before looking at Stephanie with sincere appreciation. "So do you, Stephanie, and I value that."

As they go from room to room, Stephanie is so genuinely interested, that Rob eventually loses his self-consciousness about its unfinished state and eagerly shares the details of his vision for each area. "And last but not least," he says as they return to the deck. "This is my favorite place. I love to sit out here and close my eyes while listening to the flow of the fountain. Water always seems to calm me."

Stephanie nods, admiring the softly lit stone fountain wall composed of rough-hewn tile to create a weathered, rustic look. "Me too…that and music."

Suddenly Rob bends over, picks up a remote and points it toward the window. Instantly, soft jazz music fills the space around them. Yet again, Stephanie is astounded. "I have a hidden outdoor sound system," Rob explains. "You see these 'rocks'? Well, they're really surround-sound speakers specially designed to fit into the landscape. May I?" Rob stretches his arm toward Stephanie and draws her in for a slow dance.

As soon as Stephanie presses her face into Rob's broad firm chest and inhales the warm pungent scent of his cologne, she has a déjà vu experience—like she has been in this moment before, and her body instinctively relaxes against his. As they rhythmically sway, Rob gently cradles Stephanie's body, and the soft sweet fragrance of her hair wafts around him intoxicatingly. Looking down at the curls that have been beckoning to him all day, he finally gives in and delicately twirls a soft ringlet around his finger. Stephanie gazes up as if to inquire what he is doing and their eyes lock. Without thinking, Rob bends down and slowly kisses Stephanie's lips. As she reciprocates, their gentle lingering kisses begin to mount with passion, and Rob feels himself stirring. He doesn't want to stop now but knows if he waits any longer, he probably won't.

Stephanie must also feel it, because she too begins to draw back and before Rob can apologize, tenderly puts her finger to his lips. "Please don't. This happened because we both wanted it to. I'm not apologizing, and neither should you."

Rob embraces her tightly, releasing a long sigh. "Stephanie, this is one of the hardest things I've ever had to do and believe me, there have been many, but I respect you way too much to be anything other than honest with you." He hesitantly pulls away and looks into her face.

"I want you—I really do, but the truth of the matter is that I've been through so much that I am just not ready now. Further, I feel it would be dishonorable to take one part of you and discard the rest."

When Rob finishes, tears quietly fill Stephanie's eyes. Suddenly she bursts into sobs as Rob holds and rocks her, his own eyes beginning to brim. After calming down, she sheepishly looks up at him with tear soaked eyes. "I'm so sorry...I just wanted to feel again. It's been so hard..." With that, she breaks into fresh tears. When finished, she clears her throat and takes a deep breath as Rob dashes to get some tissue. She blows her nose and begins laughing. "I guess this is not what you were expecting while preparing your pear flambé, huh?"

Rob lifts her chin and she recognizes that same firm but loving look he gives the kids when serious about a point. "Stephanie, this is way more than I could have ever expected, dreamed or imagined—and much more than I deserve. Honestly, the way I feel right now, I could say 'I love you' in all sincerity, take you in my arms, make passionate love to you and feel complete.

However, I've been working with structures long enough to recognize the misleading allure of a 'false front'. This means you'd have to be with me not just in romantic starry moonlit moments but also in the times when my bitterness silently boils inside and I don't want to deal with anyone. Believe me, I am not the nicest person to be around then. What about when you need love, compassion, and care and I'm angrily shut away, fighting demons of doubt and mistrust? Solid structures need firm foundations and materials that can weather multiple seasons and situations. That takes time, thoughtfulness and planning—lazy constructionists can create the appearance of stability and safety quickly and easily, but it always winds up costing more in the end—and not just money, but more importantly, lives."

Smiling, Stephanie gives Rob a long hug and reaches up to kiss his cheek. "You are genuine gold, cast from the mold of chivalry untold. Ride on, lone knight; shine brightly in your truth and lead to safety our war weary youth. Good night, Rob."

CHAPTER EIGHT

When Rob awakens the next morning, he feels like crap. After Stephanie left last night, he could barely sleep, with so many thoughts and feelings rushing through him. Her cries brought back memories of his mother and he felt like a helpless little boy again except this time he was the one who caused the crying. 'So here it is,' he thinks to himself, 'After everything I've tried to do I've still become my father.'

Everything was perfect until he went in for that kiss. Dalton was right about women's emotions. Rob realized that he had inadvertently cast Stephanie in the same mold as Karen because that's all he's really known. It wasn't that Karen was strong—she just didn't care. As he lies there trying to figure out how to face Stephanie after this, the phone rings.

"Hey, Rob! Oh man, you sound horrible—did I just wake you?"

"Nah, I'm just tired. I didn't really get much sleep last night."

There is a long pause. "Oh, really?"

"No, it's not what you think. After you left, things went bad in so many ways. I really don't think I'm cut out for this relationship stuff. Maybe I should just join the priesthood like you."

Dalton laughs. "You might want to sleep a few nights on that one. Although I consider it a high honor, it's definitely not for everyone. What happened?"

Rob grunts. "Man, I really thought I was doing okay--until last night. I guess I got so used to going through the motions with Karen that I almost believed

I could live like priest too if I wanted, but with Stephanie…I mean, we only kissed, but I've never experienced something so powerful. I felt I was going to burst into a million pieces; it was like she tapped straight into an undiscovered longing that was so strong, it honestly scared me. Now I understand how we can sometimes wind up in crazy situations. I'd hear all kinds stories from the guys and believe myself to be above that. After all, I'm a thinking, reasoning man, and not some mangy dog in an alleyway that jumps on anything simply because you feel the urge to. That's how my father behaved. I was so ashamed of him and hated the fact that his blood ran through my veins.

Despite this, all I'm thinking about is having that feeling with Stephanie again. I mean, I know I'm probably talking to the wrong person here about this, but I want her right now even if for selfish reasons. Why do I always have to be the guy who tries to take the 'high road'?" Most men I know do what they want regardless of consequences, but I'm probably the only non priest who sacrifices himself for everyone else's benefit but my own."

Dalton is silent a moment before responding. "You're right Rob. You are not like everyone else because you are not like anyone else. You are you. You think things through because you care and, because of that, feel more deeply than most. You don't just jump in for the moment. If you did you probably would be able to move through things more easily, but somehow I get the feeling even that would be an unsatisfying experience for you because your joy comes from making others happy and not just exclusively pleasing yourself."

There is a long pause as Rob reflects upon Dalton's words. Finally, he exhales. "Wow man, you need to go on TV with this stuff. I'm serious. You are amazing!"

"And so are you, Rob. Remember that. I think you are much too hard on yourself and now understand a little more why. You are not your father and never will be no matter what you do because you are Rob. So please stop living in the shadows of someone else's choices from long ago and acknowledge the man you are right now."

Dalton's words always seem to touch Rob in deep places. "Man, let me get off this phone before you have me crying like a baby." Although Rob says this laughingly, Dalton remains serious.

"The soul knows exactly what it needs to free itself. If we listen and allow it to do what it's supposed to, it might save us from doing a lot of other 'crazy' things in substitution. Catch you later Rob."

As Rob hangs up the phone, he mulls over Dalton's words. 'That man is definitely not from here.' He thinks to himself. Then looking up toward the ceiling he smirks. "Another angel, huh?"

* * *

When Stephanie arrives home from Rob's she is not even motivated to shower. Peeling off her clothes, she throws on a comfortable old T-shirt and climbs into bed, immediately falling into a deep dreamless sleep. The next morning she awakens with an inexplicable lightness and clarity. Recalling all that happened, she is surprised to find that she is no longer upset with Rob, or even the situation. Looking out at the slowly brightening indigo sky, she decides to go for a walk in the woods.

After a quick shower she throws on some running gear and ventures out. Although she doesn't do it often enough, she loves being outdoors just before the day breaks and all is silent but the crunch of leaves and occasional snap of a twig beneath her feet. She stops for a moment to close her eyes and stretch, deeply filling her nostrils with the rich earthy aroma. At times like this, it feels as if she is one with everything. Soon, the first few tentative peeps of awakening birds evolve into a chorus that inspires Stephanie to join in with her own melodic accompaniment. She walks on, occasionally marveling at the sighting of a cardinal or blue jay before their fluttering ascension.

Finally reaching the pinnacle of Oakwood Hill, she climbs one of the majestic oaks to get a greater panoramic view. She loves the comfort of nestling deep inside a tree; it always makes her feel special and protected, like a child sitting atop of their father's shoulders. When she was younger, she and her mom used to climb the trees in their yard and pretend they were monkeys. They would carry bananas in the pocket of their jackets and sit peacefully upon the branches, making sound effects while peeling their fruit.

She enjoyed time with her mother so much, as she was more a playmate than a parent. Most parents worried and complained when their kids climbed trees and swung from the limbs, cackling on about broken body parts, but with her mom, every day was a new adventure. Employing her boundless imagination and creativity, she made everything seem exciting. Her mom particularly enjoyed nature and would take Stephanie on many different expeditions right in their backyard. Once they caught fireflies and placed them in an empty jar that Stephanie kept on her nightstand. Enraptured, she would watch them flicker for hours, imagining they were magical fairies, making a wish each time one lit up.

That was back when she believed that anything you wished for would come true. She knows better now. Life is what you make it. If you learn to roll with the punches and laugh more than you cry, then you are ahead of the game. She has been through so much it is a miracle that she is still here at all, let alone in her right mind.

Yes, each day of life is a gift and she is determined to experience it to the fullest as a tribute to everyone she loved who is no longer able to do so themselves: her mom, Fred…her children. She owes them that much, and nothing or no one is going to stop her. In a way, she feels sorry for Rob, who wants everything to be perfect before he can fully appreciate it. There are just some things you can't build to specification, and life is one of them. You've got to take it as it is and enjoy it in its unfinished state, knowing it will never be completely fixed.

In retrospect, she is glad for what happened last night, because first, it allowed her a good cry to release all the pain she didn't even know she was holding. She had gotten so used to being numb that deep down, she hadn't fully realized all she was feeling. Secondly, she is now able to see how far she's really come and how much growth had been occurring even in the midst of her grief. All this time she thought she was stuck, but listening to Rob made her see that she really wasn't after all. She was still willing to take a chance even though just as fearful. While hurt that things didn't turn out as anticipated, to her surprise, she didn't completely unravel, which was yet another reason to have hope in moving forward.

CHAPTER NINE

Rob returns to Oakwood Public Library hoping to run into Stephanie again. They had not spoken since that night at his house a few weeks ago, and he avoided calling because he honestly did not know what to say after such a fiasco.

He goes to the circulation desk. "Hi. I'd like to return this book, please."

The woman behind the counter takes the book with an inviting smile. "Hi, I'm Stacie! I've seen you here before. You're the one who brings those adorable children to the Scrabble event. That's so sweet of you."

Rob knows she is flirting with him, but doesn't mind at all. Aside from being very beautiful, he can't help but take in her voluptuous form, especially as she leans over the counter to speak with him. "Oh, hi Stacie, I'm Rob Stephenson. I work at the local youth center on Stable Road".

Stacie eyes Rob admiringly and flips her hair. "Wow Rob, you must have quite a vocabulary to take on a game like Scrabble. I've always wanted to try it, but am not sure I'd be that good."

Rob fights to keep his eyes focused on Stacie's face. "Well, the only way you'd know is to give it a shot. Plus, I'm sure you didn't get this job in a library of all places for nothing."

Stacie gives a throaty chuckle. "Well, I guess I do have some desirable skills...but I also enjoy learning new ones too." She says, slowly licking her pouty glossed lips.

Rob looks as though he just stumbled upon the leprechaun's pot of gold. Somewhere in the recesses of his mind are the echoes of a recent conversation with Clint, but they are quickly drowned out by his screaming libido.

"Anyway," Stacie continues, lightly grazing his hand with her card. "Here's my info. Maybe you can show me some of your techniques."

Rob leaves the library with a racing pulse and only one thought in mind: Stacie needs to learn how to play—and soon.

* * *

By the time Rob gets home, he has to take another shower. Later, lounging on his couch, he finds himself thinking about both Stephanie and Stacie. He really wants to be with Stephanie, but not just physically, for she is the total package. However, that would require more from him than he is ready to give right now. On the other hand, Stacie is offering exactly what he needs at this time—quick, easy fun and nothing more—she was absolutely clear about that. He wouldn't have to be anything for her beyond their 'play dates'.

Suddenly the ideals he has been holding onto most of his life now seem outgrown. His talk with Dalton has really made him come to grips with some things. He's spent so much of his life identifying with the little boy trying to pacify his mother by being 'good' in ways he perceived were the opposite of his father that he's never taken the time to learn what it means to just be himself. If he wants to have casual consensual sex with another woman, it doesn't make him his father—it just makes him a naturally horny Rob. Furthermore, he needs to stop feeling guilty about Stephanie, when he simply told her the truth. Yes, she is upset, but is that really his fault? He has been looking through the lens of *'Not My Dad'* for so long, that he is coming to realize that he may not have been clearly seeing things for what they are. Stephanie was crying because she wanted something he is not able to give her, not because he fed her a pack of lies and then walked off without a care. Dalton is right; he is a caring and thoughtful man… nevertheless, he is a man.

As he reaches for Stacie's card, the phone rings.

"Hey, Dalton! I was just thinking about you. Well, that's not exactly true. Actually, I was also thinking about this woman I just met who works at the library and how my talk with you really helped."

Somewhat perplexed, Dalton ventures cautiously. "Um…you mean Stephanie?" Rob snickers with amusement at the obvious misunderstanding.

"No, No… her name is Stacie. She works at the circulation desk and oh man you should've seen her! On second thought… maybe not—heh heh. So anyway, after recognizing me from Scrabble Night, she leaned over, slid her card into my hand and asked me to teach her how to 'play', if you know what I mean. I was just getting ready to call and arrange a 'play date' when you phoned. Talk about timing, huh?"

Dalton waits for a few beats before responding. "Rob, you're joking, right?"

Defensive, Rob retorts, "Oh yeah…I'm sorry Father—have I sinned?"

Now Dalton becomes irate. "Oh ok, I get it…I'm your 'friend' when agreeing with and complimenting you, making you feel all fuzzy and warm inside, but suddenly become 'Father Hellfire' when I have a thought or response that doesn't align with yours? Well, please don't let me cramp your style. Go for it, and I'll get off the phone so as not to further delay your recreational adventures."

They both remain in heated silence until Rob finally speaks. "You're right Dalton, that wasn't fair of me. I've been edgy ever since that night with Stephanie. I guess I'm just frustrated. Like you said, not everyone can live like you."

Dalton responds more calmly this time. "Rob, I never asked or expected you to live like me. I spend time with you because I enjoy our friendship and genuinely appreciate who you are, but being friends doesn't mean that we always have to agree, nor does my disagreement with you automatically make it a religious issue or matter of censure. What you said really hurt me. I invest a lot of time listening and getting to know you as a person, but it seems to me that casual attire and all, I am still just an icon to you. For the record, I am a man too. I feel the same physical urges, and just because I'm a priest doesn't mean I possess some special gift of 'immunity'. Instead, I have chosen to burn as a sacrificial offering unto God, who in turn strengthens me in my weakness. I don't expect you to understand or appreciate the religious aspect of it, but it would be helpful to me as your friend if you were at least able to relate to me from a human standpoint."

Now Rob feels like a complete jerk. "Dalton, I am so sorry. I didn't mean to make you feel like that. Perhaps I have been so consumed with re-establishing my own life that I have been oblivious to yours. Please forgive me."

"Sure Rob. Just so you know, I am not an inexperienced man; I know how hard it can be—no pun intended—to feel these urges and want to satisfy them. I suppose I'm just trying to figure out where Stephanie falls in all this."

Rob thoughtfully pauses before responding. "Well Dalton, I was honest when I told her I wasn't ready for a relationship, so it's not like I'm deceiving her."

"No, you're not deceiving her, but personally I don't think you are being considerate either. This arrangement would most surely affect her at the workplace, if not beyond. Listen, I understand: you are a grown man and can do whatever you want, but do you really think it's the wisest thing to have this kind of relationship with someone from her job?"

"Probably not." Rob finally concedes. "After my encounter with Stacie I was so worked up I guess I wasn't really thinking too clearly. My only focus at the time was that I had been honest with Stephanie about my inability to begin something with her." Rob sighs heavily. So...what now?"

Dalton replies reassuringly. "Rob, that's a question I can't answer for you. However, I'm confident that no matter how difficult things may seem right now, everything will eventually work out for the best."

When Rob gets off the phone, he reflects on what Dalton said about their friendship. He was right. In this determination to live life on his own terms, Rob realizes he has also been disregarding those he cares about in the process. Conversations with Dalton are primarily focused on his own thoughts and feelings. Rarely does he takes the time to ask Dalton about his life. To make matters worse, he was about to do the very same thing to Stephanie. Some friend he is! How could he have been blinded so easily? He inwardly cringes as he recalls telling Clint how foolish—no—dumb he thought he was, and now look at him! At least Clint has youth on his side, but at 50 years old, what is his excuse? Aside from her job, physical endowments, and electric sex appeal, what else does he really know about Stacie?

He looks down at his phone. He knows he needs to stop avoiding Stephanie, but can't fathom what to say, considering all the time that has passed. Suddenly, an idea comes to him, and he picks up the phone. "Good evening Stephanie, this is Rob. I hope things are going well with you. Hey, listen; the kids have been bugging me about having you come to the center. I know you are busy, but they are looking forward to it so much that I'd really hate to keep putting them off. I'm sure you know how kids get disappointed so easily. Umm…anyway, when you get this message please give me a quick call just to let me know when you would be available so we can prepare for your visit. Thanks a lot. I'll talk to you later." He hangs up the phone and exhales nervously.

Well, it wasn't a total lie, he tells himself, but more of an exaggeration. The more accurate account was that Mariana briefly mentioned it in conversation once before moving on to the latest drama occurring at her school. Now, if she had promised them a new cell phone or some money, *then* they would've been relentless. Nevertheless, this gives him an opportunity to break the ice. After what happened, she may not care to speak to him personally, but he seriously doubts that she would leave the kids hanging.

CHAPTER TEN

Stephanie walks into Lehti's office with an assuredness she hasn't felt in a while. "Good morning Lehti!" she merrily chimes.

Smiling, Lehti studies Stephanie inquiringly, as she sits down and places a bottle of water on the table. "Well, good morning to you Stephanie! No coffee today?"

"Nope." Stephanie proudly replies. "I've started jogging in the mornings, and you'd be surprised how much energy throughout the day you get from exercising early on."

Lehti nods in agreement. "Yes, absolutely. So, that's why you have such a glow. I thought maybe you'd fallen in love since our last session." She teasingly winks.

Stephanie laughs lightly. "Actually, I guess you can say that because I have fallen in love... with life again!"

"That's wonderful to hear you say, Stephanie. Would you mind sharing what brought about this attitude?"

"Sure." Stephanie opens her bottle and takes a gulp of water. "Let me see if I can give you the short version. Do you remember the guy Rob I'd mentioned from Scrabble Night who works with the youth? Well, we hit it off and connected outside of the event. So after a night of dinner and passionate kissing, he abruptly stops just before the clothes come off, to say that he doesn't want to be with me."

"Really?" Lehti scribbles in her pad.

"Yeah. At first, I was devastated. After everything I'd been through, I decided to take a chance because I really liked him and was sure he liked me too. But when I realized that he was just scared, it made me see how strong and brave I was and how far I had come in my healing. It also helped me to be clear about what qualities I need the man in my life to have, and Rob just doesn't fit the bill. I've been through way too much in my life to live it anything but fearlessly. So the bottom line is, in a rather unexpected way I came to the conclusion that I am finally ready to start moving forward in the romance department."

Lehti looks up from her note taking. "Stephanie, it sounds like you've really been doing quite a bit of self-reflecting. Can I ask if you have confirmed with Rob about why he suddenly said he didn't want to be with you?"

Stephanie flippantly rolls her eyes. "Well yeah, but I was trying to give you the condensed story. He said something about structures, foundations and destroyed lives…blah, blah. Because he's into construction—clearly more than he is me, he was glibly using all these building metaphors while I stood there with my beating heart in hand."

Lehti prods a little more. "Stephanie, I know you want to give me a summary, but this kind of work is done best by providing as much detail as possible, so as not miss anything. Many times the big things can be encapsulated in the tiny aspects we tend to overlook."

Stephanie is slightly befuddled. "Yes, I understand that concept Lehti, for other cases, but this here is a cut and dry situation. The man clearly said that he did not want to be with me. Even after I broke into wrenching sobs, he never changed his position."

Lehti continues to burrow. "Would you have preferred him to, in that instance?"

Stephanie's puzzlement now begins morphing into irritation. "What? I'm sorry, I don't understand where you are going with this—I came in here hoping that we could celebrate my big announcement today. As you remember, that was one of the major objectives of me beginning this therapy in the first place. If I must say so myself, and I guess I do—this is a huge success for me, but instead of being encouraging, you are like a big raincloud over my head."

"I'm sorry if that's what my trying to get a greater understanding of your experience feels like to you, Stephanie," Lehti replies impassively, which aggravates Stephanie even more.

"Yes, I can tell. The sorrow is just dripping off your face. What's really going on here, Lehti? Are you threatened by my success because it may mean losing a client? With all the time we've spent together, I never thought I'd have this reaction from you now. You know I do like you, but I'm not one of those typical therapy patients who make a career out of being spoon-fed. I like to look at a situation, figure out what needs to be done, work on it, and move on. Maybe you're not used to that, but it is what it is."

Lehti patiently waits until Stephanie is finished. "This is interesting, Stephanie. I don't think I've ever seen you so angry before and I'm wondering if you had a similar reaction to Rob." Stephanie starts to say something, but Lehti interrupts. "Please let me finish my thought so as to completely understand what I am trying to say before you respond if that's okay with you."

Stephanie falls back on the couch with folded arms and nods grudgingly. Lehti carefully continues. "Thank you. First, let me advise you that a therapist's competence should not be strictly evaluated by the length of time their patients are treated, but by how effective they are in making sure their client's needs are comprehensively evaluated and addressed. For instance, if I were a medical doctor and allowed a patient to walk out of my care simply because they said they felt okay, then I'd be negligent, especially if I was aware of a pre-existing condition. Just because I am not a medical doctor, does not mean my task is any less serious, as negligence in my field can also potentially put lives at risk.

My targeted queries are the equivalent of a conscientious physician running tests to make sure the patient who says he's okay doesn't suddenly drop dead the next day. Further, Stephanie, I would like to reiterate what I told you before we began our sessions—you are not held here by anything other than your will. At any time, you are free to terminate your treatment, regardless of what I think or say. You are not a prisoner. You came here of your own accord, and you are able to leave as such.

Now, what I am trying to do, as uncomfortable as it feels, is to get you to see the picture from all angles. Sometimes we are not really seeing what we think we are seeing, and sometimes we are. Nevertheless, we won't know for sure until we are willing to fully examine it. On a final note, yes I am concerned—not angered or threatened—by your strong reaction to my questioning. In my experience, when that happens there is usually something deeper that needs to be investigated. Whether you want or feel the need to do that is completely up to you. Either way, we are out of time now, but you can take this opportunity to think about what you'd like to do going forward, and then let me know. In the meantime, I will keep your appointments on my calendar until notified otherwise. Does that sound like a reasonable plan of action for you?"

Stephanie is thoroughly embarrassed over her spontaneous tantrum, and Lehti's calm but pointed response only makes her feel worse. She knows her abrupt reaction was out of line and has increasingly been happening of late. Maybe Lehti is right, that there is something more going on with her. She pulls out her wallet and begins writing the check. "Yes, Lehti, that sounds fine, thank you." She turns around just before leaving. "I'm really sorry for what happened here today." Before Lehti can respond, she darts through the doorway.

CHAPTER ELEVEN

Stephanie walks into to a cacophonous sea of voices screeching, laughing, rapping, singing, and feels completely at home. She approaches a young man lounging on the phone at the front desk who immediately hangs up and straightens his posture upon seeing her. "Good afternoon, welcome to U.N.I. Youth Development Center. How may I help you?"

"Good afternoon. I'm here to see Rob Stephenson, please. I'm Stephanie Martin from the Oakwood Public Library."

"Yes! Ms. Martin, if you can please sign our visitor log, I'll let him know you are here. Also for security purposes, I'll need to photocopy your state or federally issued photo identification.

"Of course." She says, fishing for her wallet. "It's reassuring to know that this is truly a safe place for youth. I thought the guards and metal detectors at the front doors were impressive enough, but you sure do your due diligence here at U.N.I. I must add that your professionalism, young man, is just as noteworthy."

"Thank you so much, Ms. Martin. Honestly, Mr. Stephenson has been a positive influence not just for me, but most of us here. By the way, my name is Clint, and I'm pleased to meet you." Clint beams with pride as he stands with hand extended, which Stephanie warmly receives.

"Ms. Maaartin!" Mariana shrieks, as she runs up to Stephanie and hugs her. "Rob said we were having a visitor today, but I didn't know it was you!"

Stephanie is flooded with joy at Mariana's reception. "I'm so excited to see you too, Mariana. Thanks again for inviting me."

"Ms. Martin, Welcome!" Stephanie looks up and her heart flutters despite itself.

"Thank you, Mr. Stephenson. It's a pleasure to be here." Rob looks mouth wateringly good in his dark slacks and starched white man tailored shirt that hugs his bulging biceps and glows against his deep chocolate skin. "Come on back. The rest of the kids are in the activity room.

After taking a tour and playing an uproarious game of Team Scrabble, which Mariana, Stephanie, Tim, and Clarissa excitedly but graciously win, everyone hungrily makes their way toward the pizzas Rob ordered. No sooner than they take their first bite, the kids get to work. "So…Ms. Martin," Clarissa ventures, "Do you have any kids?" Rob shoots Clarissa a look as if to say, 'Don't start', but Clarissa pretends not to see.

Honored that the kids want to know more about her, Stephanie responds freely. "No, I don't Clarissa, but I've always enjoyed being around young people. Your thoughts, ideas, and energy really inspire me, and that's why I am so glad to be able to spend time with you all."

Mariana adeptly picks up the next leg of the relay. "Well then, are you married?" She asks, specifically avoiding eye contact with Rob, who interjects anyway.

"Hey guys, can you give Ms. Martin a rest with all the questions, please?"

Stephanie makes a motion to indicate that she is okay with it and continues. "No Mariana, I'm not married either. I guess I just haven't found the right man yet." She says that one specifically for Rob's sake.

Now it is Tim's turn, who doesn't avoid eye contact with Rob. "Well as nice and intelligent as you are, not to mention pretty, I'm sure he'll come along real soon."

53

Rob stands up. Alright, ladies and gentlemen, it is now nine o'clock, and guess what that means?"

Fabian is determined not to miss his opportunity. "Hey Rob, what's the rush? We're enjoying the company and conversation of our lovely guest. We've stayed past nine before." Rob shoots Fabian a look in reply that says the game is over; as Chen, properly primed by the others' examples, covertly closes with the execution of a ninja warrior. "Ms. Martin, will you please come back again soon? We really enjoyed your visit today."

Stephanie tentatively glances at Rob before answering. "Thank you, Chen! I've also enjoyed myself, and will definitely return, but can't say when now. Nevertheless, I will keep you all posted, ok?"

Rob walks over and opens the door wide. "Okay guys, see you tomorrow." As the kids file out, Stephanie also prepares to leave, but Rob stops her. "Um, Stephanie, can I talk to you for a moment—well actually, are you available to go somewhere to speak?"

Stephanie remains cool and collected. "Well Rob, I don't know of too many places I want to be at this hour other than home, and if it is not business related, really don't feel comfortable speaking at all."

Rob is insistent. "I promise not to keep you long. Maybe we can stop by the 24 hour diner in Asbury for a cup of coffee."

Stephanie pauses for a few beats before indifferently responding. "I don't drink coffee this late, but if you want some, then I suppose we can go. I really can't stay long."

Rob is grateful for Stephanie's concession, even if it comes with an edge of ice. "Absolutely; I understand."

As they walk into the parking lot, Rob asks. "Hey Steph, do you want me to drive there, instead of you taking your car?"

Stephanie thinks for a moment. If things turn out in any way like the last time, she would like the freedom to leave on her own accord, and not have to be uncomfortably stuck in a car with Rob to add insult to injury. So she decides to trail him in her car. As they set out, Stephanie closely follows Rob's twists and turns down an unfamiliar road. Soon she becomes concerned upon noticing they are moving away from town through a forested area she doesn't recognize. Suddenly a wild thought flits across her mind about the nature of his intentions, but she quickly dismisses it. Rob may be unfit for a relationship, but he made it very clear that night he isn't a rapist, and surely isn't a killer.

Finally, he comes to a halt at an unmarked clearing, exits his car and walks toward her. Trying to quell her resurfacing paranoia, she keeps her car in drive and slightly cracks the window open. "Um…Rob, is everything alright? This clearly is not the diner."

Rob smiles excitedly. "I know. I didn't want any coffee either, but there's something I do want you to see."

Stephanie stares at Rob in such a way that he abruptly breaks out in laughter. "Stephanie, are you serious? You look like I'm going to take you into these woods and chop you into pieces! I already know you love the forest, so it can't be that you're scared to go in."

Rob's ability to read her crazy thoughts does make her feel a little foolish. He is still laughing when she retorts somewhat defensively. "Well, you never know about these things. How many women have innocently followed someone into the woods before, never to come out again?"

Rob quickly becomes sober. "You're right, Stephanie. I shouldn't have brought you here like this, especially without warning; but as I was heading for the diner, I just kept thinking I'd so much rather be here, and changed my route. Come on let's go back to the diner where I know you'll feel safer."

Stephanie, more assured of her ridiculousness, is now gripped by curiosity and a wild sense of adventure. "Heck no—let's go!" She exclaims, grateful that in her attempt to be more comfortable with the kids, she dressed down in her dark jeans and rubber soled shoes.

Rob perks up again. "Are you sure?"

Stephanie smiles with all prior coldness gone. "I'm sure."

Rob begins to unbutton his shirt to reveal a fitted tee. Even in the tree filtered moonlight, Stephanie can see the contoured definition of his arms. Going into the trunk of his car, Rob pulls out a pair of sneakers and track pants. "Although I clearly didn't plan this, I always keep workout gear in the trunk because you never know when the mood might strike to take a run…or hike through the woods." He explains with a nervous chuckle.

Stephanie smirks with amusement. "I see. So, should I be checking your trunk for a convenient pickax or sledgehammer as well?"

Rob dramatically bows with a sweeping flourish of his arm. "Be my guest, but I'll just step aside and slip these on while you conduct your search, my lady."

Directly averting her eyes from Rob's undressing, Stephanie makes a great show of rummaging through the trunk while surreptitiously watching him from the corner of her eye. Noting the strong muscles in his legs ripple as he slides off his slacks, she begins to wonder if this will lead to yet another night of frustration for her. She pretends to finish just as he starts lacing his sneakers. "All clear!" She announces.

Rob smiles facetiously. "Whew, that's a relief! Glad to know I'm not a dangerous nut. You ready?"

Stephanie beams with anticipation. "As I'll ever be!" They venture further into the darkness using Rob's flashlight for illumination. In addition to the usual nighttime rustlings, Stephanie hears a low rumbling noise in the distance but bravely continues to follow Rob's lead. When they come to a sudden stop, her heart leaps and she stands there dumbstruck.

"Oh, my…this is amazing!" Before them is a wide cliff overhanging a turbulent ocean whose waves slap the wall below them so forcefully, it sends up a light mist of spray. In the distance is a panoramic view of twinkling lights from the streets, houses and buildings along the shoreline and beyond. Rob holds out his hand to settle Stephanie upon the rock, climbs on beside her, then turns off the flashlight. They quietly sit in the dark listening to the rhythmic churn of water below.

After some time, Rob breaks the silence. "Steph?"

"Hmmm?" Stephanie languidly responds.

Rob continues. "I'm sorry. I know that my abrupt response the other night must have felt like I was rejecting you--but I wasn't--and I would like to explain." Stephanie remains quiet, so he goes on. "I really like you, Stephanie, and want to continue getting to know you. You. This intelligent, caring, woman who electrifies me with her smile, amuses me with her quirkiness and comforts me with her presence. I don't want to assume anything with you. I want to understand everything I can about how to treat you the way you deserve to be treated.

My father used to cheat on my mother, openly sleeping around with any willing woman in the neighborhood and beyond, and it was a source of shame for us. When people would point at me, and say, 'That's Rob's little boy', it was in such a way that I felt their pity and/or contempt, and so was forced to wear the stain from a mess I didn't create. I can't even imagine what my mother had to endure as she walked the streets under scrutinizing eyes, carrying babies in succession from a man who used then discarded her like trash. What I do know was that she was often crying. Each night, I could hear her wailing into her pillow after putting us to bed. This is the most disconcerting feeling a child can have, because if the one—the only one—responsible for you is falling apart, where does that leave you?

So I promised myself I would do all I could to keep my mother happy and was determined to fill the gap my father left behind. Because of that, I really had no childhood or adolescence other than some encounters with girls who wanted to be with 'Big Rob' from the football team and occasionally chilling with the guys on the team. No one really gave me any grief either, because they knew my mother was disabled. She weighed over 500 lbs. and was diabetic.

When my brother Ricky was killed it became apparent that I could never erase the grooves of sorrow and loss created in her heart that she would play over like a familiar sad song, so I poured my helplessness into the one thing that I could do well: my work. As my business began to grow and gain success, I hired nurses and attendants to take care of my mother, but rarely spent time with her the way I used to. I felt like such a failure and even worse when she suddenly died of cardiac arrest.

Soon after, my youngest brother joined the Navy, and I was all alone for the first time in my life, with no family and no one to take care of. That's when I began to really think about starting my own family. I was 24 when I met Karen, a 19 year-old college student. She was beautiful, innocent, and made me feel for the first time that I was in love. I brought expensive gifts, took her to nice places and when we made love, I was honored to be her first. It was even more special knowing that she would eventually be my wife.

So imagine my surprise when she shows up on my doorstep one day with her father, a well-known pastor, telling me that not only was she pregnant, but also a 17 year old high school senior! I felt so stupid. She cried and pleaded with me to forgive her, already having told her father that it wasn't my fault. She wanted to be with me so badly that she lied about her age and more. Her father said he would not 'create issues' if I allowed him to host a wedding ceremony when she had graduated from high school in three months, and at which time would also be 18 years old.

When they left, my mind was racing. How could I have let this happen, how did I miss it? Finally, I realized my mistake was that I had been so consumed by not just my emotions and desire for her, but also the image of the perfect family life I always wanted. I never really took the time to go deeper. What we did is dream like kids, while acting as adults, and now the stark reality of those actions had exacted a price.

Once I got over the shock, I knew I was still in love with her and felt even more protective, so we got married and I happily became the surrogate for her doting father, feeding her every need, whim, and wish. Soon after we discovered that Karen had what was called a 'hysterical pregnancy', when a woman's body looks, feels and responds exactly as if its pregnant, but there is no fetus present. We were devastated, both in our own separate ways; she began to drown her sorrow in shopping and I worked even harder to keep up with her extravagant demands. All the while, she whined and complained that I never spent time with her.

Years later, when the business hit a particularly rough patch and money was tight, she had her father get her a job as an executive assistant in a law firm and never let me forget it. I tried everything possible to keep her happy, but it was never enough. Then one day she announced that she had been seeing her boss and wanted a divorce.

So, Stephanie, that is the long winded explanation of why I want to first, take this time to do the things I've always wanted, while gradually getting to know you—and you, me. I've learned firsthand that to accelerate this process by being physical too soon can not only cloud a situation but also complicate it."

Stephanie reaches out to hold Rob's hand and gathers her emotions. "Rob... like me, you too have been through a lot. Please know that I am here to support you however you need during this time."

Squeezing her hand, Rob is grateful for the darkness covering them, as his eyes spill with tears. "Thank you, Stephanie."

Resuming their silence, Rob feels refreshed, as if the splashing waters below are cleansing his soul.

CHAPTER TWELVE

When Dalton enters the restaurant, Rob is pleasantly surprised to see him in a pair of charcoal slacks, black shirt and nicely coordinated tie and cufflinks.

"Well now…what have we here? You had better not let The Gap see this, or you'll lose your contract."

Dalton playfully scowls. "That's fine, because 'GQ' will pick me up instead. Hey, so what's the occasion for coming to this fancy place? You know my birthday isn't for quite some time, right?"

Rob places a small black velvet box on the table between them. "Dalton, you are officially on a 'man date'."

Dalton looks down at the box and his eyebrows shoot up. "Whoa Rob, I understand things are kind of shaky with Stephanie right now, but I'm not sure this is exactly a viable alternative either. Plus I'm a priest—I don't put out on first dates."

Rob rolls his eyes. "Shut up. A 'man date' is something I came up with after realizing I was taking you and our friendship for granted. I created this occasion to say thank you and check in to see what's going on in your life. In other words, this is your time D, so stop pissing around and open the box."

Although touched, Dalton can't resist fully mining the potential comedic value of this opportunity; so, clutching the box to his chest he flutters his eyelashes and theatrically mimes a feminine voice. "Oh Rob, you do care… you really do! The answer is and will always be yes…yes!"

Just then, he turns to see their waitress standing behind him with two glasses of water and a curious look on her face. "Welcome to Soffio Di Vita, gentlemen! Is this a special occasion tonight?"

Rob immediately places a napkin over his face and breaks out in silent hysterics as Dalton turns beet red. "Ah…uh…no, I uh was just joking with my friend here."

Rob, still unable to speak, is convulsing with tears streaming from his eyes, as the waitress good naturedly smiles. "Should I give you both some more time?"

Dalton clears his throat and replies in a lower octave. "Yes, that would be great. Thank you."

The waitress, clearly seeing that she has walked in on a private joke at Dalton's expense, takes pity on him. "No worries, Sir. Please take your time."

As Rob begins slowly begins to recover from his attack, he coughs and takes a sip of water. "That serves you right, man." He says, starting to bubble with laughter again. "You should've seen your face. I wish I'd gotten a picture of that one! Well, I suppose now you'll just open the box like I initially asked without all the drama, huh?"

Dalton, still shaken by the surprise appearance, slides the box into his pocket and furtively looks around. "Um…hey man, can I just open it later, like when we leave or better still when I get home?"

Having had more than his share of entertainment, Rob decides to let up on Dalton a bit. "Yeah, sure man, that's cool. It's nothing big anyway--just a small token to thank you for your friendship and all the wise words you share with me. Although I do have some good news to update you on, I've promised myself not to bring up any of my stuff until after we've had time to talk about you."

Melanée Addison

Dalton appears more relaxed now. "Rob, I really appreciate your efforts here as well as your friendship. This really means a lot to me. Thank you."

The waitress returns to the table with a basket of warm bread. "Are you gentlemen ready now?" Rob, already looking over the menu, responds first. "Umm, yes, I'll have the salmon linguine with garlic pesto and the house salad, please."

Dalton is still trying to make up his mind. "What vegetarian dish do you recommend?"

"The vegetable fettuccine carbonara is one of our favorites."

"Then I'll try that." She makes the note, smiles and glides off.

Rob breaks open and butters his roll. "So Dalton, I don't think I ever asked you--what made you want to become a priest?"

Dalton sighs, shaking his head. "Rob, that's a long story, and definitely not dinner conversation. However, I will share what inspires me most in my ministry, and that is the example of my father, Mac. It's ironic because even though he was never a priest, people always referred to him as 'Father Mac'. His full name was Cormac Patrick Shea and he was a simple man. He met my mother at a dance when they were teenagers and loved her faithfully until the day he died.

He worked as a foreman at the iron welding factory and attended the same parish that I serve in now, St. Thomas'. He wasn't a drinker but loved to go down to the bowery and 'chat it up' with the folk there. He was a very likable man who was easy to talk to, and as a result, many people confided in him things that they would never reveal in confession. He was also very generous. We didn't have much, but anyone who needed a meal could always come to our house and eat.

My mother is also kind and caring, but not as social as my father. My father was comfortable with everyone and treated drunks with the same respect as clergy. He always held a special place for those considered outcasts and rejects, but the church would ignore these people because they considered

62

them riff raff, pure and simple and resented my father's work with them. Sometimes he would bring them to Mass and everyone would cringe as though their very presence was some form of contamination. I also got to know these people, and yes, some were heavy drinkers but I can tell you that even with all the issues they had, they would give you the shirt off their back. They were some of the kindest, loyal and truest people I'd known, they just had a lot of pain that they didn't know how to handle.

Although a devout believer, my father would never preach to them, but just sit and listen or tell a funny story to lighten their load a little, and they really appreciated him. One day, he was mysteriously found stabbed to death in an alleyway. The rumor throughout town was that one of the clergy had arranged it, and his murderer never found. To this day I don't believe anyone from Oakwood had anything to do with it, and neither does my mother."

Stunned and deeply saddened, Rob falters for words. "I-I'm so sorry, Dalton. That's horrible.

Dalton sadly smiles with a faraway look in his eye. "Yeah…it was devastating. Still, all said, he has shaped the man I am today."

Rob shakes his head. "So do you think the church really had something to do with it?"

Dalton nods. "Yes, I do. Someone there knows or knew about it."

Rob is baffled. "So, how could you still become a priest, especially in the same congregation?"

Dalton ponders for a moment. "Well, that's the other half of the long story, but the short of it is that I ultimately trust God's justice over man's wrongdoing. I answered a call from God, and that has nothing to do with anyone else's actions."

Rob studies Dalton with new admiration. "Wow…that's powerful. Thanks for sharing, Dalton."

Just then, the waitress approaches with their food. Dalton looks appreciatively at the heaping plates. "Perfect timing--I'm starving! Let's dig in, and you can give me your update."

* * *

When Rob gets home, he proudly reflects upon his evening with Dalton. Once they finished their meal, Dalton reconsidered and decided to open the box, which contained a small silver handcrafted Celtic Cross pendant he was grateful to have received.

For the first time in his life, Rob is glad to be developing relationships that connect to him in a deeper, more meaningful ways. It's not that he doesn't appreciate having the guys over on Saturdays watching the game but considers it to be more company than companionship. He treasures his friendship with Dalton because it allows him to comfortably express parts of himself that sometimes don't fall within the acceptable image of 'manliness'. However, the more he reaches for the truth inside himself, he is able to clearly see through the façade. The sum of who he is cannot be encapsulated in a static, one-dimensional image.

He used to be ashamed of his sensitivity and transparency because where he grew up it carried a stigma of femininity and weakness. When he tried to compensate by imitating the macho gesticulations he saw played out around him, he would just feel awkward and unnatural, so eventually learned to be non-emotive. That, combined with his size, made people-- especially girls perceive him as the 'strong, silent' type.

Although he sees similar struggles in Dalton, he admires the fact that he continually dares to challenge the status quo to find what he calls his 'authentic self'. Dalton, convinced that no one can find real purpose and joy until they know and live out who they truly are, often says, 'You won't get what God has for you if you're living someone else's life'. Rob is glad that he took the time to learn more about Dalton tonight, and in hindsight is grateful for the confrontation that led them to this place.

With that, he has a thought and picks up the phone. "Hi, Stephanie? Hey, this is Rob. I'm good, how are you? Really? Wow, that sounds nice. Listen,

I hope I'm not calling too late…oh? Okay. Ha ha! Well, that's good to hear. Um…so, I'm calling because I would like to ask you out on a date, but there's a catch. I want you to pick the place; somewhere that means a lot to you, that you would enjoy going to. I'll cover any and all expenses, but I want our first official date to be about what you really want and not what I think you want. Like I said, I don't want to assume anything with you. Really? Well, I'm glad you're so excited about the idea. Thank you. Okay, just let me know whatever you decide. How does this Saturday sound to you? Great! I'll see you then. You too…Good night."

CHAPTER THIRTEEN

Stephanie answers the door and bursts out laughing. "Wow, you look like the Gorton's Fisherman! What's up with this rain gear—I thought you loved water so much—that it was sooo calming to you? Come on in, Rob." She says, still giggling.

Rob swishes in defiantly. "Yeah…well, I also like to be prepared in weather appropriate situations. I'm cool with walking through the forest during a rainstorm if that's what you want, but I don't intend to catch pneumonia doing so."

Stephanie can no longer contain herself. "Rob…a rainstorm? There is a light drizzle outside!" She howls, gasping for air.

Rob remains unbending. "But they also said there could be potential thunderstorms."

Attempting to calm down, Stephanie shakes her head resolutely. First, that's not until later this evening, and secondly, I am NOT going outdoors with you in this large yellow outfit, looking like Big Bird. Granted, you can keep the duck boots, and be grateful they're not matching yellow galoshes or they'd be going too. She opens her closet and retrieves a large army green poncho. Here, put this on, if you insist on being covered. Unlike you, I won't dissolve from a few drops of moisture, so I'll forgo it to save my reputation. Now, let's go—the longer we stay here quibbling over this, the greater the chances are we will run into that big, bad 'thunderstorm' you're trying to avoid." She says, trying to conceal her amusement as Rob sulkily slides out of his rain suit and into her poncho.

As they begin the trail, Stephanie stops to takes a deep breath. "The one thing I love better than walking in the forest is walking in it during or after a rain. It smells so verdant, and everything is quiet and peaceful. It's a great time to just walk and reflect." As they continue in silence holding hands, Rob has to agree. Although everything seems hushed, he can still feel the life vibrating around them. They walk on enveloped in their own thoughts, until coming to a clearing where spread before them in a gentle mist, is a panorama of lush greenery. Finally, Stephanie speaks. "This is the place where I like to come to and think. See this tree? I usually climb and nestle inside not only to look at the view from an even greater vantage point, but I also feel protected. It's my secret little hideaway."

Rob looks up at the huge oak and then at Stephanie in awe. "Wow. You must have been some tomboy when you were younger because I sure can't see you as a little girl in a pink party dress learning to do this. What did you do—run around with the boys, challenging them to tree climbing races and other daredevil stunts?"

Stephanie smugly smiles at Rob's admiration of her prowess. "No, it was actually my mother's doing—she was the original adventurer. We would often go throughout the neighborhood exploring different things. She instilled her love of nature in me. In addition to climbing trees, we would capture bugs, lizards and snakes, examine and let them go. We weren't really into the 'girly girl' thing. This exasperated some of my friends' parents when they would come back from a visit to our house covered in dirt and scrapes with their clothes sometimes torn, but oh, we had SO much fun! I ultimately lost some play pals along the way, but it didn't matter because my mom was my best friend and greatest playmate anyway."

Rob is amazed. "That is so cool, Steph! How did your father feel about it—did he join you two?"

Stephanie's smile slightly stiffens with her response. "No, he wasn't really around much. He worked a lot and was often on business trips."

"Really, what did he do?"

"I'm not exactly sure, I just know he worked for a large corporation and was always on the go. Anyway, it actually gave us some freedom, as he wasn't really the playful type."

Where are your parents now? Rob inquires, intrigued.

Stephanie pauses for a couple of beats. "They're both dead."

The look on her face and the tone of her voice tells Rob not to press anymore, so he quickly changes the subject. "It's so beautiful and still up here, I can see why you like it so much." Stephanie's easy smile returns as she looks around. "You know it's kind of like a spiritual experience for me here. My mother never took me to church, but she taught me how to love and respect God through nature. She used to attend church faithfully when she was younger and even into her early adulthood but said that after a while she felt like there was something more than just singing songs and listening to someone lecture once a week. She wanted a deeper, more personal experience—and mind you these were in the 'peace and love' times—so she went on a spiritual trek in the mountains with some hippies and although never said so, I imagine it had something to do with smoking weed at the least, because that's what hippies did back then. She told me she had a visitation from God right there on the mountaintop, just like Moses.

She was sitting there appreciating the view when she suddenly felt this powerful energy field surrounding then entering into her. She became one with everything around her, the people, trees, grass, flowers and birds and insects as if they were all breathing the same breath at the same time. The next thing she knew there was a booming voice vibrating through her saying, 'I AM Here…I AM Here!' She started shaking uncontrollably and fell face down on the floor in tears unable to speak for hours.

No one else heard or saw anything, and after that, she never went back to her church again. Instead, she would often sit outside amongst the trees, quietly praying and listening. She often had dreams that would come true or tell me things about myself that no one else could know. At first it would spook me out, but in time I got used to it. She strongly believed that dreams were messages sent from Heaven. Any time I had a dream she would interpret it and even if I thought it was a bad one, by the time she finished explaining it to me, it was no longer scary and I would be comforted."

Rob listens intently, studying the faraway look on Stephanie's face, trying to make out her mother's in it. Suddenly they notice the raindrops becoming heavier and the sky growing darker. "We'd better start back now." Stephanie declares with a sense of urgency.

Rob adamantly insists that Stephanie put her poncho on and she does not argue, for the purposes of saving time. As the rain increases in intensity, they swiftly but nimbly descend the path of slippery rocks and mud, with Rob firmly holding Stephanie's arm to stabilize her. Finally, when they get to a wider opening, Rob briefly lets go of Stephanie's arm, loses his footing and immediately slides into a mud puddle. Once she sees he is okay, Stephanie crumples in laughter as he flails in the mud, cursing.

Still trying to compose herself, she offers assistance. "Come on Rob, take my hand." She says, her eyes moist with tears. As she anchors herself, stretching out her arm, he reaches up and jerks her down into the mud with him.

"AAAAH! Rob, I'm going to kill you!" She squeals in surprise and begins hitting him in playful mirth.

Now it is Rob's turn to laugh. "Oh, so you thought that was funny, huh? Huh?" He taunts, pinning her down in the mud, as she vainly tries to struggle under his iron grip. Soon they are wrestling in the downpour, covered in mud and laughing hysterically. Then with energy spent, they lay face to face, breathing heavily, limbs entwined.

Finally, Stephanie extracts herself and heaves her waterlogged body up with great effort. "Come on, Rob, or you are going to catch that pneumonia you were trying to avoid."

Rob slowly hoists himself up and feigns indignation, "Yeah, but it never would've happened if you'd just put your pride aside and let me look like Big Bird. So, I guess this means that you are now personally responsible for nursing me back to health."

Melanée Addison

As they trudge along, Stephanie nods grudgingly, trying to suppress a smile. "Yeah…I guess I am."

* * *

Upon returning to Stephanie's house, Rob retrieves his spare workout clothes from the trunk of his car while Stephanie showers. She then insists he does the same as she puts their clothes in the wash and makes something to warm them.

Later, with all traces of their mud match gone, they tiredly lounge on her couch with steaming bowls of vegetable soup and ginger-lemon tea. Once they finish, Rob appreciatively surveys his surroundings. "Steph, your place is so cozy and relaxing. It has an atmosphere that reminds me a lot of Lifebreath Café."

Stephanie smiles graciously. "Thank you. I get a lot of my inspiration from the various spiritual retreats I've visited over the years. I always want to feel like I am on one even when I not able to be."

Rob studies the framed artwork on the wall. "These are nice. Who are they by?"

Stephanie glances over to where he is looking. "Some are mine, and some were done by my mother."

Rob smiles, impressed. "So, you are an artist as well as a tomboy, huh? Looks like I'm not the only one full of surprises. Um, I hope you don't mind me asking, but how did your mom die?"

Stephanie swallows hard and remains quiet for a while. Finally, she sighs. "You know Rob, you've been really open with me about your history and I truly appreciate you sharing that with me. However, I have a personal philosophy of leaving the past in the past. I like to focus on the here and now and not dredge up old stuff that doesn't really even matter anymore. Now is what we have, so let's enjoy it."

Troubled by Stephanie's reaction, Rob presses cautiously. "Well Stephanie, I have no choice but to respect it, however, I think it will definitely make it hard for me to get to know you. We can't hide from our past; who we are right now is an accumulation of all that has happened to us, and if we don't look at that, then we won't ever really know--"

"We are who we choose to be, Rob—not what anyone has said or done to us." Stephanie interrupts irately. "You say you want to get to know me; I am showing you who I am—right now, right here. If that's not good enough for you then I'm sorry, but you can't have everything on your terms."

Rob contemplates Stephanie's words then reaches for her hand. "You're right, Stephanie. I apologize. I am getting ahead of myself. I did say we would take our time with this, and here I am the one pressing you. Thank you for being patient with me."

Softening with his acknowledgment, Stephanie tenderly cups Rob's face. "Rob, this is challenging for both of us. I've never met someone quite like you before and so I'm trying to figure this thing out too. I guess we'll both have to be patient with each other." As she leans her head on his chest, Rob folds his arms around her, and they quietly sit there until drifting into sleep.

CHAPTER FOURTEEN

Stephanie tentatively walks into the office. "Good Morning, Lehti."

After clearing things up with Rob, she debated whether she should call and apologize immediately or wait until her next appointment to do it face to face. Having decided upon the latter, she had not spoken with Lehti since her last episode, and still feels a little ashamed.

However, if Lehti is holding any residual energy from it, it is not obvious in her demeanor. "Good Morning Stephanie, how are you today?" She welcomingly intones in her usual melodic manner, which eases Stephanie's tension considerably.

"I'm fine, thanks for asking. Before we begin Lehti, I really owe you an apology for my behavior last time. I was definitely out of line and wrong in many ways."

Lehti smiles appreciatively. "Thank you for your apology, Stephanie, but please also know that in doing this kind of work, it is not an uncommon experience, so I don't want you to beat yourself over the head with it. Rather, think of it as an excavation of unchartered territory where you never know what will happen at any moment—whether that process will yield buried treasure or create an avalanche.

The point is, my job is to continue exploring anyway, and you should expect me to be well prepared for the task I've undertaken. What is important to me, however, is that you feel you are in a safe and comfortable environment with someone who you trust. As you already know, this is very hard work, and if those elements are not present it can make it a more difficult, if not impossible challenge to overcome."

Stephanie emphatically shakes her head. "No, that is definitely not the case, Lehti. I do feel safe and even though it's not always comfortable, still trust your judgment. I am aware of that now more than ever."

Lehti nods and picks up her pen to signal the session opening. "Okay. That's good to hear. So, please explain what has happened between then and now?"

"You were right about me jumping to conclusions concerning the incident between Rob and me. We've had the opportunity to speak and it is nothing like what I thought. Honestly, I was just hurt because I felt rejected by him."

"What changed your perception?

"When he revealed some past experiences that made him hesitant to jump into something right away, it all made sense. I guess I was so focused on what I wanted that I couldn't see anything beyond that."

Lehti stops scribbling and looks up. "So what did you want, Stephanie?"

Stephanie quickly realizes she may have unexpectedly treaded upon that 'avalanche' territory Lehti was referring to as she feels the first rumbles of uneasiness shudder through her but it is too late--Lehti has already begun her excavation.

"Well..." she pauses while trying to collect her thoughts. "I wanted...I wanted to feel loved." She concludes uncertainly, but Lehti is persistent.

"Please describe what that feels like for you."

After remaining quiet for a while, Stephanie nervously shakes her leg as her stomach begins to churn. "Lehti...I can't do this. Please... not today."

Lehti studies Stephanie with concern and nods yieldingly. "Okay Stephanie, but please at least tell me what is happening. You don't look well."

Stephanie shakes her head, trying to fight back rising tears. "I...my stomach hurts. I don't know...I don't know..."

Lehti's voice remains calm and measured. "What do you need me to get for you, Stephanie?"

Dazed, Stephanie tries to stand up and gather her things but immediately starts swooning. "N-nothing. I just have to..."

"Stephanie!" Lehti rushes over to steady and guide her back onto the couch. "Please, just lay back and be still for a few moments. I'll dim the lights while you rest for the remainder of the session, and then let's see how you feel, ok?"

"Okay.", Stephanie responds weakly as she takes a sip from her water bottle, and closes her eyes. Her head is spinning, and breathing, rapid. Taking slow, deep breaths, she lets her mind float into nothingness.

In what seems like only a minute or two, she hears Lehti's soft voice. "Stephanie?"

"Yes." She opens her eyes and carefully sits up.

Lehti intently observes her from the chair. "How do you feel?"

Stephanie reaches for her water bottle again. "Much better, thanks. I don't know what happened...that just came out of nowhere. Maybe I should get checked by a doctor."

Lehti searches Stephanie's face thoroughly. "Have you ever experienced this before?" Stephanie pauses then nods with sudden recognition. "Yes... but not for a while...a long while."

Lehti nods conclusively. "Well it definitely wouldn't hurt to see a doctor, but it appears that what you had was a good old fashioned anxiety attack. I am glad you are feeling better. So, let's pick up next time. Until then, please take care of yourself and let me know what the doctor says."

As Stephanie stands up again, her legs are a little shaky, but overall she feels much stronger. "Thanks so much, Lehti." She says gratefully, handing the check over. "I'll see you soon."

* * *

Stephanie steps outside as the cool morning breeze hits her face. While walking to her car, she decides to call in sick, as she desperately needs a mental health day. Lehti was right; she hadn't been doing her reflection and journaling much lately and instead, pulling more and more hours at work. Nevertheless, what really set off today's episode was Lehti's questioning— what does love feel like to her? Although it seemed like such an elementary question, she was stumped. She could've easily said being held and kissed, but somehow she knew that Lehti was going for more than that.

She recalls her relationship with Fred and is surprised at how less frequently she thinks of him now and that realization strikes a pang of guilt in her. She doesn't want to admit it, but Rob may be eclipsing Fred's memory. Not long ago she was sure no one could ever come into her life and do that. She wanted to talk to Lehti about that some more, instead of: 'What does love feel like to you?' What did she expect her to say?

She picks up her phone and calls out. In the place she's in today, all she'd need is one dig from Stacie and she'd be either in jail or looking for a new job. She decides to go to Lifebreath for breakfast where she can eat, relax and reflect while doing her journaling assisgments. With a smile, she remembers how she and Rob played with abandon the forest like two kids on a wild expedition. She really, really likes Rob. He is so much different from Fred. With Fred, their excitement was vicariously lived through the young people and all he brought to her intellectually and culturally, but with Rob, their energy is more physical than cerebral. She likes that but isn't sure how much longer she's going to be able to hold off. She laughs to herself. What a time for role reversal! Usually, it's the man pressing the woman, who is trying to hold out, but one more of those mud wrestles or even cuddles on the couch and she's going to have to tie him down and have her way. To her defense, they do say that women in their 40's suddenly get a burst of sexual energy, and this must be what's happening to her. Whatever it is, it had better work out soon or she is going to be doing more than snapping at people.

CHAPTER FIFTEEN

Rob and the kids file into the room and excitedly wave to Stephanie. Delighted to see them as well, she briskly makes her way over.

"Hey, guys! How's it going?"

Mariana pipes up, as usual. "Great, Ms. Martin! We're now having weekly Scrabble challenges at the center. In addition to tracking our scores, Rob made a chart for us to see if we are also improving our vocabulary skills and game strategies. It's fun!"

"Yeah," Clarissa agrees. "And at the end of the year, we're going to be honored at the annual award ceremony in categories like, *"Best Sportsmanship, Player of The Year,* and *Most Improved."*

"Wow, that's great!" Stephanie enthuses.

Tim smirks with his usual cocky swagger. "Well, I've already started reading the dictionary in my spare time, so don't y'all be mad when I walk away with all three awards!"

Fabian scoffs in response. "Whatever, man. I'm just doing this to improve my freestyle flow, for the ladies you know, so when they see me in the place...it's Ready, Set Go!"

Chen smiles and pulls something out of his bag. "Here Fabian...you can borrow my dictionary."

Everyone bursts out laughing at Chen's surprise attack. Stephanie then looks across the room to see Stacie sashaying in their direction with one of her winning smiles. Upon her approach, all three boys' eyes widen in-synch while the girls stare, suspiciously guarded. All the while Rob is standing there looking dazed and confused.

"Hello everyone!" she croons, with a lingering glance at Rob. "You all are having so much fun over here I figured this must be where the party is. So, how do I get an invite?"

Stephanie quickly steps in with a fake smile. "Hey guys, this is Stacie Bennett, and she works here at the library with me. Stacie, this is Tim, Chen, Fabian, Clarissa, and Mariana who are all here from the U.N.I. Youth Center and this is their Advisor, Rob Stephenson."

Everyone politely says hello, but Stacie is not content to leave just yet. "Oh Rob, yes...I know Rob already." She says with a cryptic grin and a flutter of her eyelashes.

Now all the females, including Stephanie glare at Rob quizzically with raised eyebrows as the males smile at him with open admiration. Rob's eyes briefly bulge as he breaks out in beads of perspiration. "Oh well, yes...w-we...I was returning my library book and we, we...chatted about Scrabble...Night."

Stacie is delighted with the stir she is so effortlessly creating. She looks at Rob and chuckles, giving him a playful tap on the arm. "Yes, we did, and I said I would love to join you guys in a game once I learn how to play."

She concludes with a slow, meaningful smile then glances at Stephanie who remains as cool as a cucumber.

"That sounds great Stacie, but as we are starting to get underway now, it won't be today. Kids, please say goodbye to Ms. Bennett and thank her for stopping by. See you tomorrow, Stacie." Stephanie then turns to the kids, who for varying reasons are in a tumult. "Okay now, it's time to get your heads clear and game face on! Guys, drop and do as many pushups as you can in one minute and ladies its jumping jacks for you. Rob, you monitor the guys, and I'll watch the ladies.

Everyone excitedly scrambles to find a clear place to perform their exploits. When the minute is up everyone begins buzzing about how many they did and how much more they could've done, etc. Rob looks gratefully at Stephanie for the welcome diversion, but she is pokerfaced. "All right, I'll be back after the game to see how you did. In the meantime, do your best, and remember to have fun!"

* * *

Rob hangs up the phone and falls back on the couch in exasperation. He's already left three messages for Stephanie, including one about the kids wanting to see her again, but she has not responded. He knew he messed up the moment he saw Stacie wiggling her hips in their direction with a look in her eye that her beauty pageant smile could not disguise. Now he truly understands the saying, 'Hell hath no fury like a woman scorned'. He had to experience this with Stephanie first, then Stacie, and now it's back to Stephanie all over again. At times like this, he really envies Dalton. To add to the increasing female drama in his life, even the girls at the center have been giving him an undercurrent of attitude. The guys, however, are more than ok, patting him on the back and high-fiving him every time he passes by. Even Clint is seriously thinking about paying off the book fines he's accrued since junior high school and renewing his library card.

However, for Rob, not only is this frustrating, but embarrassing. Everyone now thinks he is this player, which is the last image he wants to be projected to the kids, particularly the females. One of his major reasons for coming into this work was to be a positive, stable male role model to compensate for many of the missing or wandering fathers most of them were stuck with, just as he had been. Still, no matter how many times he's insisted that nothing transpired between him and Stacie, her award winning performance left an indelible mark in everyone's mind, including Stephanie's. Short of stalking her at the library or her home, he is just going to have to wait for the next Scrabble Night to see her.

He picks up the phone one more time. "Steph, this is Rob again. Listen, I understand that you are upset, but I can explain everything if you just let me. I want you to know that nothing really happened, Stephanie. I care about you too much for that. However, I will not call again and instead wait to hear from you when you're ready. Have a good night and sweet dreams."

In the following three weeks, Rob is on pins and needles. During this time, the kids also seem a little more subdued, but that's most likely because of his own energy. Although he has not heard from Stephanie yet, he often imagines her perched in her oak tree, overlooking the scenery and going over things in her head. Despite her prolonged silence, he believes that once she finishes working things out, she will realize what they have is truly special. They share a unique connection that most do not often find. He knows she felt it from the beginning, just as he did. Whatever she has been through and now doesn't even want to talk about clearly has really affected her. Therefore, he will continue to give her the space to sort her feelings out.

* * *

Unfortunately, when Scrabble Night does come, Rob is sick in bed with a stomach bug and has to call out. After a couple of weeks more with no word, he can no longer take it and Stacie or not decides to go to the library to speak with Stephanie and sort things out.

When he walks in, sure enough, there is Stacie behind the desk. Nevertheless, in his urgency to see Stephanie, he is prepared for anything she has to throw at him. "Hi Stacie, how are you? I was wondering if I could speak to Stephanie, please."

Stacie, in place of her eye batting and purring, gives Rob a restrained smile with a look in her eye that he can't quite make out. "I'm sorry, Rob...I really am."

Rob's heart drops into his stomach. "What is it, Stacie?"

Just then, he sees Stephanie distractedly going through some papers while quickly approaching the desk. She is regally clad in a deep purple wrap dress and diamond accessories with strappy stilettos. Her makeup is luminously applied in complementary tones and her beautiful tangle of curls is brushed and elegantly upswept into a chignon.

"Hey Stacie", she starts, still glancing down at her papers. This is the revised report. When Jeff comes, please tell him I'm running just a few minutes behind, but will be out soon."

The look on Stacie's face causes her to turn around, where she sees a crestfallen Rob standing behind her. However, if she is surprised, she doesn't miss a beat. "Oh, Hi Rob! It's good to see you. I'm sorry to be so brief, but I'm in a rush right now." As she begins to hurry off, suddenly she turns back. "By the way, we missed you and the kids at the last Scrabble Night, so hope to see you at the next. In the meantime, please give them my best." With that, she disappears, as Rob and Stacie stand there in stunned silence.

"Rob, I'm so sorry. This is my fault, but to be honest, I did not know there was anything going on between the two of you. When I asked Stephanie beforehand, she gave me a completely different impression. I know I can be a flirt, but I also do have certain standards."

Rob stands there trying to control the emotions boiling inside him. "Who's Jeff?" He calmly asks with an unconcealed flash in his eye.

Stacie, sensing his energy, treads carefully. "Jeff Santos. He's a big real estate mogul Stephanie met at some business event. He's been taking her out a lot lately. Listen, Rob, I get off in half an hour. Why don't we go somewhere and just talk—that's all because whether you believe it or not, I am concerned about you right now."

Rob stares right through her. "So, he's coming here to pick her up?"

Stacie is now afraid she has said too much. "Rob, please don't say or do anything rash. Just wait for me at the U2 Lounge down the street, because you seriously look like you're going to kill someone right now and I don't think being in jail is going to benefit those kids who look up to you."

At the mention of the kids, Rob begins to snap back. After a few moments of silence, he mutters, "Yeah, I'll meet you there.", then walks off. Exiting the building, he notices a tall, distinguished man getting out of a chauffeured town car, heading in his direction. His wavy black hair is framed with silver highlights, and he is sporting an expensively tailored business suit.

"Excuse me," Rob calls out, briskly striding over to the gentleman. "Are you Jeff Santos?"

"Yes, I am.", the man responds as he covertly searches Rob's face for recognition.

Rob coolly lifts his hand and extends it in greeting. "Nice to meet you. I'm Rob Stephenson. From what I hear, we're both good friends of Stephanie Martin. She's great, isn't she?"

Jeff's face slightly relaxes at the revelation of their connection. "Yes, she is a wonderful woman. I'll give her your regards, Rob." He says with a smile.

"Please do." Rob smiles stiffly in return and walks off.

* * *

As he enters the U2 Lounge, the blood is pulsating through Rob's head as he feels that familiar feeling of rage creeping up. "Hey, give me a double shot of brandy straight up." He orders the bartender, who upon seeing Rob's size and the menacing look on his face, quickly obliges. Rob not being a heavy drinker, has never had anything like this before, but he'd heard it ordered plenty of times while out with the guys, so he figures it must be potent—a man's drink. When the bartender places it in front of him, he immediately knocks it back like he'd seen it done on TV and tries not to choke as the burning sensation spreads down his throat. He wants so bad to ask for a glass of water, but figures this pain is a better distraction for the one that is ripping his heart apart right now.

'Damn, that Stacie!' He is going to give her a good piece of his mind when she comes in. She couldn't leave well enough alone and realize that he hadn't called her for a reason. No, she had to come over, in front of the kids no less, and announce that they already 'knew each other', which wasn't even true. He knows nothing about this woman. Stephanie clearly knows more about her than he does, which is most likely why she is so upset. She's probably heard all the salacious stories of men who were trapped by the net of her allure; In light of that, of course, it would easy to believe that he was just another fish who greedily swam toward her line. Well, he is going to milk every bit of information out of her before telling her what he really thinks.

"Another double, please!" Rob says with a slight slur, and the bartender looks concerned.

"Okay guy, but we have an hourly drink limit here, just so you know."

Rob glowers at the bartender in response, who in turn, refills Rob's glass, subtly shaking his head. Now the wiser, he takes this one in more slowly. He looks up to see Stacie coming toward him, all hips and lips. Maybe he won't say anything harsh to her after all, he thinks, as he yearningly watches her rhythmic sway.

"Oh, Rob..." She places her hand over his with doe eyed sympathy.

Between that and the drinks, Rob begins to feel better already. This is the kind of remedy needed for a broken heart. "Steph—sorry—Stacie, please. I understand. It happened and you apologized. So, tell me more about Stephanie and this Jeff guy."

Stacie in her remorse is eager to please. She orders a fruity daiquiri from the ogling bartender. "Well, as you know Stephanie is a pretty private person, but as far as I can tell, she's been seeing him regularly for almost a month. As you know, he has a lot of money and often sends her flowers with a catered lunch because he knows that most times she doesn't get out like she should. He also has been coming to pick her up after work and take her to the city. From what I've heard, so far they've gone to the theater, on a yacht, and to his friend's art gallery event. I'm sure there've been more, but this is all I've been able to glean from the talk floating around. Obviously, I'm the last person she'd share her personal life with, so although I don't know anything more about the nature of their relationship, my guess would be they're getting serious at this point."

Rob empties the rest of his drink, and after hearing this needs more. "Excuse me, bartender?" he says a little too loudly, as he is well on his way now. The bartender shakes his head and starts to say something, but Stacie puts her hand on his arm and looks up with full charm. "It's alright. He's with me." Glancing down her blouse, the bartender smiles at her gratuitously as he pours Rob's drink then glares enviously at him before walking off.

"Like I said before, I really apologize, Rob. I was teasing Stephanie because although I saw she was attracted to you, I was sure she'd never do anything about it, and decided to mess with her a little bit. It wasn't the nicest thing to do, I admit, but I never would've done that if I knew you two had something going. Plus, I was attracted to you and clearly not too shy to let you know. Based on our chemistry that day, I thought you were feeling me too. From what I've observed, you don't seem to be the kind of guy that would play Stephanie like that, so I had no evidence of a relationship between you two."

Even in his inebriated state, Rob has to admit that Stacie is right. He definitely was returning her vibe that day at the library and with Stephanie's secrecy not revealing anything else, she was just making herself known to him. Actually, he has to admit that he is flattered, as judging by the stare of almost every guy in here, she is quite a looker. Now that he has had a general conversation with her, she also seems to be a decent person—just a very sexually assertive one. "No, I'm not that kind of man, which is why I took your card but never called. Anyway, it doesn't even matter anymore. I guess it's over."

Stacie leans in and slowly slides her hand on the inside of Rob's leg. "But I'm still here."

He looks down at her ample bosom. Feeling the warmth of her hand penetrating his thigh, he stares into her inviting eyes, then at her glossed pouting lips. Removing a large bill from his wallet, he places it on the counter and leads her out the door.

CHAPTER SIXTEEN

The next morning Stephanie wakes up, lazily stretches, then nestles back under the covers. Lying there, she goes over yesterday's events in her mind. She knew Rob was standing there all along because she saw him when she first came out of her office. She orchestrated the whole scene—initially pretending not to see him, mentioning Jeff's name, and then appearing nonchalant upon 'discovering' he was there. From the look on his face, it apparently made its mark.

She rolls her eyes as she recalls the ease in which she pulled it off. Stacie isn't the only one with feminine wiles; she just doesn't use hers in such an obvious and trashy way. The only thing she hadn't orchestrated was Rob running into Jeff and introducing himself as her 'good friend'. Although he wasn't overbearing about it, he definitely was curious as to what constituted their 'good friendship'. He must have been able to tell from Rob's demeanor that it meant more than that, at least to him.

With Rob's face, you can always tell what is going on, which is why she knows something happened between him and Stacie. He was stuttering and sweating so much, she thought he was going to have an epileptic fit when Stacie flashed her horse-toothed, gloating smile as if to say, "That's one more for me!" Well, they can have each other. Rob isn't the only fish in the sea. She may not be a brick house like Stacie, but she is definitely no dog either. On top of that, she knows how to play the game too, but clearly uses more discrimination in her approach.

When she met Jeff at the Business Leaders Community Forum, she could tell he was interested but didn't throw her tits in his face and start licking her lips. Instead, she engaged in intelligent conversation while maintaining eye contact that said, 'Yes, I'm interested too'. Sure, they were talking business, but at the same time, there was another conversation going on. Therefore, when he invited her to dinner and the theater, it was no surprise.

She admires Jeff. He is a man who likes to work hard but play harder, and she appreciates that. He isn't big into nature or anything like that, but sure loves to spoil her. Each time they go out she is treated like a queen. He is a widower who had been happily married for 30 years before losing his wife to breast cancer two years ago.

However, if she is honest she has to admit that she enjoys Jeff's company, complete with upgraded lifestyle and pampering, but just doesn't feel that same spark of connectedness or deep attraction she did when with Rob. On the other hand, Jeff is crazy about her and wants to introduce her to his kids and family as his 'current friend and future wife', with which she is definitely not comfortable. She knows she could commit to Jeff if she chose to, but also wonders if it would be the best decision. Although impressed by Jeff's power and success, she is even more so by the fact that he is genuinely a great person in spite of it. She is also flattered that someone who could have anyone, wants to be with her. She is not from high society, wealth or fame, but he still values her, and that speaks a lot of his groundedness.

After pondering all this, she decides to tell him she is finally ready. He deserves it, and so does she. Life is short and there is only one go round here, as far as she knows. Being the kind of man Jeff is, she is sure he won't waste too much time, either. He has already said she would be the 'perfect wife' for him--very sociable, beautiful, but grounded, intelligent, culturally aware and laid back. She realizes that you can't have everything in life, but if a good portion of it is there, then it is most likely about as good as it is going to get; anything more than that is 'gravy'. Life is unpredictable. Look at what's happened so far to her—her mother, her father, the man she thought she would marry and have a family with—POOF—all suddenly gone.

Rob is nice, and they had some great times in the short span they spent together, but ultimately he really doesn't know what he wants. He wants to take it slow with her but go fast with Stacie. In other words--have his cake and eat it too. Well, he has just found out the hard way that life does not work like that; at least not with her.

Her cell phone rings. "Hey Babe, it's me. How'd you sleep last night?"

Stephanie smiles at the thought. "After you--like a baby."

Jeff chuckles with satisfaction. "Me too. It was a struggle to get up and leave you for my early morning meeting, but I left something on the table for you."

Stephanie feigns exasperation. "Jeff, I hope you didn't make breakfast for me again—you could've used the sleep, you know."

Jeff blows a kiss over the phone. "Don't worry, it wasn't breakfast this time, but hopefully it will fill you up just the same. Gotta run, baby—I'll call you later. I love you."

"Love you too." Stephanie lies.

She hangs up the phone and pops up to see what he left. On the table is a card with a red velvet box. In it is a beautiful gold pendant necklace with two linked hearts, each encrusted with Stephanie and Jeff's birthstones— diamond and ruby. The card says:

Stephanie,

I know it hasn't been that long, but I can't help feeling as though we already are one—our two hearts beating together. You have given me joy I never thought I would find again. Sometimes I look in your eyes and can tell you've been through a lot, although you don't speak of it. You don't have to. Just let me spend the rest of my life making yours better.

Love, Jeff

As she reads it, tears begin slowly sliding down her cheeks, until she finally collapses on the table in heartwrenching sobs.

* * *

Rob wakes up blurry eyed the next morning with a splitting headache and churning stomach. Stacie is comfortably nestled in the blanket beside him. He slowly peels his tongue from the roof of his mouth, which is cottony and putrid. The taste makes him want to throw up. Surveying the room, he tries to recall the night before, as he notices his clothes loosely tossed over an upholstered pink vanity chair. He peers over and studies Stacie's face. She looks like a sleeping baby doll with her un-glossed, but still dewy pink lips puckered and snoring lightly. Even without makeup, she is breathtaking. As he gets up, she stirs slightly but doesn't awaken. Upon entering the bathroom, he jumps in horror at his reflection in the mirror. His red-rimmed eyes are bloodshot, and his face ashen gray. Suddenly, he begins to heave and lurches to the toilet just in time, as bitter greenish bile shoots out. Once emptied, he stays there painfully gagging until sure he feels safe to step away.

Flushing the toilet, he rinses with mouthwash from the medicine cabinet, splashes his face, and sits on the side of the bathtub to collect his thoughts. The last thing he remembers is talking to Stacie at the lounge. He feels like such a loser. After all this time, he finally has sex and it is a complete waste because he was so drunk.

Nevertheless, the one thing he clearly remembers is Stephanie breaking his heart into a million pieces. How can she already be serious with this Jeff guy in so short a time? He was trying to give her space to sort things out so they could eventually reconnect, and all the while, she was in someone else's arms—and most likely their bed. In light of this, it is unbelievable he has gotten all this flak for simply flirting with Stacie. Well, at least now he has truly earned Stephanie's contempt. Not that she even cares, having virtually flicked him away like a bug from her shoulder.

"Rob?" Stacie sleepily calls from the room. "Are you okay?"

Oddly feeling self-conscious, Rob wraps a towel around his waist before stepping into the room. "Uh…yes. I just was washing my face."

Stacie looks like a little girl, sitting in the bed with tousled hair, sleepily rubbing her eyes. Even with her shiny pink lace trimmed nightie, her 'sex-kitten' appeal is diminished, and for the first time, Rob begins to wonder how old she really is. He contemplates why a woman with so much natural beauty feels the need to vamp up her sex appeal the way she does, but after working with youth for some time, he could probably make a pretty educated guess.

"Well, that's good, because you sure weren't last night." She says with a smirk caught between amusement and disappointment.

Rob cautiously comes over and sits on the bed beside her. "Stacie, what happened last night?"

Stacie looks at his worried face and chuckles. "Don't worry Tiger, you never even got out of the cage."

Rob rapidly blinks several times trying to process this. "What do you mean?"

Stacie gives a long stretch and smiles. Well, for starters, we had to take my car, as you were three sheets to the wind. Then, I had to keep pulling over while you got sick all over the road. By the time we got here, you were barely able to stand and passed out on my bed. So, I took off your pants and shirt and tucked you in. By the way, you thought I was Stephanie and kept apologizing, saying you loved me. That sure does wonders for a girl's desire level, even if you were able to make it happen."

Rob is stunned. "Oh my God…Stacie, I'm so sorry. I don't know what to say. I think you're beautiful, I really do, and am obviously attracted to you—"

"Yes, I got the memo already. You don't love me. Don't worry, I understand. I don't exactly ooze lovability in that type of way anyhow. That's not what my specialty is."

Although she says this with a light, playful air, Rob detects undertones of hurt and feels like a complete jerk. "No, it's just that I don't really know you that well yet. I'm sure you're a very lovable woman. Look how you took care of me when you could've just left me out on the side of the road."

Stacey rolls her eyes. "Rob, I didn't say I was a monster either. I do have feelings."

Rob squirms with discomfort. He is digging himself in deeper with every turn. "I'm sorry Stacie; I didn't mean it like that. Personally, I think you are worthy of the same love as Stephanie, but the problem may be that deep down, you don't really think so. How old are you anyway?"

Stacie's eyes fly open with astonishment. "What? Are you really asking a woman her age? That's a no-no, Rob. You should know that."

"You'd be surprised," Rob mutters under his breath. "I'm just asking because without your makeup you look really, really young."

Stacie tinkles with laughter. "Well, not that you'd have to worry about that now, rest assured I'm well over 18. Thanks for the compliment, though.

She takes one last stretch then throws the covers back. "I'm starved. You want some bacon and eggs?

Rob carefully shakes his head. "Even if I did, I wouldn't trust putting any food in my stomach right now. However, I will trouble you for a steaming cup of black coffee and two aspirin."

Stacie hops up, throws on a tiny pink satin robe and slips into her fuzzy pink slippers. "Sure. After I eat and shower, I'll take you back to your car and you can continue to forget this night never happened."

Rob holds out his arm to stop Stacie in her tracks, smiling with admiration. "Stacie, I think you're a sweet and wonderful woman. I really want to thank you for everything."

He reaches out to give her a hug but she immediately pushes him back half-jokingly. "Ugh! Get outta here! I'm not hugging you--you smell like ol' man Willie on the corner with all that alcohol coming from your pores."

Rob busts out in laughter. "Okay, you got that. But just know that I still appreciate you anyway."

* * *

Slowly composing herself, Stephanie jumps into the shower, throws on her sweats and goes for a run. She needs to calm down. Ever since that day in Lehti's office, she's been experiencing what her doctor calls, 'stress related anxiety". Even when still, her heart would suddenly palpitate with sharp pains. Other times, she'd simply bursts into tears for no reason at all. Although she carries her prescribed anti-anxiety medication, she has not yet worked up the nerve to take it after reading all the potential side effects. She has instead, chosen to exercise as a safer alternative. So far, she has successfully hidden it in the presence of others by either excusing herself to the restroom, going for a walk or simply closing her office door when at work. Nevertheless, her episodes have become more frequent, and she fears that Jeff or even worse, her job will find out.

At the end of her run, she decides to stop at Lifebreath for some decaf coffee and a coconut carrot muffin. As she enters, she sees Dalton sitting at a table reading. "Hey there, stranger!" he cheerfully greets, upon noticing her.

Knowing that by now Rob must have obviously told him what happened, she is guarded by his response but still plays along. "Dalton! How are you?"

He smiles back unpretentiously. "I'm doing well, Stephanie, thanks for asking. Hey, have you had the butterscotch scone yet?"

Remembering their last conversation, she smiles. "No, I haven't, but I have a hankering today for the coconut carrot muffin."

He nods accommodatingly. "I hear ya. Well, if you don't mind, please feel free to join me. I'm just doing a little Light reading over here." He chuckles to himself at his private wordplay. Stephanie briefly hesitates, unsure of where this could lead, but doesn't want to be rude, as he seems genuinely pleased to see her. "Sure thing. I'll be right there." Her stomach begins to quaver slightly, but she surreptitiously takes some deep breaths to quell it.

She returns with a now lavender-chamomile tea and muffin, and notices that Dalton has been reading The Bible. "Oh, are you a Christian?" She asks, grateful for the opportunity to lead their discussion in a different direction.

Dalton closes his book and smiles "Yes, I am. Actually, I'm a priest."

Stephanie begins laughing at his joke, but after a moment realizes there may not be one. "Really?" She asks with a hint of disbelief on her face.

Dalton smiles and nods understandingly "Maybe you've never seen one dressed so casually before, but I generally prefer this attire in informal places."

Stephanie is still processing Dalton's revelation. "I don't think I remember you mentioning that when we met."

Dalton takes a sip of his coffee and clears his throat. "No, I didn't. I usually don't offer that information in my introduction: 'Hello, I'm Dalton the priest…and you are…?' He chuckles again. "If it comes up naturally, of course, but otherwise, I don't press it."

Stephanie is intrigued. "So how did you and Rob become friends then? From what I understand, he's not religious at all."

"Well, religion is not my only sphere of knowledge or area of interest. We actually met at an event here and hit it off right away. The rest is His story."

Although Dalton is completely finding his clever quips amusing, Stephanie is oblivious. "Wow…that's crazy."

He tilts his head inquisitively. "Is it? Why do you think so?"

Stephanie quickly shakes her head. "No, not crazy like that, but more like unconventional. Please don't take this as an offense, but you don't really seem like a priest, not that I know that much on these matters. I'm just surprised because we all had such an intense conversation at Rob's where he and I'm sure myself, said some things that had to be offensive to you, and you never said anything. I can't even believe you read the book.

Dalton shrugs and shakes his head. "It's one of my favorite books, and I actually suggested it for Rob to read."

Stephanie is stunned. "What! You were the friend who recommended it?"

Dalton holds up his palms. "Guilty as charged. Stephanie, my faith is not just a static set of beliefs, rules, and regulations, and that's that. I have an ever-evolving, personal relationship with God through Jesus Christ, and believe it or not, He's not just in church or a particular person with a collar, He's everywhere."

Stephanie instantly perks up. "That's what my mother believed! When she was younger, she used to go to church all the time because she believed God was only there, but later, she discovered Him in Nature; and He would speak to her there too."

Dalton smiles at Stephanie's enthusiasm. "Yes, but make no mistake. He has a special Presence and Power in His Church and established Himself it for a specific purpose. We should not overlook that. The problem comes when people apply their own understanding of what that means and begin to abuse their authority to manipulate, stagnate and oppress others for their benefit. But, yes, He will make Himself known to anyone who is truly looking for Him, anywhere."

Stephanie finds herself comforted by this conversation and the calm and loving energy from Dalton. She feels like she can tell him anything and not be afraid or ashamed, and now easily sees how he and Rob could become friends. "Dalton, I really enjoyed speaking with you. I wish that we could have remained friends, but under the circumstances, I do understand. Still, it was a pleasure knowing you."

She gathers her things to leave, but Dalton reaches out and gently places a hand on her arm. "Why Stephanie, we've always been friends." As she looks into his eyes, she feels warmth radiating through her and something powerful begins to draw her into a cloud of understanding. Instinctively knows she is in the Presence of God, right there in Lifebreath Café. "I am always here for you. Remember that." Transfixed, she nods, unable to speak.

Then just as suddenly, she and Dalton are looking at each other with a quiet awareness of what has just taken place, as they reverently bask in the hushed silence that envelops them in the midst of a busy café.

* * *

Stephanie walks back absorbed by what just transpired with Dalton. Until now, she had never shared a deep spiritual moment with anyone but her mother. After her death she did not want to and instead has kept her faith private, preferring to experience God on her own through meditation, or like her mom, in the midst of nature. Nevertheless, she has to admit that it felt awesome when God's Voice spoke directly to her through Dalton with a force that immediately dispelled every fear, rambling, and muddled thought, leaving nothing but clarity behind.

She arrives home, showers again and dresses for work. On her way out, she stops at the table, re-reads the card, and places the pendant around her neck. The most difficult thing she finds, however, is having the courage to live that clarity out in the real world.

* * *

By the time Rob returns home, he feels much better and is ravenous with hunger. He quickly showers, shaves, dresses then decides to go to Lifebreath to eat rather than cook. When he gets to the door of the café, he runs into Dalton, who is on his way out.

"Hey man! Where've you been?" Dalton inquires. "I've been trying to call you."

"Yeah, I guessed that," Rob says sheepishly. "My phone died."

Dalton looks at Rob and a ripple of concern crosses his face. "Is everything alright?"

Rob is in no mood for his fighting pride today. "Hey, are you on your way to somewhere important?"

Dalton places his hand on Rob's shoulder and steers him inside. "Not anywhere that can't wait. What's going on?"

Rob motions for Dalton to hold on as he approaches the counter. "Hello, can I have two orders of the veggie and cheese omelet with home fries, whole-wheat toast, and a large lemongrass tea?"

Dalton shakes his head in amazement. "Wow, two orders! What did you do to work up an appetite like that—or should I even ask?"

Rob chooses a nearby table. "Man, you would not believe the day I had yesterday. I still hadn't heard anything from Stephanie so finally decided to go to her job. As I am at the desk asking Stacie to speak with her, she rushes right by all dressed to kill and asks Stacie to tell her date when he arrives, that she's running late. Then she turns to me with this fake smile and says, 'Oh Rob, good to see you — gotta run — tell the kids I said hi.' and flies off like nothing. Can you believe that?"

Before Dalton can answer, Rob's order is called and he goes to retrieve it. When he sits back down, Dalton patiently waits as Rob hungrily attacks his plate. A few moments later, he continues. "So, I'm standing there ready to tear that place down when Stacie starts begging me to meet with her after work because she wants to talk. Man, I wanted to hurt somebody so bad, I knew I had better get out of there fast. I agreed to meet her at the U2 Lounge and on my way out, guess who I run into? Her 'date', Jeff Santos, you know, the real estate bigwig?" Dalton nods and Rob goes on. "So I go over, introduce myself and tell him that Stephanie and I are really good friends. You should've seen the look on his face trying to figure that one out.

Then I walk to the lounge and proceed to get so drunk that Stacie has to practically carry me to her house as I vomit all over the place and finally pass out on her bed. But, get this: the whole time she told me I kept calling her Stephanie and apologizing, saying that I loved her! Dalton, what kind of fool am I? Please tell me—because I really need your insight and wisdom now more than ever."

Dalton looks at Rob with heartfelt empathy. "Well, Rob...it sounds to me like you are simply a fool in love. Join the rest of the human race."

Rob waves his hand dismissively. "Except for you and your friends, of course."

Dalton shakes his head admonishingly. "Perhaps; but we have a whole set of other challenges. Nevertheless, this is not about me. I am really sorry to hear this happened to you, Rob."

Rob polishes off the rest of his plate then takes a sip of tea. "Yeah, me too. I can't get over what an idiot I made of myself in front of Stacie. Still, all things considered, she was pretty good about it. I think she's real cool, although yesterday's episode clearly killed any chance of an opportunity with her. Meanwhile, Stephanie's parading around town with this big shot who's effortlessly buying her the kinds of things that would break me. Stacie said he even sends her catered lunches with flowers. Who can top that? Hell, I'd leave me too."

Dalton sighs. "Rob, you are so much more than your financial net worth. I truly believe that what you offer Stephanie, money cannot buy, and deep down she knows that."

Rob's eyes widen in disbelief. "Really, because from my perspective, her 'depth' has been comfortably snuggled in some rich man's bed all while I've been stuck in a holding pattern."

Feeling Rob's pain, Dalton ventures delicately. "Believe it or not, what she's doing is out of hurt, and all this man's 'parading', as you say, is a wonderful diversion from it. Although this has caused you great suffering, as your friend supplying the wise counsel you just asked me for, I would suggest you not retaliate by doing something equally as foolish to complicate matters even more. Just be patient and see what happens."

With that, Rob is beside himself. Laughing incredulously, he stands up and starts to walk off, then abruptly turns back and leans into Dalton, speaking through gritted teeth. "I DID that Dalton, and look what happened. What should I do now, wait for them to get married?"

Dalton gently puts his hand on Rob's arm to calm him down and motions for him to sit. Rob reluctantly lowers himself into the chair and glowers.

"Rob, I know you're seething mad. I understand and I'm not trying to mitigate or dismiss the reasons why you feel that way. All I'm asking, as someone who cares about you, is to try to be as level headed as possible. You have a lot of lives invested in you, and can't just throw them all away over one person's actions. Please."

Again, an inference of the youth brings Rob back to his senses. "Dalton, you're right. I'm behaving like a madman over a woman I didn't even know a few months ago. Granted, we had a great connection and I grew to care about her immensely, but she is not the whole of my life's existence, and I feel like I've been making it out to be. Now that I think about it, it is the kids who have been most impacted by not only the consequences of my thoughtless actions but also my attitude in dealing with them. I know how it feels when the adult you are connected to starts to lose balance, and for some of these kids, I've been the only model of stability they've ever known. Before now, I never even considered how selfish and single-minded I've been!" He resolutely slaps the table and stands. Man, D… I've got some ground to cover."

Relieved, Dalton smiles and also rises from his chair. Without warning, Rob turns and ambushes him with a long, tight bear hug. "I've never done that before, but after each conversation with you, I always want to. So there! I know I've been getting all sappy on you lately, but you only have yourself to blame."

Dalton laughs with appreciation. "Well if it's between this and you going on a rampage, then sap away!"

CHAPTER SEVENTEEN

Stephanie looks up from the computer and answers her ringing cell phone.

"Hello lovely, guess who?"

Stephanie smiles playfully and responds in a sexy voice. "Oh, hi Johnny baby, I've been waiting all day for your call. I've missed you so much."

There is a brief pause and then Jeff, trying to sound blithe says, "Ha. Maybe that would've been funnier if I had not yesterday's experience with your 'good friend' Rob."

Stephanie rolls her eyes in exasperation. Men. She chortles with amusement to deflect Jeff's indirect accusation. "Yeah well, first of all, we had that conversation already and secondly, you started this whole thing with your little 'guess who' game. Was that a set-up or what?"

Jeff stiffly laughs in response. "You got me! I guess I need to be more careful next time, huh sweetheart?"

Stephanie feels the friction increasing and realizes that she probably shouldn't have joked with him like that. "Well…all kidding aside, I really do miss you, Jeff."

Jeff responds with piqued interest. "Oh, yeah? You wanna show me how much tonight?"

Stephanie chuckles throatily. "Sure, if you can handle it."

Melanée Addison

Jeff is officially back on track. "Ooh, baby! Now that's what I'm talking about."

They both heartily laugh as the tension disperses.

"Jeff?"

"Yeah, babe."

Stephanie fingers the pendant around her neck. "Thank you for the beautiful necklace and the card. It was very touching."

Jeff lovingly smiles. "Baby, that's only the beginning of what I have for you. You're worth so much more to me."

Stephanie closes her eyes and nervously bites her lip. "Sweetheart, I have something I want to tell you. Can we go somewhere quiet tonight?

Jeff hesitates. "Steph, are we okay? I mean, if I said or did anything--"

Stephanie interrupts. "No baby, don't worry. It's all good."

Jeff breathes a sigh of relief. "Well then! I'll call for my table at Giordiani's and have a car waiting for you outside. What time will you be ready?"

"No later than 6:30."

"Great, then I'll make 7:00 reservations and meet you there. I love you."

"Okay, love you too." Stephanie hangs up the phone and stares off in deep thought, absently toying with her pendant.

There is a sudden knock at the door and she jumps. "Yes, come in.", she calls out.

The door opens and it is Stacie. "Hi, Stephanie. If you have a moment, I'd like to talk to you, please."

Stephanie definitely has no time for this today. She shakes her head apologetically. "I'm sorry Stacie, but I have a meeting that I need to prepare for."

Stacie concedes with a smile. "Okay. Maybe we can do lunch tomorrow, then?"

Stephanie smiles tightly in return. "Hmm…let me check my calendar and get back to you, ok?"

Stacie nods deferentially. "Sure."

As Stacie leaves, Stephanie ponders her sudden shift in attitude. Gone is the usual sashaying or flippant mannerisms, and frankly, it leaves her wary of her motive for this uninvited visit. On the other hand, she wouldn't be surprised if Rob has already dogged her too, and now she's coming in here with her tail between her legs realizing that cheaters never win. Whatever it is, she's not dealing with it today, and tomorrow doesn't look good either. She is fed up with other people's drama playing out on her stage. They need to get a therapist or handle things on their own, and leave her out of it—she has a life to live.

She looks at the clock. There is exactly one hour to finish her work, freshen up and meet the car outside for her special night with Jeff. She exhales and nervously touches her pendant, hoping she is truly ready to make this big announcement.

* * *

As Stephanie is escorted to the table, Jeff stands up and insists on personally pulling out her chair instead of the waiter. Once she is seated, he greets her with a peck on the lips then nods to the waiter who ceremoniously uncorks a bottle of Dom Perignon Brut and fills their glasses. He nods again and the waiter dutifully disappears. Jeff smiles and attentively studies Stephanie, captivated. Looking deeply into her eyes, he raises his glass. "To new beginnings, and better days". Stephanie bashfully smiles and lifts her glass in return. "To new beginnings, and better days." They clink and quietly sip.

Still maintaining eye contact with her, Jeff lifts his hand as a signal to the waiter hovering nearby, who then quickly disappears into the back. "So, shall we order and then talk about whatever is on your pretty little mind this evening?" Stephanie smiles and studies the menu, settling on the Insalata de Suzanna for starters, and Melanzana alla Parmigiana as her entrée. Jeff selects Lobster Bisque for his first course and the Costellata di Vitello w/ Risotto Porcini and Agnoloti Di Spinach for the main course.

Stephanie looks up to see the waiter approaching with a voluminous spray of huge red roses accented with baby's breath and fern leaves displayed in an ornately engraved flared silver vase. As the waiter makes his way across the room, all eyes follow the lavish arrangement and fall upon Stephanie in awe as she graciously receives it. "Jeff…" She tries to continue, but her eyes begin to water, and she chokes up.

Jeff takes her hand and gently squeezes it. "Baby, you don't need to say anything. Just receive it. I'm just happy to be with you."

Tears are now streaming from Stephanie's eyes and her chest begins to tighten. Quickly grabbing a napkin to dab her face, she clutches her purse and forces her quivering lips into a smile. "Excuse me…"

Moved by her emotional response, Jeff's eyes begin to mist. "Of course, sweetheart; take your time. I'll inform the waiter of our selections."

Unable to speak, Stephanie nods and briskly makes her way toward the restroom, then secretly slips outside and ducks into an isolated area, where she bursts into agonizing sobs.

A short time later, with eye drops administered, makeup reapplied and anti-anxiety pill popped, she glides back into the dining area with a cool ease, kisses Jeff slowly and tenderly and sits down to her appetizer. Looking over at the breathtaking arrangement, she warmly places her hand over Jeff's. "Baby, this is amazing beyond belief. Thank you so much."

Jeff tenderly runs his finger alongside Stephanie's face. "Stephanie, you make me feel like a king. Sometimes I feel like I don't deserve you."

Stephanie smiles and for the first time honestly responds. "I feel exactly the same way."

* * *

After covering the floors, windows, and doorways with plastic sheeting, Rob puts on his work jumpsuit, gloves, goggles, and mask. He then picks up his sander to begin stripping the walls of the spare bedroom. The familiar drone of the motor and rasp of sandpaper makes him feel like he is finally starting to come back to himself. Aside from cost, the major reason he bought this house knowing the time and effort involved in restoring it was that it would be therapeutic for him. With everything that has been going on, he welcomes this now more than ever. He needs the kind of focus this work requires in order to keep his mind off other things.

It is also a recharge for his confidence to feel the accomplishment of a job well done. If only life were this way. Then he could simply envision a design, lay out a plan, and finish it accordingly. This is why he loves construction so much. For the most part, what you see is what you get. Sure, there are glitches and unforeseen challenges in the process, but it is more like solving a puzzle, where's always a solution; you just have to find it.

With people, it is not so simple because things don't always turn out as you desire. You can plan something, work on it as hard and long as you want and what you wind up with is completely different. Well from now on, he is sticking to what he knows best.

After finishing, he cleans up and surveys his progress with appreciation. Now feeling energized, he wants to go out and do something but is not exactly sure what. He briefly considers Lifebreath Café, but wants something a bit more exciting tonight, and ponders other options.

Showered and dressed, he goes into the kitchen to make a nice, hearty meal. Dalton would cringe, but he is definitely feeling a thick juicy steak with roasted new potatoes and grilled asparagus topped with creamy asiago sauce. He goes into the living room and turns on some lively music to get him started when he notices Stacie's card sitting on the side table.

He gets his cell phone and dials.

"Hello?"

"Heyy Stacie, this is Rob."

"Rob who?"

"Umm…the Rob who was just in your bed—well, Rob from the youth center."

"Rob…?" Stacie ventures tentatively. "Stephanie's Rob?"

Rob shakes his head, starting to regret the phone call already. "Not anymore, remember?"

"Oh, sorry…you know what I mean. What's up, Rob?"

Deflated, Rob mentally plans his next renovation project. "Huh? Oh… nothing. I was just wondering…if you wanted me to teach you how to play Scrabble—for real."

Stacie pauses for a moment and then laughs. "Rob. That was a pickup line. I already know how to play Scrabble, and quite well, I might add. Wow, where've you been hiding—under a rock?"

She starts laughing again and Rob imagines his head turning into a huge lollipop with the label '*Sucker*' on it, like in the cartoons he used to watch. "No. Try a 26 year marriage, Stacie…that's where I've been hiding." He responds irately.

"Wow Rob, calm down. I was just kidding with you. You've got some temper there, huh? Or are you still upset over the Stephanie thing? Probably so.", she answers her own question before he can respond. "Yeah, sure. You sound like you need to get out--but out, out—not Scrabble out." Why don't you take me dancing tonight?

Rob starts to pick up again. "Sure! Well, I don't really know too many places like that around here. It's been a while."

'Like since never', Stacie thinks to herself and chuckles. "Don't worry, that's my job. Just be here by 8:00, because I want to grab something to eat first. And, Rob?"

"Yeah?"

Stacie pauses with a smirk that he cannot see. "No drinks for you tonight. Ok?"

Rob has to smile despite himself. "Don't worry. You won't have to enforce that one. See you at 8!"

Feeling like he just got his 'mojo' back, Rob goes over to the television and selects the 'Disco Music Channel' on his cable system. He then cranks up the volume and begins reviving the smooth moves he used back in the day. While gyrating to the beat, complete with arm flails and Jackson 5 spins, he gets confident, tries to do a Soul Train split, and feels a sharp pull in his back. "Aaaargh!" He shouts, reaching toward the couch like a drowning man for a life raft, and slowly slides to the floor. The longer he lays there hoping the pain will subside, the more exciting Scrabble seems. He gingerly rolls over and grabs his cell phone from the coffee table.

"Hello?"

"Uh, Stacie…" Rob starts and then lets out an agonizing groan as he tries to shift.

"Rob! What happened?"

Rob tries taking shallow breaths to staunch the pain before speaking. "I don't think we're gonna do dancing tonight, sweetie."

* * *

"Aaaah!" Rob sighs in relief, as Stacie finishes massaging medicated balm into his back. "That feels so much better. Oh my, thank you so much, Stacie. You sure have some magic fingers there." Rob says dreamily as he lays on the floor fully relaxed.

As Stacie tilts her head and purses her baby doll lips into a pleased smile, a glimmer of sadness escapes from her eyes. "So I've been told."

Rob smiles apologetically. "I feel guilty for having you rush over here like this."

Stacie shakes her head in protest. "Don't be. What you should feel is lucky you keep a spare key outside. Who knows, if I didn't come, you might have been still lying in this same spot tomorrow soaked in piss. Wow, Rob... you're way older than you look. You might even qualify for one of those medical alert necklaces they sell on T.V. You should at least look into it."

Suddenly, Rob feels his 'mojo' get up and crawl under the couch for refuge. "Thanks, Stacie. You think they'd throw in a wheelchair with that too?" He says with a sarcasm that is lost on her.

"I dunno. Probably doesn't hurt to ask."

Rob gives her a dead stare and then changes the subject. "You know as I was laying here on the floor practically soaking in my own urine, I had a thought. "How is it that a beautiful girl like you is even available on a Saturday night?"

Stacie smiles and rolls her eyes. "For the record Rob, I'm 28, okay? I could've easily had plans. That's not a problem. I'm just tired of the same old stuff. I'm getting too old for that now. I recently broke up with my boyfriend Steve, who surprise—was cheating on me with God knows how many women. It just seems that most of the men who are after me only want one thing. Personally, I'd rather stay home—or even play Scrabble—than to have to deal with that anymore. I mean Rob, I saw the way you looked at Stephanie that day and how you cried over her. I want to be loved like that.

Rob is stunned. "I cried?"

Stacie shrugs dismissively. "Yeah, I left that part out, figuring you already had enough humiliation for one day."

Rob remains silent, so she continues. "It seems like everyone just wants to use me as a human blow up doll, but no one really sees who I am inside. I know you're probably thinking it's because I come off that way, and maybe you're right, but that's how I've always been, ever since I was young. I would flirt and guys would fall at my feet. It felt powerful to know that I was the one that every woman feared and every man desired. I guess I've just gotten so used to having that kind of control that it has become second nature to me."

Something Stacie said catches Rob's attention. "Stacie, how long have you been using this power over males?"

Stacie looks up in thought. "I dunno, maybe since around 11 or 12 years old. I was a fast developer and definitely the first in my school to have these." She looks down and smiles. As soon as I did, I became popular and the source of countless schoolyard fights. You always heard my name on people's lips—even teachers.

The girls hated me but envied my power and popularity with the boys, so they kept me close, hoping to increase their chances too. The whole time I thought I was so special because all the cool boys wanted to take me to the back of the school and feel my tits. With all the fuss made over my looks and body, I never even had the chance to develop my own personal identity. When people mentioned my name the only image that ever registered was 'Tits and Ass." Rob nods, fully comprehending, as Stacie continues. "So that's what I became: Stacie—flirty, sexy, cute and bubbly—exactly what every man wants, right?"

Rob shakes his head in sorrow and shame. He slowly sits up and hoists himself up on the couch next to her. "That's not the Stacie I've come to admire. This desirable woman before me is sweet, sensitive, intelligent, warmhearted and funny. You've been done a disservice, Stacie, and I'm so sorry that even I played a part in that. Like I said before, you deserve to be loved just as much as any other woman. However, as a man, no matter how old I may be—when you start throwing that image around, flirting and tempting us, then you too are complicit in your depersonalization.

You have a beautiful face and a gorgeous body, but my personal advice would be to uncover the former and cover latter a bit more. You don't need to wear all that makeup. I've seen what you look like without it and it's so much more real and appealing. You want to know the truth? Deep down, every man wants a live blow up doll—even me, but that's just fantasy. When it comes to real life, we want something genuine to match us in our own fragile, imperfect reality."

Stacie listens to Rob intently. "Rob, you are quite a man. I hope you don't mind me saying this, but Stephanie is so stupid. When I first saw you, I wanted you as a challenge—mainly to soothe my ego over Steve. You were handsome, sexy and seemed like a really nice guy to be at the library playing Scrabble with all those rough looking kids. Although it was clear you had a heart, I was going for something a little below that." She laughs. "Now, I realize that I might be passing over my very own Rob for this reason."

"You want to know something I've never told anyone before?" Rob listens quietly and she goes on. "I don't even like sex all that much. I just like to make a man weak because it makes me feel powerful, and I kinda get off on that, but now what I really want is for a man to hold me tenderly and tell me he loves me, particularly when he's not pounding me like a porn star. I want a man who will honor and respect me and whose baby I would be proud to carry." As her eyes begin to mist, Rob also feels a swell of emotion rising.

She looks up at Rob with quiet gratitude. "Wow, I never really get to speak like this to anyone, you know? Let alone a man." Then she smiles at him with her autopilot seductiveness and Rob realizes it is going to take some time for her to break that habit. "Well, Stephanie better come to her senses soon, because old or not, I will snatch you up in a second—and you know I will!"

Rob heartily laughs and points to the jar of medicated rub on the table. "Now, would you really want this to be the future you'd have to look forward to?"

Stacie doesn't miss a beat. "In a blink, baby! And if you wind up with me, that would be the only future we'd have to look forward to!" Rob laughs again, stands and holds his arms out toward Stacie. "Do you think you can oblige a reformed 'ol' man Willie' this time?"

As Stacie hugs him tightly, she feels like a fragile little girl who after wandering for so long, has finally begun to find her way home. Rob squeezes his eyes shut, but is unable to stop the one tear that slides down his cheek.

CHAPTER EIGHTEEN

Rob is relaxing in his den the next Saturday afternoon watching the game when the doorbell rings. Reluctantly he gets up and goes downstairs. He is honestly not in the mood for any company today. It had been a particularly long week and he just wants some space where he doesn't have either listen to or solve anyone else's problems.

Looking through the viewer, he is relieved not to see anyone. It is probably just the package he'd been expecting. He opens the door and stares in shock, unable to utter a word.

"Rob…" She begins penitently.

His mind is racing a million miles and crashing into the walls of his skull. Everything feels like it is moving in slow motion, and for a moment he wonders if he is just dreaming because this simply cannot be happening.

Seeing his reaction, she makes another attempt. "Rob, I'm so sorry for showing up unannounced, but I really needed to talk to you, and didn't want to risk you hanging up if I called. Can I please come in?"

Rob remains frozen in place, his numbness slowly giving way to reality.

"How did you find me, Karen?"

She offers that familiar smile and as much as he wants to hate it, strangely he finds his anger inaccessible.

"With much effort and a little paid help." She says with a wink, hoping to lighten his mood.

Rob sighs, and finally swings the door open. "Come in. Would you like something to drink?" He asks with distant politeness.

Karen's amused expression causes her dimples to deepen, and against his will, the ice around Rob's heart begins to melt. "Always the gentleman... Yes, I'll have something cold, please."

Rob pads barefoot into the kitchen still trying to process all that is happening. One thing for sure, she still looks great, which makes being caught unshaven in his sweatpants and dingy white tank, even more of an atrocity.

When he returns, she is looking around with too comfortable a curiosity for his liking. "Nice place you have here. It's totally your style. I'm glad to see that you are finally pursuing and getting what you want in life."

Rob feels the embers of a slow burn beginning to stir. "So, what brings you here, Karen?"

Karen takes a dainty sip of her drink and pauses before answering. "Rob, I want to make amends. Clearly, things did not end well, but I feel like there has been too much between us to leave it that way."

Rob has been trying hard, but can no longer help himself. "Oh, so what happened to your Prince Charming? Did he ride off without you?"

Karen sighs and tightly shuts her eyes, but Rob can still see the beads of moisture glistening through her lashes. "Rob, I understand I probably deserve some of this, but it is still hard to have to do...so, please."

Instantly feeling remorseful, Rob collects himself. "I'm sorry, Karen. Go on."

"Well, as a matter of fact, he did; and truth be told, it was the best thing that could've happened for me. I was falling apart long before I got with Aaron, which is why things happened the way they did. I began drinking—socially at first, but then at times and in places that didn't even call for a drink. I had been hiding it so well, that I even fooled myself into thinking what I was doing was okay. Oh, I had a hard day, I am stressed, I need to sleep, I need to wake up...you get the point. The breaking point came when Aaron left, and I was all alone with myself for the first time. My father didn't even want to deal with me anymore. Anyway, to make a long story short, I joined AA and have been sober for nearly a year now.

Once I started to get clear, I saw not only how much I was hurting myself, but how deeply I had hurt you, and that, believe it or not, was even more unbearable than my own pain. Inevitably, I knew I was going to have to come here, not just for my healing, but also yours. I am so sorry Rob for the way I treated you and the pain and suffering it has caused."

Rob's heart begins to swell and tremble but refusing to give in to tears before her, he quickly chokes it down.

"Karen, thank you for reaching out to do this, and I apologize for my earlier attitude. Have you also reconciled with your father? You know deep down, he loves you too."

Karen's face brightens and she reaches over to squeeze Rob's hand. "Actually, yes I have, thanks for asking. I've even rejoined his church and am becoming an ordained minister, which brings me to my other reason for coming to see you. God has placed a message on my heart for you."

Rob is instantly put off by this statement. "Karen, you know good and well I don't go for all that stuff...I didn't then, and I still don't."

Karen nods yieldingly. "Rob, I'm not here to make you 'go' for anything. I need only deliver the message. What you do with it is up to you."

Annoyed, Rob shakes his head and rolls his eyes, but he cannot deny the obvious change in Karen's countenance. If she believes this will help, then he will hear her out and get it over with. "Sure...go ahead, then." He says, stifling a sigh of exasperation.

Karen begins to fix upon Rob with a deep intensity, but somehow it seems like as though she is looking beyond him. He just hopes she does not try to pull off any of that crazy babbling and jerking stuff, because if so, he will shut her show down with lightning speed.

"Rob, all your life you have carried the burden of taking care of others; your mother, your brothers, me, and even now, these children. It has been a heavy load, and God is now asking you to let Him take care of you. Stop hiding in the lives of others, and let Him be the Father you have always longed for. He sees and loves you dearly, but you keep fighting off the very thing you need and have even been asking for: Rest; not an earthly rest, which is temporary, but a complete rest that can only come from surrendering to Him. Don't let pride destroy your life, Rob. Trust Him, for He can protect not only you but also those you care about much more than you ever could. You think you're open and transparent, but you are hiding...come clean, Rob, and stop hiding, says The Lord."

Rob listens with vacillating emotions. Her words seem spot on, but are they really from God or someone who has lived with him for 26 years? There was nothing here she couldn't have heard directly from him, or have figured out from being a part of his inner life. As for his work with the kids, she already said she did a lot of research to find him and even paid people to help her, so even that should be no surprise for him to hear. It is amazing how these people take the weak and vulnerable, use obvious facts, then attribute it to God. If he didn't really believe that she was convinced of this charade, he would be enraged; but clearly, this is how she was brought up. It's really not her fault. Nevertheless, all this aside, he has a quivering feeling inside that he can't seem to shake. Seeing Karen after all these years and then bringing up all this stuff all at once has really done a number on him.

Sensing his state of mind, Karen gets up and gives Rob a tight hug. "I should get going now. Thank you so much for not turning me away, and opening yourself up to listen."

Feeling vulnerable, Rob continues holding onto Karen. Even after everything, her closeness gives him a familiar comfort, and he begins sliding his hands down her body and softly kissing her neck. "Kar...let's just--"

"Rob." Karen gently pushes him away. "We can't...for many reasons."

Frustrated and angry, Rob snaps. "Oh, so now you get all holy, after years of turning me away and running into the arms of another man. Karen, I loved you... I LOVED you and you threw it all away!"

Tears are now sliding down Karen's face. "Yes, Rob. I know that, and I messed up. I messed up! Whether you believe it or not, I am a different woman now. I am not the confused and angry girl crying out for attention anymore, but you...are still a rescuer. Only I don't need a rescuer, because I have a Savior, and truth be told, you don't have space for a woman who doesn't need to be saved.

I will always love you Rob, and be grateful for all you have given me in many ways. I will also always regret that I didn't have it in me to do the same for you at the time. I hope you have allowed me to do so in small measure with this visit. Please know those were not my words I shared with you. To be completely honest, I really didn't want to contact you. I was too ashamed, but because I knew this was not just about me, I did."

Although he certainly does not agree with her angle on this 'rescuer' crap, one thing is for sure: Karen is not the same woman who hurt and left him years ago. This is a kinder, gentler, woman before him. 'Isn't life funny?' He thinks to himself. 'The people we wanted all along can sometimes only become so once they're no longer with us.'

CHAPTER NINETEEN

Stephanie wakes up, slides out of bed and grabs her purse. She opens the bottle of pills and swallows an extra one—just in case. Then she looks down at Jeff sleeping soundly, without a care. She cannot stop thinking about the close call she had at dinner the night he gave her the roses. Even after a full week of consistently taking her pills, she still can't tell him what she had intended to say. She knows he is getting tired of sleeping at her apartment when his house is obviously more accommodating, but she isn't prepared to be presented to his children and parents at this time, and most definitely not in this state. Sure, they know about her, but that doesn't mean she wants to be padding around their place in a bathrobe after screwing Jeff all night.

He has been patient with her as always, which only makes her feel worse and wonder what her hang-up is. Here is a man who provides her with everything the world has to offer. He wants to take her to his luxury properties around the world, and she would never have to work again. He is loving, kind, generous, and here she is acting like some crazy mental escapee. What more could she want? Not everybody has to experience an otherworldly connection to be in love. She admits she felt that kind of connection with Rob, and where did that get her? Love is different for each person because each person is different. There is no one size fits all. She truly loved Fred for who he was, and she can love Jeff for the person he is too. He doesn't press or ask for anything other than her presence in his life. It is time for her to get over herself.

Jeff shifts, reaches out and immediately opens his eyes when he feels her absence. "Baby?" He looks up sleepily. "You alright?"

Her heart instantly melts. He even wants her in his sleep. She slides back under the covers and curls into him. "I'm more than alright. I'm with you." He sighs deeply squeezing her tightly to him, then lifts her hair and begins softly kissing the back of her neck. She lightly moans then gives a throaty chuckle. "Haven't you had enough yet?" His body answers before he does. "Never."

* * *

Stephanie carefully smooths the skirt of her garnet colored silk shirtwaist dress and delicately lowers herself on the couch so as not wrinkle it and crosses her legs demurely.

"You look very nice today Stephanie," Lehti notes. "I love your pendant. It's gorgeous."

Stephanie proudly fingers it with a smile. "Thanks. My boyfriend gave it to me."

Lehti's eyebrows slowly rise as she quietly waits for more information.

Stephanie, amused by Lehti's reaction, laughs. "Yes, Lehti, it's official...I have a boyfriend now."

"Well, good for you Stephanie! Is this the reason why I haven't been seeing you lately?"

Stephanie tilts her head and smirks. "Pretty much, yeah. He's a prominent businessman, so I've been accompanying him to a lot of evening functions that we don't get home from until late, so it's been kind of difficult for me to awaken that early."

Lehti nods. "Do you want me to change your present time slot?"

Chewing the side of her lip, Stephanie looks apologetic. "Well, actually Lehti, I was thinking of stopping my sessions going forward."

This time Lehti doesn't seem surprised. "Really?"

Stephanie nervously continues. "Yes. When I came to you, I specifically wanted to work out the trauma from the loss I experienced and be able to move on with my life. I think I have now achieved that, and I really want to thank you for taking this journey with me."

"Well, that's great Stephanie. As I've said, you've made great strides in moving forward and I'm really proud of you. By the way, did you ever go to the doctor about your attack?"

Stephanie's eyes briefly dart away. "Yes, I did. The doctor said that I have been experiencing 'stress related anxiety' but told me that I was on the right track by exercising."

Lehti is unmoved. "So, have you been exercising, Stephanie?"

Stephanie fights not to squirm in her seat. "Well basically, yes. I mean, I've obviously missed some times, but I haven't given up the effort completely."

Lehti keeps pressing. "And did he prescribe any medication for you?"

Stephanie unconsciously bites her lip again. "Well, he offered a prescription to take if needed, but like I said, he was happy that I was already addressing it through exercise."

Lehti nods but doesn't look convinced. "Have you had to use it?"

Stephanie has had enough. "Lehti, what's with all the questions, especially now? Does it really even matter?"

Lehti is unruffled by Stephanie's outburst. "Stephanie, we've been through this before. You're here now, so for my records, I am doing a closing interview. I am not judging you. I am only gathering as much information as possible before I close your file. Regardless of what you say, you still don't have to come back if you don't want to. I'm not going to have you committed or anything unless of course, you are a danger to yourself or someone else."

Stephanie calms down a bit but is still edgy. "Yes, Lehti. I've had to take them; and before you ask me, I have had other incidents but am working it out. I don't need therapy for every little thing. The main point is I have gotten over the necessary hurdle. Everything else is just life; plain and simple."

Lehti looks up from her pad and studies Stephanie. "Stephanie, you seem to be taking my questions personally. Do you think I mean you harm in asking them?"

Stephanie sighs impatiently. "No Lehti, I think it's just that because I'm better now this whole questioning process is kind of annoying. I believe it had its purpose at one point, but I am not in that place now. I'm not saying that I'm perfect, but I just don't think it is necessary for me to continue therapy any longer."

Lehti finishes scribbling then puts down her pad and pen. "Point taken. Well, perhaps then we should end your session here."

Stephanie turns to look at the clock behind her. "I think that would be good, thank you. Really...thank you Lehti for everything, and if anyone ever asks me for a good therapist, I will definitely refer them to you. You've been amazing." Stephanie retrieves her checkbook for the last time and hands Lehti her fee.

"Thank you, Stephanie. I'm glad you feel our time together has served you well. Take care."

Stephanie walks out with a mixture of aggravation and relief. She understands that it is her job, but that woman is relentless! It's as if she wants to know every single nuance of Stephanie's thought life. Maybe these types of things entertain and titillate her. She knows she is married, but you have to have some kind of emptiness of your own to want to bore into someone else's life like that. As for her, she would never have the room to be able to listen to all the stuff that people go through. She doesn't even have the wherewithal to listen to her own self beyond a certain point. After a while you realize it's time to get off the couch and live your broken, crazy life out in the real world with real people and make real mistakes instead of sitting there sifting through the sands of your life reminiscing, theorizing and hypothesizing about what happened and why and what it really means, blah, blah, blah.

In a way, she feels sorry for Lehti, spending her life tied to other people's pain and confusion, day after day. Personally, that alone would drive her crazy. She is glad she got out when she did or she would've been like one of those people, trapped in the hole of helplessness waiting for the next morsel of sustenance to be dropped down. No, she is the type who would instead build a ladder, create a rope, or do whatever to climb the hell out of there instead of slowly wasting away. That's how she's come this far. With all the stuff she's been through she could have easily given up, but that's not who she is, and look—things are turning around for her yet again. She has a beautiful life with a wonderful man to look forward to and refuses waste a second more of it.

* * *

Stephanie walks into her office and checks her messages. She is so excited that Jeff's latest development, 'The Tribal Tower' is finally complete and can't wait to attend the private reception and tour this evening to celebrate. She is particularly interested in this venture, as it is a hotel which integrates various world cultures into its décor and cuisine. One of the things she most appreciates is that Africa is presented as a diverse, abundant continent with numerous developed countries and cultures, as opposed to the often one-dimensional portrayal of a swath of dried land and naked indigenous people with spears, beating drums and chanting. The main attraction is a restaurant called 'Motherland' that features a revolving menu of cuisine from South Africa, Senegal, Liberia, Ghana, along with other cultural restaurants and gift shops that carry handcrafted fair-trade items from all over the world. Everyone is so looking forward to the opening that they are already at full capacity for the first six months.

There is a knock at the door. "Come in," she responds.

Stacie cracks open the door and peeks in. "Hey Stephanie, do you have a moment?"

After putting her off for weeks, Stephanie figures she'd better get this over and done, and now is a perfect time, as after leaving Lehti's, she is already in 'house cleaning' mode. "Yes Stacie, as a matter of fact, I do. Step in, please. What can I help you with?"

Sensing Stephanie's undercurrent of impatience, Stacie hesitantly continues. "Well…it's about Rob actually—"

Stephanie abruptly slams her palm on the desk and stands up. "I knew it…I knew it! Wow, Stacie, I know you have no problem with being brazen, but this here takes the cake. How dare you come in my office trying to commiserate with me of all people over a man who you practically knocked me down and stepped over to get to? What did you think was going to happen? Did you think that after you screwed his brains out he was going to profess his love and marry you?

Stacie's face reddens and her eyes water as she trembles with rage. "You Bitch. You stupid ass Bitch." She says with quiet fury. "You think you know everything, don't you? From the moment you came here, you holed yourself up in this office day and night, hiding from life, all the while resenting people like me, who are not afraid to go after what they want.

For the record, I never even kissed, let alone slept with Rob—not that I didn't try—and you know why? Because after you stepped on him like a roach that day, he got drunk and cried like a baby over you, although I have absolutely no idea why. You walk around here acting like you have it all together, but for the record, it is oh so clear that you are just a boiling hot mess.

Then you have the nerve to come at me? When I specifically asked if you were seeing Rob beforehand, you yourself invited me to come by on Scrabble Night and talk to him. So, what did you really expect Stephanie; because unlike you I was clear about what I wanted. I don't have men jumping through hoops like a damn circus act, trying to figure me out. Now you got this rich guy spoiling the hell out of you because for some reason he likes you too, but you're just playing him because it's obvious that you still want Rob. So, who's really the low down one, Stephanie? Personally, I could care less about you. I only came in here because I felt sorry for Rob's sake about what I did that night, and to tell you what you wouldn't allow him to say for himself; but now I hope he will come to his senses and realize that it truly is the best thing for him not to have wound up with you." With that, she turns and walks out, leaving Stephanie standing there flustered and speechless.

* * *

Stephanie stares out the window of her office, unable to focus. Since her earlier altercation with Stacie, of all kinds thoughts are running through her head. Although she already took a couple when she woke up, she has to pop two more pills just to calm down. She hopes that Stacie hasn't gone and run her mouth off to Aline or anyone else in the office about what went down between the two of them. The last thing she needs right now is to be in the center of some crazy office drama. She has always been careful to maintain a professional image, which has served her well, allowing her access to high-level business events like the one where she met Jeff. Even if Stacie chooses to be low and gossip, she will simply ignore it and move forward. She has things more important to focus on than what some trashy wannabe Diva has to say about her. Knowing what she does about Stacie's questionable life choices, she should be the last person to talk about anyone else's.

She reaches to answer her phone and smiles when she hears Jeff's voice. "Hi Baby, sorry I couldn't call you earlier. My morning meeting ran over and I had to run straight to lunch with the General Manager of The Tribal. How's your day going so far? Did you get out for lunch today?"

Stephanie is touched by Jeff's concern. This is exactly what she needs right now. "Hi sweetheart, I'm so happy to hear from you. Today is your big day and I am too excited to eat. Anyway, I'm saving my appetite for the reception."

Jeff sighs with apprehension. "Baby, this is *our* big day, but I don't want you to be weak on that account. I really need you to start eating more often. I knew I should've had lunch sent over for you."

Stephanie purrs soothingly, "Jeff, honey, I'm okay. I don't want you to worry about me, especially today. It's only a couple of hours more. I'll be fine. I love you and will see you soon." Jeff blows a long kiss in response. "I love you more and can't wait for you to know how much. See you soon."

* * *

Stephanie walks into The Tribal Tower and is greeted by various wait staff dressed in their homeland's cultural attire, presenting signature beverages and cocktails. On stage, a band is playing world music accompanied by dancers. The pulsating, vibrant atmosphere makes Stephanie's body hum with a primal energy, and instinctively she thinks of Rob, who would absolutely love this place. She eagerly receives some of the deliciously aromatic offerings presented to her and reads the back of each country's flagged toothpick, which contains the official name and description of the sampling. Then sipping her exotic cocktail from a gourd shell, she slowly walks around, taking everything in.

"Stephanie!" She turns to see Jeff waving. She radiantly smiles and strolls over to the group of people he is standing with, ready for an evening of presentation.

Later, when everyone has gone and the cleaning crew is hard at work, Jeff takes Stephanie in his arms. "Baby, I have something I want you to see. Come on."

He takes her hand and leads her to a darkly tinted glass door in the back of the lobby. When he presses his hand onto the identification pad, it immediately opens to reveal an elevator. Fascinated, Stephanie follows him inside, in quiet anticipation of what awaits. When the doors open, they step out and motion-detecting lights gradually illuminate the space in a soft ambient glow. Stephanie is speechless as she realizes they are on the roof under a glass dome, surrounded by the night skyline.

Jeff proudly looks on, satisfied by her reaction. "This is the only place I did not include on the tour because no one publicly knows it exists yet. I wanted you to be the first to see it. He escorts her to each room to survey the luxurious furnishings and amenities. When they are finished, he says,

"This, my love is the most expensive rental in the Tower and is named 'Suite Stephanie', after my very own sweet Stephanie. It is specifically designated as a honeymoon suite, and I want us to be the first to christen it."

He takes a blue velvet box out of his jacket pocket and slowly drops to one knee. "Stephanie, you have made me happier than I can remember being in a long time, and I want us to enjoy even more together. I know you think I spoil you, but that's only because I want you to experience a fraction of what you make me feel every single moment of every day. I love you Stephanie and I know you love me too, so let's just declare before others what we already know in our hearts." He opens the box to reveal a large sparkling princess cut diamond nestled in platinum filigree "Stephanie, my love…will you marry me?"

Stephanie's eyes fill with tears, and her heart bursting with joy, she says, "Oh Rob, YES!"

Jeff looks as though he has been struck with an iron rod. "What?" He quietly whispers.

In that moment, Stephanie realizes what she has just said, and everything begins moving in slow motion. She mutely stares wide-eyed at the devastated look on Jeff's face as he sinks to the floor, eyes brimming with tears and confusion. "Stephanie, what are you doing to me?"

Stephanie stands there unable to think. Her heart is rapidly drumming and the room begins to spin. Panicked, she darts into the elevator and frantically presses for the lobby, eyes blurring with tears. As the doors are closing, she hears Jeff's heartbroken cries. "Stephanie! Stephanie!"

She runs out of the hotel choking with sobs and flags a taxi. She can barely speak to give the address, she is wailing so hard. When the taxi drops her off, she thrusts at him several large bills and jumps out, still crying.

CHAPTER TWENTY

Rob walks in the door, relieved to be home from a particularly trying day, and wishes it were Friday instead of Thursday. He wonders if there is a full moon hiding behind the cloudy night sky because everyone's energy was haywire today. There were two fights at the center, one involving Clarissa and another girl in the bathroom, and the other was initially between two guys from separate teams during the basketball game, but it quickly erupted into a melee with the members of both teams going at it. It was so out of control that police and ambulances had to be called in.

After turning on some smooth jazz music to calm his frayed nerves, he walks into the kitchen, pours himself a glass of wine and begins setting up the spices and condiments necessary to prepare his meal of grilled salmon steak glazed with hoisin sauce and stir-fried string beans with scallions and garlic soy sauce. After a day like this, he especially welcomes the relaxation that cooking brings him. There is something meditative about the repetitive sounds of chopping and scraping. In addition, the fragrant smoldering aromas always put him in a joyous, expectant mood.

In the middle of his culinary inspired bliss, he suddenly has a thought of Stephanie and wonders how she is doing. He remembers what Dalton said about her being in pain and trying to find an escape for it, and hopes that wherever she is, she is at least happy. It is clear that she has been through a lot and deserves to experience joy, even if it isn't with him. He recalls her story of the calm and protection she feels when sitting in the middle of that oak tree on the hill and wants her to experience that peace even after she climbs down and puts her feet on the ground.

Although it hurts him to lose her, he truly hopes that this Jeff guy is treating her right and not controlling or manipulating her with all his gifts and luxurious outings. He didn't get that feeling from him, but you never know with these rich guys. They always have a public face that they buy and a private one that they hide. If this is the case, then he would feel more miserable if even a misunderstanding between the two of them left her worse off than before she met him. That was his initial fear and the reason why he didn't want to approach her in the beginning. Nevertheless, the chemistry between the two of them clearly overrode that resistance. His heart begins to flutter as he recalls their night by the deck, how everything felt so right. Maybe he should have just given in instead of fighting it. Everyone isn't Karen, and he is no longer a dreamy-eyed, inexperienced 24 year old, but an older and wiser man. But that is all water under the bridge at this point. He has to focus on what is and not what could've been.

After he has eaten and cleaned the kitchen, he takes a nice long hot shower, slips into his boxers and T-shirt, and goes upstairs to watch TV. While watching the sports show his mind keeps wandering. Finally, he goes downstairs to the bedroom to cap off this crazy day and his wandering thoughts with a good night's sleep. As he drifts into a deep sleep, he dreams he is holding Stephanie in his arms again, and the same feeling of that first night begins to overtake him. In the background, he hears church bells ringing louder and louder until he finally wakes up, realizing it is his doorbell. Knowing that no one finds his house by mistake, he groggily jumps up and stumbles downstairs, wondering who it could be.

He opens the door to find Stephanie there bawling, her dress wrinkled and wet with sweat and tears. His heart drops to his stomach as he pulls her inside. "Stephanie, what happened?"

She lunges and grasps him tightly, unable to speak through her sobs. He quietly holds her, occasionally rubbing her back.

After a while, she calms down. "Oh Rob, I'm so sorry. I have made such a mess of things and hurt so many people. I just don't know what to do anymore... I don't know what to do. I was so scared because, from the beginning, you moved me in places I didn't even know existed. I've lost so much in my life, I didn't know if I could ever recover from losing you too.

You wanted to know about me before. Now I need to tell you everything so you can understand.

When I was nine, my abusive father bashed my mother's head in and then shot himself, all while I was home. After that, I was placed with my father's sister who blamed me and my mother for what happened and basically ignored me. When I was 12 her husband began molesting and forcing me to have sex with him until I ran away at 17 to live with an older man who verbally and physically attacked me. I stayed with him for five years because I had nowhere else to go. When I finally got pregnant, I thought he would calm down because of the baby, but it seemed like he beat me even more frequently and harshly. One time he came home from drinking, convinced the baby was someone else's. I told him I was rarely allowed to leave the apartment, so it couldn't be, but he still beat me so badly that I lost the baby.

The hospital referred me to a battered woman's shelter where I stayed on to join their job-training program and was ultimately hired as a clerk in an elementary school. I attended college and worked my way up to becoming a teacher. At that time, I was engaged to my live-in boyfriend of seven years, but came home and found him in our bed with another man when he had gotten the return date from my teacher's conference mixed up.

Sometime later, I met Fred, a new science teacher at my school who was everything my previous relationships were not. He was loving, gentle, kind and very patient. He wanted to marry me but I told him that I refused to be trapped. However, when I became pregnant and wanted our child to be part of a loving family, I relented. We planned a beautiful fairy tale wedding with the help of his mother and sisters. It was one of the happiest times of my life. I couldn't believe everything was finally coming together for me. Then the night we were coming from our wedding rehearsal dinner, our car was struck by a drunk driver who instantly killed Fred, nearly killed me and I lost the baby. As if that wasn't bad enough the doctors told me I had experienced so much internal damage that I never would be able to have children again.

As soon as I was physically able, I left with no word or forwarding information. I wanted to forget everyone connected to that part of my life, so I moved here for a clean start and began working at the library, keeping to myself. I enjoyed my job and that was enough for me. I started therapy to work through the trauma I experienced, so it wouldn't follow me forever.

There have been other opportunities with men before, but I never entertained them. I just wanted a peaceful, quiet life with no more loss and no more pain. Then you came and I couldn't shake it off like I'd always done. Something within me kept rising like bubbles and it scared me like crazy. I'm so sorry about what I did to you with Jeff, and I—"

"Shhhh..." Rob places his fingers gently over Stephanie's lips. "That's enough for now, Steph. It's okay. You need to rest."

Stephanie looks up at Rob with red-rimmed swollen eyes. "Rob, I just want you to know that I do love you. Jeff just proposed to me, and I called him by your name because I wanted it to be you."

Rob leans down and tenderly kisses Stephanie. "Steph, I love you too. I'm here now and it's okay. He holds and gently rocks her as she cries with relief. Later, when Stephanie has showered and is swimming in one of his T-Shirts, she climbs into bed with Rob and instantly falls asleep in his arms.

* * *

Early the next morning, Rob awakens and watches Stephanie sleep. With tousled curls falling over her face, she looks like a beautiful angel who has just landed from Heaven onto his bed. Playing back everything she told him, he finally sheds the tears he could not last night. A rush of protectiveness overtakes him and he wants to hold and keep her safe forever. "I love you so much, Stephanie." He whispers to her soundly sleeping form, but she doesn't even budge. He kisses her forehead and plays with her ringlets until finally, she begins to stir. Opening bleary eyes, she looks around, confused. When she focuses upon Rob gazing at her with adoration, she smiles, sighs with relief and snuggles her head into his chest.

Rob softly rubs the back of her neck. "Steph?"

"Hmmm?" Stephanie groans sleepily.

"Let's get married--now. Today."

Stephanie jerks her head and stares at Rob in wide-eyed surprise as tears begin to fill her eyes. She then throws her head back on his chest and cries convulsively. Still rubbing her back, Rob is unruffled. "Is that a yes, then?" He says, smiling.

She lifts her head, laughing and crying at the same time. "Yes!, Yes!" She gasps through tears and kisses him on his lips, then all over his face as they giggle together.

"Well, I don't know about you, but I do not want to wait one more second until I can call you Mrs. Stephanie Stephenson or Martin-Stephenson or however you want to put it as long as you're my wife!" Rob exclaims, jumping up from the bed.

Stephanie excitedly jumps off after him. "You know, we may both get fired for this, but let's take the next couple of weeks off and go somewhere far away!"

Rob is tickled by her enthusiasm. "Well, that's a great way to start a marriage—both of us being unemployed! Let's call out for a few days instead and go to a resort, so we can still be married and keep our jobs."

As Rob gets ready, Stephanie feverishly makes phone calls in search of an available justice of the peace and to her delight, finds one who is able to see them this afternoon. Next, they rush to Stephanie's house so she too can pack and get dressed. They then go down to the courthouse to obtain their license. Afterward, they visit a nearby jewelry store to purchase the bands for their ceremony. Rob's is a wide titanium band with three diamonds going across the middle, while Stephanie chooses an antique style with two rows of diamonds in a white gold setting. Upon arriving at the Justice of the Peace, they are flushed with joy and anticipation. Stephanie shines splendidly in a simple off shouldered flouncy white cotton sundress with large red flowers and a large black patent leather buckled belt. Her curly hair is in a loose upsweep and adorned with a red flower. Rob is striking in an open neck white linen Chinese collared tunic, black linen pants and a red rose pinned to his shirt.

The ceremony is touching, as they gaze into each other's teary eyes, vowing to love, protect and take care of each other for life. As they leave the courthouse husband and wife, life around them seems different. Quietly walking down the steps hand in hand toward the car, Stephanie turns to Rob. "Honey, let's not go anywhere--I just want to go home, if that's okay with you." Rob looks down at Stephanie instinctively knowing that she means the farmhouse and his heart swells with joy. "I'd be honored and delighted Mrs. Martin-Stephenson." Stephanie smiles back placidly. "That's Mrs. Stephenson to you, Sir."

* * *

When they arrive at the farmhouse, Rob makes great ceremony in carrying a laughing, kicking Stephanie over the threshold. When he puts her down, he briefly recalls it was the same place where just hours ago, she fell into his arms distraught. So much has changed since then. She no longer has to feel lost and alone, for he is here to take care of her now. He reaches down and gently pulls her close. "Stephanie, thank you for changing my life forever." As they hug tightly, Stephanie feels his heart beating hard, and knows that he is nervous. Slowly, she pulls herself away and looks up at him. As soon as their eyes catch, everything disappears and they slowly kiss until all the hunger and passion that had been contained is unleashed and they uncontrollably began to devour each other with abandonment, biting, licking grunting and groaning until they both burst in shouts of ecstasy and lay breathlessly spent in each other's arms.

After they shower and change, Rob prepares a simple meal of black bean burgers, sweet potato wedges and a large salad, which they voraciously consume, then finish with a rich thick coconut-banana smoothie slowly sipped on the deck overlooking the fountain. Slurping the last of her drink, Stephanie sighs with contentment. "This almost doesn't seem real, and yet I feel like I was always supposed to be here."

Rob nods in wonder. "I understand completely. Like it's too good to be true, yet so natural. I feel like this was how my life was always intended to be only I'm just discovering it now."

Stephanie smiles in agreement and then changes the subject. "So, when are we going to tell Dalton and the kids?"

Rob studies the fountain in thought. "Well, we'll probably tell Dalton tomorrow, but I would like for us to have a celebration here and invite the kids. You know they were a big part of this too—especially Mariana."

Stephanie can't help but chuckle as she envisions Mariana's exuberant response to their news. "That's a great idea! We could even have Dalton do a ceremonial exchange of vows for everyone to witness."

Rob looks adoringly at Stephanie. "If it were up to me, we would have one every day just to remind me of what an incredibly lucky man I am." Then a thought hits him, and he becomes troubled. "Steph, what are you going to do about Jeff at this point? You know if he hasn't already, he is going to contact you."

Stephanie continues staring into the cascading waters, thoughtfully tapping her glass, already knowing that he has. "I've made such a mess of things for him that this could be the final blow to his devastation. I don't think I should say anything until we've talked face to face. What do you think?"

Rob gazes searchingly at the sky then turns to face Stephanie. "Steph, I trust your judgment on however you want to handle this. Still, as I don't know him, my main concern is your well-being. If you feel like you would be safe, then fine. I just don't want anything to happen to you. Who knows what he's liable to do under these circumstances?"

Stephanie nods. "Well, I won't rule anything out, but I also think I know him enough to not feel threatened or in danger. He's never even given me a hint of that possibility. Just the same, I will meet with him in public and you can be nearby if that makes you feel better."

Rob smiles with relief. "Yes, it would. Thank you."

Stephanie reaches over to touch his face. "No, thank you for putting up with my craziness and the mess it has created."

Rob clutches her waist and firmly draws her in with a long passionate kiss. "I'll do all that and more, to have you as mine."

Stephanie feels a stirring under the intensity of his ardent stare. "Mmm... Rob, we'd better at least try to make it to the bed this time."

Rob, however, is already underway. She moans lightly as he slowly kisses her neck with hands grazing her body. Then with one hand, he whips the soft, thick throw off the lounge set and gently lowers Stephanie onto it, continuing to lingeringly explore every inch of her body until she is carried away on waves of frenzied pleasure. Afterwards, he begins to gradually make his way, slow and measured, savoring every sensation that fills his body, fervently whispering in Stephanie's ear while she gasps declarations of affection in return. Soon with bodies trembling beyond control, they cling to each other, roaring in raptured release.

CHAPTER TWENTY-ONE

Rob and Dalton clear Stephanie's apartment over the weekend, moving her belongings into Rob's house, where she selects what she wants to keep, setting the rest aside for donation. She uses the room Rob recently renovated as her yoga/meditation room, embellishing it with items from her apartment. While decorating, her phone rings and she answers it.

"Stephanie, this is Jeff. Please don't hang up. I've been trying to call you for several days now. I need to speak with you."

Stephanie's heart begins racing with apprehension at the sound of his voice. She is not prepared for this now. "Jeff. Yes, we do have to talk, but I am away for few days. Can we meet in the library courtyard on Wednesday during my lunch break?"

Jeff remains silent for a few beats before offering a strained response. "Sure. 1:00, right?"

"Yes," Stephanie confirms. "I'll see you then."

After hanging up, she turns around and is startled to see Rob standing in the doorway. "Sorry." He apologizes. "I was coming to ask you a question and didn't want to interrupt your conversation. That was Jeff, right?"

Stephanie nods. "Yeah. He surprised me by calling from a different number, figuring I wouldn't pick up if I saw it was him. He was right. I knew we had to speak, but I wasn't ready just yet. Now I'd rather just get it over with, so we can both move on. We're going to meet at the library courtyard tomorrow at 1:00, so I hope you can make it."

Rob walks over and hugs Stephanie. "Don't worry, I'll be there." He looks around at the room. "Wow, you've wasted no time in spiffing this place up. I like what you've done with it. You've quite a flair for design yourself, Mrs. Stephenson."

Stephanie looks around satisfactorily. "Thanks, I like it too. I guess this is one of the many areas where we complement each other. However, just know that you have officially been relegated as the house cook because that is one of the areas where I dare not compare."

Rob smiles graciously. "Baby, I love your cooking but will relish every opportunity to spoil you with my meals, since you enjoy them so much. I'd also like for us to cook together sometimes and can show you some things I've learned along the way."

"Oh, that sounds like fun!" Stephanie gushes. "I'm so glad we made this decision, Rob. I think we are going to have a good life together." Rob tenderly kisses Stephanie on the lips. "I agree, Mrs. Stephenson."

* * *

Upon returning to work, Stephanie tries to be low-key, but people obviously notice the ring. Once the word gets out, she is flocked with many surprised well-wishers, but Stacie avoids her like the plague. Stephanie knows that at least for the sake of work, she is going to have to try to figure out how to navigate their relationship, but for now, her focus is on sorting things out with Jeff.

She looks at her computer's clock for the fiftieth time, dismayed that it is only 12:38 p.m. There is so much nervous energy bouncing within her that she wonders if she should just sit outside and gather her thoughts beforehand. Rob called earlier assuring her that he would be nearby and ready to protect her if needed. Truly, that is the least of her worries, for she knows Jeff would not threaten or harm her. If anything, she is the one who has been doing all the injuring up to this point.

She has had such a whirlwind of excitement with Rob these past few days that she almost forgot about Jeff. Now the flood of guilt and anxiety that had been on reprieve returns with vengeance, and she pops a pill for the first time in days.

Furthermore, now that she rethinks it, Rob watching from a distance actually may not make things easier. She hopes he does not misinterpret anything and unnecessarily intervene to make things worse, which Jeff does not deserve. The fact of the matter is, she had been telling this man she loved him and given him every indication of wanting to be together. She needs to own up to that. Nevertheless, she still decides to remove her ring to avoid adding insult to injury. There is already enough to wade through.

She looks at the clock. It is 12:44, so she gathers her purse, notifies Aline, and walks into the courtyard. Breathing in the floral fragrances while listening to the gurgling fountain, she calms down a bit and looks around. In the midst of the manicured shrubs, flowers and grass is a brick paved area whose umbrella covered outdoor café tables draw those who want to read outside and/or bring their own food. Seeing this as an opportunity, she suggested the idea of having an indoor café or at least a food cart to provide another way of raising revenue for the library's community services, but it is still under board review.

She sits at a table and surveys the area to see if she can spot Rob, but notices nothing. 'My personal ninja at work', she thinks to herself and chuckles as she imagines him suddenly jumping out of the shadows in full gear and weaponry ready to defend her at a moment's notice.

While continuing to wait uneasily, she regrets not having brought a book, so she wouldn't just be sitting here with her mind racing, anticipating Jeff's arrival. However, now that the moment has arrived, knowing Rob is around makes her feel better, despite what she previously thought.

She pulls out her phone to see if there are any messages from either Jeff or Rob but finds none. She checks the time again; it is 12:55. When she looks up, Jeff is walking toward her in his usual business attire with a confident stride and demeanor she knows belies what he is truly feeling, for he is a businessman down to the end. As he approaches, she stands up to greet him with a kiss on the cheek and the scene of Judas and Jesus flashes before her.

Jeff surveys her admiringly before sitting down. "You look great."

Stephanie has been glowing since she and Rob got together, but obviously, isn't going to offer that information. "Thank you. Jeff, I appreciate you still wanting to talk after what happened. Honestly, I think it was a shock to both of us, as I obviously did not expect for things to go that way."

With her first mention of the incident, she notices cracks in Jeff's armor as the pain resurfaces on his face. "I've been going over and over it in my head, trying to figure out what I missed, what I didn't see, and I just never imagined or expected this would happen, that we would be here like this." His eyes begin to tear. "What happened? Were you seeing him all along?"

Stephanie's heart aches for him, but she fights the urge to reach out and comfortingly grab his hand. "To be honest, we had been sort of seeing each other until right before you and I met when I hastily broke things off for matters I won't go into. At the time I really thought it was over between us and was prepared to move on with my life. I never intended to deceive you, Jeff. Please believe me."

Jeff unrelentingly presses on, wanting to know everything. "So, are you seeing him now? Do you really love him, because Stephanie, all this time you said you loved and wanted to be with me and I believed you with all my heart. I invested my life's hopes and dreams in us being together.

Anyway, I've been thinking; I know especially at this stage of our lives, that we all come with baggage we think is neatly packed away, but sometimes when we find a tie here or a sock there, we realize we hadn't included everything as planned. I still love you Stephanie and meant every word I said to you from the beginning until now, and just because your life is not neatly packed and travel ready, doesn't mean I do not want to take this journey with you anymore. We can sort it out together, because that's what marriage is, Baby."

At the simple sincerity of Jeff's words, Stephanie's eyes fill with tears and Jeff offers to her what she refused him. Grabbing her hands in his, he looks her squarely in the eye. "Stephanie, please marry me. I still want you to be my wife."

No longer able to contain herself, Stephanie begins to sob and prays that Rob does not take this moment to appear. "Jeff, please, please hear me out and try to understand. I care so much about you and yes, even love you. You are one of the most beautiful souls I have ever met. You have been nothing but gentle and kind and loving to me, even now, after all of this. However, I would be doing you more harm in the long run if I agreed to be your wife. You asked me if I loved Rob because in your mind you are looking at it as an either/or situation. How can I love Rob and say and I love you at the same time? Yet, I have come to understand that there are different kinds of love. I did not lie when I said I loved you, but have discovered that I am in love with Rob in such a way that it would ultimately do you or any other man a disservice if I were to be with anyone other than him. I know this is a hard thing for you to hear and under the circumstances, not easy for me to say. I didn't understand this when we became involved, but I do now, and care way too much for you to inflict any more pain at my own expense."

Jeff is crushed but nods with resignation. "I don't know what more to say, Stephanie. After this, I may very likely be telling the next woman the same thing, and then perhaps will understand, but as for now, I really don't."

He stands up and gives Stephanie a kiss on her cheek with tears in his eyes. "I wish you all the best. Call me if you ever need anything." With that, he turns and walks away, leaving Stephanie feeling numb. As she sits there for a while, she begins to wonder if Rob ever did show up after all. Either way, she welcomes this space to process what just happened. Although it was painful, she is relieved to have been true to her heart. Even if Jeff does not understand right now, she is grateful that he at least respects it. She truly admires him more than ever and hopes he finds a love worthy of him.

She checks the time and decides to run over to Lifebreath for some coffee and lunch before heading back to the office. Now that she's gotten that out of the way, next on her list is Stacie; but that is for another day and another time.

* * *

When Rob returns to the center, everyone is in an uproar to welcome him back, especially the kids. There are endless questions concerning his

A Broken Hallelujah

sudden and mysterious disappearance, but Rob wants to surprise them, so he and Stephanie arranged that he would not wear his ring until the 'party' that the center and kids are being invited to. He smiles every time he imagines the look on their faces when they realize the true reason they are there.

"Hey, Rob, man—where you been? Don't tell me it was you who had an 'emergency' appointment this time." Clint walks into his office with a huge welcoming grin.

Rob smiles back, returning his greeting with a brief handclasp. "Ha Ha. You wish. I told you I ain't goin' out like that."

Clint starts laughing. "I hear you man; let me tell you firsthand, it is no joke. That and our last conversation really made me think about slowing down myself—not the standstill place that you're at—but just a little more paced than I've been going. I'm getting too old for this stuff and need to start thinking about settling down with a wifey."

Rob smirks at Clint's comment. "Just so you know, settling down with a 'wifey' is not the same thing as having a wife."

Clint gives him a mischievous look. "I know that man...you don't have to pay nothing when you leave!"

Rob shakes his head. "Well, I suppose we should start slow with you, so I'll consider that progress."

Clint jerks his head in a single nod. "Exactly!"

With that, Rob changes the subject. "Hey, listen, man, I'm having a party at my house in a few weeks and would like for you to come. Oh, and tell the other Saturday Night guys that this will not be a sports event, so to dress with a little more class than usual."

Clint is thoroughly interested. A party, huh? Will there be any females there?"

135

Rob smiles at Clint's one-track mind and instantly thinks of Stacie. That could be a match made in Heaven—or Hell, depending on the perspective. "Please don't come with those expectations. It's not that kind of party."

Clint's eyes widen. "Oh wow, Rob—now I get it—refusing the panties and all. Hey, that's real nice of you but I don't think this is for—"

"Shut up Clint," Rob interjects. "I'm just saying don't show up trying to make this your personal hook-up connection."

Clint still seems a little tentative. "Well, will there at least be food and drinks at this 'party'?"

Rob is now beginning to question his offer. "Hey man, relax. It's just an invitation, not a court order for child support. Come by if you want to, but if not we're still cool, okay?"

Clint relaxes a little. "Yeah, that's cool. I should be there, though. I'll tell the guys too. What time is it going to be?

Rob smirks. Six o'clock---EST, not CPT, thank you."

Clint looks perplexed. "Wow, that's kind of early for a party. What is it, more like a barbecue, then?"

Rob fights his growing exasperation. "Yes, kind of like a barbecue, but a little more classy—meaning no jeans or sneakers."

Clint starts laughing. "Slacks and shoes? Man, please don't tell me this is one of those fancy parties where we have to eat scraps from toothpicks because I need some real food—on a plate bigger than the palm of my hand."

Rob is done. "Come and find out. Now, get out my office with your 500 questions. I've got work to do, and close the door when you leave. Buh-bye!"

* * *

Stephanie rushes home from work with a new excitement and decides to surprise Rob with a meal. After changing out of her work clothes, she goes into the well-stocked kitchen and begins looking around. She opens the freezer and realizes that apparently, Rob is more of a carnivore than she thought, as she surveys the rows of different meats stacked before her. "Ugh.", she says to herself. "I sure hope he doesn't eat pork, because if so, I may have to get my own cooking utensils." She finally decides upon stir-fried vegetables over noodles and makes a mental note to pick up some tofu to add to their food supply. He prepares vegetarian meals so well it was easy to believe that he was practically one himself.

Just as she finishes, Rob walks in, grabs Stephanie around the waist and plants a big kiss on her. "Mmm...mm, that smells good, what do we have here?" Stephanie beams with delight. "I made some stir fried vegetables and noodles, Chinese style. However, if you want to add meat to yours, you'll have to cook it yourself. I do have my boundaries."

Rob gently kisses the back of her neck. "Baby, I'll eat fresh grass out your hand, if you're feeding it to me."

Stephanie laughs with a wink. "You don't know the full range of my diet yet, so don't make promises you can't keep. As a matter of fact, I do like raw grass—it's called wheatgrass and very good for you; so, because you offered with such conviction, you WILL try it."

Rob makes a face, and she starts laughing even harder. "Welcome to my world, baby!"

While eating, they share the details of their day. Curious, Stephanie is anxious to go first. "So Rob, were you actually in the courtyard earlier?"

Rob puffs up with pride. "Ha, you didn't see me, right? I told you I'd be there, but I know how to stay hidden. I would make a great private detective."

"Or stalker." She quips.

Rob laughs heartily. "See, the list of options is expanding already!"

He then becomes serious. "Yes, I was watching and honestly, when I saw how much that man cared for you, I knew he wouldn't hurt you, so I moved a little further away to give you privacy, but stayed around because I promised I would be there for you. When I saw you were finished and he left, I wanted so much to come and hold you but realized this was the time for you to process your emotions privately and I didn't want to interfere with that."

Stephanie is amazed. "Wow, it was like you were reading my mind! That's exactly what was happening." Rob leans over to give Stephanie another kiss. "That's because we're connected. I feel what you feel."

Stephanie nods. "He said he still loved me and asked me to marry him again. I didn't have the heart to tell him that I already was—to you."

Rob listens intently. Well, from what I could see, it wasn't easy for you, also; you must have cared about him a lot, Steph."

Stephanie bites her lip. "I did and told him that, but I also said that the way I feel about you supercedes any other feelings and that wouldn't be fair to him. It was so hard, Rob. I never wanted to do that to him, but I was more relieved that he was even still gracious when he left and told me to call him if I ever needed anything."

Rob slightly furrows his brow. "Steph, at the risk of sounding a little overbearing, maybe even jealous, I hope that you don't take him up on that. From the perspective of a man, that's the 'open door' move, which basically means that if we ever get into an argument, hit a dry spell, or you begin to feel dissatisfied for whatever reason, he's letting you know that he'll still be there to take you back. I've seen many a woman fall for that and mess up their marriage or relationship along the way. Most of them were my ex-wives friends, and I personally feel that may have even been an influencing factor somewhere along the line in the destruction of my own marriage. Although it seems innocent at face value, it can ultimately be catastrophic to a relationship."

Stephanie reassuringly places her hand over Rob's. "Don't worry, sweetheart. That door is closed, not just for me, but to also allow him to move onto someone who can give him the love he deserves. Still, though I am confident no one can take me away from you, I won't test it."

Rob looks at Stephanie adoringly. I feel the same way, baby."

Stephanie smiles then changes the subject. "So, what about you--how did your day go?"

Rob shakes his head, laughing. "As soon as I walked in, everyone mobbed me, especially the kids, asking all kinds of questions. There was even a rumor going around that I had quit and the kids were very upset."

Stephanie is appalled. "Who would start a rumor like that?"

Rob shrugs dismissively. "Who knows, but you know how some people are—creating drama wherever they can. Anyway, everyone is now buzzing about the party and I can't wait to unleash our surprise. You know I was thinking, and I'm not sure how you would feel about this, but one of my co-workers would be a perfect match for Stacie and so I am thinking about inviting her as well, but obviously, the final word rests with you."

Stephanie inwardly cringes at the mention of Stacie's name from Rob, but out of respect for how he dealt with her and Jeff's situation, remains cool. "Well, that would potentially keep her off your trail if it works out, but I didn't tell you that Stacie and I had a blow-up last week, and it was not pretty at all."

Rob raises his eyebrows in surprise. "What? Are you serious? What happened?"

Stephanie, recalling how things went down, is now hesitant to rehash the details. "Um...well...I guess it started with a little misunderstanding on my part. Stacie said she wanted to talk to me about something and mentioned your name. Thinking she was actually going to ask me for some sort of relational advice for the two of you I kind of came down hard on her, but she returned with full fire. We haven't really spoken since."

Rob is at a loss for words. "Oh wow...ok. Well, I guess that's that."

He tries to appear nonchalant, but Stephanie perceives otherwise. "She told me nothing happened between the two of you. Is that true?"

Rob wonders if and how much Stacie revealed about the night he got drunk and passed out in her bed, but decides not to go there, just in case. "Yes, that's true, we never even kissed but, to be completely honest, there was a brief flirtation between us a while ago that I never followed upon because of my feelings for you. However, when I got to know her beyond the façade, I found her to be a truly nice young woman, and thought she would be a great match for Clint."

Now Stephanie is surprised. "Clint? You mean that sweet young man who works at the front desk?"

Rob smirks with cynicism, wondering what kind of front he put on to make Stephanie get that impression, but doesn't want to blow up his spot. "Well yes, he was helping at the front desk when you came to visit that day, but he actually is the leader of the teen boys group at the center. I know he looks younger, but actually, he and Stacie are around the same age and both recently mentioned to me that they were looking to settle down. That's the only reason why I thought of her, but don't worry about it. He can always just stop by the library on his own if he's really that interested."

Stephanie sits quietly before finally speaking. "Stacie told you her age?"

Rob instantly regrets having brought this whole thing up in the first place. "Well, yeah she told me when she found out what an 'old man' I was. I suppose at that point, I became more of a father figure to her. I don't think she would've told me if she had considered me otherwise." He says this hoping to diffuse Stephanie's unease, but apparently, it does not work.

"Well, I happen to know that Stacie distinctly prefers older men, so that doesn't even sound right. Still, I will say in her defense, she was the one who initiated the reconciliation between us on your behalf, and I should consider that. Let me talk to her first to see how it goes, and then decide if it would be best to invite her or just leave it alone." She was also tempted to remind Rob of what he had just said about her, Jeff and closed doors, but decided against it when she realized that unlike him and Stacie, she actually did sleep with Jeff.

Rob continues in his nonchalance. "Yeah, whatever you want to do. It doesn't really matter to me; I was just trying to look out for Clint." Then he rapidly changes the subject. "So anyway, Mrs. Stephenson, how does a nice candlelight bubble bath sound to help you unwind from your day? I'll run the water while you get ready."

Stephanie purrs and slowly leans in, playfully nipping Rob on his ear before breathlessly whispering, "Only if you're joining me, Mr. Stephenson."

* * *

The next day at work, things return to normal. With all the questions about Jeff avoided, and she and Rob's elopement answered, everyone is back to business as usual—everyone except Stacie, who is unusually quiet and withdrawn, not just with Stephanie but in general. Normally the office's social butterfly, Stephanie is one of many who notices the change in Stacie's demeanor, as well as her subdued appearance and attire.

"Maybe she got religion." Aline jokes during a conversation in Stephanie's office. "Honestly, she's been like this all week, Steph. I don't know what happened to her, but I'm telling you, it seems like she's had some sort of conversion to make changes this drastic."

Stephanie muses over Aline's comments. "Or maybe she's depressed for some reason," she offers.

Aline nods with clarity. "Yeah, that's a more likely explanation. However you look at it, if Stacie leaves her house without makeup, it's gotta be either an act of God or the devil."

Stephanie tries not to laugh at Aline's comment, and instead tightly purses her lips as if thinking. "Well, I'll talk to her and see if I can get a feel for what's going on."

Aline's eyes instantly widen. "*You're* concerned about Stacie? Well, what do you know? Miracles ARE abounding in this place, after all. Praise Jesus!" She does a little shuffle with uplifted arms.

Stephanie is unmoved. "Save it for your church choir, Aline. That stuff doesn't work here."

Nevertheless, Aline is undeterred. "Apparently it does. I don't care what you say Stephanie, prayer works!"

* * *

Stephanie picks up the phone to call the front desk. "Hi Stacie, this is Stephanie. Aline is on her way over to relieve you. Can you please come into my office for a moment? Okay, thank you."

When Stacie appears in the doorway, Stephanie invites her in and asks her to close the door. "Stacie, first off I owe you an apology for how our interaction went last week."

Stacie stares at Stephanie unflinchingly expressionless. "You shouldn't apologize if that is how you feel."

Stephanie is slightly taken aback by her response. Well, I think we both said things to each other that we really didn't mean, and—"

"I meant what I said, Stephanie because I believe it is true and have no regrets about it. You, on the other hand, said things about me that you meant although they were not true. You may not appreciate it, but I have been open about my life, warts and all, and made no apologies for it. I have shared information with you freely, but you have taken my confidence and judged me with it. At the same time, you kept your own life hidden while believing yourself to be above reproach, and I personally can't respect that.

While I am not a prude and can at times be flirtatious, you had the nerve to portray me as a shameless whore as you yourself were stringing two men along. Furthermore, it was only my truth that caused you to open your eyes and from the looks of things, start cleaning your act up. Yet after all

142

this, you still sit here and piously tell me that we both said things we didn't mean? You knew I was right then and you know it now, so no, I will not accept your apology because it's phony and dishonest. Be real, and then we can talk. Until then I really don't have much else to say to you beyond our working relationship."

She then gets up to leave, but Stephanie stops her. "Stacie, please. Okay… I'm sorry. Yes, you're right; you did ask me about Rob and I didn't say anything because I wasn't sure myself at that time about how I felt, and what or if I wanted to do anything about it. And yes, I was threatened by your expressed desire to pursue him, and that there should have been a clue to me, but I'm not like you. I've been so used to stuffing things down because it was the only way for me to get through my life without going crazy. It is true that I did resent not only your ability to be honest and open about yourself, but also because you are the type of woman that gets whatever she wants just by showing up, and I have had to fight for everything I've had. That's not your fault, but I made it out to be, and for that, I am truly sorry for any pain I have caused you in doing so."

Stacie stands there defiantly, fighting back rising tears. "You know, you and everyone else in the world think that because I have these huge ass tits and a curvy body that everything I want simply floats to me on a magic pillow. If so, then why am I the one spending my nights alone crying myself to sleep, while you have a wonderful husband lying in your bed? You think I don't have to, haven't had to fight all my life too, Stephanie—fight grown men off because they lusted after my well-developed, but still pre-pubescent body—and most times unsuccessfully? Fight glares from females who feel threatened by my very presence, and the men who confirm their fears by staring at me like a magazine pinup, even while holding their hand? Even now, I'm fighting you here in my place of employment over this.

No, we may not have had the same type of battles Stephanie, but before you go running your mouth off about how damned easy you think my life is, think about that." With that, she walks out leaving Stephanie sitting there with tears of sorrow and regret in her eyes.

CHAPTER TWENTY-TWO

Rob walks into Lifebreath excited about his meeting with Dalton on the details of their secret wedding ceremony. "Hey, there buddy, Good Morning!" He greets with a huge grin.

Dalton, however, receives this ebullient welcome with a wary look. "So this what marriage does to you, huh? Perhaps I did come out with the better deal, after all."

Rob laughs heartily and slaps him on the back. "Hmm…I don't think so my friend, but we'll never know now, will we?"

Dalton chuckles, shaking his head. "No, I guess we won't. Anyway, let's go over the plans for your big day—well, your second big day. Not that I really have to ask...but how are things going so far?"

Rob beams with joy. "Wow man, this is what every marriage should be like. It's great! Steph and I flow so easily that everything just feels natural between us. I'm really enjoying it."

Dalton is thoroughly pleased. "I am so glad you two did this. It's clear to see that you were made for each other. Didn't I tell you to wait it out, and if it was meant to be, you would know?"

Rob nods in awe. "Man, you were so right—as usual. I tell you, you've got some serious connections up there."

Dalton graciously smiles and changes the subject. "So, what's the order of events here?"

Rob opens up his portfolio and pulls out some papers. "This is what Steph and I came up with: The party will start at six o'clock, so we'll have the food set out buffet style to allow people arriving at that time to begin eating immediately as well as give time for those coming a little later not to miss anything. We're going to have Luke from Saturday Sports Night serve the drinks. He occasionally moonlights as a bartender, so this will help him make some extra cash in tips and keep the kids from trying to sneak into the alcohol. We'll also have music playing from the system inside. I've already gotten some song requests from the kids and am in the process of making up a playlist. Steph doesn't want to come out until the ceremony, but I'll be around to greet everyone and make sure they're comfortable, etc. Then at 6:45 I'm going to make an announcement that we have a special presentation from the kids."

Rob laughs conspiratorially. "They're in the ceremony and don't even know it. I've asked them to either write or choose a piece to read of what love and/or unity means to them, and they've got some good stuff so far. So, that will go until 7:00 or when the last presentation is over, at which point you'll make the announcement of one last presentation by me. Stephanie will be standing by inside and that will be her signal to start 'The Bridal Chorus' and walk out to where I'll already be on the platform waiting for her. Next, you'll perform the ceremony where we will say our prepared vows, exchange rings and—voilà! Everyone will be shocked, amazed, and I hope pleased. Afterwards, I'll have someone put on the second playlist which starts with our first dance. When we are finished, we will invite everyone to join us on the floor to celebrate and dance the night away. What do you think?"

Dalton is impressed. "Wow, you guys didn't miss a thing. It sounds perfect! I can't wait."

Rob is bubbling with excitement. "Me either! However, this is one time I'm not going to cook and hire caterers, instead. I want to spend every moment possible enjoying my beautiful bride."

Dalton studies Rob's face with pride. "Well, who can blame you?"

Out of nowhere, Rob's stomach loudly growls and they burst out laughing.

Still chuckling, Dalton pulls out his wallet. "Whoa man! Let me buy you some breakfast before you start gnawing on my leg. I thought love was supposed to make you lose your appetite.

Rob's face slowly breaks into a mischievous smile. "Not the kind I get from my wife!"

* * *

When Rob returns home that evening, he finds Stephanie peacefully sitting on the floor of her meditation room surrounded by candles and soft drum music. He quietly goes into the bedroom to change and warm up the dinner she prepared for them.

While he is eating, she comes down to join him at the dining room table. She gives him a soft peck, then sits down and silently watches him.

Rob immediately puts his fork down. "What's up baby?"

Stephanie simply purses her lips and shrugs. "Nothing much."

Rob s right eyebrow slowly rises in response. "Stephanie."

Finally, she sighs. "Baby, you just got in from what I'm sure was a challenging day. Really, it's not that serious. Just relax and we'll talk about it in the morning when you're more rested."

Rob takes one last mouthful of food and sets his plate aside. "Steph, I don't think you realize that I go through the entire day in anticipation of this moment when I can come home and talk to you; Even if it seems like nothing to you, it is my joy, so please don't deprive me of it."

Stephanie's eyes fill with adoration, and she leans over to give Rob a soft, lingering kiss.

As she pulls back, Rob smiles with a yearning in his eyes. "However, if you keep this up, we may just have to resort to sending each other emails."

Stephanie laughs, her mood instantly lightened. "Well, I finally spoke to Stacie at work today."

As she continues, Rob listens attentively, trying to conceal his nervousness about what they may have discussed.

"Obviously she was not happy with me after our last incident but pointed out some issues that made me realize how unfair I have been to her. She also revealed some things that out of respect for her privacy, I won't divulge. The bottom line is, although I think I may have created a bit of a chasm between us, I really still want her to come to the event and definitely to meet Clint as you suggested. However, under the circumstances, I think that invitation needs to come from you instead of me."

Rob is irrepressibly curious as to what else Stacie may have said, so he covertly tries another way to retrieve more information. "I'm hearing you Steph, but I would be really disappointed at this point to find that she is holding negative feelings toward you over anything concerning me or our relationship. If that is the case, then I don't really think it would be a good idea for her to be invited at all."

Stephanie emphatically shakes her head. "No, definitely not; That's the reason I wanted to have a conversation with her first; I wanted to know that same thing, but in doing so, discovered that the root of our tension really has nothing to do with you at all, although your appearance on the scene did bring it to the fore. This is about the nature of our relationship before you even showed up. As a matter of fact, we really didn't even talk about you."

Rob is relieved to hear this. "Well, I do hope you two work it out beforehand, as I don't want anything other than joy and well wishes on our special day, and if she cannot bring that with sincerity, then I'd rather not deal with it at all."

Stephanie is persistent. "I agree, but I think that's where you would come in. Obviously, you two have developed quite a rapport and it's clear she truly admires and respects you. I think if you invite her with that understanding, it would be better than coming from me. I know this seems like a complete about face, but I really do want the best for her."

Rob shakes his head in awe. "Stephanie, you truly are something else. You have such a beautiful, loving and genuine heart for people. That was one of the very first things that drew me to you, you know."

Stephanie smiles teasingly. "What? You mean it wasn't my banging body and knockout good looks?"

Rob heartily laughs. "Oh, believe me, that was a part of the package too, but truthfully, you captured my heart long before you stirred my desires. But now that I have both..." He slowly begins sliding his hands around her waist.

Stephanie responds by wrapping her arms around his muscular neck and pressing her body into his. "Shhh..." She softly hisses in his ear, "Put it in an e-mail."

* * *

The next morning Rob sits up with a start and looks at the clock, realizing he slept later than usual. He is surprised that Stephanie didn't wake him before leaving, but knowing her, would've wanted him to get more rest.

As if on cue, the phone rings. "Wake up sleepyhead." Stephanie purrs. "While I wanted you to sleep a little longer, I'm also making sure you won't be late today at my expense."

Rob smiles and stretches. "Woman, I'd swear you've got some secret superpower locked away somewhere. How is it that you knock me clean out then just pop up and start your day so early with all this energy?"

Stephanie giggles. "Baby, *you* are my special power and I must have drained it to the last drop because you were snoring like a grizzly bear all night. I was afraid that if I did try and wake you, you would've mauled me."

Rob grunts. "Oh, you would've liked that."

Stephanie laughingly agrees. "You are so right! Anyway, it's time for you to start getting ready now. Have a great day, and I'll see you tonight. Oh, do you want anything in particular to eat?"

Quickly dismissing the first thought that pops into his head, he says, "Not really. You've been doing such a great job so far that whatever you make is fine, as long as it's not raw grass."

Stephanie chuckles. "Okay, got it. I love you."

Rob wistfully looks over at the empty space next to him. "I love you too and am missing you already. See you tonight."

Rob hangs up the phone and gingerly gets out of bed, as his back pain starts up again. As much as he doesn't want to admit it, he is having a hard time keeping up with Stephanie and is either going to have to increase his workouts or purchases of medicated balm. He runs a hot shower and stands underneath the pulsing water hoping the steam will loosen some of the tension in his back and legs. Afterwards, he rubs in some medicated balm and gets dressed.

"Man, aging is no joke." He says to himself, remembering Stacie's comments. He may outwardly look younger than he is, but somebody obviously forgot to send that memo to the aching muscles in his body.

While he still has Stacie in mind, he decides to give her a quick call. "Heyy Stacie, this is Rob Stephenson. I hope you have been doing well. Listen, I know you are aware that Steph and I recently got married, and although I never asked or expected it, I want to take this opportunity to personally thank you for speaking to her on my behalf. Considering that you two have not always seen things eye to eye, I really want you to know how even more impressed I am with who you are as a person. Anyway, Steph and I are having a celebration of our union, and want you to come, especially as you have been the main catalyst in us reuniting in the first place. So, please give me a call when you are able and I can give you more details. Okay, talk to you then."

A few minutes later, as Rob prepares to leave the house, his phone rings. "Hi Rob, this is Stacie. I saw you called."

"Oh, hey Stacie, that was fast. I hope I didn't disturb you. I know you're at work."

"No, I didn't go in today, actually."

Rob notices that Stacie does not sound like herself. "Oh? Are you sick?"

Stacie replies impassively. "Yes, I guess you could say that. Sick and tired, is more like it."

Rob is now very concerned. "Stacie, what's going on? Are you able to meet with me later this afternoon for a little while? I get a break around 4:30. We can meet at Lifebreath Café. Do you know where that is?"

Stacie is quiet for a moment. "The hippie place?"

Rob smirks in amusement. You never have to guess what's on her mind. "Yes, the hippie place."

"Yeah, I've seen it. I'll meet you there."

* * *

When Stacie walks in, Rob is pleasantly surprised to see that she has taken his advice. She is wearing a pale grey linen dress with a hemline just above her knees, topped with a soft pink cashmere cardigan. From what he can tell, her only makeup is a light pink gloss on her lips. She dons diamond studs and a delicate matching pendant for accessories. Even modestly dressed she looks stunning and still turns heads, but this time more so for her natural beauty.

Rob stands up to give her a peck on the cheek. "Well now, look at you!" He gushes with fatherly pride.

Stacie genuinely smiles for the first time in days. "You like?" She slowly twirls around.

Rob nods approvingly. "It's very nice, Stacie...very nice."

Now Stacie is beaming. "Thank you. I went to one of those boutiques and the salesperson was very helpful in picking outfits that work best for my body type. It is different, but I'm starting to like it. Plus, the looks I get now are not so lecherous, and that's a relief."

Rob smiles appreciatively. "Hey, do you want anything to eat? They have coffee, tea, sandwiches, even pastries—and everything here is all natural."

Stacie wrinkles her nose in response. "No thanks. That sounds too healthy for me. I like my chemicals. Plus, I have this insatiable craving for a bacon cheeseburger and fries, which I'm figuring is not sold here. But thanks anyway. I really just wanted to catch up with you and get the details of your event. By the way, Congratulations! So, fill me in."

Rob pauses reflectively, trying to figure out how to broach the situation between her and Stephanie. "Okay...well, we're having what most people think is just a party, as I haven't revealed to my job yet that Steph and I got married. In fact, like mostly everyone else, they didn't even know we were dating. Anyway, in the middle of the event, we are going to surprise them with an 'impromptu' wedding ceremony. It's going to be a blast, and as I mentioned in my message, I'd love for you to be there. Still, there is one concern that I need to bring up if you don't mind."

Stacie, knowing what is coming next, remains straight-faced. "Go ahead."

Rob appears uneasy, but presses on. "I'm sure as you would expect, that Stephanie and I talk about what's going on in our lives. Well, she was upset the other day and in her own words told me she realizes that she has been treating you unfairly. She also insisted on not giving me the specifics of your conversation because she didn't want to violate your privacy, and frankly I not only respect but appreciate that. However, what she did express was that because of her actions, she is concerned that you may not feel comfortable attending.

Now, I would like to speak from my perspective. "I realize that I am coming into this in the middle of a relationship that had already been established, for better or worse. So even if I wanted, it would not be my place to make a judgment based upon the existing dynamics. As much as I admire and appreciate who you are and all you've done for me Stacie, Stephanie is my wife and my first concern. And so what I guess I'm trying to say is yes, while we both have agreed that we would like you to be present at our ceremony, if you are not able to do so without even the residue of these issues surfacing, then we would absolutely understand and respect that. So to put it the way you would: This is our special day to share with those we care about and I don't want any drama occurring, real or perceived."

Stacie intently listens until he is through. "Rob, I really respect you telling me this. I also don't want anything other than for the two of you to feel joy on this wonderful occasion, and not have to be worried about mine or anyone else's energy or actions. It is true that Stephanie and I have had some tension, more so lately, and I did tell her about the things she said that hurt me. Although she did apologize a few times, honestly, I was not as gracious as I would've liked to have been in accepting. It was just that day, in particular, she was the straw that broke the camel's back in terms of everything I'd been dealing with for a while."

"You know, everyone always assumes because I look the way I do, that life is easier for me than most. Well, the older I get I am realizing that while some things may come more easily to me, like unsolicited attention and unwelcome overtures from men, the things that I really want are just as elusive for me as with anyone else. I have no shortage of men trying to court and woo me into bed, but then afterwards, I ultimately find that I was just one in a string of encounters they were having for one reason or another. It's also disgusting how many married men approach me, and it's really making me lose hope that there truly is someone like you out there for me Rob. I'm not mad at Stephanie for finding you; she was one of the lucky ones. I just wish people would stop presuming they know what I'm about and treat me appropriately. See, with you, I can be myself because you're not judging me simply based on my looks. I just want to have that experience more often."

As Rob listens, he makes a mental note to have a long chat with Clint beforehand. "Stacie, please don't give up hope so soon. You've only recently switched courses and I'm sure as you continue walking this path, what is yours will arrive in time. I mean, look at Steph and me—I am almost twice your age and I've now just found this wonderful woman. The reason why is because I wasn't being true to myself. I spent years going down a road that I should've gotten off a long time ago, but then again if I had, would I even have met her? Who really knows how this thing works, but all I can say is the best way for you to be happy with someone, is to first be happy with yourself. Love yourself for who you truly are and not who others think you are or should be and all will be well."

Stacie smiles appreciatively. "You know, you should be a therapist or something. You're good."

Rob grins as he recalls similar conversations between Dalton and himself. "Well, it does help to have someone to talk to, but I also think we can see other's solutions much more easily than our own—especially when we've already made the mistakes. He checks the time. Hey, listen, Stacie, I've got to run, but I really appreciated being able to speak with you. Think about what I said, and let us know what you want to do, okay?"

Stacie stands and gives him a big hug. "No. Thank you, Rob. I always feel so much better after talking to you. See you later."

CHAPTER TWENTY-THREE

The day of the celebration is beautifully bright and breezy, which exactly matches the mood of Rob and Stephanie, who are filled with excitement, anticipation and more than a little nervousness. Everything is already set up, with catering tent, platform and chairs all in place. Even Rob is dressed in his fitted white cotton tunic with gold embroidery around the neckline, white linen pants, and matching leather sandals. Stephanie remains in loungewear, deciding to put on her dress later, as her appearance will not be for quite some time.

They spend this extra time checking and re-checking all the details that could, if not dealt with, derail the order of events. Rob is yet again testing the sound system's MP3 connection and going through the playlists when the doorbell rings. Stephanie, who has been looking over his shoulder, is grateful for something else to do and rushes to answer it.

"Dalton!" They simultaneously exclaim with joy.

Dalton stands there for a moment temporarily caught off guard by their overenthusiastic response to his appearance, but quickly recovers. "Wow, now that's what I call a greeting! Hey, let's do that again, shall we? One... Two...Three!" Playing along, Rob and Stephanie recreate their response then crack up laughing.

"Boy, are we glad you're here!" Rob says as he comes over to clap Dalton on the back with his usual welcome.

However, with a solemn look, Dalton holds up his hand in protest. "Hey man, I'm sorry, but you can't touch me when I am wearing the ceremonial robe. I don't know if you remember, but we spoke about this a while ago. Still, I must be clear about the protocol in these situations." He then extends his ringed finger toward Rob, who looks uncertain.

Dalton smiles reassuringly in response. "It is considered a sign of respect to kiss the holy ring in greeting when a fully attired priest enters your home to perform a service." Rob glances at Stephanie who looks just as confused, then back at Dalton whose face remains friendly but firm. Finally, with furrowed brow and puckered lips, he haltingly leans toward the ring, careful not to brush against Dalton.

"Psyche!" Dalton shouts and quickly pulls back his hand, cracking up uncontrollably. Stephanie, grateful it wasn't her, joins in.

"You are going to Hell, Dalton!" Rob exhales with relief. "What kind of priest are you anyway, telling lies to innocent people like that?"

Dalton is doubled over, trying to catch his breath. Finally, he responds in gasps. "First...you don't even... believe in Hell, and secondly...I told you... I'd get you back for that time at the restaurant! Whew! You should've seen the look on your face! Oh man! I wish I could've captured that. Where's the video guy when you need him?" Finally calming down, he claps Rob on the back. "Okay man, I guess we're even now, huh?"

Rob still simmering over being so cleverly bested, especially in front of his wife, menacingly raises his eyebrow. "You think?"

Now Stephanie intervenes, pretending not to have enjoyed the trick as much as she did. "Oh Rob, come on baby, let it go." She unsuccessfully tries to suppress a giggle. "You have to admit, we needed that. Dalton, before you came, we were wound up with nerves."

Rob still feigning anger, hovers over Dalton with a determined stare. "On the advice of my beautiful bride, you get a reprieve today, but watch your back, Father Pants on Fire."

Dalton coolly smiles back and blows on his finger as if it were a smoking gun, pretending to put it back in his holster. "So, now that I've won this round, let's get down to business."

As they run through the details of the ceremony, including the vows they had memorized, the doorbell rings again.

"Stacie! Wow, you look amazing!" Stephanie coos admiringly as she opens the door. Stacie is radiant in a classily fitted sleeveless tangerine dress with gold accessories and gold T-strap open-toed heels to match. Her face is lightly bronzed and lips tinted with tangerine gloss.

"Thank you." Stacie smiles graciously as they carefully exchange hugs.

"Come on in. Stacie, this is Dalton, our good friend and the priest who will be performing the ceremony. Dalton, Stacie is a co-worker and good friend of mine who graciously offered to help me dress and prepare my makeup for today."

"It's so nice to meet you, Stacie." Dalton offers his hand to Stacie, who reverently receives it with a slight bow.

"It's nice to meet you as well, Father Dalton."

Dalton starts to say something but decides to leave it alone.

After Rob and Stacie greet and hug, Stephanie excitedly takes her hand, leading Stacie to the stairway. "I want you to see my dress so you can tell me how you think I should wear my hair with it." Rob watches them ascend the stairs already engrossed in their plans, delighted that they had worked things out so well.

* * *

As Stephanie is carefully hidden away upstairs with Stacie, Rob takes over the rest of the details, including helping Luke set up behind the bar and Greg, also from sports night, who offered to record the event for free, get situated. He then directs the caterers who go right to work, getting started.

When the kids arrive with Clint, he has them run through their readings on the stage, even prompting them how to enter and leave. Wanting everything to be perfect, he leaves nothing to chance. Finally, it is six o'clock and the guests slowly start trickling in. Rob at the last minute recruits the kids to welcome and direct those entering toward the food and the bar. At 6:45, as planned, Rob announces the youth presentations. First up is Mariana, who looks adorable in a navy blue bohemian tunic and white slacks. She wears black mascara with red lipstick and her usually unruly curly black hair is tightly pulled back into a conservative bun.

She walks up to the microphone with confidence and flair. "Good evening ladies and gentlemen. My name is Mariana Robles, I am sixteen years old and from the United Neighborhood Initiative Youth Center where our loyal advisor Mr. Stephenson has asked my friends and me to present you with some writings on the topic of love and unity which I hope you enjoy. If so, please hold your applause until the last speaker has finished so that everyone is able to clearly hear. Thank you." A few people clap on autopilot but instantly stop when they realize their faux pas. Nevertheless, Mariana smoothly continues. "The title of my piece is:

United Together

United we stand, divided we fall; I give you my heart, my hand, my all.

Together we'll stroll down the walkways of life, Laughing and singing—conquering strife.

I know I can make it as long as you're there for the of rest of the days we both will share."

Next up is Chen, who nervously takes the microphone from Mariana. He has on a white man-tailored shirt, dark slacks and a blue striped tie. "Hello, My Name is Chen Li Soong and though I am from China, I wrote a traditional Japanese poem, called Haiku. The title is:

'New Life'

Two hearts beat in one

Sanguineous pathways emerge

To create New Life

When he finishes, Clarissa comes up for the microphone. She wears a simple black dress with ballerina flats and in what Rob assumes is for the occasion, considerably lightens up on her dark eye makeup, but still keeps her piercings. Hi, my name is Clarissa Kellison and the poem I wrote is called,

Flesh of My Flesh

Flesh of My Flesh

Bone of My Bone

You're mine to Have and Hold

Not to Oppress, Rule or Own

I look into your eyes and see the best of me

Unfolding in exquisite clarity

We are inseparable; our umbilical tie inseverable

Forever joined by spiritual love and destiny

When Clarissa is done, Tim swaggers onstage and takes the microphone. He sports a white polo shirt with khakis and fresh white sneakers. "Good evening, my name is Timothy Warren, and the piece I've composed for this occasion is called, I Got You."

I Got You

Wherever you are, wherever you'll be I got you, and I know you got me

You don't have to fear the darkness at night

Because you'll see that I'm near

Like a bright shining light

So keep walking on Tall, proud and strong

In all that you do

Trusting deep down inside that I always got you

When he finishes, he pauses with a smile for effect, holds out the microphone for Fabian, then struts off like a proud peacock.

"Buenos Noches, My name is Fabian Feliciano and the piece I wrote is in Spanish, which I will recite first then read the English translation. It is called, "Te Amo Por Que"".

Te Amo Por Que

Te amo por que

Las estrellas brillian en tu ojos

Te amo por que

Me haces reconocer

Que maravilloso es este mundo

Contigo en el

Melanée Addison

Te amo por que

Mi corazon no save otra manera

Solamente te amo por que

In English:

I Love You Because

I love you because

The stars shine in your eyes

I love you because

You make me realize

How marvelous the world is

With you in it

I love you because

My heart knows no other way

I just love you... because.

Once Fabian finishes, everyone comes back onto the stage as the crowd enthusiastically stand to their feet, roaring with thunderous applause that lasts for over a minute. Then, as rehearsed, they each step forward to take an individual bow. Finally, with hands clasped they bend in unison before swinging their left arms toward Rob who walks onto the platform vigorously clapping with pride as they file off.

"Aren't these young people amazing?" Rob asks the crowd, who again begin applauding with confirmation until Rob holds up his hand to continue. "Mariana, Clarissa, Chen, Tim and Fabian are just a few of the magnificent young people from the U.N.I. Youth Center. At this time, I would also like to take the opportunity to introduce my wonderful, trusted friend and colleague, who works alongside me in this very challenging but rewarding vocation, Clint Teele. Come on up Clint!" Clint surprised by the unexpected announcement, quickly makes his way onto the platform, graciously waving in acknowledgement.

After he leaves, Rob scans the faces before him with swelling emotion. "Well there's one last very special presentation I have for you here, and to help me with that, I would like to introduce my good friend, Dalton Shea." Dalton comes up and realizing that Rob in rehearsing the kids' presentations earlier, inadvertently switched the original plan around, but no stranger to impromptu speeches jumps right in. Placing his hand on Rob's shoulder to keep him from walking off, he says, "Let's please give Rob a hand for this wonderful event that he has put together." Everyone again breaks out in polite, grateful applause.

"The theme for this event is Love and Unity, and I am so happy to be able to be here to share this momentous occasion with you all. As I look around, I see the faces of everyone who has been touched by Rob's example of just that. As most of you already know, he is a loving person who constantly goes out of his way to make sure others are comfortable and well taken care of, and he is definitely a person of community, often reaching out and bringing together those who would not normally have the opportunity to connect, as is evidenced by this occasion. As one of his good friends, I know that he is thrilled to see you all here, as am I, and so without further ado, we bring you Rob's latest and greatest presentation." There are a few beats of silence and Rob begins to get nervous, but Dalton's firm hand reassuringly gripping his shoulder keeps him calm and steady.

Then on cue, the music begins, and the doors to the deck open as Stephanie steps out, resplendent in a one-shouldered white sari with gold embroidered trim. Her accessories are a pair of dangling gold earrings, choker and cuff. Her curls are pulled into a loose upsweep with stray ringlets cascading around her shoulders adorned with a white orchid. Her makeup is glowingly applied in gold tones with her dark eyes beautifully accentuated in liner and mascara. She carries a bouquet of white orchids wrapped with gold ribbon.

As she slowly makes her way toward the platform there is a collective gasp of shock and awe followed by murmurs of surprise. As she fixes upon Rob who is staring, clearly dumbfounded by her beauty, she wills herself not to cry, as she can't remember if her eye makeup is waterproof.

Soon sniffles are heard throughout the crowd as people begin to realize what is taking place. As she reaches to the platform to join a watery-eyed Rob, Stacie who had been inside the entire time turns off the music and begins to cue the next playlist for later. Afterwards, she watches the ceremony through the open door as Dalton begins to speak. From where she is standing Stacie can see the girls from Rob's group, amongst others steadily wiping their eyes. Once Dalton finishes, Rob and Stephanie prepare to say their vows and turn toward each other, as Rob begins.

"Stephanie, my life, my love, my lady. Ever since you showed up in what seemed unexpectedly but now I know was perfect timing, I have not been the same. Before you, I thought I had seen all I cared to and was convinced that no one could ever move me again, but suddenly I find myself continually overtaken by the limitless depth, beauty, and texture that this life has to offer and that is all because of you. You have changed the axis and rotation of my world, and I'll never be able to fully express all you mean to me. In short, it's not that I'm nothing without you, but that I'm just so much more of everything with you. I love you."

Now it is Stacie's turn to tear up, and reaching for a nearby tissue box, she dabs her eyes as Stephanie begins reciting her vows.

"Rob, for as long as I can remember, I have been a runner, a fighter, and a wanderer. Having lost so much so early, I never trusted anything or anyone to stay, and therefore continued to move through the shadows of existence. However since you've come into my life, I finally feel safe to enjoy the marvel of all that surrounds me. You are my rock and the grounding force that holds me together. Your consistent love and dedication at times when I least expect or deserve it has been overwhelming. Being a creative soul, words have always come easily to me, but now as I stand here looking into your eyes, they have all fled and what I'm left with is the silent awe of how deep my love is and the amazement that you are mine."

When they finish their personalized vows, Dalton has them repeat the traditional ones, and finally exchanging rings, presents them as man and wife to deafening applause and shouts of joy as they exchange a long, passionate kiss. Afterwards, Rob grabs the microphone triumphantly. "So, you all thought this was just going to be a party, huh? Well, we gotcha!" More roaring applause follows. He then gives the microphone back to Dalton who says, "And now the new Mr. and Mrs. Robert Stephenson will have their first dance together after which they invite you to join them on the dance floor and really get this party started!

There is a raucous response, which dies down once Stacie starts the second playlist. 'A Simple Song' by Melanée Addison, fills the air, as the teary-eyed, kissing bride and groom glide across the floor, oblivious to everything around them, caught up in their magical moment. After the song ends, a popular dance tune plays and the kids practically storm the dance floor in excitement not so much to dance to their recognized song choice as to get the opportunity to speak to Stephanie and Rob and express their amazement at what had just taken place.

Once Stacie is assured the playlist is progressing as planned, she makes her way out to join the crowd on the dance floor. Stephanie, upon seeing her, rushes over to give her a long hug, profusely thanking her for not only helping to create her stunning look but also for willingly filling in all the gaps they had not foreseen in their initial planning. Rob soon follows and leads her over to Clint who is immediately stunned by her beauty, but ever the smooth operator tries his best to play it off. Rob asks him to personally look after 'he and Stephanie's very special friend', before reassuring Stacie that she is in good hands with Clint, as he is practically his personal protégée.

Then retrieving his wife from the grip of the kids, they go around and greet each of their guests, most who are still trying to recover from the shock of their ambush wedding. The only people not surprised, but still thoroughly overjoyed by the occasion are Stephanie's co-workers, who faithfully maintained their secrecy as requested.

After the guests are gone and the clean-up is finished, Rob and Stephanie go upstairs, peel their clothes off, and too tired to talk or even shower, crawl into bed, instantly falling asleep.

* * *

When Stephanie and Rob awaken late the next morning, they sit in bed going through the highlights of yesterday's event. Stephanie gushes over the kids' presentations that she and Stacie watched through the glass doors of the deck. "They were something else, weren't they? What talent and creativity were expressed in their writings. I was especially drawn to Fabian's Spanish poem; it sounded so romantic!"

Rob proudly nods in agreement. "Absolutely, but you know who surprised me the most? Chen! Did you hear that word he used—what was it, sanguineous? I clearly had to look that one up in the dictionary! I'm telling you this dude is quietly coming up from the rear, and I'm willing to place my money on it that he will be the 'Scrabble Champion' by the end of the year. Of course, I won't tell the kids that."

Stephanie purses her lips in thought. "You're probably right, but overall, I just enjoyed the wonderful imagery they each brought to their piece. Tim's part about 'walking on and being strong' made me feel like he was secretly writing it to himself, and it was clear to see what Clarissa's experience with love has been like—not to oppress or own? Even Mariana I am finding is a hopeless romantic, but that shouldn't really be a surprise. What command and poise she showed yesterday! I admire her energy and drive to achieve the best, and I am certain she will.

Rob, I can't wait to come back to the center and ask them about the inspiration behind their poetry and see what else they may be working on." She then has a thought that shifts her mood. "Rob, this is the kind of thing that I miss so much about working with kids. Fred and I used to do this very thing; sit and talk about our kids; what they did and said and what we thought they needed to get where they wanted to be. We spent hours discussing how we could give it to them, be it with encouraging words, academic assistance or counseling. We saw a great many lives begin to change from those conversations, including ours. I don't know how you feel about me telling you this, but I still miss him, especially during times like this."

Rob gently wipes the tears that have begun to fall down Stephanie's face. "Steph, when people have become a part of us they never leave, even when we can't see them. We always carry them inside. That's what I was trying to tell you before. We can't divorce from our past, whether it's been positive or negative. It will always inform on some level our thoughts and actions. I may not have become the man I am today if my father had not done what he did to our family. Personally, I am filled with joy when I hear that in the midst of all the pain and loss you experienced that you've had these wonderful moments in your life with someone who loved you very much. I am grateful for the time that you had with Fred because in part it has made you the woman that I have completely fallen in love with. I don't wish to erase your fond memories of him, but to do them honor in continuing to love and care for you as he did while he was here."

With Rob's words, something deep within Stephanie gives way and her quiet sobs soon break into wails of released pain and grief, submerged for years. As her body convulses with emotion, Rob holds her tightly, quietly rubbing her back and smoothing her hair. When she finally stops, she quietly lays on his lap in deep thought, while Rob absorbedly alternates between twirling locks of her hair around his fingers and releasing it. Finally snapping out of her reverie, she turns her head and smilingly peers at Rob. "Hey, what are you doing up there?" She sniffles.

Rob looks down at her with a loving smile. "I can't help it, I love your hair. It's so beautiful and playing with it relaxes me."

Stephanie bursts out in laughter. "Oh yeah? Well, you wouldn't say that if you had to struggle with it every day trying to get it to lie down. However, since you enjoy messing with my hair so much, why don't you help me wash it sometimes? I could seriously use the help, especially when I have to slather it with conditioner to comb through and detangle it."

Rob looks as though someone handed him a six-figure check. "Really, Steph? I would love to do that!"

Stephanie smirks. "Yeah, okay…we'll see how long your love affair with my hair lasts after a couple of sessions of untangling snags and naps. Speaking of which, didn't Stacie do an awesome job yesterday?"

Rob shakes his head with admiration. "First let me say, baby, you looked so ravishing yesterday, that I literally thought I was going to pass out when you walked through those doors! I still don't know how I remained standing. Stacie did an amazing job on all levels, and things would not have gone as smoothly without her."

"I know!" Stephanie enthuses. "I told her that same thing. We've got to get her a thank you gift."

Rob snorts with laughter. "I think we already did! Did you see her and Clint last night? I know I told him to look after her, but he gave it a whole new meaning. It was like she was the Queen of Sheba, and she was eating it up too. I'm so happy to see that they hit it off so well."

Suddenly an idea occurs to Stephanie. "Rob! You know what? We should invite them over for dinner soon."

Rob vigorously nods, caught up in Stephanie's enthusiasm. "Yeah, then we could talk to see where their heads are and give advice or redirection if necessary."

Stephanie smiles, shaking her head in amazement. "Look at you--you're worse than me, 'Father Hen'! I said, invite them to dinner, not get all up in their business like they're teenagers. These are not our kids we're talking about here. They are adults, just like us."

Rob narrows his eyes, casting a side-glance at Stephanie. "Hmmph! Well, clearly you haven't spoken at great length with either one of them. Trust me they need just as much if not more intervention than the kids. Also, as I am the matchmaker, I'm personally invested in making sure this goes right because I can guarantee you that neither one of us will hear the last of it if it doesn't."

Stephanie breaks out in a cackle. "That much you are right about!" Do what you feel is best baby...but can you first please invest in making me some breakfast? I am starving!"

CHAPTER TWENTY-FOUR

Monday when Stephanie gets into her office, she calls Stacie at the front desk. "Hey Stace, I just wanted to know if you are free for lunch today--my treat. Excellent! I'll meet you up front at 1:00. See ya."

As they walk out the building, Stephanie turns to Stacie. "So Stacie, since it's on me, where do you want to go?"

Stacie doesn't wait even a moment before she eagerly blurts, "Chowmommas! I've been dreaming about their 'Down Home' Turkey Burger and candied yam fries since you called me this morning."

"Oh, really, what's that?" Stephanie tries to sound enthusiastic as she silently prays that they at least carry a decent salad on their menu, but Stacie is already in food ecstasy.

"Whaaat? That's a turkey burger with macaroni and cheese baked inside topped with collard greens and cranberry sauce served with a side of deep fried yams brushed with a candied glaze."

Stephanie is now fighting to keep her rapidly declining appetite. "Okay... well, Chowmammas it is! Let's go!"

As they continue along, Stacie looks at Stephanie's face, amused by the valiant effort she is making to accommodate her, knowing that this clearly would not be her personal choice. "Hey Stephanie, I just want to say I really appreciate this. I know this is not like the crunchy hippie place you and Rob like so much, but you should really let yourself go a little sometimes.

Like, think about it: when was the last time you had a real good, juicy hamburger?"

Stephanie ponders a few moments. "Stacie I can't even remember, it's been that long, but just so you know, I do love burgers and eat great ones all the time, but they're just made with ingredients other than meat. You should expand your horizons too, you know?"

Stacie smirks knowingly. "I did—at your wedding event. I mean it was good, but I never had…what was that, Indian food?"

Stephanie raises her eyebrows in surprise. "What, you didn't like the food? There was plenty of meat!" Stacie wrinkles her nose. "You mean curried goat? I am so sorry sister…I am not eating anybody's goat. I did, however, try the chicken, which was very good, but what was with all that chickpea and spinach stuff? Anyway, I put a little over my rice and it was okay, but in my opinion, that's not the kind of food that makes you wanna jump up and slap your mama."

Stephanie nods diplomatically. "Well, it's clear that we definitely have two distinct differences when it comes to food tastes. However, since you were a good sport about it, I will take your advice and try something from their artery clogging vegetarian options."

Stacie smiles with excitement. "Oh Stephanie, you're going to love it! This place gets rave reviews all the time. I suggest you go for their macaroni and cheese, collard greens and candied yams with cornbread. You could also throw in their potato salad which is to die for! I've been there so many times and that is what always runs out the fastest."

As they enter the restaurant, the aroma filling the air catches Stephanie off guard and she reflexively licks her lips like a Pavlovian puppy. "Omigosh it smells so good in here!"

Stacey nods emphatically. "What did I tell you? No one can resist this place!" Once seated and their orders placed, Stephanie opens her purse to remove an envelope. "Stacie, this is just a small token of my appreciation not just for your invaluable contribution to our ceremony, but also for putting up with me all this time. I am honored to have someone like you as a friend, and hope to be as good a friend to you as you've been to me."

Stacie purses her lips with amusement. "I hope not. I wasn't always a perfect friend to you either, especially considering what happened at that Scrabble Night, so let's both of us just start fresh from here, okay?"

Stephanie affectionately places her hand over Stacie's. "Deal."

Stacie opens the card and reads it, blinking back tears. "That was so beautiful. You really have a way with words, Stephanie. Thank you."

Stephanie eagerly waits as Stacie opens up the envelope inside the card. "Stephanie! Omigod! Thank you SO much!" She leans over and hugs her, elated."

Stephanie chuckles, pleased with her joyous response. "I'm glad you like it. It's from Rob and me. We thought not only would you appreciate a full day of pampering at the Ocean Hills Resort, but couldn't imagine anyone more deserving of it."

At this point, their food arrives and they immediately begin heartily attacking their plates in complete silence.

Finally, Stephanie, halfway through her meal says, "I can't believe how good everything is. I don't know what they put in here, but I think it might be worth a heart attack."

Stacie nods in silent agreement, her mouth filled with food.

When they are able to slow down their pace a little, Stephanie asks Stacie, "So how are things going with you and Clint? From what I saw, you guys hit it off quite well."

Stacie smiles elusively. "He's cute... and sweet...but he's not ready for me yet."

Stephanie is baffled. "What do you mean?"

Stacie chuckles with recollection. "Well, from the moment we met he was buzzing around, asking all kinds of questions trying to figure me out right away. Then he occasionally would drop a line that he thought was smooth, but unfortunately for him, he's only used to wowing these trifling club chicks. He's confused because he doesn't know what to do with a woman like me; I don't fit the pattern of what he's used to.

While I graciously received all his flattery and attention, it was clear I was not impressed by his facade, which only made him try harder. I would tell him to relax because having watched him in unguarded moments especially with the kids, I've already seen that underneath his act, deep down he really is a good guy with a great heart. However, I won't because I want him to work hard and even wear himself out for this. If there's one thing I've learned by now, it's that a man only values those things he's invested serious effort in obtaining, and from what I can see, Clint has been playing it easy up to this point.

So if he is real about having something meaningful, then his actions over time will tell. Right now, he's going through all these charismatic 'playa' moves, estimating how long it will be before he breaks me down into his bed, but what he does not yet understand is that this is a completely new game here. Like I told Rob before, I've had enough encounters at this stage to last me the rest of my life; I'm done with that. I want something different and I am willing to wait to get it. So no, I'm not immediately writing him off; I will continue to enjoy his company while giving him the opportunity to learn how to treat me according to how I deserve to be and not from the reference point of his previous experiences."

Stephanie listens in amazement. "Wow, Stacie, that's powerful. You got all of that from one meeting?"

Stacie calmly looks at Stephanie and says, "I know it seems so, but this didn't just come from nowhere. I clearly see my journey in his. As I watched him, I saw how, by my own posturing, I was scaring off the very thing I wanted. I'd like to take credit for this awareness, but to be honest with you, it was Rob who showed me how I was working against myself, and he's probably doing the same with Clint too. Stephanie you really have one amazing man there."

Stephanie smiles appreciatively. "I know." She studies Stacie thoughtfully. "You know Stacie, to my own embarrassment I have to be honest and say that I totally miscalculated you. You are truly a force to be reckoned with!"

Stacie nods graciously. "Thank you. I must admit, while over the years many have underestimated me, no one has done it more frequently than myself, but those days are over now. Say hello to Stacie 2.0!"

* * *

When Rob gets into work, he barely sits down before Clint pops in his doorway. "Hey, Playa! Look at you, the 'Original Mack'—we've been sleeping on you dawg!"

Rob looks up with mild annoyance. "Now would you like to try communicating that thought in English?"

Clint saunters into Rob's office and lounges in his usual seat. "Yeah, you know what I mean...you marry one and pass the other onto me. Don't get me wrong--I'm not mad atcha, it's exactly what I asked you for and everything I wanted."

Now Rob is fully exasperated. "Clint. I'm serious. You need to stop saying stuff like that. I am a married man, so please respect my wife. I will, therefore, say it again and for the last time. Stacie and I never had anything whatsoever beyond a friendship. This is how these stupid rumors are spread around here.

Furthermore, you need to grow up if you want a serious relationship like you say you do and realize that your adolescent inspired Ebonic expressions are not going to cut it anymore. Seriously, man, I'm trying to look out for you, but you are also going to have to work with me because now it's not just yours, but my reputation on the line here."

Seeing Rob's frustration, Clint immediately calms down. "Hey Rob, I'm sorry. I was just kidding with you, but you're right. I apologize for disrespecting you and your wife, not to mention Stacie. She's really great, man. Thanks for introducing us."

Rob settles down himself. "You're welcome. Clint, I did it because I know although you like to joke around a lot, deep down you are a good man. You just need some fine-tuning here and there. Both Steph and I really care about Stacie as a friend and believed we were making a good choice in bringing you two together. Please don't prove us wrong."

Then Rob switches to a lighter note. "So tell me, how are things going between you two?"

Clint leans back in his chair. "Yeah, it's great, man. I can tell she's really into me. It's not that I'm not used to having beautiful women, but she is the real deal. Those Saturday Night dudes were eye hustling all night, trying to get up in there, but not on my watch. Anyway, yeah, she's definitely feeling me. I told her I wanted to take her out to a fancy restaurant so I could get to know her better, and she was smiling all up in my face. I've got to pace myself, though, 'cause I don't want her getting caught up too fast. That happens a lot with me and chicks…you know how it is."

Rob listens patiently. "I hear you. Well, just take it slow and enjoy yourselves. There's no need to rush anything."

Clint nods. "Yeah, I'll give it like three weeks or so before I make my move. By then she'll be tearing my clothes off, you know?"

Rob shakes his head. "No, actually I don't want to know. How you guys go about this physically is your own business." My concern, however, is that you build a strong enough foundation to support the various levels of your relationship. If you feel that it will be in three weeks, well, then that's for you to decide. On another note, Steph and I would like to have you two over for dinner soon, so let me know when is good."

Clint gets up and gives Rob a handclasp. "Yeah, that sounds great man, thanks a lot. Listen; let me start getting prepared before the guys get here. I'll catch you later, and thanks again for everything, Rob. I really appreciate it."

Rob smiles warmly. "No problem. I'll talk to you later."

* * *

A few weeks later, Rob walks into Lifebreath Café with a slight limp. "Good morning."

Dalton looks up from his coffee. "Wow, man...no offense, but you look beat. I hope this is not the other side of marriage showing up."

Rob slowly sits down and shakes his head with a wan smile. "Man, that woman is wearing me out! I've upped my workout routine and even stopped eating meat, but still can't seem to keep up with her."

Dalton chortles with amusement. "One more plug for vegetarianism! I've been telling you for a while that you get so much more energy from the vegetarian lifestyle, but now I suppose you're finding out for yourself the hard way! Seriously, be patient Rob. Stephanie has years of that lifestyle to your few weeks of meat abstinence. Don't worry, it'll get better."

Rob still appears discouraged. "Yeah, but will it make me any younger? I think this aging thing is what's really getting to me. It's sapping my manhood if you know what I mean. I just can't do what I used to. It's frustrating, especially at this point in our marriage. We're still supposed to be newlyweds, for god's sake! Oh—sorry about that."

Dalton ignores Rob's perceived infraction. "Well, you know they've got pills for that. There's now a whole wave of resurrected 70-year-old playboys out there, so I know you'll be fine. You just need a little support from time to time and there's nothing wrong with that. Just go see your doctor and he'll give you a prescription." Rob nods reluctantly. "Yeah, I guess you're right. I hate going to the doctor's, though. Although it's been a while, the last time I went I felt like a prison bride."

Dalton breaks out in laughter. "Yeah, I heard about those tests. I'm certainly not looking forward to it myself. Anyway, how's everything else going?"

Rob shrugs impassively. "I suppose it's going well. Stephanie is doing great, especially as she and Stacie have become closer now. She really hasn't had a friend like this before, so she's excited about that. Work is fine, considering the usual drama. Everything else is good; it's just that this thing is hanging over me like a shadow. But enough about me—how are things with you, D?"

Dalton smiles at Rob appreciatively. "Not bad, thanks for asking. I've just launched an intervention and educational outreach program for those struggling with substance abuse and their families, so I'm really looking forward to seeing how that comes along. There seems to be some interest right now, but that always tends to happen at the beginning. However, I am praying this doesn't ultimately wind up as another dead-end program and really does make an impact. This is not an easy population to successfully reach."

Rob looks at Dalton understandingly. "Yeah, I know. Many of our kids' parents, as well as some kids themselves, are struggling with this issue. Please give me the information so I can send some referrals your way."

Dalton is encouraged. "Wow, thanks, man, sure thing. I really appreciate that."

Rob shakes his head. "No, I am really grateful for all that you do personally and professionally in our community. Speaking of which, let me order some tea and be on my way, I have a few extra things to take care of today. I'll catch you later."

* * *

When he gets home, Rob showers, changes and meets Stephanie in the kitchen as usual. "Hey, babe." He says, giving her a kiss. "So what's on the menu today?"

Stephanie puts down the book she is reading. "Well, I want to start experimenting with different recipes and liked the food from our ceremony so much that I decided to re-create the Indian curry vegetable stir fry—so, tell me what you think." Rob digs in and takes a mouthful. After a few chews, he begins coughing and immediately reaches for his glass of water. He takes a couple of gulps and smiles. "Wow...it's good baby, it has lots of spice in it."

Stephanie looks concerned. "You think so? When I tried it, I thought it wasn't enough, so I added some more. Oh, Rob, I'm sorry! I wanted this to be a perfect reminder of our special day."

Rob leans over to kiss Stephanie. "You are a perfect reminder of our special day; this is just the icing. It's really good, though, Steph; I like it. So anyway, how did your day go?"

Stephanie suddenly becomes excited. "Omigosh Rob! We have to go to Chowmommas one day. Stacie and I went there for lunch today and the food was sooo good! I had the mac n cheese, potato salad, candied yams and collard greens with cornbread. Everything was absolutely delicious."

Rob studies Stephanie with amusement. "Oh was it now, Mrs. Health Freak? I thought that was 'heart attack' food. It's just like what I grew up on, but most likely not as good as my mother's meals were. Nevertheless, we soon shall see, won't we?" He shakes his head and chuckles. "So Stacie got you to eat at Chowmommas, huh? Watch out, because if she has her way, you two will be wolfing down bacon cheeseburgers and fries in no time."

Stephanie smirks. "Oh, she's already begun her campaign on that already, but I am prepared with my counterattack. When she and Clint come over, I'm going to sneak fresh kale in their fruit juice! Anyway, I know you want to hear what she said about Clint. Although her first impression was that he was sweet with a good heart, she insists that he will have to prove himself if he really wants to be with her. In the meantime, she's taking it slow in order to see where he really is."

Rob slaps the table with glee. "Atta girl! She is on it. I'm so proud of her."

Stephanie beams with his response. "I know, I told her the same thing. She really has her head on straight so I'm not concerned and strongly suggest that you don't get mixed up in their business either."

Rob nods in agreement. "You're right, Steph. I tried to talk to Clint earlier today and he is still trying to play 'Joe Cool' although it is clear that he has already been reeled in. Underneath that rapidly crumbling smooth exterior, he looks like a deer caught in headlights." He laughs, slapping his knee in mirth.

However, Stephanie stares at him with head tilted and eyebrows furrowed in thought. "Hmmm...now why does that sound so familiar? Oh, yeah! You mean like how a certain man was after meeting a particular woman in the local library, huh?"

Rob abruptly stops and with a slow smile says, "Oh, that's low, Mrs. Stephenson. If I can remember correctly, there was a time not too long ago in a neighborhood café when a beautiful woman fell prey to the irresistible charms of a distinguished gentleman, herself."

Now Stephanie laughs and after giving Rob a long lingering kiss points to his glass on the table. "Well, what do you know, Mr. Stephenson? I think they're putting something in the water."

CHAPTER TWENTY-FIVE

Rob just finishes preparing the food when the doorbell rings.

"Oh no!" Stephanie exclaims, "Are they here already? I haven't made the juice yet!"

Rob calmly massages her shoulders. "Don't worry, take your time. I'll keep them company in the living room. When you are done just bring the drinks in there, and we'll chat for a while before eating. The food will keep warm in the oven until we're ready."

Stephanie relaxes and gives Rob a peck on the lips. "Thanks, baby. I'll be in shortly."

When Stephanie comes in with the drinks, Rob, Clint, and Stacie are doubled over in laughter.

"Hey, guys!" She sets the tray down on the coffee table and welcomes Clint and Stephanie with a hug. "What's so funny?"

Wiping tears of laughter from his eyes, Rob explains. "We were just talking about our wedding party. Who was that lady gyrating with Tim on the dance floor? She was definitely having flashbacks from her flapper days!"

They break out in laughter again. Clint quips, "From the looks of it that probably wasn't all she was having."

Stephanie waves her hand dismissively. "Oh, that was Stella. Leave her alone, she's sweet! She is a volunteer who helps me organize our monthly community meetings. She's been supportive in getting people together to discuss and resolve issues around here." She then begins handing out the drinks. "These are some green apple spritzers I made. I hope you like it."

Everyone graciously takes their glass, but Stacie studies hers uneasily. "Stephanie, what exactly is in here? I usually don't drink things that are green colored."

Stephanie refrains from rolling her eyes. "Well Stacie, just think of it as a soda, except that it contains natural coloring and no chemical preservatives."

Clint takes a tentative sip then raises his eyebrows in surprise. "Hey, this is good, Stephanie! Stacie, you should at least try it first to see if you like it."

With all eyes on her, Stacie hesitantly takes a sip, smacks her lips and waits for what seems like forever to Stephanie before responding. "It's not bad. I guess I could do this."

Stephanie heaves an internal sigh of relief, inwardly rejoicing that Stacie didn't outright reject her mainly vegetable juice disguised with fruit. Suppressing a smile, she and Rob exchange surreptitious glances as she quickly changes the topic. "So Clint, I hear you run a young men's group at the center. How's that going?

Clint sips a little more of his juice before answering. "It's challenging, but we are slowly making progress. You know, it's tough for males at this stage because they want so badly to be a man but they don't always have the tools to usher them into successful manhood, and the things they associate with it are often very childish and dangerous on many levels. So, all I can do is talk to them and tell them of my own experiences to give them guidance as well as help them seek employment opportunities."

"Unfortunately, in these neighborhoods, fast money talks the loudest, even if it comes with the risk of imprisonment or death. Yet with each friend they have to bury slowly comes the awareness of what I've been saying— for some. The rest are still consumed with either vengeance or dreams of ghetto glory. Nevertheless, I take my success in small measures. If I can save just one from jail or murder, then I believe it's worth it. Because someone saved my life, I feel I have no choice but to invest it in doing the same for others."

Stephanie nods and glances over at Stacie, who is raptly listening, her eyes filled with admiration. "Wow, that's amazing, Clint. I really respect what you do and the circumstances you have to do it under. I know it's not easy, but I am sure it is worth it."

Clint smiles at Stephanie with appreciation. "Thank you. It is."

Now Rob interjects, "Hey, let's all finish this conversation over some food, shall we?" With that, he ushers them into the dining room.

"Wow," Stacie gushes when she walks in. "This table is beautiful! It looks like it belongs in one of those fancy restaurants. Does it come with a waiter too?"

Rob pulls out her chair and waves his arm with a flourish. "At your service, mademoiselle!"

Stacie sits and looks over at Stephanie, clearly impressed. "Okay now... this is how you do it, huh?"

Stephanie chuckles, nodding in agreement, as she lowers herself in the chair that Rob has pulled out for her.

Clint also remains standing with his hand on his hip, looking at Rob with mock expectancy until Rob lightheartedly responds. "Clint my man—that treatment was only for the ladies. Unless there's something I don't know about, you're going to have to seat yourself.

Clint shrugs and sits down. "Well, you can't knock a dude for trying!"

Rob goes into the kitchen and brings out platters of grilled tenderloin steaks, cheesy garlic mashed potatoes topped with chives and grilled asparagus. He presents a large bowl of mixed lettuce accompanied by various salad toppings and dressings. For Stephanie and himself, he has prepared a delicious soy-based meatloaf with mushroom gravy. Everyone is delighted and enthusiastically digs into their meal.

Stephanie, curious of the developments since their last conversation, attempts to glean some more information. "So Stacie, have you been anywhere interesting lately?"

Stacie, aware of Stephanie's intentions, falls right in. "Yes, I have actually", she says, looking at Clint, smiling. "Clint took me to a beautiful waterfront seafood restaurant at a hotel in Asbury that featured a live band. Not only was the food delicious, but I had a blast dancing the night away."

Clint joins in, laughingly. "Yeah, I found that out the hard way when we met at the party. If I didn't know any better, I'd swear you were training for the Olympics or something."

Stacie smiles exultantly. "Well, what can I say? I love music—next to food of course. So, that was the perfect experience for me, a combination of my two favorite things."

Stephanie casts another covert glance at Rob before continuing. "Wow, that was really classy, Clint, not to mention thoughtful to take Stacie somewhere meaningful for her."

Clint beams with Stephanie's compliment. "Yeah, well you know...I like to show a lady a good time when I appreciate her, and I enjoy Stacie very much. She has a lot of qualities I like. She's funny, smart, and best of all, keeps it real at all times."

Stephanie and Rob look at each other and burst out laughing, knowing exactly what he means, having been the recipients of her brutal honesty themselves.

Stacie looks at them skeptically. "I hope that's a compliment."

Rob smiles at her reassuringly. "It most definitely is."

After dinner, Rob serves his homemade strawberry cheesecake with coffee and tea as they continue their conversation.

"I was telling Rob that I can't wait to get back to the center to speak with the kids about their poetry," Stephanie says. How did they feel after receiving that standing ovation?"

Clint shakes his head, recalling that night. "Man, they were wound up! Between having their presentations so well received and your surprise wedding ceremony, they couldn't calm down from the excitement and held freestyle rap battles during the entire ride back. Even the Chinese guy got involved. He needed a little work on the styling, but his vocab was impressive and he caught on to the rhythms quickly. Then Mariana took on Tim, and although they ruled it a tie, I personally thought she won."

Stephanie shakes her head in admiration. "That girl is like an atom bomb waiting to blow, she has so much talent within her."

Rob nods in agreement. "Yeah, but I haven't seen her around for a few days, which is unusual for her. I hope everything is okay. She's one of the consistent ones." Clint responds with reassuringly, "Yeah, but even the consistent ones have their spells now and then; and for some reason, it always seems to happen around a huge success. However, when their heads begin to deflate, they eventually float right back in like nothing."

Rob smiles gratefully. "You're right, man. I guess sometimes I just get a little overprotective." He then looks at Stacie, who has been silently observing. "Now you see why this is my right hand man and capable partner in this work."

Stacie looks over to Clint who is staring at her, captivated. Holding his eyes, she agrees. "Yes, he is a good man."

* * *

The next morning Rob surprisingly wakes up before Stephanie, who apparently has slept through her alarm. "Steph baby, wake up. You overslept." He gently nudges her, but Stephanie doesn't budge. "Stephanie!"

Rob calls a little louder, shaking her shoulder. This time, she sleepily opens her eyes but doesn't move. "You overslept, Steph. C'mon, get up or you're going to be late for work."

Stephanie remains there blinking, too exhausted to move. "I am so tired; I don't know if I can make it through today. Plus, I don't feel well. I knew I shouldn't have had that cheesecake last night."

Rob is concerned. "Baby, do you want me to make you some mint tea to settle your stomach?"

Stephanie's face upturns. "No, I think I just need to rest here for a moment. I'll get up. Rob, I have to stop eating like this. I've gone off both my diet and exercise routine, and it is wreaking havoc on my system, not to mention my waistline. I seriously need to get back on track. No offense, but I'm not really used to eating rich foods so often, even if they are meatless. I prefer simple, fresh meals with lots of vegetables. That cheesecake really did me in, and--"

Suddenly she pops up and runs into the bathroom where she instantly throws up last night's cuisine. Rob pours her a glass of hot water from the faucet and gives it to her when she is finished rinsing her mouth. "Here take this to flush your system out." She slowly drinks the water and sits against the wall for support. "Please call the office to tell them I am sick today."

When Rob comes back, he finds her on the commode, doubled over. "It's coming from both ends." She groans. Rob wets a washcloth with cold water and wipes her sweaty brow, then comfortingly rubs her lower back.

"Rob, I'll be okay... please just leave me alone for a moment. I'll be out soon." Rob looks down at her helplessly. "Okay, I'll be in the room if you need me."

Finally, she comes out, weak and pale. "I just need to take a shower and relax today, that's all." She says in response to the worried look on Rob's face when he sees her.

"Steph, I'm going to stay home with you. You don't look well at all."

"Other than being sick, I'm fine, Rob. You don't need to stay, but thank you. I am going to be resting and taking it easy anyway, so it's best if I am alone. I'll call you if I need anything, okay?" She goes into her drawer and takes out some loungewear. "I'm just going to shower and lie back down, and then you can get ready."

When she goes back into the bathroom, Rob picks up the phone and dials. "Hey Dalton, listen I need you to do me a favor. Please drop by to check on Stephanie at some point today. She's not feeling well but insists that I don't bother her. I don't want to crowd her but am concerned because she doesn't look good at all. I also have to take care of that stuff this morning, so I won't be able to hang around too much longer. Yeah. Sure, I'll let you know. Thanks, man. I really appreciate it."

* * *

When Rob walks in that evening, Stephanie is waiting at the door. "Hey baby, how are you feeling?" He says, leaning in for a kiss.

To his surprise, Stephanie moves away. "We need to talk."

"Okay." Rob looks confused as he sits on the couch. "What happened, Steph?"

Stephanie stands over him with folded arms. "Did you really have Dalton come over today to check on me? I specifically said I wanted to be alone, and you disregarded my wishes. Rob, just so you know I lived alone for quite a while before meeting you, and quite successfully too. I am your wife, not your child. I know we're married, but you need to respect my boundaries."

Rob stares at her, incredulous. "Are you serious Stephanie--you're upset because I cared enough to make sure you were all right? Yes, I sent Dalton to check in on you because I would not be home all day and wanted to make sure that when I did arrive, I wouldn't find my wife passed out on the floor—or worse. You know, you've got to do something about this independent spirit of yours, because it really doesn't work well for marriage. You want to live as if you're single but carry around my name for decoration? No, that name means that you are a part of me, Stephanie. If something is wrong with you, then something is wrong with me. I am sorry if you don't understand that, but I hope you will. I'm going to change and then will be up in the den to relax. Therefore, I would also like to be left alone. I'm not hungry tonight, so please feel free to put the food up and go to bed without me. Now does that feel single enough for your comfort?"

Stephanie stands there teary-eyed and speechless as he turns, goes up the stairs and slams the bedroom door.

* * *

The next morning Rob wakes on the leather couch in his man cave with a foggy head and dry mouth. As he sits up, he knocks over the empty bottles of beer he drank the night before. He gets some water, then sits down to mull over last night's episode with Stephanie.

So many things are coming at him that for the first time he feels like he may have rushed into marriage too soon. He is experiencing stress at work, issues with his body and now pressure in his marriage. He thought he was doing all the right things, but just like with Karen and his mother before that, does it really matter in the end? He realizes he came down on Stephanie too hard, but everything just boiled to a head in that moment.

He'd already had a challenging day beginning with Stephanie's illness; then he gets to work and receives a call from Mariana's mother informing him that she would not be coming to the center anymore because of neglecting her responsibilities at home. On top of that, Stephanie hadn't answered her phone all day, probably in retaliation to Dalton's visit, but he didn't know that at the time. Although Dalton said she seemed fine when he stopped by, he was still worried.

So when he finally comes home anxious and concerned for her, she shows up at the door with an attitude? In any case, he knew he was going to have to apologize for his actions so they could talk this through rationally. Although he loves Stephanie very much, sometimes she makes it so hard to do just that.

He goes downstairs and finds the bed empty. Then he goes into the kitchen and sees a note on the table.

'Rob, I am so sorry for last night. I realize that I have probably been cranky lately because I have not been taking care of myself the way I am used to. Please forgive me for taking it out on you. I love you and appreciate all you do. I went for a run this morning to get back on track. I hope that we can talk when I return. Your wife always and forever, Steph.'

Rob's eyes fill with tears as he slides down into the chair, reading her note over again. "I love you so much, Stephanie...I love you so much."

After he showers and gets dressed, Rob makes a fruit salad tossed with honey and lime and a green smoothie for Stephanie's return. She was right, he is going to have to scale back on these rich meals and from now on, they are both going to eat more simply: vegetable soups, stir fries and salads, not to mention smoothies and plenty of water. This will do them both good, and he is grateful that she is such a good influence on him concerning his health.

The door opens and Stephanie walks in flushed. "I think I pushed myself too hard." She explains to a concerned Rob. "It's been a while, so I should've allowed myself to gradually build up to where I was before."

After guiding her to the couch, Rob offers Stephanie the smoothie, which she refuses and asks for water instead, which she quickly gulps down. Again, Rob gets a cool cloth to wipe her face. "Steph, just lie back until you feel stronger. You're probably dehydrated. I'll get you some more water."

Soon she begins to get her strength back. "I'm okay now, baby, thanks." "You got my note, I see. I am so sorry my attitude last night. It was uncalled for; you were only showing concern. Do you forgive me?"

Rob smooths Stephanie's hair and gently kisses her lips. "Always...no matter what, Steph. Please know that. I am also sorry for speaking to you like that. I was just so worried. I don't want to lose you, Steph." He hugs her tightly, blinking back rising tears.

Stephanie rubs his back soothingly. "Don't worry baby, you won't."

* * *

As soon as Rob gets to work, he receives a call from Stacie that Stephanie was rushed to the hospital after passing out in her office. He bolts out of the center without a word and drives to the hospital with single-minded focus.

When he arrives, a doctor is speaking to Stephanie in the examination room. "Mr. Stephenson?"

Rob lunges for Stephanie with a long hug of relief. "What happened?"

The doctor is serious as he shakes Rob's hand. "I'm Dr. Mortimer, Mr. Stephenson. I was just giving your wife some unexpected news."

Rob's heart drops into his stomach as the doctor continues. "Mrs. Stephenson is pregnant." Rob feels himself go lightheaded and grabs a nearby chair for support. "What?"

Dr. Mortimer continues. "Her gestation stage is currently at six weeks. However, I must let you know that not only because of her age, but also due to the internal damages she's sustained from prior trauma, this is a high-risk pregnancy for both mother and fetus, and unfortunately, under those circumstances, I am recommending a voluntary D&C to terminate. I know this is a lot, so I will leave you to talk for a moment and will be back shortly."

Rob stands there for a moment, staring at Stephanie speechless. However, Stephanie is beaming with tears in her eyes. "Rob, did you hear? We're going to be parents! It's a miracle! The doctors said it would never happen again and look!"

Rob sits down trying to process everything. Finally, he ventures cautiously. "Stephanie, didn't the doctor just say this pregnancy puts you at risk?"

Stephanie waves her hand dismissively. "Yeah, the doctors also said I would never get pregnant again, and I believed them, but not this time. I know this happened now because it was meant to be. It's God's gift to us, Rob, don't you see? He knows how much we love and want children and is finally allowing us to experience parenthood together. So, no...I'm not listening to any more doctors. I am listening to my heart."

Rob remains silent, his mind reeling in all directions.

Finally, Stephanie replies edgily. "Well, this is not the response I expected from you. You yourself said how much you always wanted to have children; so, here we have this joyous moment before us, and all you can see is gloom and doom? This is our child we are talking about, Rob...OUR child!"

Rob suddenly snaps back. "Yes Stephanie, but you are conveniently overlooking one simple fact. You can die from trying to have this child who also may die, and then I've lost you both! Are you factoring that in as well, because I sure am!"

Dr. Mortimer returns and they quickly become hushed. "So Mrs. Stephenson, should I schedule a follow-up appointment for termination?"

Stephanie is indignant. "No, Dr. Mortimer, but you can schedule me a follow up appointment with the obstetrician so my baby can live."

Dr. Mortimer looks over at Rob, and then back to Stephanie. "Well, the final decision is up to you. It is my responsibility, however, to let you know of the risks and possible outcomes. You can get dressed and I will write a referral for Dr. Samsone. Take care, Mr. and Mrs. Stephenson."

* * *

Rob and Stephanie drive in complete silence, each absorbed in their own thoughts. When they arrive home Stephanie tensely asks, "So, are you coming with me to the doctor's visits or am I going it as a single mother?"

Rob glares at Stephanie. "Does it really matter, Stephanie? Does it really matter what I feel, do, think or say—as long as you get what you want?" With that, he walks up the stairs to his den and slams the door. After several minutes, he comes back down. "I'm going to see Dalton. I'll be back later if you care to know."

After he leaves, Stephanie breaks down in tears and picks up the phone. "Hi, Stacie…yes, I'm okay. I just found out that I'm pregnant, but Rob got upset and left the house, and I don't know what to do…" She then collapses in hysterical sobs. When she somewhat regains her composure, she picks up the phone and answers Stacie who has been calling her name repeatedly. "Yes, I'm here. I'm sorry…I just feel so alone. Okay, I would appreciate that very much. I just don't know what else to do. See you soon."

* * *

Rob storms into Dalton's office at St. Thomas' parish in distress. "Dalton man, what the hell is going on? It's like everything is falling apart at the same time. This is too much for me, and I hate to say it, but I really wish I would've just stayed single. Every time I get involved, I fall fast and then wind up having all these issues.

I love Stephanie, but as I told you from the beginning, I just don't think I can really give her what she needs…especially now when it matters the most. This is just like my mother and Karen all over again. Maybe it's just my fate to keep failing at what I want the most. Why even try? What is it for? Now I see why some men just up and leave. It's not that they don't feel love; it's just that the failure is too great to bear, and not so much for themselves, but for the ones they care about the most. I know Stephanie needs me right now, but Dalton, how can I fight for her and myself at the same time?"

Dalton remains quiet for a moment. "This is hard, Rob so I am not going to try to sugar coat it for you or pretend I have the answers because I don't. All I can do is be there with you as your friend and pray for you as a man of God. However, I encourage you not to give up or even think about it, because you need the strength to fight now more than ever for your life and future with this woman you love. I know this may sound trite, especially to you, but I truly believe that everything happens for a reason; that no matter how painful things may be, there are no mistakes."

Rob blankly stares ahead, his emotions frozen with pain. "Yeah, well I wish I had your faith because I sure do need it right now. I just don't see things the way you and Stephanie do. She thinks this is an act of God—a gift, she calls it. What a way to send a gift, wrapped up in death. From what I see, there is no rhyme or reason to any of this; if you do good you die just the same as someone who is evil, so why do we even differentiate as though it matters?"

Dalton listens intently before responding, "Well, if you truly believed that, then why are you always so personally insistent upon doing the right thing yourself? Rob, your whole life dispels exactly what you are saying—why invest your time and energy in these kids, why love Stephanie, why reach out and help others at all if they are all just going to die anyway? The fact of the matter is I don't think you really do believe that, although it would be easier to. Yes, Rob, we are all going to die eventually, but in between birth and death, there is the joy of love and life—of giving it, receiving it, and sharing it. It is this hope of joy that compels us to fight. Although it appears that you and Stephanie are waging opposing battles, really you are each fighting for the same thing in your own way. Once you realize this, it may be easier to put things in perspective concerning both your feelings."

As Rob sits in silent thought, he feels a peacefulness fall over him. "Dalton, I really appreciate you so much. I'm beginning to think maybe there is something to what you've got here. I don't know for sure, but I might come by one day and check out one of your talks."

Dalton smiles warmly. "It's every Sunday at 11 a.m. Consider this an open invitation."

* * *

When Rob returns home, Stephanie is gone and this time there is no note as to her whereabouts. He calls around and finds that she is out with Stacie. As he walks around the house, he instantly retracts his wish of wanting to have stayed single. He takes in the various signs of Stephanie's presence and smiles. Even with all the challenges, he would have it no other way. She belongs with him—of that, he is certain. He picks up the sweatshirt she flung over the couch earlier and inhales her scent. He needs her and is prepared to do everything in his power to make sure they both come through this stronger than ever.

Yes, he is scared and does not know what lies ahead of them, but like Dalton said, as they are here right now, this is an opportunity to experience the joy of their love, rather than dwell on the fear of what could happen.

Rob goes into the kitchen to prepare a simple meal of stir-fried vegetables over brown rice. When Stephanie walks in, her eyes are red and swollen from crying and Rob feels like the biggest jerk in the world. "Stephanie, can we please talk?"

She nods weakly.

Taking her hand, he leads her to the couch to sit down. "Stephanie, I realized I disappointed you today by my reaction to the pregnancy, and I am sorry. Like I told you earlier today, I do not want to lose you. I love you so much, and I'm scared Steph. However, I thought about it and I want us to experience what we do have—the joy of our lives now and expectancy of what is to come. Please know that I am and will be here for you and our child in every way you need me to. I am so sorry, baby… that won't happen again."

Stephanie smiles with exhaustion and places her hand over Rob's. "It's okay, baby. I understand more than anyone how it feels to lose something you've wanted so much for so long, but I've also realized that you can't let it keep you from believing because once you do, you've lost yourself as well. I love you Rob, and want you to know that we will go through whatever life holds for us, together."

With tears in his eyes, Rob gently kisses Stephanie's forehead, then helps her up. "Come on baby, let's eat, then rest upstairs. It's been quite a day."

CHAPTER TWENTY-SIX

Over the next several weeks, Rob and Stephanie's lives revolve around work, doctor's visits, and holiday preparations. Closely monitored and strongly advised by her obstetrician, Stephanie takes it easy, with no stretching, lifting, or strenuous activity. She faithfully employs uterus-toning tonics and Kegel exercises to strengthen her cervical area and better her chances of carrying full term.

When Rob isn't out conspiring with Dalton on some secret he won't reveal, he is hidden away in his workshop. Stephanie, on the other hand, is frequently out with Stacie, selecting furniture for the nursery and fawning over adorable baby outfits. Together, Rob and Stephanie excitedly prepare for their upcoming Thanksgiving Day Feast with Stacie, Clint, Dalton, and the kids, minus Mariana, who Stephanie is extremely saddened upon hearing is no longer in attendance at the center. Nonetheless, they are looking forward to a great time, with much to do in advance.

Excited to spend their first Christmas together as a family, they each have been secretly buying gifts and hiding them in places where the other is off limits, such as Stephanie's meditation room and Rob's man cave and work area.

"Hey, Steph!" Rob calls out as soon as he walks in the front door.

Stephanie carefully approaches the stairs and peers over the banister. "Rob, what's going on?"

Rob dashes up the steps looking like a boy who just learned to tie his shoes. "Look at this and tell me what you think. It's a Christmas present for Dalton." He pulls out a box and opens it to display a huge, black leather bound book with a gold Celtic cross embossed on the cover and gilt-edged pages. Stephanie gasps in admiration. "Oh wow, it's beautiful!"

Rob studies The Bible with pride. "See, I even had it personalized with 'Father Dalton Shea' on the bottom. He'll get a kick out of that. He has a Bible on the desk in his office already, but it is beaten up with pages falling out, so I thought this would be a good replacement. I went into a store that sells religious articles and asked the salesperson what kind of Bible would be good for a Catholic priest, and they led me to this one. It is in Latin as well as English."

Stephanie nods appreciatively. "He will love this, Rob. It's a great gift."

Rob smiles with satisfaction. "I'm glad you approve because it will be from both of us."

Stephanie starts to reach up and give Rob a hug, but he bends down to give her a kiss instead. "Careful, mama…remember, we've got some precious cargo to protect there. Speaking of which, let's get you off your feet so I can give you a massage."

* * *

The house is festive in autumn colors with gold leaf accents. Rob and Stephanie bustle about to create a traditional Thanksgiving Day feast, complete with turkey and trimmings of cornbread stuffing, gravy, biscuits, cranberry sauce, candied yams, macaroni and cheese, as well as string beans, collard greens, mashed potatoes and maple glazed roasted carrots. Desserts are apple, sweet potato pie, as well as Rob's celebrated cheesecake with vanilla ice cream for accompaniment. Beverages include apple cider, fresh berry spritzer and homemade rum-spiked eggnog for the adults.

When the doorbell rings, Stephanie excitedly rushes to greet Clint, Stacie, and the kids, as Rob takes their coats and ushers them inside.

"Where's Fabian?" Rob asks, upon entering with their beverages.

The kids quickly exchange glances as Clint shrugs. "I don't know. When I told him about it, he said he was coming, but never showed up at the center today. The kids say he hasn't been in school that much either."

Rob gives Tim a long stare. "So...you don't know anything at all?"

Tim vigorously shakes his head. "Nah. Listen, I told you...I'm staying straight. I just go to class and leave. I don't even speak to no one like that no more."

Rob studies him a little more then decides to let it go, although not entirely convinced. "Well, I'll do a little more investigating next week, but for now, let's enjoy ourselves on this great day of Thanksgiving."

Just then, the doorbell rings again. When Dalton enters, he warmly greets everyone. Rob invites them all to the candlelit table, which is already set with food. Before they begin, Stephanie asks Dalton to say a prayer of blessing. When he is finished, everyone grabs the dish closest to them and passes it onto to the next person. Soon everyone's plate is filled and they begin to dig in.

While they are silently eating, Stephanie speaks up. "Hey guys, I think that in keeping with the spirit of today, we should each say why we are grateful this Thanksgiving, and because I came up with the suggestion, I'll start." Everyone nods in agreement. "Well, first I am grateful to be here with all of you. We specifically invited you here today because you are a special part of our lives, and I am happy for that. Secondly, I am lucky to have such a wonderful husband to share this and every holiday with, and my prayer is that each year we will have more new great experiences to add to this one."

When she is done, she nudges Rob who smiles at her lovingly and then proceeds. "Well, like Stephanie, I am thankful to be here with all of you. It really means a lot to have you present, and although there are a couple missing from our midst, we will enjoy ourselves on their behalf. I am also grateful to have this moment with my beautiful wife and the expectation of so much more for all of us to celebrate as time goes on. I couldn't ask for more."

Rob looks at Dalton, who clears his throat and takes a sip of his drink. "I am truly, truly blessed to be here with such wonderful people—Stacie and Clint, although I recently met you, I know that you have been a huge support for Stephanie and Rob in many ways individually and as a couple. Therefore, I am honored to join you in creating a unit that will not just expand our circle, but also the capacity of these young people and all those who will come behind them. Tim, Clarissa and Chen, you are amazing. I got just a little taste of it at the wedding ceremony, but I know there is so much more inside of you and am grateful to be surrounded by such talented visionaries. I am confident that you will all go on to make your mark in this world, and so thank you for allowing me to be a small part of history in the making."

Tim, deeply touched by Dalton's comments, falters a little in his delivery. "Well...man, I don't even know what to say now. Um...I am...grateful to have you all in my life." He begins to get a little emotional as he continues. "I don't really hear these kinds of things outside of the center or from anyone who doesn't work there, so thanks. I am especially grateful for Rob and Ms. Mar—Stephenson—sorry...inviting me here. I am also grateful for Clarissa and Chen who are still hanging in here with me. It's not always easy, and sometimes I do wanna give up, but knowing they're in this too encourages me to go on. Thanks."

Next up is Clarissa, who unlike Tim does not fight back her tears. "Rob, I don't know what I would've done without you this year. I know I got into some fights and didn't always have the best attitude, but you never gave up on me. You stuck in there and always said good things to and about me, even when I didn't deserve it, and because of that, I am trying to be better because I want those things to be true and make you proud of me.

I would also like to thank Mrs. Stephenson for bringing Rob the love and happiness he gives away so freely to others, especially us bad ass kids!" Everyone laughs as she continues. "Also thank you, Father Dalton, for your words, which I could just say are kind and leave it there, but when you speak, I really believe that what you say is going to happen. I don't know how to explain it, and maybe I'm just weird, but that's just how I feel. I'm also glad to be here with my fellow soldiers, Tim and Chen with Clint holding us down as usual. Stacie, I did not like you when I first met you...but you seem okay now." Stacie smiles good-naturedly at Clarissa, and with sincerity says, "Thank you, Clarissa."

Chen follows. "I am so glad to be here today. The food is good and everyone so hospitable. We don't have this day in my country, but it feels a lot like our celebrations where everyone is together and caring for each other with a lot of food. I am thankful that I have you and times like this to remember when I miss home."

Clint looks directly at Rob as he begins. "Well, as for me...I am grateful for second chances." He turns his gaze to Stacie for a moment before continuing. "And also to have people in my life who see and believe in me sometimes more than I do myself. Rob, Stephanie, and Stacie, you may have possibly saved my life a second time. The first time was a street worker from the gang violence initiative, but this time you all came in at just the right point to snatch me from a fate worse than death, which is living with unused potential. I'm not there yet, but can at least see more clearly the direction I am moving in. Tim, Clarissa and Chen, I know firsthand how hard it is to try to build for the future when you've first got to find out how to make bricks from the dust and rubble of your current life, which is why I admire you all the more for pushing forward, not perfectly but consistently. By this, you inspire me each day to keep going, because if you ain't giving up, then neither am I. So, just know that we are in this thing together. Thanks for keeping me on the path, all of you. And Dalton, you seem like a real great person to know, so I am grateful for the opportunity to meet you again and look forward to building that unit you mentioned."

When he finishes, everyone looks at Stacie expectantly, so she jokingly quips, "I see...saving the best for last are we? Well, I hope I don't disappoint." Everyone chuckles. "Okay...where to start...I am truly appreciative for having met some wonderful people this year as well as rediscovering the ones I thought I already knew." She smiles at Stephanie. "This feels like a year of change to me, like somehow we are being prepared for greater things up ahead, and I am excited to see what the future unfolds for all of us here individually and together."

Rob reaches over and affectionately squeezes Stephanie's hand. "Sweetheart…that was a great idea! Thank you so much. This is what my mother used to call 'giving people their flowers on this side'. That means too many times, we often don't express how others touch our lives until they're gone. However, now that we do know how we feel about each other in the land of the living, let's continue our celebration with dessert and games!"

* * *

As the snow gently falls outside, it finally begins to look and feel like the holiday season is in full swing. After Rob lights the fireplace, he and Stephanie cuddle while watching classic Christmas movies. When the doorbell rings, Rob reluctantly gets up to answer it, leaving Stephanie comfortably nestled on the couch. He soon comes back in, grinning from ear to ear. "Now I see why you didn't want us to shop for a tree together." He places a small potted Norway Fir tree, about three feet tall, on the coffee table.

Stephanie excitedly sits up and inspects the sapling with a satisfied smile. "I wanted it to be a surprise. This is not just a Christmas tree, but also our Memory Tree, which is so much better. We can keep it on the table for now, but it will grow at least a foot every year, so eventually we'll plant it outside as a living symbol of our journey together. I thought it would also be a good idea to make an ornament capturing each year's experience. This way, every holiday season we can have a personal keepsake to pass on to our child, who hopefully will continue the tradition—a *real* family tree!"

Rob shakes his head in awe. "That is one of the greatest ideas I've ever heard." He draws her to him and kisses her forehead affectionately. "I am so glad you are in my life, Stephanie." Stephanie rests her head on Rob's chest with tears in her eyes. "Thank you, Rob, for giving me something to celebrate."

CHAPTER TWENTY-SEVEN

Stephanie awakens with a tingling sensation and fluttering heart. "Rob... Rob." She whispers in his ear.

Rob slightly stirs but doesn't open his eyes. "Hmm?"

Stephanie is persistent. "Rob...baby...wake up."

He finally opens one eye and smiles sleepily at Stephanie. "Merry Christmas, baby."

Stephanie hovers over him, grinning like the Cheshire Cat. "Merry Christmas!! Are you ready to open your gifts?"

Rob gives a long groaning stretch then pulls Stephanie toward him and begins to undo her buttons. Slowly opening her plaid nightshirt, he gently kisses her stomach. "Wow baby, thank you. Two priceless presents wrapped in one precious package. This is the best Christmas ever!"

Stephanie gazes at Rob adoringly then gives him a slow, sweet kiss. "I love you, Robert Stephenson—with all my heart." She snuggles against him as they lay quietly savoring their time together.

Finally, Stephanie speaks. "I did get you something else, you know."

Rob feigns astonishment. "You mean there's more? Oh, baby...I don't know if my heart can take it!"

Stephanie laughingly slaps his arm. "C'mon Rob, I'm serious…let's open our gifts now. I can't wait anymore!"

As they make their way downstairs to their little Christmas tree, now decorated with lights and ornaments, Stephanie grabs a medium sized box and proudly hands it to Rob. "You go first."

Still feeling mischievous, Rob takes the box, holds it to his ear, and waits. "Hmm…no ticking…are you sure it's for me?

Stephanie is beside herself. "Rob!" She exclaims in playful exasperation. "Just open the gift please."

Rob chuckles and pulls away the wrapping paper. Once he is able to see the label on the box, he stops and stares incredulously. "Stephanie, this is the new Xenon Via 3000 HD Digital Video Camera. It hasn't even been released yet…how did you get it?"

Stephanie beams with pride. "Oh, I have my ways…"

Rob continues tearing away the paper and opens the box to inspect the contents. Fascinated, he begins reading through the features, oblivious to everything else until Stephanie finally clears her throat to snap him out of his technological trance. "Oh…Baby, I'm sorry. Thank you so much. This is amazing! Can you please just give me a few moments to set it up so we can capture the rest of this on camera?"

Stephanie smiles and rolls her eyes. "I should've known this was going to happen. Sure, take your time. I'll cut up some fresh fruit for us in the meantime. And, Rob?"

Rob distractedly looks up from his manual. "Yeah, babe?"

Stephanie begins buttoning up her nightshirt. "No exposed shots, please. The last thing I want to do is present our Christmas video to the kids and unknowingly show up on it half naked—or worse."

Rob smiles with a wink. "You got it, baby. That'll be our other Christmas video!"

Rob is finishing up just as Stephanie brings in a bowl of fruit salad topped with whipped cream. He switches on the camera and adjusts the settings before focusing it on Stephanie, who has just shoved a large strawberry in her mouth.

When she realizes what he is doing, she quickly puts one hand out to block the camera and the other to hide her mouth, covered with cream. Chewing, she wipes it away and gives Rob a warning look. "Really Rob, on my first shot, I have to be introduced like this?"

Rob is like a child with a new toy. "What do you mean baby? That's what it's for. I'm just testing anyway. I'll erase it if you like, but just know I'm not going to make this a staged thing. I want to look back and see things as they really are, not like some fake TV show."

Stephanie grudgingly concedes. "Okay, okay. You can keep it. Just remember to be careful where you focus. I don't want a reality TV show, either."

Rob smirks impishly. "Well, I'll try, but you do know where my eye naturally travels."

Stephanie nods with a knowing grin and hands Rob another box. "Yes, I am aware of that, which is why I also bought this."

Rob opens it to reveal a motion-sensored tripod, as Stephanie continues. "So, now you can use this to capture the both of us as we really are."

Once he has set up the tripod and finalized all settings, Rob goes to the tree and brings Stephanie a thin, flat package. She opens it and gasps. "Oh...Rob...."

He proudly looks on as she studies the handcrafted picture frame featuring a large photo of them kissing after exchanging vows. It is made with a mosaic of colorful glass tiles. Bordered around the photo are Scrabble tiles that spell out their names. "I'm glad you like it."

Her eyes brim with emotion. "Honey, this is so beautifully created, and tells our story in a unique way, just like the tree. I don't know what to say... thank you seems too paltry."

Brushing away a falling tear, Rob softly kisses her face. "Steph that is exactly how I feel about you. How ironic that we meet over a word game, but the expression of our love defies every word that has ever been created. So, don't thank me; just keep loving me from the deep, unspoken places of your heart, and that will be more than enough."

Stephanie stares at Rob in awe. "Who are you, Rob? Sometimes you seem like a dream to me. I've never met anyone like you before and don't believe I ever will again."

Rob rubs Stephanie's back soothingly. "Well, you won't have to worry about that, because I'll be around for a long time. C'mon, let's finish opening our gifts. We have to get ready to leave soon. There's one more for you down in my workshop. I'll be right back."

Stephanie takes his hand. "Wait, I have another gift for you as well, and it's your turn anyway...so here."

Rob sits down, opens the box, and pulls out a navy blue football jersey with the number '01' printed on both sides. On the back, above the number, it says, 'DAD'. Now Rob fills with emotion as he silently holds it in his hands, turning it over.

Stephanie gently puts her hand on his shoulder. "That's your celebration shirt for when we finally make our touchdown, Big Rob."

Rob nods, places his hand over Stephanie's, and smiles, unable to speak. Blinking back tears, he gives her a long hug then goes down into his workshop.

He returns carrying an ornately carved oak rocker with sleigh runners. Inscribed upon the headrest is, *'For Stephanie Stephenson: A Mother's Love Knows No Bounds'*. Stephanie speechlessly stares at the chair, tenderly fingering the inscription. She lowers herself in it, closes her eyes and slowly rocks as tears slide down her face.

Rob sits at her feet watching intently, imagining, as she is, the baby who will soon be cradled in that chair. They remain silent, each taking in the reality of what is to come. Finally, Stephanie opens her eyes, reaches out for Rob to help her up, and hand in hand, they ascend the stairs.

* * *

Rob and Stephanie arrive at St. Thomas' parish to a crowd much larger than they expected and as a result, have to wait a while to enter. Rob wraps his arms around Stephanie to shield her from the cold as the line slowly progresses. Once inside the sanctuary, they look around appreciatively, taking in all the fine architectural details of the old Catholic church.

Stephanie shakes her head. "Rob, I can't believe it took us this long to come here. After all the support Dalton has given us, we should've done this much sooner."

Rob nods in agreement. "You're right Steph, but we are here now, so let's not beat ourselves up over it."

Soon Dalton approaches the pulpit to welcome everyone to Christmas Mass, which opens with a beautiful choral selection from the youth, followed by several hymns from the adult choir. As the music and heavenly voices fill the room, Stephanie's eyes begin to tear, and she feels the same sensation of God's presence surrounding her, like that time at the café. She turns to look at Rob, who is quietly taking everything in. He smiles and gently squeezes her hand to reassure her that he is okay.

When the choir is finished, Dalton recites prayers from a book, which the congregation repeats in unison. Not knowing what to say, Rob and Stephanie listen, respectfully following suit when everyone kneels upon the red cushions in front of them, sits, or stands.

Melanée Addison

Finally, Dalton begins his sermon on what the miracle of Christ Jesus truly means beyond this special day of commemoration. Stephanie and Rob are quickly drawn into the message, finding it relatable in typical Dalton style. After the service is over and the crowd around him eventually dwindles, Rob and Stephanie tentatively make their approach.

"Oh wow...hey guys!" Dalton embraces them with shock and pleasant surprise. "I'm so glad to see you here! Wait just a moment; I want to introduce you to my mother." As he excitedly approaches a group of women talking, Rob and Stephanie exchange amused glances as they observe Dalton in a new light.

Looking like a valedictorian on graduation day, he returns leading a petite, silver haired woman with a kind face. "Rob...Stephanie, this is my mom, Abigail Shea."

Mrs. Shea grasps their hands with genuine pleasure. "My Paddy has spoken so much about the two of you. I am so glad we finally meet. Did you enjoy today's Mass?"

Rob and Stephanie nod in unison. "Yes ma'am, we did very much." Rob offers, but Mrs. Shea waves her hand dismissively.

"Please, call me Gail. I already feel like we're old friends. Would you like to join us for Christmas supper?"

Rob and Stephanie again exchange glances before Stephanie graciously smiles. "We would love to, Gail."

Dalton is elated. "Great! First, let me go to the office to gather my things, and then we'll be on our way."

He begins to rush off, but Rob stops him. "Dalton, can we come also? We have something for you."

At this point, Dalton notices the package in Stephanie's hand. "Sure! Mom, we'll be right back."

As they enter Dalton's office, Stephanie is impressed. "Wow Dalton, your office is gorgeous! I love the stained glass skylight. It feels so cozy and peaceful in here."

Dalton humbly nods. "Thanks, Stephanie. I enjoy being in here myself."

Rob stands next to Stephanie, who then extends the package to Dalton. "Dalton, we would like to present this gift to you. It is not much; just a simple token of our appreciation for who you are and all you have done for us. I hope you enjoy it."

Thanking them, Dalton opens the package and gazes in wonder. "You have no idea how special this is to me. Exquisite as it is, it would not mean as much from anyone else. The fact that you chose something which represents the core of my life, shows that despite our differences in belief and my laid back, sometimes comedic disposition, you really see and honor me." His voice chokes with emotion. "I love you both very much."

Stirred by Dalton's response, Rob clears his throat and takes a deep breath. "We love and appreciate you for the amazing man you are... on every level."

* * *

Mrs. Shea is a gracious host, and they automatically feel at home. Stephanie is glad that Dalton is a fellow vegetarian because, in addition to the traditional roasted bird Gail prepared, there are all kinds of meatless dishes for her to enjoy. Rob and Stephanie revel in the food as much as the conversation, as Mrs. Shea is an easy talker. "I am so glad my Paddy has such good friends like you. You know, he's just like his father, Mac."

She gets up and returns with a framed photo of Dalton's father. "Wow!" Stephanie remarks as she studies it. "Dalton you look exactly like your father."

Rob nods his head in agreement, marveling over the resemblance.

Mrs. Shea looks on wistfully. "Oh, my Mac was just a bit more than Paddy's age when he was taken from me, but I thank God for sparing my son, or I don't know what I would've done. Talk about the miracle of Jesus! Did he tell you?" Rob and Stephanie glance at Dalton then back at Mrs. Shea, shaking their heads.

Mrs. Shea looks at Dalton reproachfully and continues. "Growing up, he didn't always believe like he does now, but my Paddy was literally brought back to life, just like Jesus! He was declared dead for 35 minutes, but Father John, rest in peace, would not stop praying until he finally came back, just like that!

It was on the news, and everyone called it the 'Miracle of St. Thomas'." Her eyes fill with tears as she recalls. Since then, he has faithfully continued the mission of his dad, who everyone called 'Father Mac' although he never was a priest. I thank God for allowing me to experience His grace, even in the pain and loss. I still miss my Mac dearly, but each time I look at Paddy, I know that he is still here with us in spirit."

Rob and Stephanie study Dalton as if meeting him for the first time, while Mrs. Shea chastises him. "Dalton Patrick Shea--I don't know why you don't talk about this more often; it is an opportunity for people to see the power of God right before their very eyes and know that He is real."

Dalton comfortingly pats his mom's hand. "Okay Ma, I will...I will." He looks at Rob and Stephanie fixedly. "It's true. While I was dead, I had a vision of Jesus surrounded by a blinding white light. He lovingly placed his hand over my heart and began sucking the black sludge of death from my body into his. I could see it sliding into his heart and clogging it, causing it to beat slower and slower. I couldn't move, but heard myself screaming for him to stop, as I didn't want to be the cause of his death. Eventually, it did stop, and I began sobbing uncontrollably over the fact that I had killed Jesus, who was only trying to save me.

The next thing I knew I was in a hospital bed with my mother tearfully embracing me, shouting praises to God for bringing me back to life. I should have been rejoicing, but couldn't stop crying in agony over Jesus' death. It was then that I finally understood, and knew that I was being given a second chance for a reason. My father didn't have that opportunity, but I would use the one I had for both of us. So, here I am—a living testimony of God's love and mercy."

Rob and Stephanie listen in stunned silence while Mrs. Shea emphatically nods in agreement. "So when my Paddy speaks about the miracle of Jesus, he knows firsthand."

When Rob and Stephanie arrive home that night, they shower and quietly lay in each other's arms, each reflecting upon the day's events until eventually drifting to sleep.

CHAPTER TWENTY-EIGHT

Stephanie comes out of the bathroom in her wedding dress and twirls around. "How does it look?"

Rob carefully examines her from all angles. "You definitely look a little more voluptuous than the last time you wore it, but I'm not complaining."

Stephanie nonchalantly shrugs her shoulders. "Well, that's to be expected under the circumstances. I just want you to make sure that nothing is falling out or rising up more than necessary. I don't mind coming as a curvy Cleopatra to the New Year's Masquerade, but I definitely do not intend to look like a sloppy Cleo*fat*ra.

Rob laughs. "Baby trust me... you are full in aaall the right places, and look great. Is Stacie still coming over to do your make up? If she can't make it, Clarissa would surely be an easy stand in for this one."

Stephanie slaps Rob's arm playfully. "Rob, leave that girl alone. She's at the age where creative expression is at its height. You need to encourage and redirect it; not make fun of her. She looks up to you and would be devastated to hear you speak of her like that."

Rob waves his hand dismissively. "No, she wouldn't. She's a tough cookie, and I joke with them like that all the time. You're such a softie. I hope you are not going to coddle our child like this. The world is a rough place and we don't need to raise someone who is going to faint at the slightest offense; they'd never get up off the floor."

Stephanie lifts her chin defiantly. "Yes Rob, I know more than anyone how tough the world can be. This is why a child needs to have a foundation of love and security. Without it, they truly will faint and not be able to get back up. If I did not have my mother there for my first nine years, I don't think I could have ever made it to this point. The world is harsh enough and the last thing a child needs is to be 'toughened up' by those who are supposed to nurture and care for them. That's all I'm saying."

Rob decides to leave it there, already seeing where this could possibly lead if he doesn't, and instead changes the subject. "So, what do you think of my outfit? Do I look like a respectable Antony?"

Stephanie looks him over carefully. "You look good, but it would be more realistic if you wore a skirt or short robe instead of those pants. I have a white wrap skirt that would go perfectly with your tunic, or we could just take a white sheet and make it work."

Rob puffs his chest out and folds his arms obstinately. "I am *not* wearing anybody's skirt or dress. I may not be fashionably accurate for that time period, but I've got my pride and manhood to protect in this day and age, so I'm going to put this little gold wreath on my head and everyone will get the picture. That's as far as I'm willing to go for this occasion, period—discussion over."

Stephanie wraps her arms around Rob soothingly. "My man, the powerful Mark Antony, has spoken and so it shall be."

Just then, the doorbell rings and Rob opens the door to Clint and Stacie dressed as a cheerleader and football player, respectively. He breaks out in silent hysterical laughter, particularly at Clint who in addition to baring his hairy thighs is wearing a stuffed bra and hideous blonde wig with garish make up, no doubt applied by Stacie. After calming down, he quickly ushers them into the dining room for fear that Stephanie would see them and give birth right there on the floor if not warned in advance. So, after informing her of 'Cheerzilla' downstairs, he calls Stacie up to help Stephanie with her makeup.

When they arrive at The Center, everyone gets a kick out of Clint's outfit and Rob is even more thankful that he stuck to his decision to wear pants. The kids are particularly amused and playfully tap the padding that is supposed to be Clint's butt, in addition to popping his legs when he walks by. At first, he takes it good-naturedly, playing like an offended woman, but after one strike too many, he begins to make threats of physical harm to the next person who slaps his legs in passing. However, his inert intimidations only incite the kids and he is harassed even more throughout the night. The event features a talent contest and fashion show where a panel of youth judges vote for best costume, which Clint unanimously wins. As midnight approaches, everyone counts down and toasts the New Year with plastic flutes of sparkling cider. Afterwards, the kids wait for rides from their parents or an escort home by a staff member. Leaving those details to Clint, Rob takes a tired Stephanie home to sleep.

* * *

Rob comes home from work to find Stephanie soaking in the bathtub. "Hey baby, how are you feeling?"

Stephanie's look says it all. "I feel tired, achy and can definitely do without this part of pregnancy. My body is swollen, my breasts are sore, and even the soles of my feet feel extra sensitive. It seems like as soon as I get over one stage, there's a completely new set of ailments waiting. But listen to me—this is what I wanted, right? So all considered, I won't complain."

Rob kneels by the tub and gives Stephanie a tender kiss. "I wish I could take it for you, Steph. I really do. I hate to see you suffer like this. Can I get you some tea to drink?" Stephanie smiles appreciatively at Rob's concern. "Thank you, baby, some mint tea would be really nice."

Later, as they lie in bed, Stephanie turns to face Rob. "Baby, I recognize how hard this must be for you, dealing with the challenges of a high risk pregnancy and I want you to know how much I appreciate your love and support, especially considering that we cannot be physical the way we used to." She chuckles apologetically. What a way to begin a marriage, huh? We start going full steam and then nothing. How are you doing with that?"

Rob gazes at Stephanie and lovingly traces the side of her face. "Well, you know how much I enjoy you. I won't lie about that, but right now that's not my focus. My priority is your well-being and making sure our child arrives safely. Believe me, I've held out for lesser things, so I'm okay. Thanks for asking."

Stephanie smiles gratefully. "I know sometimes I can become consumed with my feelings at your expense, and I don't want to seem selfish. I really want to be there for you the way you are for me, and…"

Rob places a finger upon Stephanie's lips. "Shhh…Stephanie. I can handle it, whatever it is. I hope you know this is not a sacrifice but is what I truly desire. What I also want is for you not to worry about anything, especially now, and allow me to enjoy each moment with you. Please."

Stephanie's body slowly relaxes as Rob begins smoothing her hair, and eventually, she drifts into a deep sleep. Rob studies her peaceful face as silent tears slide down his own.

Rob is startled awake by the sounds of Stephanie's cries. He pops out of the bed to find her bent over in pain with the front of her gown covered in blood. They immediately rush to the hospital where the doctor informs them that she has miscarried. Distraught, Stephanie is sedated and scheduled for release in the morning. As Rob goes home to get her a change of clothes, his mind is numb. Upon returning to the hospital, he leaves a message for Dalton, Stacie and Clint to let them know what happened then tiredly settles in a chair to wait for Stephanie.

* * *

Once home, Stephanie sleeps a lot, mainly due to the pain medication. Rob tries to get her to eat, but she only drinks water and goes back to sleep. Rob keeps everyone updated through phone calls, but does not want to see anyone, as they are both in shock and grief. After a few days, Stephanie finally agrees to broth and tea, but barely takes in much of that. She doesn't say much, and worried, Rob eventually asks Stacie to come by, thinking maybe Stephanie would feel more comfortable speaking with a woman about this. When he tells her Stacie is coming by, Stephanie doesn't react either way but continues silently staring ahead.

When Stacie arrives, she hugs Rob and sits to talk with him before going upstairs. Rob remains on the couch in helpless fear, as he's never seen Stephanie like this before. With everything she has already been through, he hopes this doesn't take her down for good.

Rob has never seriously prayed before, but remembering Dalton's story, he gets down on his knees. "Dear God, I know I am probably the last person who should be asking you for anything right now, but I honestly don't know what else to do. Please help me to fight this battle and win so that I can be there for my wife, who I do not want to lose. I am starting to see that you are more powerful and real than I ever imagined before and I really need help. If you could bring Dalton back from the dead, I know you can do anything." He begins to sob. "Please God I am so sorry for anything I have ever said or done against you, but I really, really need you and so does Stephanie. Please help us…please. I will do anything; I just want us to live this life we've fought so hard for." Afterwards, he wipes his eyes, gets up and calls Dalton.

Stacie sits quietly with Stephanie, holding her hand before speaking. "Stephanie, at a time like this I know there's not much to say, but I just want you to know that I am here for you in any way I can be. I've been in this situation before, myself." Stephanie slowly looks away from the wall she has been focusing on, toward Stacie as she continues.

"I was raped by a friend of my father's, at thirteen years old. I never said anything because I was convinced that no one would believe me. Everyone assumed because I was built and flirtatious that I was also sexually promiscuous. Ultimately, I guess that's what Charlie banked on too. So when I ran into him one day after school and he invited me to the local burger joint to get some food I really didn't think too much of it, not only because he was my father's friend, but honestly I had never noticed him looking at me like the others did.

Anyway, I was more focused on getting my favorite burger, fries and a milkshake. So, we ate and talked about school and I even confided to him that I was having trouble with some of the boys in my school trying to bed me. He said that young boys didn't even know how to handle themselves, let alone a beautiful young woman; that I should not give in because one day I would meet and marry a nice man who would respect me. I really appreciated him telling me that.

When we were driving back, to cheer me up, he told me he had a nice piece of jewelry at his house that he wanted me to have, so I begged him to let me get it even though he initially insisted on taking me home. Eventually, he relented and when we got there he told me to wait in his bedroom while he used the bathroom. I was filled with excitement as I imagined the kind of jewelry a man his age would have—diamond earrings or a fancy necklace and began daydreaming of showing up at school looking rich, making the girls who called me trashy even more jealous.

When he came back in completely naked, everything went blank. I was too confused to react. He locked the door and told me to take my clothes off. I didn't know what to do; my mind was racing. I stood there shaking and crying with my heart beating through my throat. I couldn't believe this was happening to me. Then quietly but more firmly, he told me again to take off my clothes. I did, and while trying to cover myself, I felt for the first time in my life, dirty and ashamed. He pulled me to him and said, "I'm going to show you how a real man is supposed to love a woman so you won't have to keep messing with these little boys no more. You've got way too much to be wasting on them."

As I started crying harder, calling for my father, he wiped my tears, rocked me and softly said, "I'm your daddy right now, and I'm gonna take special care of you, baby girl." I know it sounds crazy, but he was so gentle with me that after a while I convinced myself he really was doing me a favor. When I later figured out I was pregnant, I didn't know who to tell because I never really had any friends like that. I was also scared that my father was going to kill me, Charlie or us both, so I kept quiet and continued as nothing had happened.

Because I had always been active, I was able to get away with wearing large tops stretchy leggings, and sneakers. I even continued to take dance classes after school just to prove that everything was normal. It may have been due to the day I lost my balance and fell forward during a routine, because soon after I began spotting, although I didn't know the implications at the time. Then in class one day, I started having major cramps and went to the bathroom to find blood running down my legs. I tried to wipe it up, but it just kept coming. Eventually, the waves of pain became stronger until I was on the floor screaming, and someone ran to get a teacher. I was rushed to the hospital and my parents were notified. It was horrible—everyone looked at me like just another sad statistic. My father was never the same with me again and my previously apathetic mother accusingly tried to monitor my every move.

Yet, in all this, do you know what the worst thing was for me? It was the forgetting. One moment a life is growing in me, and in the next, there is nothing there. How do you go back to normal after that? No one ever really seemed to understand that. Maybe because it was hidden from their view, it didn't really matter as much." Tears begin to flow down her face. "I had milk in me that was supposed to nourish another life and the doctor just gave me pills to dry it up like nothing. He said I was lucky this had happened because I could now go on with my life, make wiser choices and do better for myself. I know he thought he was helping, but my baby had just died and everyone was avoiding it like a bad dream.

Years later, I came across an article about women who suffered from miscarriages donating their breast milk to nourish abandoned and sick babies and how it helped them not just feel useful, but also honor why they had that milk in the first place. I wish I could have done that because maybe it would've helped me deal with my grief more easily. To this day, I don't even know if it was a boy or girl, to give it a name, so on that date each year I buy a dozen red roses surrounded by baby's breath to remember that although a short time, 'Baby X' did exist, and I was its mother."

They remain in silence until Stephanie finally says in a hoarse whisper, "Am its mother. "You ARE that child's mother and nothing will ever take that away." They stare at each other in unspoken recognition, then embrace in sobs over the abrupt loss of their children.

* * *

As Stacie descends the stairs, Rob is alarmed when he notices that her eyes are red and puffy from crying. However, she smiles and squeezes his arm reassuringly. "She'll be fine—just give her time, space and be available only when and how she asks you to be."

He nods and hugs her gratefully with tears in his eyes. "Thank you so much, Stacie. Tell Clint I'll be in touch soon."

He slowly goes up the stairs, apprehensive of what awaits. As he approaches the bedroom and hears Stephanie in the shower, he is so encouraged that he goes back down to make a light meal of vegetable soup and salad with a smoothie, in the hopes that she will finally begin eating again. While he is still fixing the food, Stephanie comes in with a tentative smile and sits down. Rob smiles back and continues his preparations. Keeping in mind what Stacie said, he decides to let her speak when she is ready. When finished, he simply places their food on the table and begins silently eating while covertly watching to see what Stephanie does. At first, she hesitantly takes a couple of spoonfuls, but slowly builds in momentum until she has hungrily devoured everything.

Afterwards, she sighs with satisfaction and looks gratefully at Rob. "Baby, thank you so much for having Stacie come over. She was very helpful in giving me perspective and direction. Therefore, I've decided to take a leave of absence from the library, donate my breast milk, and volunteer at the hospital caring for sick newborn babies."

Rob listens, nodding supportively. "Steph, I am here however you want me to be. I've also decided to take some time off to give you whatever assistance you need at this stage. Just please let me know."

Stephanie purses her lips and stares at Rob unswervingly. "I want us to begin looking into adoption. I am still a mother Rob, and there are children out there who need exactly that. In the meantime, I encourage you to continue doing what you have been. Don't stop just for me. I will be better in time. I also know that this was your child too and just because you weren't carrying it doesn't make your loss any less. Please know that I am here for you as well. However, ultimately we will need to grieve and heal in our own personal way, which may mean finding additional support outside of each other to fully get through this."

Rob reaches out to squeeze Stephanie's hand. "Steph, thanks for acknowledging this and being honest about where you are. Yes, this is hard for me too, but I've been speaking with Dalton and he's helping me through, so I think we'll both eventually be fine. I'm still going to take time off because I also need to sort some things out, and we will look into adoption once we've gotten through this. I love you."

Stephanie smiles through tears as she hugs him, "I love you too, Rob.

CHAPTER TWENTY-NINE

Rob quickly answers the phone, glancing nervously at a sleeping Stephanie. "Hello?" He murmurs into the receiver.

"Hey Rob, what happened this morning? You didn't show up."

He quietly slips out of the room to go downstairs. "Hey D., I'm sorry about that, but Stephanie had a bad night and I wanted to stay to make sure she was okay. She's been having crying spells a lot lately."

Dalton pauses a few beats before speaking. "What about you?"

Rob replies dismissively. "Oh, I'm hanging in there. I'll be okay, but my main concern is Stephanie right now. You do understand, right?"

Dalton softly sighs. "I'm trying to Rob, but frankly I don't see the logic in you completely neglecting yourself to take care of Stephanie so attentively. The crying spells are just her going through grief; that's natural and inevitable whether you're there or not. You need this time just as much as she does—even more. In addition, you told me Stephanie herself said it was important that you both equally take care of yourselves. If I didn't know any better, I'd think you were trying to avoid your own feelings of fear, which although understandable is definitely not productive for the long run."

Rob's lips tighten. "Well, maybe you don't know better, Dalton. Did that ever occur to you? I don't think I need to be questioned or analyzed on why

I am taking care of my wife who just had a miscarriage; so if that seems inappropriate to you, well then I don't know what else to tell you."

Dalton closes his eyes to remain patient. "Rob, I do understand your desire to be there for Stephanie, but as you have specifically asked me to help you through—

"Exactly!" Rob interjects with frustration. "I asked you to help me, Dalton, not criticize me. It doesn't seem like you really do understand."

Dalton tries another route. "Okay Rob, I will respect however you feel you need to do this, but I am only trying to be here for you so that ultimately you can continue to be there for Stephanie, even beyond this situation. I love and care about the both of you. I know that this is a scary thing to have to walk through, but I cannot do it for you, Rob. I'm just trying to be there the best way I know how and I apologize if you feel anything I said was offensive."

Rob calms down with Dalton's apology. "Listen, Dalton, I'm sorry man. I am going through all kinds of emotions right now and taking it out on you. I really do appreciate you making the time and commitment to be here for me like this and apologize for leaving you hanging again. Just give me a little more time to make sure that Stephanie is out of the woods, and then I'll pick back up again. It won't be too much longer—I promise. I'll call you when I'm ready, okay?"

Dalton takes a deep breath, shaking his head helplessly. "Okay, Rob…I'll talk to you soon."

* * *

Stephanie bounces in flushed with joy, as Rob is preparing their meal. "Hey, baby!" She greets him with a passionate kiss on the lips.

Rob smiles, happy, surprised and flustered all at once. "Wow, that hasn't happened in a while. I guess it went well, then."

Stephanie flings her coat on the back of the chair and sits down. "It was wonderful! After my interview, they ran tests and informed me that they are starting a new program where mothers who are not able to, after meeting me and giving written consent, will allow me personally breastfeed their babies if needed during my volunteer hours. They believe this will help them feel more of a life connection and increase their chance for survival."

"I am SO excited, Rob! Even if it's not my own child, it will prepare me for when we do get our baby. They want me to come back next week when the results are in and begin meeting with some parents who have signed up. For the first time in weeks, I am finally feeling like I have hope again."

She then gets up and wraps her arms around Rob's neck, pressing her body into his. "And for the record...that's not the only thing I'm feeling."

Rob cautiously smiles. "Wow baby, that's great, but, um...do you think it's too soon? I mean yes, I want to, but..."

"You're scared." Stephanie finishes his thought. "I understand. I shouldn't have just sprung it on you like that, anyway. I know this is a process for you too. Well, let's just start to slowly prepare ourselves for it, okay?"

Rob softly kisses her reassuringly. "Steph, you know I want you. That hasn't changed a bit. I just want to make sure that you're fully healed before we jump into anything. I know what the doctor said before, but please just go for one final check-up first."

Stephanie looks deeply into Rob's eyes and gives him a long, tight embrace. "Rob, I love and appreciate the way you always put me before your own needs and desires. Thank you so much, baby."

Rob smooths her hair, kisses her forehead then breaks into a mischievous smile. "Yeah well, just make sure you go to the doctor soon because Valentine's Day is coming up and you can show me all your appreciation then."

* * *

Stephanie walks into the darkened house, turns on the lights and calls out. "Rob? Rob…are you here, baby?" When she doesn't hear a response, she cautiously ventures up the stairs. "Rob?" She opens the bedroom door, looks inside and nearly collapses when she sees Rob standing there in his black satin lounge pants smiling in the midst of soft music, candlelight and rose petals. She smiles and sighs with relief. "Oh my god, baby, I was so worried! Your car wasn't in the driveway and the lights were out, so I figured you weren't here but I didn't get a call from you. Then I remembered I'd seen Dalton's car at the hospital earlier and all kinds of thoughts started running through my mind…"

Rob comes over and holds Stephanie comfortingly, murmuring softly in her ear. "Happy Valentine's Day, Steph. I wanted to surprise, not scare you. Clint's car is in the shop and he had plans to take Stacie somewhere special tonight, so I let him borrow mine. Come on, this is defeating the purpose of why I set all this up in the first place. The water's probably getting cold." He opens the bathroom door and Stephanie notices on the floor is a trail of candles and rose petals that lead to a steaming bubble bath. Next to the bathtub is a table with a bucket of champagne and fruit, and a beautiful bouquet of red, white and yellow roses. Rob takes Stephanie's coat off and slowly unbuttons her blouse, while softly kissing her neck, eliciting a groan of arousal from her. "I've missed you so much that I promise to make this last for as long as I can."

After sinking into the soothing waters of their whirlpool bathtub, Rob pours them each a glass of champagne then drops a large ripe strawberry inside and proposes a toast. "I know you can't have too much of this under the circumstances, but I figured one glass couldn't hurt during our special celebration."

Stephanie takes a sip as she immerses herself in both the lush bubbles and Rob's embrace. "Mmm…baby, this is wonderful! I love the flowers-- especially the colors you chose. They blend gorgeously."

Rob glances over at them, softly nibbling Stephanie's ear. "Thank you, but I chose them for more than that. The red symbolizes the fire and passion of our love, white is the purity of our friendship and the yellow for the hope that lies ahead of us."

Stephanie turns around, speechlessly gazing into Rob's face. "Like I said from the beginning—you surprise me more and more each time. I guess the only thing I should expect from you is the unexpected, huh?"

Rob smiles, puts down his glass and begins to massage her shoulders. "The only thing you should expect from me is that I will love you deeply for the rest of my life—how I do that…well…remains to be seen. Baby, you move me in new ways every day, so my surprises are a direct result of your love."

Stephanie purrs with satisfaction as she quietly sips, luxuriating in the balmy water and soft glowing lights. Soon Rob's hands continue to travel in soft caresses over her body and passions ignite as they begin re-discovering each other, making love throughout the night until both they and the candles are drenched.

* * *

Stacey picks up her tray of smothered steak tips with mashed potatoes and corn and nervously looks around until she finally spots Stephanie waving to her. "Hey Steph, sorry I'm late. It took forever for Aline to relieve me, but I told her I had to take extra time because I was meeting you here. She wants me to tell you that she understands why you haven't returned her calls, but is still praying for you and would like to talk whenever you're ready."

Stephanie nods appreciatively. "Tell her I said thank you and will reach out at some point, but between you and me, I just am not ready to do that right now. To be totally honest, I feel a little embarrassed. Despite what the doctors' said, I made such a huge deal about this pregnancy and even attributed it to God's intervention. To now have nothing to show for it doesn't leave me with much else to say to myself, let alone anyone else."

"On the other hand, I am so happy to have started this program! When I'm with these precious little souls I realize how much we really have in common. We're both struggling to live this fragile life and have been linked together to make that happen. In other words, we are feeding off each other for survival. It's a connection like I've never experienced before. I mean, I have one with Rob, but this is on a completely different level. I can't fully explain it--it's like it transcends the fact that these babies haven't even come from me. It does, however, confirm what I've already known: that I am a mother, regardless of physicality. It's amazing Stacie, and I owe it all to you for helping me discover this."

Stacie appreciatively squeezes Stephanie's hand. "Well, I am grateful to you because I feel like I'm healing more deeply by just hearing about your experiences. So, thank you for having the courage to step out during such a difficult time to do this."

They quietly smile at each other then Stephanie changes the subject. "So, how was your Valentine's Day?"

Stacie closes her eyes and sighs with the memory. "Magical! Clint had already told me that we were going out for dinner and dancing, but what he didn't say was that it was going to be on a yacht! Oh my goodness, Steph, it was beautiful! It had these huge picture windows and skylight in the dining area where it felt like we were surrounded by stars. Then he had a dozen roses delivered to our table as the DJ sang 'You Are The Sunshine of My Life' in dedication to me. Everyone started clapping afterwards and I swear Stephanie, I thought that man was going to get down on his knee next—which I'm glad for his sake he didn't, but it was wonderful. After that, we danced the night away. I had the greatest time, and it didn't hurt driving around in Rob's luxury vehicle either. How was yours?"

Stephanie smiles cryptically. "Oh, it was quiet. We just stayed at home and relaxed. It was good to simply spend time together and work toward getting back to normal, you know?"

Stacie clicks her tongue sympathetically. "Absolutely; that's what's most important now. There'll be plenty of time for going out and all that other stuff later."

Stephanie nods and checks her watch. "Hey Stace, I'm sorry…I've got to get back now, but thanks so much for agreeing to meet me here. I just had to see you and catch up. I'm glad things are going well for you. Obviously, I've been tied up lately, but I'll call you soon and hopefully have you and Clint back over again."

As they stand up to hug Stacie says, "Don't worry, Steph. Take all the time you need. I'll be here whenever you're ready."

* * *

Stephanie comes home to find Rob on the couch in his den dozing with the TV on. "Hey Babe, how's it going?"

Rob groggily sits up to give Stephanie a kiss. "Better now. I'm sorry I just reheated some leftovers for dinner today. I felt a little lazy. You know, after doing it for over 30 years, I think I could get used to not working. Maybe I should just retire."

Stephanie rolls her eyes with disbelief. "Yeah, right; you not working—especially with the youth—I don't think so. Give it another week and you'll be chomping at the bit. But yes, you do need and deserve this time of rest." Then she bursts out in laughter. "You'd better store up all your energy now because I'm sure those kids are already plotting to burn down the neighborhood in protest if you wait too much longer."

Rob shakes his head, joining in. "You ain't lying about that! Clint tells me they're bugging him every day, asking about my return, but I don't call him my 'right hand man' for nothing—I know he's holding down the fort over there and probably doing it even better. Anyway, enough about me... how were things at the hospital today?"

Stephanie's mood suddenly changes as she plops down on the couch. "Everything went great with the babies, but those cackling hen nurses need to mind their business. You would think with all the sick people they have to tend to they wouldn't have time to be spreading rumors, but I guess not."

Rob is perplexed. "Why, what happened?"

Stephanie rolls her eyes. "They were gossiping about me like I am the only woman they've ever known to have a miscarriage. It was so embarrassing, Rob! I went toward the nurse's station to ask a question and overheard them talking about how they felt sorry for me and wouldn't want to be in my place for anything. Then they started in on you, saying they feel sorry for the father too; how you can't even do anything about the situation because you are not supposed to say anything to me about it. How the heck do they know what we talk about, anyway?

Nosey busybodies are what they are, and I should report them, but I'll just leave it alone. I need to keep my emotions clear to focus on those babies and their healing so will instead ignore their piteous glances and ignorant mutterings."

Rob looks confused. "But Stephanie they have so many other patients there, how do you know they were talking about you specifically?"

Stephanie exhales in exasperation. "Really Rob? Because they mentioned my full name, that's why! What do you think; that I'm imagining all this like I'm going crazy or something?"

Rob hugs Stephanie consolingly. "No, No baby—of course not; I just asked because I wasn't clear, that's all. Now that I am, I find it totally unacceptable and am going to say something. Even though you are there in the capacity of providing a service, you are also a patient and they need to respect the confidentiality of that, even amongst themselves. Don't worry about it baby, I will take care of this. You just keep your mind on what you are supposed to be doing."

Stephanie grabs Rob's face and covers it in kisses. "My knight in shining armor rides to the rescue! Thank you, baby."

Rob grins exultantly with Stephanie's response. "Anything for you, my queen—and those kisses too!

* * *

Stephanie walks into the private lounge and gives Dalton a grateful hug. "Thanks so much for agreeing to see me. I feel bad because I know Rob would be upset if he knew I was doing this, especially after the fuss I made over honoring each other's space, but Dalton, I don't know what else to do. I really think he's depressed."

Dalton squeezes Stephanie's hand reassuringly. "Don't worry Stephanie. Please know that as a friend, I am always here for you both without giving preference to the other. As a counselor, however, I have to give deference to Rob. I'm sure you understand."

Stephanie nods, her eyes filling with tears. "I know this has been hard on both of us, but I think I've been so wrapped up in my own healing process that honestly, I really haven't been paying as much attention to his; plus, he really doesn't speak much about what he is going through and instead prefers to dote on me. This is why I specifically made it a point to tell him that we each had to focus on ourselves during this time—but you know Rob."

"However, now that I am coming out of my fog and stabilizing, I'm starting to see that he hasn't been taking care of himself as much as I thought he was, so I just need to check in with you and get your perspective. No offense to you Dalton, but I really think at this point he needs to see a psychiatrist who can officially diagnose and perhaps prescribe him something, at least in the interim. This is not my husband. He's so listless and just lays there watching TV most of the time—or sleeping."

"At first, I was grateful that he was relaxing and taking time for himself and happy to eat leftovers or to come home and cook for us. However, I think over time, the lack of interaction and activity he was used to has caused him to sink into a state of lethargy. I'm afraid that if I don't intervene soon, he may go even deeper. He doesn't want to talk about returning to work and rarely answers his phone anymore."

"When I suggested that in addition to you, he meet with a psychoanalyst or psychiatrist for an evaluation, he didn't exactly snap at me, but very firmly said that there was nothing mentally wrong with him." The tears that had been welling up in her eyes finally spill over. "Dalton, I am his wife. I know he's not fine, and I'm scared that the man I love is being chipped away more and more each day. In all this, he insists he's still meeting with you, so I just need to know what you think about this."

Dalton studies the floor a moment before responding. "Well Stephanie, like I said, I really cannot divulge anything Rob and I discuss, but will say this much. You both have been on an emotional roller coaster even before your marriage and the miscarriage. While you share a lot in common, please also realize that you are not the same and have individual ways of dealing with life challenges. Even if Rob does need to see a professional therapist, that has to be his decision, not yours. As painful as it may be, you have to allow him the space to work things out his way and just continue being there to support, not criticize it. In getting to know Rob over time, I have had to learn that lesson myself. Anything he perceives as pressure will further shut him down and push him away. So, this may not be what you want to hear, I think it's the best advice I can give now."

Stephanie nods solemnly. "You're right. It isn't what I want to hear, but probably what I need to. Thanks again, Dalton." As they stand and hug in parting, Dalton says, "Stephanie, remember that I am always here for you as a friend. Any time you need to talk about anything, just call me.

* * *

Stephanie returns home that evening to a dapperly dressed Rob, head cleanly shaven with a new sparkling diamond stud in his ear. He reaches down to give her a passionate embrace and kiss. "Come on baby, get dressed—I'm taking you out tonight!"

Stephanie stands there with a stunned smile, trying to take it all in. "Rob... you look great and very sexy with your bald head, not to mention that earring."

Rob beams with pride. "Thank you. In addition to seeing a new patch of grays crop up, I wanted a fresh, clean start and figured this was the best way to do it. I was nervous at first about how you would take it, so I am glad you like it. Do you really, or are you just saying that?"

Stephanie looks at Rob and licks her lips. "Robert Stephenson, I am not lying-- you look so good that if I wasn't famished, I'd decline your offer and stay home to devour you instead."

Rob laughs heartily. "Well then, we'll save dessert for home. Seriously, baby, I know I have not been the easiest to get along with lately. I've just been going through this aging thing, which is really showing more by having such a young, vibrant and beautiful wife. I just want to be able to make you happy in every way I can."

Stephanie gratefully hugs Rob and gives him a tender kiss. "Robert, you need not feel self-conscious about your age or anything else. I am completely happy, turned on and satisfied in every way by you. I just want you to take care of yourself as well as you do me. That is the only thing I'm really concerned about."

Rob smooths her hair reassuringly. "Well, I don't want you to worry Steph. It may not look perfect but trust that I am working it out. So, come on and get ready because your new, sexy husband is taking you to Chowmomma's tonight!"

* * *

Rob and Stephanie arrive home laughing, joking, and full of life.

Rob joyfully embraces Stephanie, tenderly kissing her forehead. "Steph, I am so glad we went out tonight. It's been a while and I know we've gone through a lot, but I want us to get back to having fun again. Plus the food tonight was almost as good as my mother's, so I did enjoy it...but not as much as I'm going to enjoy dessert with you!"

Stephanie squeals with laughter as he suddenly lunges and begins tickling her. Soon their playful wrestling develops into urgent kisses and caresses. Still giggling, Stephanie murmurs, "Rob, remember this is just how we began...not even able to make it into the bedroom."

Rob smiles mischievously and then scoops her up. "Oh, we're making it to the bedroom tonight, baby, but not too much further than that." He says, carrying her up the stairs.

Once inside, Rob gently lays Stephanie down and begins to undress her, slowly kissing and licking her body. Groaning in anticipation, she reaches out for him, but he entwines their fingers together and continues to explore. When frenzied with passion, she excitedly begins clawing and grasping for him again, he abruptly draws her tightly to him and whispers, "Steph, I can't."

Slowly, Stephanie's body relaxes. The taste of tears fills her mouth when she gives him a reassuring kiss. "Rob, please…it's okay, baby…it's okay." Soon her drops mingle with his, as he helplessly cries in her arms for the first time.

* * *

The next morning when Stephanie awakens, she quietly studies Rob's sleeping face. Her emotions begin to stir again as she recalls his anguish hours earlier. Before this, she had no idea how much of a blow the miscarriage dealt to Rob's perceived manhood. She is well aware that like a woman, a man's foremost desire is to procreate--to leave behind a sign of his presence in this world. No one deserves that opportunity more than Rob does. In the drive to establish a sense of motherhood from her loss, she minimized the impact of Rob's denied fatherhood--yet again. Now she sees why he doesn't want to return to work—it must be a painful reminder to be involved in the lives of other people's children so close to losing his own. Tears slide down her face as she finally begins to comprehend all he has held inside to tend to her needs. Suddenly, the reality of his comments on marriage finally hits home: their pain is one and the same.

Rob begins to stir. Quickly wiping her face, she smiles as he slowly opens his eyes.

"Morning, baby." She greets him with an affectionate peck on the lips.

Smiling back, Rob pulls her into a tight hug then kisses her forehead. Good morning to you, my love…Steph, are you ok?" He inquires, noticing her watery eyes."

Stephanie blinks back tears. "Just overwhelmed with joy that I am your wife and marveling in how lucky I am to have you."

Rob gives a small sad smirk. "Even if I can't fulfill your needs?"

Stephanie looks at Rob sternly. "Robert, I really wish you would stop talking like that. I don't think or feel that way at all, so please don't put it on me. I meant what I said before. I am fully satisfied and more in ways than I never thought imaginable--in the bedroom and out, so please stop narrowing your worth to me as simply being physical, because it's not. I want you to understand that in my eyes, your greatest value is your heart, your mind, and your spirit—not your body. I know as well as you that our bodies will at some point fail us, but our love doesn't have to."

Rob quietly traces Stephanie's face with his finger as tears fill his eyes. "I love you so much, Stephanie. I want you to always know that—no matter what."

Stephanie hugs Rob reassuringly. "I do, baby...I do."

CHAPTER THIRTY

Dalton and Rob walk into the brightly colored sunlit room and sit to wait for assistance. Rob smiles at Dalton with sincere appreciation and a bit of sheepishness. "Hey man, I know it's been a while, but like I said, I just wanted to make sure Stephanie was coming along first—which I am happy to say, she is. She seems to be getting stronger every day, so now I finally feel comfortable enough to focus on me."

Dalton purses his lips and looks firmly at Rob. "That's not the way it's supposed to work, Rob—but as we've been through this before, I am not going to say anymore on it. I am just glad that you're here now. How've you been feeling?"

Rob shrugs with nonchalance. "A little tired understandably, but if you must know, I'm also happy to report that in between worshipping Stephanie, I have been getting plenty of rest."

Dalton starts to say something in reply, but decides against it, and simply shakes his head.

Just then, a nurse enters with urgency. "Mr. Stephenson, we've gotten the results of your tests back—your white blood cell count is dangerously high and your kidneys are shutting down as we speak. You need to be admitted right away."

Rob stares at the nurse stunned, trying to comprehend her words. "What are you talking about? I have to be home today or my wife will be worried."

The nurse shakes her head resolutely. "I am sorry Mr. Stephenson, but that would be against our medical advice. Under the circumstances, your life is seriously at risk. If you want, we can inform your wife, who can—

"NO!" Rob fiercely growls. "Don't you dare! I don't care what you say—I am going home NOW!" As he starts for the door, suddenly he collapses and being unable to revive him, a medical team is called to rush him into emergency services.

Sometime later, Rob groggily awakens to find himself attached to an intravenous drip and Dalton at his side. As he tries to get his bearings, his eyes clearly indicate what he is struggling to express verbally, due to his brain feeling like a ball of cotton.

Dalton reaches out and places his hand on Rob's shoulder. "No, Rob... Stephanie has not been contacted yet, but I think that she should be. She needs to be involved in the decision making at this point."

I also want to let you know that I consider any promise I made to you around this, nullified. We can no longer pretend this is something you can simply rest your way through, especially now. Well...I won't. As a friend, I tried to respect your process, but in hindsight have allowed it to harm others--most damagingly you. If anything worse happens as a result, I truly don't know how I can live with that."

Rob looks at Dalton's pained face and nods with resignation. "Okay." He mumbles, his eyes brimming with tired tears. "But before you go, just tell me this one thing...why does God hate me so much?"

Dalton looks at Rob perplexed, caught off guard by his question, but Rob continues, undaunted. "I mean, with all that sacrificing and praying you've been doing most of your life, you must have some secret knowledge to share by now. C'mon, tell me, Father Shea...what have I done in my life so bad to deserve this? Maybe because I refused to shamelessly sleep with scores of women, the way my father did. Perhaps I have been too faithful to my marriage vows or did not abandon my mother and brothers in their time of need. Oh yes, I know! It was that I nurtured and encouraged kids who were abused and tossed away like trash. What, Dalton—tell me, Damn it!"

"Yeah well...you want to know what I really think? There isn't anyone 'up there' running things—there can't be! If so, he would truly be incompetent, don't you think? I think we're the crazy ones--making up all these stories that never really seem to check out, and yet, we still go on reciting them to ourselves, each other, and worst of all...our children. Until one day, we find ourselves lying in a bed, dying from doing good while all those who could give a shit simply put us in the ground and continue telling the same old damn fairy tales. Yeah...that's MY story. How do you like it?" Rob lies back, spent from his tirade.

Dalton remains silent for a long time as he ponders Rob's words. Finally, he speaks.

"Rob, do you know why we become so angry when life doesn't go our way?"

Rob stares at Dalton vacantly, too exhausted to respond. He is out of answers right now, anyway.

Dalton looks down at Rob with tears in his eyes. "It's because we think it's ours. When I was dead—even before—as I lay there dying, I came to the utter realization that this thing wasn't mine. It was slipping from my grasp and I couldn't just change my mind, reach out and get it back. It was then I that I really understood that all the power we think we have is just an illusion. There's a saying, I think it's in the Talmud. 'We don't see things as they really are; we see them as we really are'. This means that it doesn't matter if we say there is no God and produce theories and evidence ad infinitum to prove our viewpoint. Well, at least it doesn't matter to God because He knows who He is. More importantly, He knows who we are. We are the only ones running around in the midst of our illusions of self-imposed grandeur."

"However, in the end, each man will have to come to the awareness that we were created by God for God; and whether we choose to worship Him with our will or curse him with our mouths, we will still always belong to Him. We are His Creation, and the indisputable testament of this is that our very act of respiration is imbued with His glory—every breath we take is a 'broken Hallelujah' unto Him—our hard wired form of praise. Listen: (breathing in) Hah (breathing out) Leu. So it really doesn't matter what we say or do, because the whole time that we are here, we're glorifying Him with each inhalation and exhalation, and when it's over, it still returns to Him because it was His all along."

"When my father was here, I thought he was mine—that I possessed him—so when he was murdered I was infuriated with everyone, especially God. How dare He allow them to take what belonged to me, and so mercilessly? At that point, I began my tirade against God and man alike. If someone could just come and take what I treasured like nothing, then I was going to do the same. In my rage, I was indiscriminate—everyone was fair game. The things I did to others as well as myself, during that time were unspeakable; it is only God's forgiveness that even allows me to go on living with the knowledge of it."

"However, even before I could come to that point, when I was sent to rehab and could no longer drink or drug my anger and pain into submission, the reality of my savage acts tormented me day and night. In my soberness, I hated myself for committing them, and I hated myself for feeling guilty over them in the first place. Were the people who killed my father feeling guilty? Were they being tormented like me? I didn't think so at the time and cursed the conscience that relentlessly pursued me. As soon as I was discharged, I went on the streets and got a big score. I won't say what I had to do to get it, but for me, it was my last hurrah anyway—my big F.U. to God and everyone, including myself—or so I thought."

"Well, here I am now in a collar listening to others' confessions and absolving their sin...me. It's absolutely incredulous that I should be here at all, let alone in this capacity. But then I breathe in and back out and remember: It's not mine...it's not mine."

As Dalton is speaking, tears uncontrollably stream from Rob's eyes until no longer able to hold back, he finally breaks down in anguished sobs.

Dalton reaches over to embrace Rob, whose cries have now escalated into heart wrenching howls, and his own eyes spill with tears of compassion as he fervently prays for the pain of the little boy who got lost inside the man, and the man who got lost in the corridors of life.

* * *

Dalton walks into the ward as Stephanie is preparing to leave. "Hey Dalton, what are you doing here? We've got to stop meeting up like this you know… people will talk." She quips with a wink.

Dalton tries to smile lightheartedly in response, but his eyes give away what his words do not.

"Dalton…what's wrong?" Stephanie forces herself to remain calm, despite her rapidly increasing heartbeat.

Dalton knows there is no other way to start this. "Stephanie, please come and sit down first."

Stephanie is now barely able to contain her rising panic. "Dalton, please just tell me…where's Rob? You were supposed to meet him today. Just tell me NOW!"

Noticing the nurses starting to gather, he gets right to the point. "Stephanie, Rob collapsed earlier but is now stabilized in the emergency room. I came to bring you to him."

Stephanie calms down slightly but is still terrified. "Oh my God! What happened—is he okay?"

Dalton nods but doesn't say too much more. "I believe he wants to speak with you."

Stephanie quickly gathers her things and quietly follows Dalton, her mind racing in all directions. Upon seeing him, her eyes fill with tears. "Rob, honey, are you okay?"

Rob tries to smile nonchalantly, but can't stop his lips from quivering. "Hey, baby...I just got a little dehydrated, but am fine now. The doctor said I contracted a bacterial infection and need a dialysis treatment.

Stephanie is stunned. "What? Did they say how this happened?"

Rob closes his eyes and sighs. "Stephanie...I have Stage 4 Cancer."

Stephanie swoons and her knees begin to buckle. As she tries to grip the bed railing for support, Dalton catches and gently leads her to the nearby chair. She stares in shock and disbelief as tears slide down her face. "Rob, what are you saying to me?"

Rob's eyes also begin to well, but he forces himself to be strong. "What I'm saying Steph, is that I have been and will continue to battle this and ultimately, we will be okay."

Stephanie nods then pauses in confusion. "What do you mean 'have been battling this'? How long have you known, Rob?"

Rob looks away. "Stephanie, I didn't think it would get to this point so fast. I thought I could handle it without worrying you, especially when we found out you were pregnant."

Stephanie now begins violently trembling, and Rob is unsure whether it is from fear or rage. "You knew even before I'd gotten pregnant?! She shakes her head with incredulity. I can't believe what I am hearing—all this time you knew you were sick while leading me to believe that nothing was wrong? All the times I asked you to get a check-up when I saw you losing weight and sleeping for hours on end, I'm thinking you're depressed, and now you tell me that I've actually been watching you die right before my eyes, Rob? Is that what you're telling me?" You too, Dalton? When I came to you in complete distress, you looked in my face and told me how much you cared all while keeping this lie!"

"Stephanie," Rob and Dalton begin simultaneously, but she is beside herself.

"Right now, I have nothing to say to either of you." She shakes her head in tearful astonishment. "Isn't this the ultimate irony of deception--the man who professes to love me with all his heart, and a goddamned priest!" Grabbing her purse, she dashes out.

"Stephanie!" Rob screams. As Dalton tries to catch her, the nurses rush in to calm Rob down.

When Dalton returns he finds Rob waiting impatiently. "Did you get her?"

Dalton shakes his head with resignation.

Rob slowly closes his eyes and sighs. "Call Stacie from my phone—she's probably going to see her."

Dalton picks up Rob's cell phone and dials Stacie's number. "Hello Stacie, this is Dalton. I'm wondering if you've heard from Stephanie recently. No, she's left the hospital already and I am trying to reach her. Well, actually, everything is not okay, but I'll have to explain later. If you do hear from her, please have her call Rob...or me. Thanks."

Rob's rubs his eyes in exasperation. "Dalton, what am I going to do now?"

Dalton squeezes Rob's shoulder reassuringly. "Give her just a fraction of the time you yourself had to adjust to this shocking news. Rob, I know your intentions were good, but Stephanie is absolutely right to feel the way she does. You should not have under any circumstances kept this from her. I also have to take the legitimate blame for continuing that deception when I had other choices.

Rob sighs wearily. "You know, man, I don't understand this thing called life, but that doesn't mean I'm going to let it get the best of me, either. I will fight and win this battle for Stephanie's sake. She's been through so much already, and just doesn't deserve this."

Dalton nods in agreement. "No one understands it, Rob. Believe me, the person who says they do is a bigger liar than the two of us put together.

The good news is we don't need to understand it, but simply surrender it to The One who does."

Just then the doctor comes in. "Mr. Stephenson, I understand we've received your consent for treatment, so someone will be in shortly to get you prepared."

Rob tries to smile. "Thank you, doctor. I apologize for being a jerk earlier."

The doctor nods empathetically. "Don't worry, Mr. Stephenson. I can't say I wouldn't react the same way under the circumstances but am glad you've changed your mind. Take care."

As the doctor leaves, Dalton stands up and gathers his things. Hey man, it's been a long day. Why don't you stop trying to figure things out for now and just let yourself be taken care of? I'll be here to check on you tomorrow, and I'm sure Stephanie will too."

Rob nods, stifling a yawn. "Yeah. See you tomorrow, D. Thanks for everything."

235

CHAPTER THIRTY-ONE

When Rob awakens the next day, Stephanie is by his bedside. "Rob, I'm so sorry about yesterday, but I felt like my whole world just suddenly blew apart. Nothing seemed real anymore, and I simply freaked. Please forgive me. I know you were only trying to protect me, but from now on, we are in this together."

Rob breaks down in tears. "Steph, I'm so sorry baby. I never meant to do this to you…I don't know what I was thinking. From now on, not only will you be aware of, but will have the first say in everything that concerns our lives."

Stephanie embraces him in a tight grip. "I love you so much, honey. My first and last say is that we will come through even stronger. So just know, you are not going anywhere Mr. Stephenson—not on my watch."

Rob caresses Stephanie's face as she gently wipes away his tears. Pressing his hand against her face, she tenderly kisses it. "Sweetheart, if you're up to it, some of the kids are waiting downstairs with Stacie and Clint to see you."

Rob starts to say something and then breaks down in sobs.

Stephanie consoles him. "It's alright honey. They just want you to know how much they care and are also in this with us. I'll go tell them you send them your love and will arrange another visit if, and when you're ready. After, I'm going to check in with the doctor to see what's going on, but I'll be back soon, okay?"

Rob nods and valiantly tries to smile.

* * *

When Stephanie comes back from the waiting room, she asks to speak with the oncologist. "Hello, Mrs. Stephenson, I'm Dr. Holmes. I understand you've been through quite a lot recently. You're a remarkably strong woman."

Stephanie solemnly nods. Thank you, Dr. Holmes, but I suppose we all do what we have to when needed, right?" Dr. Holmes nods in agreement. "Absolutely; As Mr. Stephenson has given you power of attorney, I would like to update you on what has been happening with him up to this point. In early October he was diagnosed with an aggressive Stage 3 prostate cancer, at which point he chose to be treated with hormone replacement therapy in place of the chemotherapy and radiation we recommended. He appeared to be responding well at the time, but when he suddenly stopped his treatments, the cancer rapidly spread throughout his body. Now his organs are shutting down and personally, I think he is too weak for chemo. I'm so sorry to have to tell you this: There's really nothing else we can do for him at this point but to make him comfortable as he probably only has at most a few weeks left."

Stephanie calmly stares at the doctor. "I understand. Thank you, Dr. Holmes."

Dr. Holmes carefully studies Stephanie before proceeding. "We can recommend some great hospice choices that would give excellent care to Mr. Stephenson and allow some of the load to be taken off you so that you can begin to make arrangements. We also have a grief support group here to help you work through your emotions during this trying time."

Stephanie nods. "Thank you. I would like to take him home now."

Dr. Holmes tilts her head and squints, trying to understand her statement. "Well, Mrs. Stephenson, under the circumstances, you would have to make hospice arrangements first. If you need, we have an on-site planning team that can help you with the paperwork and other decisions."

Stephanie continues to gaze unwaveringly at Dr. Holmes. "So, let me see if I understand this. You can provide me with a team to plan for my husband's death, but have nothing to offer me to plan for him to live?"

Dr. Holmes' face cringes sympathetically. "Mrs. Stephenson—"

"No, please," Stephanie holds up her hand with patient insistence. "I have heard and respect your medically trained professional perspective. Remember, I've been through this before and your colleagues were proven right, despite what I felt. However, do you see the ludicrousness in what you are telling me? I have all kinds of supports to help my husband die, but should I desire, even hope for him to live, then I'm on my own? How do I even begin to trust to leave him in any care with such a perspective? If I do, will the nurses care for him with respect for the life that he fully possesses now, or would they already consider him as dead? How can anyone heal in that type of environment?"

"Further, I am willing to believe and will continue to do so until there is no more reason to, that my husband will live and want him to be cared for accordingly. If that means I'm on my own then I will be on my own, loving his life until there is no more if that is to be, but I simply refuse to send him to a place that is preparing for him to die. I do again, truly thank you, Dr. Holmes, for all you and this hospital have done for both me and my husband up to this point, but I am taking him home to care for him alone."

Dr. Holmes looks at Stephanie and sighs with resignation. "Okay Mrs. Stephenson, I understand. Because it is against my recommendation, I will need you to sign an 'against medical advice' release and ask that you give it another day to allow him to stabilize for when you do bring him home. Please know that you still have access to these resources, so feel free to call at any time if you change your mind." She then stands up to shake Stephanie's hand. "I thank both you and Mr. Stephenson for entrusting us with your care." Stephanie smiles with a composure she cannot comprehend under the circumstances. "Thank you, Dr. Holmes."

* * *

Rob studies Stephanie's face searchingly as she enters the room. "So?"

Stephanie forces herself to hold his gaze. "Well, the good news is that you'll be coming home soon."

Rob squints and waits. "And the bad news is?"

Stephanie sighs and finally relents. "Rob, we both know what we are up against here, but that's not going to be our focus, is it? Let's just look at how we need to move past this and continue on with our lives."

"Okay." Rob reluctantly replies. "Can you still tell me what the doctor's determination was?"

Stephanie briefly glances downward before responding. "She said that she doesn't think you are well enough for further treatment—"

"And is sending me home to die." Rob finishes. They stare at each other in silence trying to grasp those uttered words hanging between them.

Finally, Stephanie speaks. "Baby, we don't have to accept this. Like you said, we are going to do everything in our power to fight it. We hear stories every day of people receiving diagnoses like this and still overcoming the odds. Look at Dalton! You are here now and I'm not looking at any other option."

Rob nods in agreement, although his eyes hold a tinge of fear. "Neither am I." Suddenly he lets out a bellow of pain and Stephanie panics. "Rob, baby what is it? What's wrong?" When he doesn't respond, Stephanie frantically runs out for assistance and returns with a nurse who after an assessment, administers a syringe with painkillers into his arm. She continues to monitor Rob until his pain subsides and he begins to drift into a stupor.

"Mrs. Stephenson," she whispers. "Can I please speak to you outside for a moment?" Stephanie worriedly studies Rob, whose eyes have already closed, and numbly nods.

"First let me say that I'm so sorry for what you are going through. My husband was also diagnosed with stage 4 cancer but has been in remission for nearly a year. Can I speak candidly with you?"

Stephanie nods again, feeling a ray of hope begin to rise within her.

"I've heard that you are planning to take Mr. Stephenson back home to care for him by yourself, but from the perspective of a trained medical professional who has already gone through this, I personally think it would be better if he received hospice care."

Hearing this, Stephanie's facial expression immediately changes as she starts to interject, but the woman, old enough to be her mother, stops her with a raised finger and gentle but firm look.

"Mrs. Stephenson, I understand when you hear the word hospice, you think only of a place primarily preparing for your husband to die, but I want you to know it is so much more than that. In a hospice facility, he can receive 24 hour care from those who are sensitive to the situation you both face. This frees you to focus on being there to support him in other ways. On the other hand, if you try to do everything on your own, not only will you quickly burn yourself out, but he will be unable to receive the critical attention and pain-management medications someone in his situation needs. Believe me, as a wife, I struggled with the same thing myself when having to admit my husband, but as a medical professional, I knew he would have access to better resources than I could personally give him. Please understand that the outcome of my husband's situation is atypical to the norm, but I personally think you'll have better leverage fighting with a team rather than trying to take everything upon yourself. I really hope you don't feel that I am intruding, but I just want you to have another viewpoint."

She takes a small pad out of her pocket and begins to write. "I also want you to know that if you need to, you can always call me at home or at work. My name is Felicia Franklin, but everyone calls me Lee."

Tears slide from the corners of Stephanie's eyes as she takes the number. "Thank you so much, Lee. Please call me Stephanie. I really appreciate it and will call you soon to find out more information."

Lee nods. "Please stop by the Nurses station before you leave and get some pamphlets to read over." She then looks at Stephanie with a loving sternness. "I'll also expect you to come by for a nice home cooked dinner soon. Then you can meet my husband." Stephanie smiles gratefully, feeling looked after for the first time since this ordeal began. "Yes—absolutely, Lee."

When Stephanie arrives home that evening, she is completely exhausted, as she has not had a decent night's sleep since Rob had cried in her arms. When she looks back over the events from October all the pieces seem to finally fall into place—Rob's initial response to her pregnancy, his 'secret' visits with Dalton, and even the pain, weakness and impotence he blamed on aging. On one hand, she understands his desire to protect her, but on the other, is still very upset because if he had told her earlier they most likely wouldn't be in this situation now. However, that is irrelevant at this point. They have yet another battle to fight together and she is determined not to lose this one. She decides to admit Rob into hospice and closely monitor how he is being treated. If at any point she feels like it is anything less than what she would give, she will look at other options. For now, all she has the energy to do is take a quick the shower and roll into bed. Tomorrow is another day and she can figure out everything else then.

CHAPTER THIRTY-TWO

Stephanie walks into Rob's room the next morning and greets him with a kiss. "Good morning, baby. How are you feeling today?"

Rob studies her carefully. "There's a bottle on the ceiling and it's almost full."

Confused, Stephanie glances at where Rob is focused. "What bottle, baby? I don't see anything."

Rob looks at her like she is dull. "The bottle that is swinging from the ceiling filled with smoke. We should climb on the bed and grab it before we can't see anymore." He tries to get up, but when the tubes restrict him, he impatiently reaches to remove them.

However, Stephanie gently places her hand on his chest. "Hey, I've got a better idea. I'll go get a ladder and then we can climb up to get it together, okay?"

Rob grins, delighted with her suggestion. "Yeah! That's what they do in the place where ladders go between Heaven and Earth."

Stephanie forces herself to remain in the moment. "Okay then! I'll be right back." However, Rob is too absorbed in his image to even notice. The moment the door closes behind her she begins sobbing uncontrollably.

"Stephanie?" It is Lee. Stephanie is so overcome that she cannot even reply.

Consolingly placing an arm around Stephanie, Lee guides her into a private room and reaches for a box of tissue. "Sit here for a moment. I need to check on my last patient, and then we can talk." Stephanie, who had just begun to calm down, gratefully nods then starts to cry all over again. Lee reassuringly squeezes Stephanie's shoulder before hurrying out.

When she returns, Stephanie is more composed though still distraught. Lee offers her a bottle of water from the mini-fridge and silently watches as she gratefully gulps it down. They sit in silence until Stephanie begins to speak and tears roll from her eyes afresh. "He's having hallucinations."

Lee nods knowingly. "It's a scary thing to have to watch the one you love in this state. There are no words for it."

Stephanie miserably agrees as she wipes her eyes. "I feel like I'm losing him already and I don't think I can handle it. I honestly don't know if I can go on if that happens, Lee. I've surprisingly made it through so much in my life already, but I don't think I would with this."

Lee studies Stephanie attentively. "Well then, let's not even entertain that possibility. As rough as this day has been let's remember that he is still here in it, which means there is the opportunity for tomorrow to be a better one. I am saying this Stephanie because these are the things I've had to remind myself during my journey with Milton, and although it seemed like a bottomless pit at times, there were better days. Nevertheless, you're doing the right thing in allowing yourself to express the fear and pain you feel now. When I see others bottle it up or remain in complete denial, they are the ones I worry about being able to handle things over the course of time. We cannot escape the fact that this is a painful experience you are going through, so the more you allow yourself to let your grief out, the better you will be able to manage the bad days and enjoy the good ones."

Stephanie tightly embraces Lee. "Lee, I can't even begin to thank you. I feel much better now."

Lee smiles affectionately. "There's no need for thanks, dear. That's what I'm here for. You remind me so much of my daughter, Celina who we lost when she was hit by a drunk driver."

Stephanie cringes at Lee's story. "I am so sorry. That's how I lost my fiancé and unborn child a few years ago. I also lost my mother when I was nine. I knew we easily connected for a reason. Thank you for showing up in my life at just the right time. You're like an angel to me."

Tears fill Lee's eyes. "That's what I thought when I first saw you. When you come by I have to show you Celina's picture so you can understand better."

They stare at each other with curious wonder. "Life sure is a strange thing isn't it?" Stephanie remarks, but Lee shakes her head.

"I don't think so; in fact, I think it is very purposeful. Listen when I tell you this: Everything happens for a reason at the time it is supposed to."

Stephanie smiles, shaking her head incredulously. "You sound just like a dear friend of ours." At that moment, her cell phone begins to ring and she looks down at the number. "Wow, what a coincidence!" "It's Dalton, the friend I was just speaking to you about. Hold on for a second, Lee. Hey, Dalton! Well, to be honest, I'm not exactly sure how I'm doing. Sure, I'd love for you to stop by, especially since you're already here in the building. You would be a most welcome sight for us, particularly at a time like this. Okay, great. We'll see you soon."

Switching off the line, she looks at Lee in amazement. "Isn't it something how this stuff happens?

Lee smiles with a nod. "Divine signs are often given to us, but most times we are too absorbed in our own reality to recognize them until they become blindingly bright, and unfortunately sometimes not even then. From what I can see, you are very loved Stephanie...very loved." She looks down at her watch. "Well, break time is over. I've got to get back, but I'll come by and check on you later."

As Lee gets up to leave, Stephanie grabs her hand. "Thank you so much, Lee...for everything." Lee squeezes her hand back. "You're welcome Stephanie, but I believe you are the gift I should be grateful for."

* * *

Stephanie hesitantly grasps the handle and takes a deep breath before opening the door. Rob, lying in a peaceful haze, calmly smiles as she walks in. "Hey babe, you just missed Mom and Ricky! They got the bottle down for us."

Stephanie stares at him, dumbstruck. "O-okay baby...that's nice."

Rob, however, looks right through her, lost in recollection. "You should have seen her...she was beautiful. She looked so happy, Steph! I miss them so much." Tears begin to flow from his eyes and Stephanie holds his hand consolingly. "Stephanie, they looked so peaceful. I'd never seen my mother like that before."

Oh by the way...I heard our song playing from heaven, except it was more beautiful than we'd ever heard before because the angels were singing it."

Stephanie looks confused. "Our song?"

"Yes, Steph...our wedding song, except the words, were different. I'll give them to you.

Just then, there is a knock at the door. "Come in," Stephanie calls out, grateful for the interruption. "Hey there, Dalton!" She enthuses with a flood of relief.

Rob also smiles with the pleasure of seeing his good friend. "Hey Dalton, guess what? I saw my mother and brother today!"

Dalton doesn't blink an eye. "Wow, you did? Tell me about it!"

Stephanie feels like she has suddenly been transported into a scene from 'The Twilight Zone'. Is she going crazy or is it everyone else? "Okay you two, I'm going to give you some space. I'll be in the cafeteria."

Rob looks at Stephanie with a sly smirk. "Don't worry; I'll be here when you get back."

"Funny." Stephanie forces a smile, but at the same time, those words meant in jest hold a reality she cannot escape, and her stomach lurches with fear. By the time she reaches the cafeteria, Stephanie's appetite is long gone, but she forces herself to get a toasted bran muffin with the cup of coffee she's ordered. As she sits there distractedly picking at it, a flurry of thoughts flood her mind. She is so lost in contemplation that she doesn't even notice when Dalton sits down and startles when he calls her name. "Wha—what happened? Is Rob okay?" She pops up from the chair as her stomach begins to drop.

Dalton quickly places a reassuring hand on her arm. "He's fine. He just fell asleep."

Stephanie nods and slowly sits back down. "Wow, that was quick. Those drugs are really doing a number on him, don't you think?" she inquires, trying to ease into the conversation she wants to have with him.

However, Dalton shakes his head. "Well, it wasn't that quick. We spent about twenty minutes together, and yes, while the drugs do cause him to drift in and out, at least he's not in pain."

Stephanie sighs deeply. "You're right. I am truly grateful for that. So…what do you think about his story?"

Dalton studies Stephanie for a moment. "You mean, you want to know if I think it's true, right?" Stephanie holds his eyes without answering.

Finally, he slowly exhales. "Stephanie, thanks to my adorable doting mother I am convinced that you think way too highly of me. I can't tell you if what Rob saw was real or not, the same way no one else ever will be able to confirm my vision. He believes it is real, and that's what matters most to me, as it has brought him the first real sense of comfort I've seen since this ordeal began."

Stephanie knows she is appearing selfish and judgmental, but Rob is not Dalton's life—he is hers. "What I want to know is if you think this means he is really on the verge of dying, because that's what the doctors are saying, or is it just the drugs making him see these things? Please don't be diplomatic with me, Dalton. I'm here drifting alone in the middle of a dark, choppy sea clinging to splintered hope, praying for something solid to stand on. Give me something—anything!" She implores, as her panic begins to rise with the water in her eyes.

"Oh, Stephanie..." Dalton hugs her tightly, as she dissolves into heaving sobs.

"I can't lose him, Dalton!" She finally gasps. "I just can't!" She calms down and looks at him pleadingly. "Dalton...please, pray for a miracle like the priest did for you. I cannot lose Rob—I won't make it if I do."

Now tears are filling Dalton's eyes. "Stephanie, that's exactly what I've been doing. I've been praying and fasting, begging for God to heal Rob, but to be totally honest, I can't help feeling like I'm praying more for my own sake, because not only do I not want to lose my best friend, but I also don't want the devastation of knowing that I would be responsible for it. Honestly, I don't know if I would ever be at peace with that, Stephanie. I'm so sorry. I wish I would've said something sooner. I was just afraid that if I did, Rob would shut down and lock us both out. Or maybe, in reality, I was the one who thought too highly of myself."

As Dalton hangs his head in shame, Stephanie picks it up and forces him to look into her eyes. "Dalton, whatever happens, I want you to understand this clearly. I do not in any way blame you for how Rob chose to handle his sickness. I cannot at this point say I'm not upset with him, because I am his wife and good intentions or not, he chose to shut me out at a time when he could least afford to. I have to deal with that and the repercussions. However, though it hurts deeply, my pain is not greater than my love for Rob, so it is my love that will always fight for rather than against him.

No offense Dalton, but in my eyes, this is not about you at all, so I want you to immediately drop that heavy load of guilt you have been needlessly carrying. Yes, I want a miracle and will go to the ends of the earth if necessary, to get one. I also clearly know that you are not God nor am I expecting you to be. I am, however, asking for a friend who is willing to stand by my side to fight this battle with the both of us—that's what I really need." Dalton looks at her with tearful gratitude. "Well then, that's exactly what you have, Stephanie."

* * *

As Stephanie starts back to check on Rob, her phone rings. "Hey, Stace." She says in a tired voice. "Yeah...today has been a rough day. Rob is hallucinating from his drugs and talking about seeing his dead mother and brother. I don't know what to do, anymore. It's like I'm already by myself now. Well, you're welcome to come by, but he's in and out of sleep mostly. Don't worry, I understand about Clint. We're all having a hard time with this and dealing with it in our own way. If you guys just want to sit with me in the waiting area, that's fine too. Under the circumstances, I may not feel like talking too much but could use the company just the same. Okay, I'll see you later. Thanks."

After deciding to take a long walk to clear her mind, she finally goes back to find a tear streaked Stacie sitting by Rob as he sleeps. "Clint's downstairs in the car." She whispers. "He changed his mind at the last minute. He just couldn't do it. I know he wants to be here--for you both, but he's taking this so hard, Steph. I'm sorry."

Stephanie nods. "Stacie, I understand completely, and so does Rob. We love you, so please know that whenever you are not here physically, your presence always is. In the moments when Rob is clear, we laugh over all the crazy times we've had together—and it is not over—so I want you and Clint to stop agonizing and allow yourselves to be exactly where you are. Truth be told, there is no other way to do this but honestly, and you know Rob would have it no other way."

Stacie looks down at Rob's sleeping face and smiles through her tears. "Yeah, you guys laugh about my brutal honesty, but Rob has had to set both Clint and me straight on more than a couple of occasions, so you're absolutely right about that."

Just then, a red-eyed Clint tentatively peeks in the doorway. "Hey." He hoarsely greets, shifting with discomfort.

Stephanie rushes over and welcomes him with a big hug. "Clint, I was just telling Stacie that I don't want you to feel guilty about how you're processing all this. It is a lot, and just because we handle things differently doesn't mean that our love is any less. Rob and I just want you to know that."

Upon her reassurance, a sob of pain catches in his throat and he quickly turns to leave, but Stephanie pulls him back.

"No, Stephanie." He resists. "I don't want Rob to see me like this. I need to be strong for him."

Stephanie squeezes his arm and softly replies with tears in her eyes. "Clint...look around this room. None of us are strong right now, but we're all here together, and that helps."

At that point, Rob's eyes begin to flutter open and he smiles widely when he sees Stacie and Clint. "Hey, guys!"

Clint straightens up and wipes his eyes. "Hey, Rob...How you feelin', man?"

Rob reaches over and weakly squeezes Stacie's hand. "Better now. I'm so glad you're here. How are the kids?"

Clint shrugs, throwing his arms up. "Well, you know there's always enough drama going on at the center to keep them occupied, but they miss you very much. In fact, I have some letters and cards here for you. They're all anxiously waiting for you to come back—we're all waiting for you to come back, Rob."

Rob nods trying to smile again but instead presses his lips tightly together to contain the emotion rising in him.

After a moment of awkward silence, Clint cautiously approaches Rob's bedside. "Rob, I never told you this before, but you have been like a father to me. Because I never knew my own, some old heads from around the way would occasionally step in to guide me over the years with varying degrees of success. However, you have shown me that being a man is not simply about making money and collecting women, but to respect myself and others and to live with integrity."

"I used to make fun of you all the time, but it was only because I both admired and feared you. I admired your confidence, commitment, and loyalty, but I also feared it because it put such a bright spotlight on my own mess. I knew I wasn't living right a long time ago but wasn't ready to deal with making the changes I needed to. In spite of that, you still believed and trusted me to do the right thing when it counted most." He says, glancing at Stacie.

"Although I've been an adult for quite some time now, because of you, I feel like for the first time I am finally becoming a man." His voice chokes as tears begin falling rapidly down his face. "And now that I'm on the right path, I need you more than ever. I want you to be here to witness the results of all you've done. There's so much more within me I want you to know; there are things I want to share with you, man to man; not in the childish way, I used to. I feel like I've finally found the father and friend I always longed for, and I want to give you the opportunity to be proud of me…as a son." With that, he desperately grabs onto Rob and bawls inconsolably.

Stephanie and Stacie also begin crying, as Clint's agony echoes their own. Tears stream from Rob's eyes as he embraces Clint, gently patting his back until he is able to calm down. "Clint, I have always seen who you are, and plan on being there to share more of your life's joys, but please know that I am already proud of you, no matter what. I love you, man."

Clint smiles gratefully, wiping his face. "Thanks, Rob. I love you too."

There is a knock at the door and Lee walks in. "Hello, everyone; I'm so sorry to interrupt, but Dr. Holmes wants to meet with you, Stephanie. She's in her office waiting."

Stephanie bites her lip in an attempt to contain her nervousness. "Sure, but first Lee, let me introduce you to our good friends, Clint and Stacie. Lee is one of Rob's nurses who has proven to be quite a blessing during this time."

After they exchange greetings, Stephanie gathers her things and heads for the door. "I'll try to be back as soon as possible, but please don't feel like you have to wait around if there's something you need to do."

Stacie waves her on dismissively. "Go on, Steph—we're fine. Wow, we just got here and you're already trying to kick us out." She smiles playfully. "Take your time. We're not going anywhere."

* * *

Stephanie walks into Dr. Holmes office braced for whatever will be shared in this meeting. "Hello, Mrs. Stephenson." The doctor greets. "Please have a seat." Stephanie slowly lowers herself into the chair, certain that her beating heart can be heard throughout the room. "Well, I have some good news. Mr. Stephenson seems to be greatly improving and so I think he can be safely discharged at this point. Have you made the necessary arrangements for him at your home yet?"

Stephanie's heartbeat goes from dread to excitement. "No actually, after speaking with Nurse Franklin I've decided to have him transferred to hospice."

Dr. Holmes nods and starts scribbling in her notes. "I understand. Do you need any assistance with the paperwork?"

"Yes, but she's going to help me, as you know, she's already been through this herself."

Dr. Holmes puts her pen down and warmly smiles. "Well, I'm glad to hear that you have some support in that area, Mrs. Stephenson, and again, please let us know if there is anything you need along the way."

Stephanie can't wait to get back to the room and share the good news. Lee was right; if she just rode out the difficulties, then things would get better. When she gets to the room, however, Rob is fast asleep again with Clint and Stacie by his side. "He was in a lot of pain, so the nurse came and gave him some more medicine," Stacie explains. Clint just silently stares off, lost in thought.

Stephanie's joy dampens a little as she asks, "Did he fall straight back to sleep?"

Stacie casts a quick glance in Clint's direction, but he doesn't respond. "Yeah, basically." She finally answers.

Stephanie slowly eases down in her chair. "What did he say, Stacie?"

Stacie hesitates for a few moments before responding. "I couldn't understand most of it, really, Steph. I think he was just under the influence of the medicine, and--"

"He spoke about seeing angels and bright lights." Clint cuts in quietly. "He said he wants to fly with them because he feels peaceful there."

They all sit in silence until Stacie finally breaks in. "Steph, what did the doctor say?"

Stephanie remains silent for a few more moments. "She said that he is improving and that I can make arrangements to discharge him."

Stacie brightens. "Well, that's good news, don't you think?"

Stephanie distractedly nods. "Hey guys, I'm going to run home and take care of some stuff before Rob wakes up."

Clint stands up and grabs Stacie's hand. "Well, we'd better get going too. We'll check in with you later, but you know to call if you need anything, right?"

Stephanie weakly smiles. "Of course. Thank you so much for being here. Rob was so delighted to see you; and Clint—remember what I said, okay?"

Clint gives Stephanie a long, grateful hug. "Thanks, Steph."

After they leave, Stephanie stays behind for a moment to study Rob's sleeping face. She wonders what is going on underneath those eyelids and for the first time, truly feels closed out of his world. "Please God…don't take Rob away from me. I need him so much." Her pleading tears fall upon Rob's face, but he doesn't even budge. Finally, she gathers her things and walks out.

CHAPTER THIRTY-THREE

After briefly going home to shower and change, Stephanie rushes back to the hospital hoping that Rob doesn't wake up to not find her there. On her way in, she runs into Lee.

"Stephanie, I was looking for you earlier. Rob's still in and out of sleep, but the doctor did say that he's doing much better, so we can start the paperwork whenever you're ready."

Stephanie smiles gratefully. "Thanks, Lee. I really appreciate all your help with this."

Lee affectionately places her hand on Stephanie's shoulder. "It's my pleasure. Hey, have you eaten yet?"

Stephanie shakes her head. "I haven't had much of an appetite, lately."

Lee nods sympathetically. "Well, why don't you stop by the house for a little while anyway? We'll talk and you can meet Milton."

Stephanie smiles apologetically. "I really should get back to Rob. I hadn't intended to take this long."

Lee looks at Stephanie and her heart breaks. "Stephanie, if I may be totally honest with you, it's probably not in either of your best interests to keep this bedside vigil. First, this is how burnout begins. Secondly, he's sleeping so much because he needs that rest to heal. Every time he feels he has to interact with someone, it saps his energy. Even while drifting in and out, he's aware of when someone is there waiting for him to say or do something to reassure them.

In other words, you both need this time. You don't have to come home with me, but you should have time and space so that you can both be more refreshed. This is another reason why hospice is in my opinion, healthier for both parties.

When a loved one becomes a caretaker, it is a very emotionally charged experience. First, there is the shame of having to see and be seen in such a vulnerable condition. Then the misplaced guilt can create a burden, with each party feeling as if they are not doing enough. Still, I think the greatest pressure can be on the sick person who may just want to give up but battles with the fear of their loved ones feeling abandoned. In those cases, sometimes the greatest gift we can give a suffering person is simply to allow them to go with our love and peace."

Stephanie slowly raises her brow then narrows her eyes with barely controlled impatience. "Well, as you just said, that may be the situation in some instances, but it's definitely not the case with Rob and me. He wants to be here just as much as I want him to. He has personally said this to me repeatedly. So, if *I* may be totally honest, Lee, I don't see where this conversation is going."

Lee shakes her head emphatically. "Please...please, don't take what I am saying the wrong way, Stephanie. I'm just sharing my experiences as both a nurse and caretaker. I want you to pace yourself so that you both can have the best advantage in going through this. I apologize if I offended you. Listen, I don't want to be anything other than helpful to you at this time, so from now on, you tell me what you need, and I will do my best to assist you."

Suddenly Stephanie's stomach lets out a loud growl, and they both break out in laughter, which immediately clears the tension. "Well, at this moment, it appears that I need a nice home cooked meal."

* * *

Stephanie is relieved to discover that Lee lives in walking distance of the hospital. As they enter the house the fragrant smell of cooked food welcomes them.

Lee's husband, Milton is reclined on the couch watching T.V. "Heeyy mama!" He greets Lee as she leans over to give him a kiss.

"Hey there to you, Papa! This is Stephanie, who I told you about. Stephanie, this is my husband, Milton."

"Pleased to meet you." They both say at the same time, with hands extended.

Milton gets up and gathers his things. "Weeell, Ima give you ladyfolk some space here. Stephanie, please make yourself at home. It was very nice meeting you. Mama, just bring my food to the back when you're ready."

Stephanie warmly smiles as she imagines her and Rob twenty years from now. "Thank you. It was great meeting you too, Milton."

"Come on, Stephanie." Lee leads her into the kitchen and gestures for her to sit down. "Because of my schedule, it's hard for me to come home and cook, so I make my meals in a slow cooker. It's been my saving grace. By the way, I hope you don't mind that we really don't eat meat here, especially since Milton's illness, but I have some vegetable and barley stew that will knock your socks off."

Stephanie heaves a sigh of relief. "That's perfect because I'm a vegetarian and was worried about how I was going to navigate the meat issue."

Lee smiles serenely. "Well, great—everything worked out. Let me just wash my hands and make Milt's plate, first. If you need to use the restroom, it's down the hall to the left." Stephanie pauses with a strange look on her face. "I was just going to ask you that."

Lee innocently chuckles. "Well, what do you know?"

Later, as they hover over their steaming bowls of stew with crusty wholegrain bread and salad, Stephanie unsuccessfully tries to hold herself back from greedily devouring her food. "Lee, this is the best stew I've ever tasted! Do you mind sharing the recipe?"

Lee raises her eyebrows with a knowing smirk. "I told you. Sure, I'll give you the recipe, but the real secret is the slow simmering of spices that infuses such a rich flavor into this. I had to learn how to make vegetables just as appealing as meat to Milt, or he'd never eat. He sure loved him some steak, I'll tell you, and I'd better not serve anything called a meal that didn't have some form of meat on the plate." She laughs at the memory. "I also ate my fair share, but since his diagnosis of colon cancer, we've had to switch things up quite a bit."

Stephanie shakes her head in admiration. "Well, you two sure look good for it, and you have a lot of energy, Lee to keep those long hours."

Lee waves her hand. "Oh, I've always been like that. You can't keep me still and the day I retire is when it's truly all over. Moreover, I love nursing—I always have. I feel like it's what I've been called to do, and when you discover that, it never ends because it's a part of who you are."

Stephanie nods. "I understand completely. That's how I feel about teaching, although I did stop after the car accident. Fred was a teacher too, and for me, it brought up too many painful memories."

Lee looks off thoughtfully. "Well, Celina was hit by a car crossing the street and the woman kept going. It wasn't bad enough that she was drunk, but she just drove off and left my baby there to die. Cee-Cee had just graduated from medical school and was preparing to go on a mission trip to Africa. She was so excited, and then in one brief moment, all our life's hopes and dreams for her were cut short. Although it was extremely hard, it was actually nursing that kept me going. I know I couldn't save everybody, but being able to help and comfort others even as I was in pain somehow made it better. Let me show you her picture." She goes out and returns with a graduation photo of Celina.

When she sees it, Stephanie gasps in shock. "Lee...this is exactly what I looked like when I was her age."

Lee's eyes begin to tear. "Well, you don't look that much different now. Milt said his heart stopped when you walked in the door with me, even though I'd told him about you beforehand. I guess he had to see for himself."

Stephanie looks back at the picture and studies Celina's happy, hopeful face. I'm so sorry for your loss, Lee."

Lee smiles. "Oh, she's still here, and we get signs now and then letting us know. I believe you're one of them. Now, don't get me wrong. I know you're not Celina and I'm not trying to make you into a substitute either, but I do believe we've come into each other's lives for a reason."

Stephanie nods affirmatively. "I think so too. Rob really adores you, by the way. He also lost his mother when he was fairly young."

Lee slightly tilts her head as she listens. "I see."

Stephanie glances at the clock on the wall. "Lee, I'd hate to eat and run, but I really need to get to Rob now. Still, you were right. I did need this time and space and feel much clearer on a full stomach. Thank you! We'll talk tomorrow to make arrangements for the transfer, okay?"

Lee stands up to give Stephanie a big hug. "That sounds good, Stephanie. Thanks for coming by."

Just then, they hear loud snores coming from the back room, and begin cracking up. "Just like a man…can't eat without falling asleep." Lee jokes. "I'll tell Milt you said goodbye, sweetheart. Take care."

* * *

Rob is still asleep when Stephanie comes in, so she sits and watches him, reflecting on her conversation with Lee. She hopes she isn't draining his energy by being there, but the more she ponders it, is convinced of the contrary. That might be the case with other people, but she and Rob have always energetically drawn from each other, even when they were not physically together. She has to be here to give him the love and healing energy he needs to get through this. Thinking back to how good Milt looked, she is encouraged all the more. She is so glad she went to Lee's house, for it has given her a new surge of optimism. Lee has had this effect on her from the beginning, and she wants more of it in her life.

Rob starts whispering something in his sleep. Unable to make out what he is saying, she leans closer. Listening intently, she can only vaguely make out a word that sounds something like higher or holler. Tears slide from the corners of his eyes as he smiles peacefully. Stephanie desperately wants to know what is going on, but not wanting to wake him she quietly sits back down and waits. Finally, he opens his eyes and smiles at her. "Hey, baby! I dreamed I was flying through the bluest sky you've ever seen, but you were here waiting, so I came back down."

Lee's words instantly flash before her. "You knew that?"

Rob nonchalantly shrugs. "Yeah, I was hovering between sleep and awake, so even in my dream, I felt your energy right here beside me. You know how we do." He reaches to kiss her hand. "So how are you, my love?"

Stephanie smiles with relief. Rob seems like his old self again. He *is* getting better. "I'm good if you're good. Hey, I went home to shower and change so I could spend the night here. I miss lying next to you, Rob."

Rob has that familiar mischievous gleam in his eye. "Mmm… sounds good—just don't be surprised when my heart monitor suddenly starts going into overdrive—you know how I get when you're sleeping next to me."

Stephanie laughs heartily for the first time in days. "Yeah, well just don't do anything to cause your heart monitor to go off kilter, Big Rob. Save all that for later."

Rob winks. "If you insist, Mrs. Stephenson, I'll be a good boy."

"You'd better, or we'll both get kicked out of here!" Stephanie says in a mock threatening tone, as she pulls the reclining chair closer to Rob's bed with no little effort.

Rob, however, is on a roll. "Wow, I didn't know you were so strong!" He jokes. If I had known that before, you would've moved your own furniture into the house, instead of me and Dalton. You had us thinking you were so frail and dainty that you couldn't lift anything but your favorite set of dishes."

Stephanie bursts out in laughter again. "Well, now that the secret's out you'd better watch what you say, Mister."

Rob puts up his hands and cowers in mock fear. "Yes Ma'am!"

They continue giggling as Stephanie reaches out to squeeze Rob's hand. "Rob, I'm so glad you're feeling better." Her eyes fill with tears. "I've missed you so much. I felt like I was losing you more each day. Please stay with me. Don't leave."

Rob looks at Stephanie, his own eyes misting. "I will never leave you, Stephanie; never." Stephanie smiles lovingly, and feeling comforted, relaxes into a deep sleep.

* * *

Sometime later, Stephanie is awakened by Rob's voice calling her and quickly sits up. "What is it, baby—what's the matter?"

Rob squeezes her hand with a pleading look. "Steph, please know that I love you with all my heart...but I'll be leaving here soon."

Stephanie shakily stands and tries to comprehend what he is saying. "Rob, what's going on? Are you in pain? Let me get the nurse to help you."

Tightly gripping her hand, Rob shakes his head. "Don't go. I'll have to move on shortly, baby."

Suddenly Stephanie bursts into tears, bawling hysterically as she clings to him. "Nooo! Rob...please don't say that! Oh God, I can't do this anymore...I just can't...I *won't*--not without you. I will go too!"

Rob abruptly sits up and grabs Stephanie's shoulders with a strength that belies his condition. "Stephanie, listen to me!"

Stephanie is stunned into a quiet whimper. "Baby, don't you understand by now? You are loved beyond this world. Each transition you witnessed was not a loss, but a gift to let you know that there is so much more than what you think is here. It goes way beyond what you can see. No one has left or been taken from you. They just went deeper inside to guide you into truth. They always have been and will be a part of you, Steph. You have been offered this sacred wisdom through a path many cannot accept. Here is another opportunity to realize it so you may leave behind an even greater inheritance through what has been entrusted to you. Giving up now would be like taking the cumulative wealth of all the lives deposited in you and throwing it away. I know you Steph. When the time comes you will be strong and follow your heart just as you said you would; but for now, please come here and lie with me."

Rob leans back and closes his eyes as Stephanie tearfully caresses his face. She then climbs upon his bed where they eventually drift off in each other's arms. While asleep, Stephanie dreams she is on Oak Hill climbing her favorite tree to overlook the landscape. When she gets to her usual spot she looks down and realizes that each branch which has supported her ascent represents a soul from her inner circle who has gone ahead. She then becomes aware of their collective presence embracing her—her mom, Fred, and her children. She even senses her Dad there with a loving energy, something she never thought possible. Strengthened by this, she tries to find a branch to go even higher. As she looks up, bright rays of sunlight beam through the leaves, obscuring her view. Instead of forcing it, she leans back, closes her eyes, and lets the warmth envelop her as tears of gratitude slide through her lids. When she finally opens her eyes, the sun has shifted and she sees a huge bough right above her.

Stephanie is startled awake by the loud steady ring of Rob's heart monitor and pops up from the reclining chair where she is still holding Rob's hand. She groggily stands as the staff rush in to tend to him.

"No." Stephanie calmly lifts her hand to stop them. "Let him go. I'll sign the necessary paperwork."

The doctor nods and makes a notation in his pad as the nurse turns off his machine and quietly leaves the room.

Looking upon her husband's body, Stephanie surprisingly feels at peace. As she holds his hand the tears that wash over her face are no longer from fear, self-pity, or loss, but of an inexplicable joy and awe. She is grateful to have been chosen by such a precious soul to share this earth journey and to know that his final gift on this side was to create a pathway for her to go higher and see more clearly into the other.

CHAPTER THIRTY-FOUR

So many are people flooding into the sanctuary of St. Thomas' church that Stephanie worries everyone will not be able to fit. However, Dalton reassures her there is enough capacity, even if some have to stand. From her front pew, she watches people file past Rob's body with varying degrees of sorrow—some in a state of emotionless, silent shock, and others breaking down in inconsolable tears. Stephanie chooses to send Rob off in his #1 DAD football jersey to honor not only his fathering their unborn child, but also for the role he served as a surrogate father to many. She is touched by the numerous stories people have shared with her of how Rob influenced and in some cases, even saved their lives. She is also grateful to finally meet Rob's youngest brother, Roger.

After the viewing, Dalton stands at the podium to signal the beginning of Rob's Home-going Service. The choir opens with the hymn, 'Eye on The Sparrow' at Stephanie's request. Sniffles and sobs are heard throughout the sanctuary as well as some firm 'Amen's' and 'Hallelujah's'.

When the song is over, Dalton begins to speak. "Good morning everyone—and it is a good morning, because it is God's morning, and we are in it. King David in the 118th Psalm and 24th stanza boldly exhorts, *'This is the day The Lord has made, let us rejoice and be glad in it'*. Let us remember that, as we have purposely gathered to celebrate the life of Robert Ernest Stephenson, Jr., who was not only my best friend but also my spiritual brother.

I first met Rob at a book discussion in a local café, and we instantly hit it off, delving right away into the deep issues of life and relationships. The thing is, during the entire conversation I never told Rob that I was a Catholic priest, and so he felt free to share things he later admitted he probably wouldn't have, had he known. Even though he told me he wasn't religious, when he finally did find out, it never changed the nature of our relationship one iota, for Rob was not judgmental. He accepted everyone and saw the good in both 'sinner' and 'saint'. This spoke more of Jesus' nature to me than some who wear their religiosity gleaming and dangling around their neck, and I came to admire Rob even more for the simple, loving, unpretentious person that he was. Even though he often looked to me for answers and direction, at the same time he constantly encouraged, inspired and challenged my walk as a Christian leader in ways I'm sure he never knew."

"Although he had an imposing stature that could be intimidating if you didn't know him, Rob was a gentle giant who had a sense of humor that kept us laughing to tears on many occasions. Toward the end, I am blessed to say that Rob came to personally know the God whose love he so easily embodied. Although we'd befriended each other less than two years ago, I feel like I've known him all my life. I truly don't know what I did before him, but I do look forward to seeing him again and sharing some more fun and sidesplitting laughter, this time for eternity."

"Now we will have Rob's wife, Stephanie, come up before opening the service to anyone else who wants to share their experiences of Rob."

Stephanie makes her way to the podium and gives Dalton a long hug before turning to face the congregation. "As I look over the sea of faces here, I am filled with deep awe and gratitude for you coming to celebrate my husband's life with me. It seems we all have stories of how Rob has affected us. Some of you heard a little of mine at our wedding last September. However, there's just too much for me to express how Rob has truly transformed me...too much...but I will share this."

"One day Rob caught me singing in the shower while getting ready for work. You see, usually, he would still be sleeping as I had to leave much earlier. But anyway, here I am, engrossed in my usual morning preparations when the curtain suddenly gets whipped back and I start screaming like the woman in that classic horror movie." Everyone breaks out in laughter.

"'Steph, was that you?' He asks me, stunned. 'I thought it was the radio and got up to see what station you were listening to.' So, from that time on, he often asked me to sing for him, but I was too shy and insecure and would often try to find ways to get out of it. I also made him swear not to tell anyone, lest I be publicly asked, which I was convinced would immediately send me into a dead faint." More chuckles follow.

"So, although I am violently shaking right now, I am determined to sing this in honor of my late husband. The first verse is our wedding song and a tribute to the way he saw life that I too have come to experience since meeting, knowing, and loving this special gift of God, called Rob. The second verse is the version he told me he heard from heaven shortly before going there himself."

As the organ music begins, Stephanie nervously closes her eyes and an image of her mother flashes before her. Instantly she is calmed, and her beautiful lilt rings throughout the sanctuary.

> *"It's a simple song, like falling rain*
> *Washing my soul and cleansing my pain*
> *It's a sound within, like chirping birds*
> *A sweet melody that needs no words*
>
> *Come and sing this simple song*
> *Hum it softly, or sing out strong*
> *Join me in this simple song*
> *This simple song of Undying Love*
>
> *It's an autumn wind blowing through trees*
> *Kissing the many splendored leaves*
> *It's a saving grace from the grip of fear*
> *A comforting whisper that dries my tears*
>
> *It's a quiet shout throughout the land*
> *It's the freeing touch of my Savior's hand*
> *It's a sound so sweet, from up above*
> *It's the simple song of my Savior's love*
>
> *Come and sing this simple song*
> *Hum it softly, or sing out strong*
> *Join me in this simple song*
> *This simple song of my Savior's love*

When she finishes, the room is so silent that you can hear a pin drop. Opening her eyes and scanning the crowd, she notes expressions of peace where there had been distress as everyone appears to be caught up in their own private, joyful reflection.

CHAPTER THIRTY-FIVE

In the days that follow there is a constant stream of visitors at the farmhouse. While Stephanie is grateful for their presence, ultimately, life goes on and people eventually return to theirs—jobs, families, and other commitments. Soon Stephanie finds herself home alone more often. Nevertheless, this solitude is a welcome one—a chance to rest and reflect without the distraction of hosting. Still, it has been comforting to know that so many people really care about her, which is something she didn't fully appreciate when Fred died.

She often thinks of how steeped in her own sorrow, she simply picked up and left Karoga Springs without so much as a thank you or goodbye to anyone. She will not let that happen again. In fact, she did not realize how wide her circle had become until Rob's passing, and this time vows to nurture each connection, be it through a brief note, phone call or shared moment. She thinks of all the time she'd spent running and hiding in pain, mistrust, and fear before Rob transformed her with his patient, consistent love. She also reflects upon his last words that she would leave an inheritance greater than what was left for her but doesn't fully understand it since they have no descendants to pass on any wealth or possessions. She doesn't even have a close relative. When Rob was alive she had so hoped to have her own family, but it is obvious that now she would have to alter that desire, especially since it is next to impossible for singles to adopt infants, particularly at her age.

A wave of sadness begins to overtake her as she realizes that her dream of motherhood will probably never be realized in the way she had always longed for it to be. Like Rob, she would have to find other ways to channel her mothering nature. Suddenly she has a thought and goes upstairs into the room that she and Rob had been preparing as a nursery. She hadn't been inside since before the miscarriage. A flood of emotion washes over her as she surveys the items acquired in anticipation of their new bundle of joy. She slowly walks around running her fingers over the bright, colorful decals on the wall and picks up the soft baby clothes, gently rubbing them across her face. Finally, she ventures into the corner where the chair Rob made sits and tenderly traces the words carved into the headrest: *'A Mother's Love Knows No Bounds'*. Tears slowly roll down her cheeks as she resolutely picks it up and carries it onto the deck to overlook the landscape they always enjoyed so much. Just as with Rob's jersey at his Home-Going, she would take his gift to celebrate her motherhood each day by sitting in this chair to give thanks for all the seeds God placed in her womb that allowed her to birth dreams into reality. Clearly, Rob was one of them, but there have been many others too.

As she restfully closes her eyes and rocks, suddenly an image from a dream long ago flashes of her holding a baby to her breast and feeding it. She makes a mental note to call the hospital to resume her visits to the neo-natal center. Soon her thoughts are interrupted by the doorbell, and she reluctantly rises to answer it. Although she appreciates people stopping by to check on her, she really wishes they would simply give her a call first.

She opens the door and is shocked beyond words to see Mariana standing there with a swollen and bruised face, wet with tears. Cradled inside her jacket is a tiny baby in a pale green blanket.

"Ms. Martin...I just heard about Rob."

Stephanie finally recovers enough to gently embrace Mariana and guide her onto the living room couch. "Omigod...Mariana, what happened?"

Mariana's naturally ebullient personality is subdued, and her eyes filled with a deadened pain that Stephanie recognizes all too well.

Mariana shrugs dismissively. "To make a long story short, my father beat me up."

Stephanie goes from shock to silent outrage and rushes off to make an ice pack. Upon her return, she is more composed and speaks calmly, but firmly. "Mariana, long story or not, I want you to tell me everything. Is this your baby?"

Mariana quietly nods, averting Stephanie's gaze.

Stephanie peeks into blanket and coos at the smiling baby. Oh, she's so cute! What's her name?

Mariana looks down at her baby with a sad smile. "Esperanza. It means 'hope' in Spanish."

"Perfect! Let me bring down a bassinet and get you something to eat."

Mariana is shocked. "Ms. Martin—you have a baby too?"

Stephanie looks at her sadly. "No sweetheart, but I'll explain later."

With the baby comfortably nestled and swaying beside them, Stephanie reheats one of her donated meals as Mariana shares her story.

"Ms. Martin, I've never told anyone this before, but my father has been physically and sexually abusing me for years."

Stephanie tightly purses her lips and nods. "Go on."

Mariana nervously begins picking at her nails. "Well, the real trouble came when I got pregnant by him. Once I started showing, my mother was paranoid that someone would find out what was going on and kept me home as a virtual prisoner. She stopped me from going to the center and lied to my school by saying I ran off with some boy and didn't want to come back. Because of my age, they listed me as a dropout with no questions asked. When it came time for me to give birth, she got a midwife from our country who delivered Esperanza at my house. During the whole time I was pregnant my father never touched me, but when he came into my room with Esperanza laying just inches away, I resisted, and he began punching me right there in front of the baby. At that point, something snapped and I began fighting back. I slammed him over the head with the iron and knocked him out cold. That's when my mother threw me out of the house screaming never to come back. She wouldn't even let me grab the baby's things."

As I was leaving, I ran into Tim who told me about Rob. I couldn't believe it and had to come see you. Because of everything that happened, I never even got a chance to see Rob or thank him, or...anything." She begins sobbing uncontrollably. "He was always there for me and when he needed me, I didn't have the opportunity to do the same."

Stephanie hugs Mariana tightly. "Mari, Rob knew exactly how much you cared for him without you ever having to say a word, because that's how special your relationship was. Trust me on that."

Mariana tries to smile. "I've missed him so much, Ms. Martin—he was like a father to me—a real father. I don't know what to do without him."

Stephanie smooths down Mariana's wild, wiry curls reassuringly. "You're going to take every dream, hope, and lesson he has instilled in you and live it out. That's what you're going to do. As you do, you'll hear his words guide you every step of the way, so you know he's right there with you."

Feeling comforted, Mariana nods with a smile. "Yeah, you're right." She intently studies Stephanie's face. "Ms. Martin, can I ask you for something really important?"

Stephanie puts her arm around Mariana and draws her close. "You know you can ask me anything, sweetheart."

Mariana pleadingly looks up at Stephanie. "Can you please keep Esperanza?"

Stunned, Stephanie blinks in confusion. "What? No, Mariana, I can't just take your baby. She's your child, sweetheart. I'm more than happy to help you with her, but you can't just give someone your child like that."

However, Mariana is persistent. "But Ms. Martin, you'd be a great mother! You can just adopt her—I'll sign all the papers. You even already have stuff for a baby here. Plus, you just said that I should live my life to honor Rob; well, he wanted us to go to college and experience the world outside Oakwood, and that's what I want too. No one in my family has ever gone before, and it would make everything he's done not be a waste."

Stephanie affectionately grabs Mariana's hands, squeezing them. "I am truly honored, Mariana, but I think you are not giving yourself enough credit. You are an amazing young woman! With the right support, you can successfully do both; and not only would you be, but you *are* a wonderful mother—right now."

"I can't Ms. Martin—I just can't!" Mariana cries. "Every time I think about the fact that I'm a mother at seventeen, it freaks me out. All I know about motherhood I learned from my own mother and I'd never, ever want to expose my child to that. What about when she gets older and wants to know who her father is? I did not ask for, nor do I want this kind of reminder in my life or legacy for hers." Tears fill her eyes as she searches Stephanie's face imploringly. "Please help me."

Stephanie looks into Mariana's eyes and glimpses her younger self. "Okay Mariana, I will look into the process and see what can be done, but cannot make any promises." Mariana's eyes brim with tears as she gratefully hugs Stephanie. "Oh, Ms. Martin, thank you! Thank you so much!"

Just then, the baby gives a loud wail and frustrated, Mariana quickly snatches her up, impatiently swaying back and forth in an attempt to calm Esperanza down. "See, Ms. Martin, this is what I mean about me being a good mother. Sometimes I just get so angry at this situation that I feel like I want to take it out on her. It's not fair that I have to deal with this!"

Stephanie calmly takes the screaming baby from Mariana's arms and after checking her diaper begins rubbing her back. "Mariana, she's probably hungry. Where's her bottle?"

Trying to contain herself, Mariana closes her eyes and runs her hand through her hair. "I told you my mother wouldn't let me take anything with me, and I didn't have much money. I spent all I had to get here."

"Okay... okay..." Stephanie says soothingly to pacify them both and walks out to the rocking chair. "Mariana, have you ever tried to breastfeed her before?"

Mariana makes a face. "Ugh, no."

Stephanie smiles at Mariana's youthful response. "Do you mind if I try?"

Mariana looks at Stephanie with incredulity. "Can you?"

Stephanie cracks up despite herself. "With your baby howling like this, you had better hope so. Let's see if she latches. Stephanie sits down and unfastens her blouse as Mariana looks on with a mixture of embarrassment, curiosity, and repulsion. As she brings a now red-faced Esperanza close to her breast, the baby continues flailing in exasperation. After several attempts, she finally stops. "Mariana, we have to run and get some formula. She's not responding." As she starts to rise, suddenly the baby hungrily grabs her and begins greedily sucking.

"Oh!" They exclaim in unison and Stephanie slowly settles back down as tears spring to her eyes.

Later, as she rocks a satiated Esperanza to sleep, Stephanie decides to share her own story with Mariana, who listens raptly.

When she is finished, Mariana studies the waterfall reflectively. "Ms. Martin, why do you suppose we're fed all these stories as children about 'happily ever after' when that's clearly not the case? Don't you think it's cruel to make us believe in something that doesn't really exist?"

Stephanie contemplates Mariana's question for a moment. "Well, I think we all need to believe in something ideal because without that, we'll never have anything to reach for. While I personally have not experienced the kind of 'happily ever after' as in the fairy tales, I do know quite a bit about flying high with one wing and a prayer. If can we learn to persevere in this unpredictable and often unfair life, we develop the ability to create our own 'happily ever after' rather than wait for someone to bestow it upon us. Mariana my dear, I am certain that in time you will be able to spin gold from the straws of your life and erect kingdoms of possibility from the ruins of shattered dreams. Your story has already begun and I'm so blessed to be a part of it".

As they continue in silence, Stephanie looks down at Esperanza contentedly resting in her arms, oblivious to all the painful and chaotic circumstances that brought her into the world and finally understands all Rob was saying to her.

She studies Mariana who from the look on her face is still trying to make sense of everything, and places a reassuring hand on her knee. "Baby... don't worry; it will be okay. No matter what happens, please believe it's for a reason, even if you can't see it now. All you need to do is relax and trust that you are loved and cared for on all levels."

Mariana looks at Stephanie with deep appreciation. "Ms. Martin--"

"Please...call me Stephanie. We're way beyond that now."

Mariana smiles and nods then stares off into the trees again. "Stephanie?"

"Yes, sweetheart?"

Mariana affectionately squeezes Stephanie's hand as her eyes fill with calm. "Thank you."

Stephanie gazes tenderly at her and they resume their quiet reflection.

After a while, Mariana lets out a deep, contented sigh then stands and stretches. "Stephanie, may I use your bathroom, please?"

"Of course; you remember where it is, right?"

Mariana nods, making her way.

As Stephanie watches Mariana exit, her heart breaks into a million pieces. She reminds her so much of herself at that age—too young to be used, battered and bruised—and quietly offers up a prayer of strength for the path that lay ahead of her. She thinks back to their first meeting and how Mariana had an indomitable spirit and drive for life. Recalling her poise and exuberance, it almost seems inconceivable of what she had been experiencing at home all this time. She recalls the reference in Mariana's poem to dancing and singing through her challenges, and is comforted. Mariana will be fine; it is no accident that they came together, especially now.

She suddenly thinks of Lee and marvels at how truly connected life is, especially when we're paying attention. Closing her eyes, she smiles. "Rob, I know you're still here looking out for me—for us. Thank you." She looks down at the baby who is fast asleep in her arms and goes inside to place her in the bassinet. Afterwards, she gently knocks on the bathroom door. "Mariana sweetheart, do you need some more ice?"

After a few seconds of silence, Mariana softly answers. "No thanks, I'm all set."

Stephanie decides to give her some space. So much has happened in one day. She goes upstairs to prepare Mariana's room so she can rest. Tomorrow they will go shopping for clothes and other necessities for both her and the baby. She is so grateful to have them there, especially at a time like this. It seems that for each pain and loss she experiences, God knows exactly what to provide as a balm for her soul.

She lovingly lays out some fresh smelling towels and toiletries for Mariana then adjusts the curtains to allow more light in. Finally, resting in the window seat, she gazes over the peaceful panoramic view she hopes Mariana will enjoy as much as she does. Taking in the emerging spring scenery, her eye catches something rapidly moving off in the distance. Realizing what it is, she gasps as her eyes sting with rising tears. Watching the disappearing figure until out of sight, she slowly rises, picks up the towels and gently closes the door behind her.

EPILOGUE

Outside the farmhouse there is the buzz of excitement as people mill about hugging, talking, laughing, sipping cocktails and nibbling upon appetizers passed around by the wait staff. Soft music is playing and the trees are glimmering with festive lights. Everything gradually comes to a hush as Stephanie steps upon the platform and quietly stands at the podium. She pauses to overlook the crowd in attendance before speaking.

"Good evening everyone and welcome to the grand opening of The S.H.O.W., more formally known as The Stephenson Home for Overcoming Women." Scattered applause soon escalates into enthusiastic rounds that last until Stephanie holds up her hand to continue. "I hope that show—no pun intended-- of appreciation was for you because none of this would exist otherwise. This is no longer just my house--it is ours. Because of your tireless efforts and contributions, what started a few years ago as a labor of love by my late husband, Rob, will now carry the legacy of all he lived for, which was improving the lives of others. Words cannot fully express how truly grateful I am.

I would, however, like to publicly recognize some key players who made this reality come to fruition. First, I would like to thank Jeff Santos of The Santos Group, who by his generous donations was able to not only help us finish the house's reconstruction and bring it to code but also has provided job opportunities for participants at The United Neighborhood Initiative (U.N.I.) Youth Center to train and work as anti-violence advocates in our community. Next, I would like to thank Father Dalton Shea and the parish of St. Thomas who has agreed to host a monthly community dinner and discussion group to allow our residents to become a part of the larger community. I would also like to acknowledge Mrs. Lehti Singh who has agreed to provide individual counseling and host healing groups for The S.H.O.W. I would also like to thank Clint Teele, Director of the U.N.I. Youth Center for providing volunteers for the childcare center and Stacie Teele, Director of Outreach at the Oakwood Public Library for book donations and initiating our in-house reading program. I will wrap-up with thanks to Nurse Felicia Franklin at Oakwood Memorial Hospital for providing staff for health screenings and wellness workshops.

There are so many more collaborators, individual donors, and volunteers that I wish I could call each of you by name, but we know that would take away from the event we have all been looking forward to—the Memory Tree Lighting! As I have said before, this tree will remain lit throughout the year and serve to honor those we have lost, particularly to violence, and as a remembrance that their light will always shine through us. I am confident that as we all continue in our commitment to making sure everyone has the opportunity to overcome the influence of violence in their lives, be it in their home, school, or community at large, the number of names added will decrease. Thank you all, again." When Stephanie finishes there is a standing ovation and several wet eyes in the audience.

Afterwards, everyone stands around the tree with lit candles as Dalton begins the ceremony with prayer and words of hope. As each person takes turns hanging his or her loved one's name, memento or picture in the form of an ornament, someone starts to sing 'We Shall Overcome'. Soon everyone joins in, holding hands and repeating the refrain even after the last ornament has been placed. There is a current of connection flowing and no one wants to break it.

Suddenly a loud cry rings out and everyone stops to turn in its direction. "Mommeee! Mommee!" It is Esperanza, followed by Stacie, running and excitedly waving something in her hand. "I have one too!" She delightedly cries as they approach, and everyone begins to chuckle affectionately at the friendly, outgoing Essie.

Stephanie smiles, trying to make out what she is carrying in her chubby little fingers. When they draw closer, Essie holds up her item with determined satisfaction. As Stephanie studies the object, tears fill her eyes and she kneels down to give Essie a great big hug. That's wonderful, Essie! Why don't you put it on yourself, right here in front so everyone can see?

Essie smiles widely and nods as Stephanie guides her hand over the branch then turns around, eyes beaming with joy. Everyone claps and she does a little dance, her dark curly locks bouncing as she revels in the excitement of such attention.

Stephanie laughs and gives her a tight hug. "Okay, now go with Auntie Stacie and get ready for bed."

Satisfied with her mission, Essie runs into Stacie's waiting arms, blowing kisses as she waves good night to everyone. Knowing there can be no better ending to the ceremony than this, everyone begins dispersing with hugs and expressions of gratitude. Before walking away, Stephanie takes one last teary-eyed look at the ornament's inscription, *'De Esperanza: Con Todo Mi Amor'* and smiles at the Scrabble tiles that spell out: 'LOVE ALWAYS LIVES'.

ABOUT THE AUTHOR

Melanée Addison was born in the South Bronx but has been a resident of Boston for over fifteen years.

She has spent over two decades inspiring youth in under-represented communities using the arts as a tool for knowledge, self-discovery, and empowerment. She has also performed in various theater productions throughout Boston.

Although she has published poetry and short stories throughout the years, this is her first novel (YAY!).

In addition to her passion for writing, she is a herbalist and founder of *Blue Butterfly Wellness,* where she creates and sells handcrafted, natural body care products.

Printed in the United States
By Bookmasters